One Unforgettable Night

VICKI LEWIS THOMPSON

DEBBI RAWLINS

CANDACE HAVENS

MILLS &
BOON

First Published in Great Britain 2016
By Mills & Boon, an imprint of HarperCollins*Publishers*
1 London Bridge Street, London, SE1 9GF

ONE UNFORGETTABLE NIGHT © 2016 Harlequin Books S. A.

Wild at Heart, *From This Moment On* and *Her Last Best Fling* were first published in Great Britain by Harlequin (UK) Limited.

Wild at Heart © 2013 Vicki Lewis Thompson
From This Moment On © 2013 Debbi Quattrone
Her Last Best Fling © 2013 Candace Havens

ISBN: 978-0-263-92088-8

05-1116

Our policy is to use papers that are natural, renewable and recyclable products and made from wood grown in sustainable forests.The logging and manufacturing processes conform to the legal environmental regulations of the country of origin.

Printed and bound in Spain
by CPI, Barcelona

WILD AT HEART

BY
VICKI LEWIS THOMPSON

New York Times bestselling author **Vicki Lewis Thompson**'s love affair with cowboys started with the Lone Ranger, continued through Maverick and took a turn south of the border with Zorro. She views cowboys as the Western version of knights in shining armor—rugged men who value honor, honesty and hard work. Fortunately for her, she lives in the Arizona desert, where broad-shouldered, lean-hipped cowboys abound. Blessed with such an abundance of inspiration, she only hopes that she can do them justice. Visit her website, www.vickilewisthompson.com.

To the dedicated folks who devote endless hours and abandon creature comforts so that our precious wildlife is protected. Thank you!

Prologue

July 3, 1984, Last Chance Ranch

ON PRINCIPLE, ARCHIBALD CHANCE approved of getting the ranch house gussied up for the Independence Day festivities. He was as patriotic as the next man. But the excitement of an impending party had transformed his usually well-behaved grandsons into wild things. From his position on a ladder at the far end of the porch, he could hear all three of them tearing around inside. He hoped to get the red, white and blue streamers tacked up before any of them came out.

That hope died as the screen door banged open and a bundle of two-year-old energy with a fistful of small flags raced down the porch toward him. The kid was more interested in who was coming after him than looking where he was going. A tornado in tiny cowboy boots.

"Nicky!" The screen door banged again as Sarah, Archie's daughter-in-law, dashed after him.

Giggling, Nicky put his head down and ran as fast as

his little legs would carry him. With no time to climb down, Archie dropped the bunting, tossed the nails into the coffee can and braced himself against the ladder as he shouted a warning.

Fortunately Sarah was quick. She scooped up both boy and flags a split second before he smashed into the ladder. "Those are for the table, young man."

"I gots flags, Mommy!" the little boy crowed.

"Yes, and they have pointy ends. Don't run with them, Nicholas." Sarah glanced up at Archie. "Sorry about that."

"Gabe gots flags, too!" Nicky announced.

Sarah wheeled around, and sure enough, there was little Gabe, not yet two, motoring toward them with a flag in each hand.

"I wager somebody's supplying them with those," Archie said.

"Yes, I wager you're right. And his name is Jack. Excuse me, Archie. I have a five-year-old who needs a reminder about the dangers of giving pointy objects to little boys." Confiscating the flags from both toddlers amid wails of distress, she herded them back inside.

"You're doing a great job, Sarah!" Archie called after her. He never missed an opportunity to tell her that. She'd given birth to only one of those kids, baby Gabriel, and she'd inherited the other two as part of the deal for being willing to marry Jonathan Chance. She loved all three kids equally, and she loved their father with the kind of devotion that made Archie's heart swell with gratitude.

As he turned back to his bunting chore, the screen

door squeaked again, signaling another interruption. He'd oil those hinges today. He hadn't realized how bad they were.

Glancing toward the door, he smiled. This was the kind of interruption he appreciated.

Nelsie approached with two glasses of iced tea. "Time for a break, Arch."

"Don't mind if I do." Hooking the hammer in his belt, he carried the coffee can full of nails in the crook of his arm as he descended the ladder to join his wife. "How're things going in there?"

"Not too bad, considering. I'm glad we decided to host the after-parade barbecue this year, but we didn't factor in the dynamics of having both babies able to walk and Jack putting them up to all manner of things. They'll do anything he tells them, especially Nicky."

Archie put down the hammer and nails before accepting a glass of tea and settling into the rocking chair next to her. They'd bought several rockers to line the porch, which would come in mighty handy during the barbecue. "Those boys are a handful, all right." He took a sip of tea. "Wouldn't trade 'em for all the tea in China, though."

"Me, either, the little devils." Nelsie chuckled. "Oh, you know what? I saw a bald eagle fly over early this morning. Forgot to tell you that."

"Huh. Wonder if there's a nest somewhere."

"Could be. Anyway, I thought it was appropriate, a bald eagle showing up so close to the Fourth. Maybe he, or she, will do a flyover tomorrow for our guests."

"I'll see if I can arrange it for you."

She smiled at him in that special way that only Nelsie could smile. "If you could, I believe you'd do it, Archie."

"Yep, that's a fact." They'd celebrated their forty-seventh anniversary last month, and he loved this woman more every day. He would do anything for her. And to his amazement, she would do anything for him, too.

He was one lucky cuss, and he knew it. His father used to say that Chance men were lucky when it counted. In Archie's view, finding a woman like Nelsie counted for a whole hell of a lot.

1

Present Day

FROM A PLATFORM twenty feet in the air, Naomi Perkins focused her binoculars on a pair of fuzzy heads sticking out of a gigantic nest across the clearing. Those baby eagles sure had the cuteness factor going on. If they lived to adulthood, they'd grow into majestic birds of prey, but at this stage they were achingly vulnerable.

Blake Scranton, the university professor who'd hired her to study the nestlings, was an infirm old guy who was writing a paper on Jackson Hole bald-eagle nesting behavior. He expected her firsthand observations to be the centerpiece of his paper, which would bring more attention to the eagle population in the area and should also give a boost to ecotourism.

Lowering her binoculars, she crouched down to check the battery reading of the webcam mounted on the observation-platform railing. Still plenty of juice.

As she glanced up, a movement caught her eye. A rider had appeared at the edge of the clearing.

In the week she'd spent monitoring this nest on the far boundary of the Last Chance Ranch, she'd seen plenty of four-legged animals, but none of the two-legged variety until now. Standing, she trained her binoculars on the rider and adjusted the focus. Then she sucked in a breath of pure feminine appreciation. A superhot cowboy was headed in her direction.

She didn't recognize him. He wasn't one of the Chance brothers or any of their longtime ranch hands. Her eight-by-eight platform, tucked firmly into the branches of a tall pine, allowed her to watch him unobserved.

If he looked up, he might notice the platform even though it was semicamouflaged. But he was too far away to see her. Her tan shirt and khaki shorts would blend into the shadows.

Still, she'd be less visible if she sat down. Easing slowly to the deck, she propped her elbows on the two-foot railing designed to keep her from falling off. Then she refocused her binoculars and began a top-to-bottom inventory.

He wore his hair, which was mostly covered by his hat, on the longish side. From here it looked dark but not quite black. She liked the retro effect of collar-length hair, which hinted at the possibility that the guy was a little less civilized than your average male.

The brim of his hat blocked her view of his eyes. She decided to think of them as brown, because she had a preference for dark-haired men with brown eyes.

He had a strong jaw and a mouth bracketed by smile lines. So maybe he had a sense of humor.

Moving on, she took note of broad shoulders that gave him a solid, commanding presence. He sat tall in the saddle but without any tension, as if he took a relaxed approach to life.

Thanking the German makers of her binoculars for their precision, she gazed at the steady rise and fall of his powerful chest. He'd left a couple of snaps undone in deference to the heat, and that was enough to reveal a soft swirl of dark chest hair. Vaguely she realized she'd crossed the line from observing to ogling, but no one would ever have to know.

Next she focused on his slim hips and the easy way his denim-clad thighs gripped the Western saddle. While she was in the vicinity, she checked out his package. She had to own that impulse. If she ever caught some guy giving her such a thorough inspection, she'd be insulted.

But she didn't intend to get caught, or even be seen. After a solid week of camping, she was far too bedraggled to chat with a guy, especially a guy who looked like this one. He was the sort of cowboy she'd want to meet at the Spirits and Spurs when she looked smokin' hot in a tight pair of jeans, a low-cut blouse and her red dancing boots.

He could be a visitor out for a trail ride, but if he was a ranch hand, he might come into town for a beer on Saturday nights. She'd ask around—subtly, of course. He'd be well worth the effort of climbing out of this tree and sprucing up a bit.

She was due for some fun of the male variety, come to think of it. She'd been celibate since… Had it really been almost a year since Arnold? And that hadn't been a particularly exciting relationship, now that she had some distance and could look at it objectively.

She had a bad tendency to set her sights too low, which was how she'd ended up in bed with Arnold, a fellow researcher in a Florida wildlife program. If she should by some twist of fate end up in bed with this cowboy, she could never say her sights were set too low. He was breathtaking.

He was also getting too close for her to continue ogling. She regretfully lowered her binoculars and eased back from the edge of the platform. If she scooted up against the tree trunk, he'd never know she was there.

Emmett Sterling, the ranch foreman, and Jack, the oldest of the Chance brothers, had built the platform for her. They'd also mentioned her presence to the cowhands so they'd be aware in case they rode out this way. But even if the rider had noticed the structure, he'd have no idea whether it was currently occupied.

She could be doing any number of things. She might be hiking back to town for supplies or taking a nap in the dome tent she'd pitched down near the stream that ran along the Last Chance's northern boundary. Leaning against the tree, she listened to the steady clop-clop of hooves approaching.

She needed to sneeze. Of course. People always needed to sneeze when they were trying to hide. She pressed her finger against the base of her nose.

Finally the urge to sneeze went away, but she felt a tickle in her throat. *Clop, clop, clop, clop.* The horse and rider sounded as if they were only a few yards from her tree. She needed to cough. She really did. Maybe if she was extremely careful and exceptionally quiet, she could pick up her energy drink and take a sip.

Usually while she was up here, the songbirds chirped merrily in the branches around her and the breeze made a nice sighing sound. That kind of ambient noise would be welcome so she could take a drink of her favorite bright green beverage without danger of detection. But the air was completely still and even the birds seemed to have taken an intermission.

The horse snorted. They were *very* close. If only the horse would snort again, she could coordinate her swallow with that. She raised the bottle to her mouth but was greeted by absolute silence.

That means he's stopped right under your tree, idiot. Adrenaline pumped through her as she held her breath and fought the urge to cough.

"Anybody up there?"

His unexpected question made her jump. She lost her grip on the bottle, which rolled to the edge of the platform and toppled off.

The horse spooked and the man cursed. So did Naomi. So much for going unnoticed.

The horse settled down, but the man continued to swear. "What *is* this damned sticky crap, anyway?"

Filled with foreboding, she crawled to the edge of the platform and peered down. Her gorgeous cowboy had taken a direct hit from her energy drink. He yanked off his hat, causing green liquid that had been caught in the brim to run down the front of his shirt. "Oh, *God.* I've been slimed!"

"Sorry."

He glanced up at her. "You must be Naomi Perkins."

"I am." Even from twenty feet away, or more like ten or twelve since he was still on his horse, she could see that he was royally pissed. "And you are?"

"Luke Griffin."

"Sorry about dousing you, Luke."

"I'll wash, and my clothes will wash, but the hat… And it's my best hat, too."

"I'll have it cleaned for you." She wondered why he'd worn his best hat out on the trail. Usually cowboys saved their best for special occasions.

Blowing out a breath, he surveyed the damage. "That's okay. Maybe Sarah can work some magic on it."

"Sarah Chance?"

"Right. The boss lady."

So he was a ranch hand. "She might be able to clean it." Naomi, who'd grown up in this area, had great respect for Sarah, widow of Jonathan and co-owner of the ranch along with her three sons. If anybody could salvage a hat covered with energy drink, Sarah could.

"What's in that stuff, so I can tell her what to use on it?"

"Oh, you know. Glucose, electrolytes, vegetable juice. I think it's the broccoli that turns it green. Or maybe it's the liquefied spinach."

He grimaced. "That sounds nasty."

"I don't always eat three squares while I'm working, so the energy drink helps me stay nourished and hydrated."

"You must be really dedicated if you can stomach that on a regular basis."

She shrugged. "You get used to it."

"You might. I wouldn't."

"So are you out here checking the fence?"

He hooked his damaged hat on the saddle horn and gazed up at her. "Actually, I rode out to see how you were getting along."

"You did?" That surprised her. "Did Emmett send you?"

"Not exactly. But he told us what you were trying to accomplish—documenting nesting behavior for a professor who plans to write up a paper on it. I thought that sounded like interesting work. I had a little spare time, so I decided to find out if you're okay."

"That's thoughtful." Especially when he didn't know her from Adam. Nor did she know him, although under different circumstances, she'd be happy to get acquainted. "I'm doing fine, thanks."

"How about the eagle babies? Are they all right?"

"So far." Apparently he was curious about the eagles. She could understand that. They were fascinating creatures.

"Good. That's good." A fly started buzzing around him, followed by a couple of bees. He waved them away. "They're after the sweet smell, I guess."

"I'm sure." He'd probably hoped to visit her platform and get a bird's-eye view of the eagles. Time to stop being vain and let him do that. "Listen, did you want to come up and take a look at the nest?"

"I'd love to, but I'm all sticky and attracting bugs."

"So maybe you could wash some of it off in the stream."

"Yeah, that might work."

"I'll come down. I know the best spot along the bank for washing up."

He smiled. "I'd like that. Thanks."

"Be right there." Wow, that was some smile he had going on. It almost made her forget that she looked like something the cat dragged in. She'd read that first impressions carried a tremendous amount of weight. As she started down the rope ladder, she hoped he'd make allowances.

DESPITE HAVING BEEN drenched in sticky, sweet green stuff, Luke wanted a look at Naomi Perkins. He hoped she'd be worth the possibility that he'd ruined his best hat. Had he known she possessed a hair-trigger startle response, he would have called out to her long before he'd reached her tree.

But as he'd approached, he'd assumed the platform was deserted. That was the only explanation for the total silence that had greeted him. If she'd been there, he'd reasoned, *she* would have greeted *him*.

That was the accepted way out here in the West. When a person laid claim to a portion of the great outdoors, be it with a campfire or a platform in a tree, they welcomed incoming riders. He was an incoming rider. She had to have noticed him. Yet for some reason she'd played possum.

So it was with great interest that he watched her climb down the rope ladder. First appeared a serviceable pair of hiking boots. He might have figured that.

Then came... Sweet Lord, she had an ass worthy of an exotic dancer. A man could forgive a whole bucket of that green glop landing on him for a chance to watch Naomi Perkins descend a ladder. He no longer cared about the sad condition of his hat, even though that Stetson had set him back a considerable amount of money.

She wore her tan T-shirt pulled out, not tucked in, but even so, he could tell that her slender waist did credit to the rest of her. Her breasts shifted invitingly as she descended, and by the time she'd reached the ground, he was glad he'd ridden out here.

Besides looking good coming down the ladder, she'd accomplished the climb with dexterity. She seemed perfectly at home out here by herself. He admired that kind of self-sufficiency. He'd guessed she might be that type of woman from the moment Emmett had described the job she was doing.

She'd put her honey-blond hair up in a careless ponytail. He could hardly expect some elaborate style from someone who'd been camping for days. Then she turned around, and he was lost.

Eyes bluer than morning glories, a heart-shaped face and pink lips that formed a perfect Cupid's bow. He'd never thought about his ideal woman, but from the fierce pounding of his heart, he suspected he was looking at her.

Before coming to the Jackson Hole area to work at the Last Chance eight months ago, he'd spent a couple of years in Sacramento. Although that city wasn't Hollywood by any means, he'd met plenty of women, young and old, who subscribed to plastic surgery and Botox beauty regimes. And the makeup—they wouldn't walk out the door without it. Some slept in it.

Standing before him was someone who wore not an ounce of makeup. She had an expressive face that obviously hadn't been nipped and tucked. In her khaki shorts and tan shirt, she seemed ready for adventure, like a sidekick for Indiana Jones. He didn't run across women like Naomi all that often. He felt like hoisting this treasure up onto his saddle and riding off with her into the sunset.

Not literally, of course. Sunset wasn't for several hours. Besides, that dramatic gesture sounded good in theory, but in reality he wasn't a good candidate for riding into the sunset with a woman on his horse. That implied that he'd made some pretty big promises to her.

He was a rolling stone who didn't make those kinds of promises. He traveled light. Even so, he wouldn't mind spending some time with the luscious Miss Perkins when she wasn't busy watching eagles.

Now that she was on the ground, he dismounted. "I'd shake your hand, but I'm afraid we'd be stuck together for eternity. My hands are covered with that green stuff."

"Understood."

He waved away more flies. "Time to get it off. Thanks for coming down to keep me company." Leading his horse, he started toward the stream a few yards away.

"It's the least I could do." She fell into step beside him. Their boots crunched the pine needles underfoot and sent up a sharp, clean scent that helped counteract the sweetness of the energy drink.

"Your folks own the Shoshone Diner, right?" he asked.

"Yes."

"I like the food there."

"Me, too. Now you're making me hungry for my mom's meat loaf."

"I would be, too, if I'd been trying to survive on that green junk. Listen, I didn't mean to scare you by calling to you just now. I thought nobody was up there, but I wanted to make sure." He glanced over at her to see what she might have to say for herself on that score.

Her cheeks turned pink. "I didn't realize you'd come out here because of the eagles. I assumed you'd ride on by."

"You didn't think someone riding by would stop and say howdy?"

"Sure, if they knew I was up there."

"So you were hiding from me?"

She nodded.

"Why?" He had a terrible thought. "Did you think I might hurt you?"

"No. I'm used to taking care of myself. I have bear spray and I know karate."

"I'm glad to hear it." It was the way he'd imagined she would be, resourceful and ready for anything. Very attractive traits. "But it doesn't explain why you were hiding."

She gestured to her herself and laughed. "Because I'm a hot mess!"

"You are?" He stared at her in confusion, unable to figure out what she meant.

"Okay, now you're just being nice, and I appreciate it, but I've been out here for a week. I've slept in a tent, washed up in the stream and put on clothes that were stuffed in a backpack. And then there's my hair."

"Okay, your hair might be sort of supercasual." He reached over, pulled a twig out of her ponytail and dropped it to the ground. "But the rest of you is just fine." He didn't know her well enough to tell her she looked sexy as hell. Her rumpled, accessible presentation worked for him way better than a slinky outfit. He related to someone who could survive without modern conveniences.

"Supercasual." She chuckled. "That's a great euphemism for *trashed*."

"I've seen celebrities whose hair looked way worse than yours, and it was fixed like that on purpose."

"What a gentlemanly thing to say." She pointed through the trees. "Right over there is a nice sandy spot. It's where I go in."

"Perfect." When he reached the bank of the creek, he let Smudge, the Last Chance gelding he usually rode, have a drink.

She came to stand beside him. "You're right, Luke. I overreacted to the idea of having company."

"I'm surprised you'd be so embarrassed." He finished watering the horse, backed him up and dropped the reins to ground-tie him. Then he turned toward Naomi. "Like I said, you look fine to me."

"I wouldn't have been embarrassed if Emmett had come out, or Jack. But I'd never met you." She shrugged. "I guess the vanity thing kicked in."

He gazed at her. "How did you know I wasn't Emmett or Jack?" Then he realized she must have binoculars. "Oh. You were spying on me."

Her blush deepened, giving her away.

Gradually he began to understand the issue. She'd used her binoculars to identify the person riding toward her lookout spot, which was natural. But when she'd discovered he was a stranger, she'd worried about making a bad impression. That was flattering.

"If it makes you feel any better," he said, "I wore my best hat out here on purpose. I wanted to make a good impression on you."

"You did? Why?"

"Well…" He started unsnapping his sticky shirt, starting with the cuffs on his sleeves. "I've been hearing a lot about you."

"Like what?"

"Oh, that you were this cute blonde who'd just moved back home after doing wildlife research for the state of Florida. They said you wrestled alligators and captured pythons and such." He unfastened the snaps running down the front of his shirt and pulled the tail out of his jeans. He felt her gaze on him. Well, that was okay. He wasn't ashamed of his body.

She seemed to get a kick out of the talk about her, though. "You'll have to forgive people for exaggerating," she said with a smile. "I didn't wrestle alligators. Sometimes I had to snare them and move them away from populated areas. But I never dealt with a python by myself."

"Even so, here you are out in the wilderness studying a nest of eagles. In my book, that makes you unusual."

"Sorry to disappoint you, but I'm not that exciting."

"I'm not disappointed at all. I'd have been disappointed to come out here and find you using a battery-powered hair dryer and painting your nails." If she was paying attention, she'd figure out he was attracted to her outdoor lifestyle.

"Thank you. I appreciate your saying that."

"On the other hand, I'm sure I failed to make a good impression on you, swearing and carrying on like I did. Sorry about that." He stripped off his shirt and wadded it up in preparation for dunking it in the water.

"No need to be sorry. I would've reacted the same way if I'd been showered with sticky green stuff."

Something in her voice made him pause and glance at her. To his delight, she was looking at him with a definite gleam in her eye. When he caught her at it, she blushed and turned away.

All righty, then. It appeared that taking off his shirt had been a very good idea.

2

IF NAOMI HAD realized that spilling her energy drink would make Luke take off his shirt, she would have done it on purpose. Pecs and abs like his belonged in a calendar. And unlike the shaved versions featured in muscle-building magazines, Luke had manly chest hair that highlighted his flat nipples and traced a path to the metal edge of his belt buckle.

But he'd caught her looking. He hadn't seemed to mind. In fact, she'd spotted a flicker of amusement in his eyes, which were, thank you, God, velvet brown.

"I'll go rinse this out."

"Good idea." Now, there was an idiotic response. Rinsing out his shirt wasn't merely a *good* idea. It was the *whole* idea, the reason they'd walked to the stream in the first place.

She watched him kneel on the embankment and dunk his shirt in the water. The stream wasn't large, no more than fifteen feet across at its widest point, but it ran deep enough in spots for fish to thrive, which was why the eagles were nesting here.

But she wasn't thinking about eagles now. Instead she gazed at the broad, muscled back of Luke Griffin and wondered what it would be like to feel those muscles move under her palms. Having such thoughts about a virtual stranger wasn't like her.

Except he didn't feel like a stranger. He'd come out here because of an interest in the eagles and curiosity about the woman studying them. Instead of being turned off by her rumpled appearance, he seemed to prefer it. That made him the sort of man she'd like to get to know.

At first he'd been understandably upset about getting doused with the energy drink, but apparently he was a good-natured sort of guy who rolled with the punches. Anyone would think he'd had to wash out his clothes in a stream numerous times from the efficiency with which he swirled the shirt in the water and wrung it out.

Then he set it on a nearby rock. Reaching into his back pocket, he pulled out a blue bandanna and plunged it into the water before rubbing his face, chest and shoulders with it.

Naomi felt like a voyeur standing there while he washed up. She could offer to help, but she wasn't sure that was appropriate, either. What could she do, wash his back?

At last he stood, his dripping shirt in one hand and his soaked bandanna in the other. "I'm considering whether I should put my hat in the water or not."

"I can't advise you." Wow, he was beautiful. She had a tough time remembering her name while he faced her, his chest glistening with droplets of water. Evaluating the best procedure for cleaning his hat was beyond her mental capabilities at the moment.

"I'm doing it. It can't get any worse." He walked toward her with the shirt and the bandanna. "Maybe you could find a tree branch for these."

"Sure." She took them, although she wondered what his plan might be. Hanging something to dry implied sticking around awhile. Was that what he had in mind?

Maybe he only wanted his shirt to get dry enough that it wouldn't feel clammy when he put it on, but that would take more than ten minutes. Fine with her. She wouldn't mind spending more time with this sexy cowboy. She found a fairly level branch for both the shirt and the bandanna. As a veteran camper, she was used to such maneuvers.

As she finished hanging up his stuff, he came back holding his saturated hat. "At least it won't attract flies on the way home." He looked around, found a convenient twig sticking out of a tree trunk and hung his hat on it. "I need the bandanna back. One more chore." Grabbing it, he returned to the stream and soaked the bandanna.

Naomi wasn't sure what his goal was until he walked over to his horse and started wiping its neck. Apparently the energy drink had anointed the brown-and-white paint, too. She gave Luke points for wanting to get the stuff off to keep the animal from being pestered by flies, as well.

His considerate gesture also provided her with quite a show. She wondered if he had any idea how his muscles rippled in the dappled sunlight while he worked on that horse. If she could have taken a video, it would be an instant hit on YouTube—gorgeous guy demonstrates his love of animals. What could be sweeter?

Finally he rinsed out the bandanna again and returned it to the branch where his shirt hung. "I think that takes care of the worst of it."

"You're causing me to rethink my consumption of energy drinks. I never dreamed one little bottle could create such a disaster."

He smiled at her. "Ah, it wasn't so bad. The cold water feels good."

"I know it does. That stream was a lifesaver this week when the temperatures kicked up."

"I'll bet. Now that you mention it, you look a little flushed. You can use my bandanna if you—" He paused and chuckled. "Never mind. You probably don't want to rinse your face with the bandanna I just used on my horse."

"I wouldn't care about that. But don't worry about me. I'm used to being hot."

His sudden laughter made the brown-and-white paint lift his head and stare at them. "I'm not touching that line."

"Oh, dear God." She felt a new blush coming on. "I didn't mean it like that." But he'd taken it like that. To her surprise, this beautiful shirtless cowboy was flirting with her. What a rush.

"Now you really look as if you could use a splash of cold water."

"It's my blond coloring. I blush at the drop of a hat." Or the drop of a shirt.

"It looks good on you." He gazed at her with warmth in his brown eyes.

She felt that warmth in every cell of her body, causing her to think of truly crazy things, like what it would be like to kiss him. She'd actually moved a step closer when the piercing cry of an eagle grabbed her attention.

Breaking eye contact, she looked up through the trees and saw the female sail overhead, a fish in her talons.

"Wow." Luke stared after the departing eagle. "He's huge."

"She."

He glanced at Naomi. "She? You mean her mate is even bigger than that?"

"No, her mate is smaller. Female eagles are bigger than the males." After a week of observation, Naomi could distinguish the female's eight-foot wingspan from that of her smaller mate.

"Well, blow me down with a feather. I didn't know that."

"Many people don't. They think any male creature is automatically bigger than the female, but that's not universally true."

He grinned at her. "You said that with a certain amount of relish."

"Maybe." She returned his smile. "It's fun to smash

stereotypes. By the way, did you happen to notice what kind of fish she had?"

"Looked like a trout to me."

"I thought so, too. I have to go back up and document the feeding time and the type of food on my computer. As I said, you're welcome to come up and check out the nest."

"I'd love to." He sounded eager. "But not if I'll get in your way. Or break the platform."

"You won't. Emmett and Jack were both up there together, testing its strength. They made sure it was sturdy."

"In that case, lead the way."

She walked quickly back to the tree. "This ladder will hold you, too. But we can't be on it at the same time." She started up.

"I'll wait until you give me the okay."

Climbing the dangling ladder was much easier than going down, and she made the trip in no time. "All clear. Come on up." She stood, glanced around her little research area and wondered what he'd think of it.

He hoisted himself up on the platform with another display of muscle. "What a view! Makes me want to be an eagle."

Funny, but she could almost imagine that. He had the alert gaze and restrained power she associated with eagles and hawks. "Not me. Flying would be cool, but I wouldn't like living without a roof over my head."

"I could live with that in return for the freedom of being able to fly anytime I felt like it. Yeah, the life of an eagle would suit me just fine." His glance took in the trappings of her work—the webcam mounted to the railing, the camp stool and small folding table for her laptop, her camera bag and a small cooler for her snacks and energy drinks. "Cozy setup."

"Thanks." It felt a lot cozier with him in it. At five-four, she didn't take up much room, so the area had seemed plenty large enough. Now she wondered how she'd be able to move around without bumping into him.

"Aren't you supposed to be recording stuff?"

Yes, she was, and his bare chest had distracted her from her duties. "Right." She picked up her binoculars and handed them to him. "You can help. Do you see the nest?"

"Sure do. From up here it's hard to miss." He raised the binoculars. "Big old thing, isn't it? Wow! There they are, two baby eagles getting lunch from Mom. That's impressive."

"See if you can keep track of whether one's getting more than the other." She sat down and turned on her laptop. "One of the nestlings is bigger and I suspect it's getting more food."

"That's what it looks like." Luke stood facing the clearing, booted feet spread. He looked like a captain at the helm of his ship as he studied the nest through the binoculars. "Look at that! Shoving the other one out of the way. Hey, you, you're supposed to share!"

Naomi smiled. She'd had the same thoughts, but hearing them come out of Luke's mouth made her realize how silly they were. Wildlife researchers couldn't afford to anthropomorphize their subjects. Giving them human attributes might work for Disney, but not for science.

Speaking of science, she'd better start making notes instead of watching Luke watch the eagles.

"Here comes the dad."

Yikes. She'd completely missed seeing the male eagle fly overhead. "If you'll describe what's happening, I'll just take down what you dictate."

"He came in with another fish, and that's definitely a trout. I think we're safe to say they're having trout for lunch. Now Mom's flown off and Dad's feeding the kids. Damned if that bigger baby isn't getting more of the second course, too."

"It happens. I'll bet you've seen it with puppies and kittens. They compete for the food. The most aggressive ones get the most food."

"Yeah, but when that happened with a litter my dog had, I supplemented so the runt didn't die."

She gave him points for that, too. "But these are wild creatures. If you tried to interfere, the parents might abandon both of them. I wouldn't worry too much. There are only two babies. I think they'll both make it."

"I hope so. How long before they can fly?"

"If all goes well, less than two months. They'll be on their own by fall."

"Then your job will be over?"

"It will, but this is only a stopgap until I get another full-time state job, or maybe something with the national parks."

"It's a pretty cool temp job, though. It would be exciting to see those little ones fly for the first time."

"I hope to. If I don't personally catch it with my still camera, I'm hoping the webcam will. Is the father still there?"

"Yep." Luke shifted his weight and the platform creaked. "But I think he's about done with the feeding routine. There he goes. Now the babies are huddling down."

"Unless the mother comes back, there won't be much to see for a while."

"No sign of her." Luke lowered the binoculars and crouched down next to the webcam. "So this is on 24/7?"

"Yes. Fortunately it has a zoom, so the pictures are pretty good, but quite a few researchers prefer to mount the camera on the tree where the nest is."

He glanced over his shoulder at her. "How the hell would you do something like that without freaking out the eagles?"

"You have to mount it before they start nesting and then hope they come back to that same place." She powered down the laptop to save her battery. "The professor who hired me hopes to get someone to monitor the nest next year and see if the pair returns. This year, by the time someone discovered the nest, the eggs were already laid, which meant this was the best we could do."

He stood and turned back to her. "Are you hooked up to the internet so you can broadcast it? I've seen people do that."

"So have I, but that wouldn't work here because of the location."

He glanced around. "Too remote?"

"No, too accessible. The professor doesn't want the place overrun by tourists trying to see the eagles up close and personal, which could disturb them. The Chance family isn't too eager to have that happen, either. Eventually, with proper supervision, the Chances might approve an ecotour back here, but it would be carefully planned."

"Makes sense. So this is a strictly private study."

"It is. The professor would be up here himself if he could manage it. He's the only one who gets the webcam feed, and I send him written reports."

"Am I breaking any rules by being up here?"

She smiled. "It's not *that* hush-hush. Everybody on the ranch knows about the eagles, and quite a few people in town. Fortunately, we're a protective bunch of folks around here, so the eagles should be safe."

"I think you're right about that. I've only lived here since the end of October, but I can tell it's a close community. You take care of your own."

So she was right—he was a fairly recent hire at the ranch. Getting one piece of the puzzle made her curious to find out more. "What brought you here?"

"More a *who* than a *what*. Nash Bledsoe. He was my boss when he co-owned a riding stable in Sacramento with Lindsay, his former wife. She wasn't much fun to work for after he left. Actually, she wasn't much fun to work for while he was there. I stayed because of him. Once he moved back here, I asked him to put in a good word at the Last Chance, and here I am."

"And now Nash has his own place, the Triple G. Are you headed there next?"

He shook his head. "Wouldn't be fair to Nash. I tend to move on after about a year, no matter where I am, so my time's two-thirds gone. He needs a ranch hand who'll stick around longer than a few months."

"You leave after a year?" She'd never heard anything so ridiculous in her life, unless he was trying to escape a woman or the law. "Are you on the run?"

"Nope." He smiled.

She looked into those smiling brown eyes. He didn't seem to be hiding anything. "Then I don't get it."

"Most people don't. It's just the way I like it. New scenery, new people. Keeps things interesting."

She should have known there'd be a fly in the ointment. He might be the sexiest man she'd met in ages, but if he avoided all attachments, then she literally couldn't see any future in getting to know him.

"That bothers you, doesn't it?" He sounded disappointed.

She shrugged. "Not really." At least it shouldn't. She'd leaped to some unwarranted conclusions about how this would go, and now he'd set her straight. At least he'd told her up front, so she could back off. "It's your life. You're entitled to live it the way you want to."

"Yes, I am." He sighed. "But I guess I'll pay the price where you're concerned."

"What price?"

"I…was hoping to get to know you better."

"Oh?" She wondered if this was leading where she thought it was. "In what way?"

"Well, I thought we might become friends."

"Sure, Luke. We can become friends." But from the way he'd flirted with her earlier, she didn't think he was looking for a platonic relationship. Maybe she was wrong. "You can come out here and check on the eagles from time to time, and we'll chat. Is that what you had in mind?"

"Uh…no." He rubbed the back of his neck and looked off in the distance, clearly uncomfortable with the discussion. "See, the thing is, I thought, from the way you looked at me back there at the stream, that you might be willing to go a little beyond friendship."

How embarrassing that he'd read her so accurately. "I see."

"But I can tell you don't like the idea that I don't stay around. Your attitude toward me changed."

"You act as if that's hard to understand. Do most of the women you meet like the idea of a temporary affair?"

"They do, actually." His gaze was earnest. "I tend to be attracted to women who have something going on in their lives, like you. The last thing they want is some needy guy who wants to monopolize them. So we get together, have great discussions, great sex and no strings attached."

"That must suit your lifestyle perfectly." Having this discussion while he stood there looking virile as hell wasn't helping. She didn't want to want him. He was a girl-in-every-port sort of guy. And yet…her insides quivered at the tantalizing possibilities.

"It does suit me, and it seems to suit them. I jumped

to conclusions about you, though. I thought you'd be happy to hear my exit plan, but you're not."

She cleared her throat to give herself some time to think. He was right about the signals she'd been giving off, so she couldn't blame him for putting her in the same category as his other girlfriends. Maybe she *was* in that category and hadn't realized it.

Although she'd like to settle down someday, she hadn't yet felt compelled to do that. She'd been building her career in wildlife research in Florida, but that had petered out. She hoped to get another full-time job in her field, which could be anywhere in the country. She didn't want to be either saved or tied down by a guy.

But in the meantime, she was going through a period of sexual deprivation, and he'd suggested a reprieve from that. Was it so terrible that he wasn't into making a lifelong commitment, especially when she wasn't looking for that, either?

"I need some time to think about this," she said. "After all, I just met you."

"Fair enough." He moved closer. "Just to be clear, are you saving yourself for Mr. Right? Because I'm not that guy."

She struggled to breathe normally, but she kept drawing in the intoxicating scent of Luke Griffin. "I'm not saving myself for anyone, but I…" She lost track of what she'd meant to say. This was her brain on lust, and it was fried.

"Then think about it." His lips hovered closer. "And while you're thinking, consider this." His mouth came down on hers.

She should pull away. She should give herself more time to review the situation with cold, hard logic before she allowed him to influence her by... Oh, no... he was good at this...very good. Before she realized it, he'd invaded her mouth with his tongue. No, that wasn't true. She'd invited him in. There had been no invasion at all, because she wanted...everything.

He lifted his head.

She didn't want the kiss to be over, but she wasn't going to beg him to do it again. A girl had to have some pride, which was why she wasn't about to open her eyes and let him see the turmoil he'd created.

His breath was warm on her lips. "Think about it. I'll come back for your answer." There was a movement of air and the sound of him climbing back down the ladder.

Opening her eyes, she sat down on the platform and held her hand against her pounding heart. She'd never deliberately set out to have a no-strings affair. But he'd been so sweet about it.

Still, she wasn't the type of woman he thought she was. Her answer should be no. Shouldn't it?

3

LUKE THOUGHT ABOUT Naomi all the way back to the Last Chance Ranch. He was worried that he'd insulted her by the way he'd acted. The thing was, her behavior toward him had been *exactly* like the women he'd known in the past.

In those cases, instant chemistry had been followed by a clear understanding. Sex would be purely for fun, because the intelligent ladies he'd connected with had other things to do besides take care of a man and his ego. They'd considered him a gift because he required nothing of them but multiple orgasms.

If Naomi didn't fit that category, he'd definitely insulted her, which didn't sit well with him. He knew the guy to talk to—Emmett Sterling. Emmett had helped her set up out there and might give him some insight into her character.

But he'd have to be careful. He didn't want any of the other cowhands hearing such a conversation. Luke hoped he could find a quiet moment to speak man-to-man with Emmett, but when he arrived back at the ranch he wondered if that would be possible.

Emmett, along with Sarah Chance's fiancé, Pete Beckett, had eight adolescent boys in the main corral for a roping clinic. The boys were all part of Pete's program to help disadvantaged youth. By living and working alongside cowboys several weeks out of the summer, they had an opportunity to learn discipline and routine.

Luke didn't see much of either going on in the corral. Ropes flew helter-skelter. They caught indiscriminately on fence posts and people. Clearly at least one more adult was needed in that arena.

The boys had been in residence for a couple of weeks, so Luke already knew them all pretty well. Wading into the confusion was no problem for him. He called out a greeting to Emmett and Pete, who seemed overjoyed to see him.

"I'll take these two." He motioned to Ace, a skinny, dark-haired, tattooed boy with attitude sticking out all over him, and his unlikely friend, a pudgy blond boy named Eddie who was always eager to please. Nash had been their favorite cowboy on the ranch, but Nash was busy with his own neighboring ranch these days, so Luke had stepped in. By pulling Ace out of the confusion, Luke knew he'd remove fifty percent of the problem. Ace resisted being told what to do, but he had no trouble telling everyone else what they should be doing.

Luke brought them next to the fence. "Roping is not only a skill," he said, "but an art." He'd figured out that beneath the tough exterior, Ace had the soul of a poet.

"Not when I do it," Ace grumbled.

"That's because you're treating it like a sport."

Eddie slapped his coiled rope against his thigh. "It *is* a sport." He peered at Luke. "Isn't it?"

"It can be both, I guess, but when it's done with style, it's more than a sport. It's an art form. Can I borrow your rope, Eddie?"

Eddie handed over his rope.

"Anybody can throw a loop and catch something," Luke said.

"Not me," Ace muttered.

"The trick is to make that loop dance." Luke had always loved the supple feel of a good rope. He'd been lucky enough to learn the skill from an expert roper on a ranch in eastern Washington. Luke roped the way he made love, with concentration, subtlety and—he hoped—finesse.

But he didn't like to show off, so he'd never demonstrated his skills to the folks at the Last Chance. Nash had known, but Nash would never have embarrassed him by making him perform on command like some trained monkey.

Ace needed a demonstration, though, because the kid wouldn't be interested unless he could see the beauty inherent in the task. Luke built his loop and proceeded to show him. Not only did he make the loop dance, but *he* danced, leaping and weaving in and out of the undulating circle he'd created.

He was so involved that he didn't realize all other activity had ceased and he'd drawn a rapt audience. He figured it out when he allowed the rope to settle at his feet and people started clapping. Glancing around, he saw that he'd brought the clinic to a halt.

"Hey, I'm sorry," he said. "I didn't mean to interrupt the proceedings."

"I'm glad you did." Pete surveyed the circle of admiring boys. "You've just become our new roping instructor. Welcome to the staff."

"Why didn't you tell us you could twirl a rope like that, son?" Emmett asked. "I had no idea."

"It never came up."

"He didn't tell you because he's too cool to brag." Ace's hero worship echoed in every syllable. Then he gazed up at Luke, his expression intense. "I want to learn how to do that."

"Good. I can teach you."

"Teach me, too!" Eddie's comment was followed by a chorus of others.

"Looks like you have a group of eager students," Pete said. "We'll be your assistants."

The rest of the afternoon passed quickly as Luke worked with the boys. He didn't remember he'd skipped lunch until his stomach started to growl.

As the boys were herded off to have dinner at the main house, Emmett came over and hooked an arm around Luke's shoulder. "I'm buying you a hamburger and a beer at the Spirits and Spurs. You rode in like the cavalry today, and I appreciate it."

"Thank you. I accept." Luke recognized a golden opportunity when it was presented, and he wasn't about to turn down the chance to talk to Emmett about Naomi. "Give me twenty minutes to shower and change."

"You got it. I need to freshen up a bit, myself. I'll bring my truck around to the side of the bunkhouse."

Within half an hour Luke was sitting in the passenger seat of Emmett's old but well-maintained pickup as they traveled the ten miles from the ranch to the little town of Shoshone and the popular bar. They rode with the windows down, and every once in a while they'd pass a stretch of road where the crickets were chirping like crazy.

It was one of those nights that wasn't too hot and wasn't too cold—the perfect night for lovers. Luke thought of Naomi, who was probably tucked into her tent right now. Before he'd ridden away, he'd made a quick survey and located that tent, a faded blue dome-style.

She was probably fine. Yet whenever he thought of her by herself, he had the urge to head on out there and make sure she was okay. That might not be particularly evolved, and an independent woman like Naomi wouldn't appreciate an overprotective attitude from anyone, let alone some cowboy she'd just met. Funny, he didn't usually have those protective feelings toward women, but with Naomi he couldn't seem to help himself.

Right now, though, he had to stop worrying about Naomi sleeping alone in her tent and grab this chance for a private discussion with Emmett. He didn't want to blow it. Once they arrived at their destination, their privacy would disappear.

Luke took a steadying breath. "I mentioned that

I was riding out to check on Naomi Perkins today, right?"

"I believe you said something like that. Did you go?"

"I did, and she's surviving great out there. It's pretty amazing to look at those baby eagles."

"So you climbed up to the platform?"

"She was nice enough to ask me, so I did. You built one hell of an observation spot for her, Emmett. She's really set up well."

"Good. I'm glad it's working out for her. I kept meaning to go out and I haven't made it, so I'm glad you did. She's a scrappy little thing, but I can't help worrying about her sometimes. Her mom and dad worry, too, but they've told me they've worked hard to give her room to be herself."

All that fit with what Luke had sensed about her from the beginning. "So I guess she's a modern woman who doesn't need a man around to protect her."

Emmett didn't answer right away. "If you mean that she doesn't need a man to physically protect her, that's probably right," he said at last. "She took karate when she was still in high school, and she could flip me onto my back if she wanted to."

Luke thought about that. "Good to know."

"And she takes other precautions. She has bear spray, and she makes sure her food is stowed. Naomi has a better chance of surviving out there by herself than some men I've known. But…"

"But?" Luke waited for the other shoe to drop.

"I could be way off base, but I don't think she's a

true loner. I think she'd love to find somebody to share her life, as long as it was the right somebody."

"Hmm." Well, that sealed his fate. He couldn't mess around with a woman like that. If Naomi yearned for someone steady in her life, he'd back off. His free-spirited father had tied himself to a job, a wife and a mortgage. He obviously regretted his choices. Luke had inherited that same free spirit, and he had no intention of repeating his dad's mistakes.

"Then again, how should I know what's in Naomi's heart?" Emmett said. "I'm the last person who should give out opinions on such things. I'm a divorced man in love with a wonderful woman, but the idea of marrying her scares me shitless."

"That's not so hard to understand, Emmett. Pam Mulholland has big bucks and you're a man of modest means. I watched my buddy Nash fall into the trap of marrying a woman who had a pile of money, and it was a disaster." Luke paused. "Then again, he's now planning to marry Bethany Grace, who also has a pile of money, and I think it'll be fine."

Emmett sighed. "So it all depends on the woman. And I know in my heart that Pam wouldn't let the money be a problem, but my damned pride is at stake. I can't seem to overcome my basic reluctance to marry a wealthy woman when I'm certainly not wealthy myself. I'm afraid I'll feel like a gigolo."

Luke dipped his head to hide a smile. The interior of the truck was dim. Still, he didn't want to take the slightest chance that Emmett would see that smile. But if Emmett Sterling, the quintessential rugged cowboy, could label himself a gigolo, the world had turned completely upside down.

NAOMI HAD MEANT to spend one more night out at the research site before hiking back to Shoshone for supplies and clean clothes. But the visit from Luke had thrown her off balance. She decided to take her break that very afternoon.

After clearing her platform of everything except the webcam and securing her campsite, she hoisted her backpack and made the trek into town. A night sleeping in her childhood bed at her parents' house would be a welcome luxury.

Her folks were thrilled to see her, as always, but business was brisk at the Shoshone Diner and they didn't have much time to chat. She'd anticipated that. At one time the diner served only breakfast and lunch, but recently they'd added a dinner menu.

Prior to that, the Spirits and Spurs had been the only place in town that served an evening meal. But as the tourist business had grown and the wait time for a table at the Spirits and Spurs had become ridiculous, Naomi's parents had decided to expand their offerings.

It had paid off for them. They'd hired extra help because Naomi wasn't there to waitress anymore, and both women were capable and had a set routine. If Naomi hung around the diner tonight, she'd only get in everybody's way.

So she ate the meat loaf her mother insisted on feeding her, went home for a quick shower and a change of clothes, and walked over to the Spirits and Spurs. On the way, she thought of Luke, who quite likely wouldn't be there on a weeknight. Ranch hands generally came into town on the weekend.

As she walked toward the intersection where the bar was located, she remembered the foolishly grand entrance she'd envisioned making in her tight jeans and revealing blouse. Instead she'd pulled on her comfort outfit—faded jeans and a soft knit top in her favorite shade of red. Nothing about her appearance tonight was calculated to turn heads.

Ah, well. She'd scrapped her plan to knock Luke back on his heels and make him her slave. Luke didn't intend to be any woman's slave. He was a love-'em-and-leave-'em kind of cowboy.

She'd never met a man who'd laid it out so clearly. At first she'd been appalled by the concept of a relationship based mostly on sex, with some interesting conversations thrown in, a relationship with an expiration date stamped plainly on the package.

She laughed to herself. And what a package it was, too. That was part of her dilemma. She wanted that package, even if she could enjoy it for only a limited time.

Music from the Spirits and Spurs beckoned her as she approached. During tourist season the bar had a live band every night, and Naomi loved to dance. She wouldn't mind kicking up her heels a little if anyone inside the bar felt like getting out on the floor. She could do with a little fun.

Maybe that was how she should view Luke's suggestion, too. She'd never seen herself as the kind of woman who would have a casual fling, but maybe she was needlessly limiting herself. She might be back in her hometown, but she wasn't a kid anymore. She had the right to make adult decisions. Very adult. A sensual zing heated her blood.

If the thought of parading her behavior in front of her parents bothered her at all, and she admitted that it did, they wouldn't have to know. She was living out in the woods, away from prying eyes. Luke might have to explain his behavior if he made regular visits to her campsite, but she'd let him worry about that.

As she pushed open the door to the Spirits and Spurs, the familiar scent of beer and smoke greeted her. This bar might end up being the last place in the entire world to ban smoking. Even if they did, the place was supposed to be haunted by the ghosts of cowboys and prospectors who'd tipped a few in this building a century ago. No doubt they'd bring the aroma of tobacco with them.

The band started playing a recent Alan Jackson hit she happened to like. Couples filled the small dance floor. The place was jumping, with most of the round wooden tables occupied and very few vacant seats at the bar.

Coming here had been a good idea. She watched the dancers and tapped her foot in time to the music. She'd have a beer and dance if she found a willing partner. Then tomorrow, or whenever Luke came back for his answer, she'd tell him not only yes but hell, yes. Look out, world. Naomi Perkins was ready to cut loose.

"Naomi?"

The rich baritone made her whirl in its direction. She'd last heard that voice after being kissed senseless twenty feet above the ground. She found herself staring into Luke Griffin's brown-eyed gaze. Her heart launched into overdrive.

They spoke in unison. "What are you doing here?"

"You first." Luke tilted back his hat and stared at her. "You're the big surprise. I thought you'd be curled up in your blue dome tent fast asleep."

She fought the urge to grab his shirtfront in both hands and pull him into another kiss, one even more potent than what they'd shared earlier today. "I'm staying with my folks in town. And how do you know I have a blue dome tent?"

"I checked it out before I left."

"For future reference?"

"No. In fact, that's why I hotfooted it over here. I—" He gestured toward the band. "Love that song, but I don't want to have to yell over it. Can we move outside for a minute?"

"Okay." She gulped in air and did her best to calm down. When she agreed to this affair, she wanted to appear in command of herself, even if she wasn't. He was used to sophistication, and she would exude that.

He held the door open and she walked out into the soft night air. He followed. As the door closed behind him, the music faded into background noise.

She turned to him. "Luke, I'm glad you're here tonight, because—"

"No, wait. Let me say something first. I was off base today, and I apologize with all my heart. You're not that kind of woman. I made a mistake and no doubt insulted you in the process."

Yikes, now what? Right when she'd decided to accept his outrageous proposal, he'd withdrawn it on the grounds that she wasn't *that kind of woman.*

She swallowed. "What kind of woman do you think I am?"

"The kind who needs stability. You deserve someone who wants to become a permanent part of your life, and I'm not that guy."

"Luke, I don't know what my life is going to be yet. You made me do some serious thinking today. I was shocked by your assumption that I'd want a fling, but—"

"I know you were, and I feel pretty rotten about that."

"Yes, but you see, when it comes right down to it…" She placed both hands on his chest so she could feel his heart beating and know for sure that it was racing as fast as hers. This wasn't a cold, calculated decision, after all. It was being made in the heat of the moment, and she was ready to dive headfirst into the flames.

She looked into his beautiful eyes. "I do want a fling with you, Luke." Heat sizzled through her as she plunged into the fire. "In fact, I can't think of anything I want more."

4

LUKE WAS SUDDENLY so short of breath that he was a little scared he might black out. That wouldn't be cool in front of this woman who'd said she wanted to have sex with him. But he couldn't kiss her until he stopped struggling to fill his lungs with air.

The corners of her beautiful mouth tipped up. "Apparently you didn't expect me to say that."

"No." He dragged in a breath. "That's a fact. I definitely did not."

"I've never had this kind of effect on a man before." She gazed up at him as amusement turned to concern. "Are you going to be all right?"

"I'm going to be terrific." There. That statement sounded normal. Finally trusting himself to wrap her in his arms, he nudged his hat back with his thumb and pulled her close. Damn, that felt good. "*We're* going to be terrific."

"I'll have to leave that up to you." Her eyes caught the sparkle from the bar's neon bucking bronco. "If you've spent your adult life playing the field, then I guarantee you have more experience than I do."

"Maybe." He aligned his body with hers. They fit so perfectly it was a little scary for a guy who didn't believe in perfect fits. But he'd figured that she'd be soft and pliable, warm and willing. His cock responded quickly. He'd have to remember they were standing on the corner of the town's only intersection. "But I can recognize natural talent when I see it."

Her smile widened. "You think I have a natural talent for sex?"

"I know you do, at least for kissing, which usually tells me a lot about a woman." Keeping one arm firmly around her narrow waist, he slid his free hand up through her silky blond hair. No ponytail tonight.

"We only kissed once."

"True." He cradled the back of her head. "I should gather more information before I come to any firm conclusions."

She rocked against him. "Feels like you've already come to a very firm conclusion."

"See, that's what I'm talking about." Cupping her bottom, he snuggled her in tight. "A natural talent. And, lady, sassy comments and sexy moves like that will get you anything you want from me."

"Anything?"

"Sky's the limit." He lowered his head and brushed his mouth over hers. So delicious. But he dared not get involved in the kind of kiss he wanted, the kind that would make him forget where he was.

She clutched his shoulders and joined in his little

game of butterfly kisses. "I've already told you what I want."

"In general terms, yes." The feathery touch of her lips could drive him crazy if it went on too long without some way to release the tension. "But we have to work out the details."

"We can't do anything here."

He chuckled. "No, obviously not." Although with the blood pumping hot in his veins, he'd already fantasized about coaxing her into the shadows behind the building. "We're standing in front of the most popular spot in town."

"I mean not here, as in not in Shoshone."

He nibbled her full lower lip. "You want to drive to Jackson?" He hoped not. He wouldn't be able to swing very many trips to Jackson and still handle his assigned work on the ranch. But with a hot woman in his arms, he was ready to do whatever it took to have her.

"No, nothing that drastic." She placed tiny kisses at the corners of his mouth. "I was referring to my campsite as being the most discreet choice."

"It's perfect, except you're not there." And he wanted her now, tonight. Moments ago he'd given up all hope of a relationship, but her unexpected decision and these flirty kisses had flipped the switch on his libido and destroyed his patience. He outlined her mouth with the tip of his tongue.

Her breathing had changed, signaling that she was getting as worked up as he was. "I will be there."

"When?" His fingers flexed against her bottom.

"Tomorrow."

He groaned. "That's forever."

"I can't hike out there in the dark."

"I know. But I—whoops, somebody's coming." He released her and stepped back. With luck, whoever it was would simply call a greeting and pass on by. Then he glanced over and realized that wasn't going to happen. Thank God for the shadows that should keep his aroused condition from being too obvious.

Emmett walked toward them. "Hi there, Naomi." He touched the brim of his hat. "Nice to see you."

"Hi, Emmett. It's good to see you, too. You don't usually come into town midweek."

"I wanted to treat Luke. He showed up in the nick of time and put on a roping demonstration that saved what was fast becoming a disaster."

"Ah, you would have worked it out." Luke pulled the brim of his hat back down and hoped Emmett hadn't noticed how he'd shoved it back, which was typical for a cowboy who'd been kissing a woman.

"I'm not so sure." Emmett glanced at Naomi. "Take my word for it. We had a snarled-up mess, but five minutes after Luke showed up and started twirling a rope, the kids were mesmerized. They hadn't seen the possibilities of roping until then. Pete and I aren't that fancy. This boy has hidden talents."

"Talent, singular," Luke said. "Trick roping. That's my only hidden talent."

Naomi glanced at him. "Oh, I doubt that."

"Anyway," Emmett said. "I didn't mean to break up your conversation, Luke, but your food's getting cold.

Naomi, why don't you join us? We have an extra chair. Have you had dinner?"

"Yes, thanks. I ate at the diner before I came over. But I don't want to keep you two from your meal. Let's go in."

"Excellent. You can fill me in on how the eagle project's going."

"I'd love to. That platform you and Jack built is working out beautifully."

Luke followed them in. As Emmett asked more questions about the eagles, Luke quietly ground a centimeter off his back molars. He hadn't been sure when Emmett first showed up, but he was now. The foreman was deliberately interfering in what he saw as a problem situation between Luke and Naomi.

No doubt Emmett saw Luke as the aggressor and Naomi as the sweet local girl about to be seduced by a guy who would leave her in the lurch. It wasn't like that, of course. Luke had been ready to back off and Naomi had turned the tables on him. But he couldn't very well explain that to Emmett. A gentleman wouldn't put the blame on a lady.

The foreman had every reason to misunderstand what was happening. When Luke had been hired on at the Last Chance, he'd warned both Emmett and Jack that he tended to move along after a year or so. They'd both predicted he'd change his mind, that the Last Chance had a way of getting in a person's blood.

But last month he'd turned down Nash's offer of employment and had made no secret as to why. He believed in being up front with people, so he could see why Emmett thought Naomi needed someone to step in and keep her heart from being broken.

Luke didn't want to get crossways with the foreman. He liked and admired the guy, and until now they'd had no real issues between them. But Luke would be damned if he'd allow Emmett to louse up a perfectly acceptable arrangement between two consenting adults.

He thought about his options as he ate the excellent dinner Emmett had bought him and listened to the foreman and Naomi talk about the eagles. Luke even participated in the conversation because he was interested in those birds, too. He was more interested in the woman watching the birds, but he found the eagle study fascinating. He hadn't been kidding when he'd told Naomi that an eagle's freedom of movement appealed to him.

"That nest's not as big as some." Naomi took a sip of the draft she'd ordered. "It's only about seven feet across. I've seen reports on nests that are ten feet and weigh close to two tons."

Emmett shook his head in disbelief. "That's like putting my pickup in the top branches of one of those pines. I had no idea they could be that heavy. I'd—" He stopped talking and glanced at the door. "What do you know? There's Pam. Excuse me a minute, folks. I need to go over and say hello. Maybe she can join us." He stood and walked toward the door.

Luke grabbed his chance. He kept his voice low as he looked over at Naomi. "You do realize Emmett's trying to save you from me, right?"

"I thought he might be."

"He told me earlier tonight that he thought you wanted a steady guy in your life. That's why I backed off."

Naomi sighed. "I'm not surprised he'd say something like that. He's friends with my parents, and he's a dad. He probably sees me as being like his daughter, Emily."

"Ah. Okay, I get that." Luke thought about the blonde woman who was in training to eventually take over Emmett's job when he retired. Emily and Naomi had several things in common besides their coloring. They were both only children who had been raised to be independent and fend for themselves without leaning on a man. They both enjoyed testing themselves with physical challenges.

But Emily was now married to Clay Whitaker, who ran the stud operation for the Last Chance. Emmett might figure that Naomi, having similarities to his daughter, also should find herself someone like Clay.

He glanced at her. "Maybe Emmett knows what he's talking about. Maybe I should just—"

"Don't you dare back off because Emmett thinks I'm just like his daughter. I'm not."

The defiant sparks flashing in her blue eyes gladdened his heart. She thought for herself, and that was a quality he admired. "I'm sure you're not just like anyone."

"Nobody is. We're all unique, which means we get to choose our own path. What you and I decide to do is none of Emmett's business."

The tension that had been tightening a spot between Luke's shoulder blades eased. "And you won't be upset if I tell him that?"

"No, but I think I'm the one who needs to tell him."

"I'll tell him." He started to add that it should be a man-to-man talk but decided that might not sit well with Naomi. She liked being in charge of her destiny.

"No, you work for him and I don't."

"But he built you a research platform."

"Well, one of us needs to say something. Uh-oh. Here he comes. And he doesn't look happy."

"Bet it has something to do with Pam." Luke noticed that Pam Mulholland, the woman Emmett cared for but couldn't bring himself to marry, was being helped into her chair by a guy Luke didn't recognize. The barrel-chested man dressed in flashy Western clothes and what looked like an expensive hat. "Or that guy."

Emmett returned to his seat, his expression grim. "It's my own damned fault," he muttered to no one in particular.

"What is?" Luke asked. "And who is that guy with Pam? I've never seen him before, and if that's the way he normally dresses, I doubt I've missed him."

"You haven't missed him." Emmett picked up his beer and drained the contents. "Name's Clifford Mason. Just flew in today from Denver. Booked a room at the Bunk and Grub."

Naomi looked over at the table where Pam and the newcomer sat. "Does Pam normally go out to dinner with her B and B guests?"

"No, she does not." Emmett smoothed his mustache. "Far as I know, it's never happened before."

Luke could see Emmett was seething with jealousy and was doing his best to keep a lid on his feelings. "Is he on vacation?"

"No, he's been in contact with both Pam and Tyler Keller, Josie's sister-in-law." Emmett looked over at Naomi. "I don't know if your folks told you that the town hired Tyler a while back as a special-events planner to bring in more business. She's been doing a great job."

"I think Mom and Dad said something about it. And I certainly see the results in the increased tourist trade. So this guy is connected to an event?"

Emmett nodded. "Something to do with special preparations for the Fourth of July celebration. All very hush-hush. They want to surprise the good people of Shoshone."

"Well, then." Luke sat back in his chair. "It's only a business dinner. He'll be around until everything's set up, and then he'll leave. No big deal, right?"

Emmett scowled at him. "It wouldn't be if I hadn't seen the way he looked at Pam, like she was a helping of his favorite dessert."

"That's understandable." Naomi seemed to be trying to soothe the troubled waters, too. "She's a beautiful woman. But there's no way she'd prefer a citified dandy like him to you, Emmett. She probably went to dinner with him to be polite."

"I'd be willing to believe that if she hadn't flirted with him right under my damned nose."

Naomi smiled. "Emmett, that's the oldest trick in the book. She's trying to make you jealous. Everybody knows how you feel about her. And she's made no secret about how she feels about you, too. Why not end the suspense and propose to her?"

"Can't bring myself to do it. Doesn't seem right when she has so much and I have so little."

"Love?" Naomi asked with a twinkle in her eye.

Emmett snorted. "'Course not. Money's the problem, not love."

Luke checked on Pam and Clifford's table. "Then you're leaving the door open for the likes of him. I agree with Naomi. I'm sure Pam would rather have you than that character. But she might be tired of waiting for you to get over this hang-up."

Emmett muttered something that could have been a curse.

"I have an idea." Luke tucked his napkin beside his plate. "Go over and ask Pam to dance. Stake your claim."

The light of battle lit Emmett's blue eyes as he pushed back his chair. "All right, I will. That sonofabitch probably can't dance a lick."

Luke grinned. "If he could, he wouldn't dress like a peacock."

"That was brilliant," Naomi murmured as they watched Emmett amble over to the table.

"Let's hope it works." Luke thought it might. He hadn't spent his adult life romancing women without learning a thing or two. Pam looked surprised, but she left her chair and walked to the dance floor with Emmett.

Luke pushed back his chair. "That's our cue. Dance with me, Naomi Perkins."

Laughing, she took the hand he offered and soon he had her right where he wanted her, in his arms. He'd had a hunch that she'd be a good dancer. He thanked the series of coincidences that had given him the opportunity to dance with Naomi. What a joy.

Her breath was warm in his ear as she twirled with him on the polished floor. "Did you talk Emmett into dancing for his sake or yours?"

"I figured it would help us both out." He spun her around. "I couldn't leave here tonight without at least one dance."

She brushed a quick kiss on his cheek. "I knew you had more hidden talents."

"Anything I have is yours for the taking." He moved her smoothly across the floor in a spirited two-step.

"I'm taking it."

"When?"

"I'll be up on my platform by ten in the morning. After that, it's up to you."

He twirled her under his arm. "Are you sure we can't manage something tonight?"

"Positive. You're going home with Emmett and I'm sleeping in my parents' house."

He brought her in close for one precious second. His heart hammered so loudly he could barely hear the music. "I want you so much."

"I want you, too." Her cheeks were flushed. "And I will have you. And you'll have me. Tomorrow."

The music ended, and he held her close. "Promise you'll think about me when you're lying alone tonight."

She gazed up at him, her lips parted as she breathed quickly, recovering from the exertion of the dance. "Only if you'll promise to think about me."

"That's an easy promise."

"I think I should leave now." She eased out of his arms. "See you tomorrow."

He watched her go and fought the urge to follow her outside for one last kiss.

"That was a good idea you had." Emmett came over and clapped him on the shoulder. "We dance great together, and I don't think she'll be flirting with that Clifford guy so much now. Thanks, son."

"You're welcome. Ready to go home?"

"Yeah. I made my statement." He reached for his wallet and tossed some bills on the table. "Let's leave."

Back in Emmett's truck, they rode in silence for a couple of miles. But finally Luke decided he needed to clear the air. "I know you're worried about me getting involved with Naomi."

Emmett blew out a breath. "I wouldn't be, except you keep talking about leaving. I wish you'd rethink that, Luke. Frankly, I've never quite understood it."

"I have more things to see and do. Too long in one place and I get restless, wondering what's on the other side of the hill. When you start getting attached is when you're reluctant to leave, and then you slowly settle into your rut."

"I suppose you think I'm in a rut, then."

"From my vantage point, yes, but if you're happy, that's all that matters. I was born a wanderer, just like my dad."

Emmett slowed down so that a family of raccoons could cross the road. "So he travels all over the place, too?"

"Nope. He got mired in a mortgage, car payments, a lawn that has to be mowed, a fence that has to be painted, a garage that has to be cleaned. My mother wanted all that, and he became trapped by those things in order to please her, or at least keep the peace. He never went anywhere. He warned me that he was a cautionary tale."

"Hmm. So your father is miserable?"

Luke nodded. "Not completely miserable, but he has regrets. He sighs when he glances through the travel section of the newspaper and he watches every travel documentary he can find. He even clips out coupons for discount travel adventures that he can't follow up on."

"Excuse me for saying so, Luke, but unless he's an invalid, he could still travel. What's stopping him from going?"

"Like I said, the responsibilities at home, and my mother, who has no interest in traveling." But as Luke laid it out for Emmett, he had to admit that his father was an adult with free will. If this was his passion, he could find a way to make it happen. Maybe it was easier to stay home and complain.

"You know, son, could be he's using your mother as an excuse not to go."

"Maybe. He might be scared to actually go now. I see your point, but that only emphasizes mine. I don't want to tie myself to the same things that weigh him down, whether he's allowing that or not. I'd rather avoid being in that mess in the first place. I wouldn't be good at settling down, and I know it."

"I suppose, with an example like that, you don't think so."

Luke had the feeling that Emmett had more he could say, but he was refraining from saying it. That was okay with Luke, because they'd strayed from the topic, which was his intentions toward Naomi and hers toward him.

So he tackled the subject again. "Naomi knows all about my wanderlust. She and I are attracted to each other, and I've told her I'm not a forever kind of guy."

"Yes, but she might think she can change you."

"I don't think she wants to."

"All women want to get a man to settle down. It's the way of the world." Emmett spoke with certainty.

"It used to be, Emmett, but not so much anymore. Naomi's like a lot of women—not sure where she's going, what her next job will be. She wants to stay flexible. She's no more ready for a husband than I'm ready for a wife."

"She told you that?"

"She did. And she's not the only woman who's said the same kind of thing. I don't want to go behind your back, Emmett, but I intend to spend time with Naomi, and she's heading into it with her eyes wide open. In fact, she likes the idea that I won't be begging for her hand in marriage."

Emmett was quiet for at least a full minute. "Her folks wouldn't appreciate knowing about this."

"I'm sure they wouldn't."

"So I won't tell them."

"Thank you."

"I won't pry into your activities during your free time, but I expect the same amount of work out of you that I've always had."

"You'll get it. But I have an afternoon off coming, and I'd like to take it tomorrow."

"Guess I don't have to ask where you'll be going."

"No. And…I'd like to borrow a horse. If you can't lend me one, I understand, but I—"

"You can borrow the damned horse." Emmett sounded gruff. "Smudge can always use the exercise."

"Thanks, Emmett."

"You're welcome. And if you have any more bright ideas regarding Pam, don't keep them to yourself."

Luke smiled. "I won't."

5

NAOMI HAD EXPECTED to toss and turn, but she slept great. She loved camping, but there was something to be said for a good innerspring. As she packed up for the hike back to the campsite, she thought about what likely would be happening there in the next few days and searched around for items she wouldn't normally take camping.

Lacy underwear topped the list. Then she threw in a see-through nightgown that she'd never considered wearing while sleeping in a tent. She had a perfume bottle in her hand, ready to pack it, when she came to her senses.

Good grief, had she completely lost her mind? Fragrance of any kind was a no-no. She was in bear country, for God's sake, not at a beach resort.

For that matter, she might want to forget the see-through nightgown, too. It was the sort of thing a woman wore when she emerged from the bathroom of a luxury suite and sashayed over to the king-size bed where her lover waited, his gaze hot. When two people were crammed into a small dome tent, transparent lingerie lost most of its impact.

With reality smacking her in the face, she pulled out her lacy underwear, too. She was doing field research on a nesting pair of eagles, not arranging a romantic tryst with the man of her dreams. Luke had suggested this arrangement after catching her at her rumpled worst. If she got all fancy on him, he might laugh.

Or worse yet, he might wonder if she was trying to snare him with her feminine wiles. Then he'd turn tail and run. He'd proposed a straightforward liaison where they both understood the parameters. Seductive clothing could easily send the wrong message.

Because she could cut cross-country to the campsite, her hike was only about five miles. Hiking always helped her think. As she walked, she examined her knee-jerk response to this situation with Luke.

She'd automatically reached for the accepted female lures—fragrance and suggestive clothing. She'd reacted as if she needed to make herself more desirable to him. Oh, yeah, Luke would have been suspicious of her motivation for doing that.

She was suspicious of her motivation. Before this affair started, she might want to search her conscience to make absolutely sure no hidden agenda existed. This relationship couldn't be a bait and switch where she accepted his invitation to a no-strings affair and then subtly tried to bind him to her.

Hiking across a sunny meadow filled with sage and wildflowers, butterflies and songbirds, was perfect for soul-searching. She did a mental practice run through the scenario. For a few weeks, she would enjoy Luke's company and his gorgeous body. They'd have great sex and watch the eagles together. She'd become used to having him around.

But the eagles would leave the nest. Luke had already said that was about the time he planned to head for parts unknown. She'd have to bid him goodbye without making a big deal out of it. Could she?

Well, of course she could. After she'd graduated from college and before starting her first job, she and some friends had spent the summer backpacking through Europe. They'd had an amazing time, but that trip had ended and the friends had scattered. They kept up through emails, but their summer of bonding was only a memory now.

Had she been sad when the trip had ended? Of course. Would she like the chance to do it again? Definitely. But that wasn't possible. Everyone's lives had taken different turns.

She vowed to think of this time with Luke that same way, minus the continued email connection. She doubted he'd want that. For the next few weeks, she'd pretend to be on vacation with Luke Griffin, her traveling companion on the road to sexual adventure.

Satisfied with her conclusions, she hurried toward the campsite. Fortunately it was as she'd left it. The tent was secure. After stowing her food supplies in a canvas sack attached to a pulley, she hoisted it out of bear reach. Then she opened the outside tent flaps to air it out and tucked her clean clothes in another canvas sack inside the tent.

At last she was ready to check on the eagles. With her computer, her camera and her binoculars in a smaller backpack, she climbed the ladder to her platform. Like an absent mother coming home to her children, she was eager to see what had happened to her charges while she'd been gone.

And like that same mother, when she looked through her binoculars and spotted the two nestlings, she was sure they appeared bigger than they had the day before. Her scientific self knew that one day wouldn't have made much of a difference. Yet they seemed to be moving around more. The larger of the two lifted its fuzzy head and looked in her direction.

"Hi there," she murmured with a smile. "Miss me?"

The nestling turned, giving her a profile view, and blinked.

"Someday you're going to be a magnificent eagle with a snowy head and talons strong enough to grip a small deer. I won't recognize you."

She wouldn't have any artificial means of tracking them, either. She agreed with the professor's decision not to use telemetry to keep tabs on these birds after they left the nest. Radio tracking could help researchers learn about the eagles' habits, but Naomi disliked anything that might interfere with their normal behavior.

Yet at times like these, when she felt a kinship with the creatures she'd been studying, she longed for a way to trace their journey after they left this meadow. She thought she'd be able to recognize the parents if they returned next spring. The male had a scar above his right eye, and the female was missing one toe on her left claw. But even if the babies came back here, too, they would have changed drastically by then.

Lowering the binoculars, she set up her folding table and camp stool. Then she turned on her computer and checked the webcam feed. She hadn't updated Professor Scranton recently, so she sent him a report and received an immediate and grateful response.

The guy could easily be in his nineties, and he had done his share of fieldwork in his day, but now health issues prevented him from doing the research for his paper. He'd told Naomi that her information provided the energy boost he needed to keep writing.

Even so, he'd urged her to take breaks and not neglect her normal life while observing the eagles. She'd assured him that at the moment, she didn't have a particularly exciting life and would be happy to spend most of her time focused on the nest and its occupants. Of course, that had been before Luke Griffin had ridden under her tree.

But Luke didn't want her to drop everything for him, even if she'd been so inclined. He actively *wanted* her to be involved in her career, because that guaranteed she wouldn't become needy. She began to see the sense in what he'd been trying to tell her. He was a man for the new breed of independent women, of which she was definitely one.

An eagle's shrill cry caught her attention. Raising her binoculars, she watched the female glide into the nest with another fish in her talons. Feeding time.

Naomi grabbed her digital camera and took several shots. Then, using the webcam image, she sat at her computer and made rapid notes.

After the female left the nest again, Naomi scanned the area with her binoculars for no particular reason, except…a feeling. Something about the scenery had changed. The more she'd worked in the wild, the more her senses had sharpened, so maybe she'd known he was coming even before he'd appeared.

Through the powerful lens she watched Luke riding toward her, exactly as he had the day before. He had the same relaxed style, and although his shirt was a different plaid than the one he'd worn yesterday, he looked very much the same. But nothing was the same.

She lowered her binoculars, unwilling to spy on him today. He was no longer a hot stranger to ogle as a distraction from her research duties. He was Luke, the man she'd agreed to have sex with. And he was coming for her.

LUKE RODE INTO the clearing and wondered if she was watching him through her binoculars. He couldn't remember ever starting an affair this way, where they'd discussed the issue and had come to the conclusion they'd go for it a good twelve hours before anything actually happened.

Usually the decision was made during a passionate make-out session, and there wasn't much logic involved until later. After they'd had wild sex, he would gently explain his position on commitment, and because he'd chosen wisely, the woman in his arms would thank him for not expecting anything permanent.

Everything was different with Naomi, probably because they'd met out here, under the blue Wyoming sky, and he was fascinated by the nature of her work. In the past he'd hooked up with business types who'd been looking for a hot cowboy in a country-and-western bar. That had to be the source of the difference. His other lovers had come looking for someone like him.

When he'd heard about Naomi's eagle research and her wildlife background, he'd been so intrigued that he'd made a point to connect with this interesting woman. That had put him in the unfamiliar position of trying to impress *her*. He seemed to have done a decent job so far. He couldn't speak for her anticipation level, but the twelve hours since they'd decided to become lovers had ramped up his libido considerably.

Still, he might want to add some style to his entrance. Slapping his hat against Smudge's rump, he urged the gelding into a gallop and cut across the meadow, heading straight for her tree.

He didn't dare look up to see how she was taking this frontal assault, because he had to keep his attention on the terrain. Racing toward her wasn't all that bright, perhaps, but it had chutzpah. A few yards shy of the platform, he reined in his horse in a spurt of dust.

Very showy, if he did say so. He kept a tight hold on Smudge, who was prancing and blowing like a stallion. Tilting his hat back with his thumb, he glanced up. "Howdy, ma'am." He might sound casual, but his heart was pounding like crazy.

"Howdy, yourself." Grinning, Naomi leaned over the railing. She looked adorable, with her hair in a high, flirty ponytail. "That was quite—"

"Stupid?"

"I was going to say dashing."

"Dashing." He squinted up at her. The sun created a halo around her blond hair, but he knew she was no angel. Desire tightened his groin. "That's what I was going for. Dashing."

"You achieved it. You looked like a Hollywood cowboy."

"You should see me twirl my lariat."

"I'd love to."

He couldn't seem to stop staring at her. The sunshine fell on her like a spotlight, turning her into a blonde princess. If he hadn't pushed his horse into a gallop on the way over here, he could have ground-tied him and ascended to the platform as any decent Hollywood cowboy would do.

As the ache for her grew, he longed to climb that ladder and claim his prize. But Smudge needed a cooldown. And while Luke was at it, he might as well settle the horse into his temporary quarters.

"Are you coming up or do you want me to come down?"

"I'll come up. Let me get Smudge sorted out first. How are the eagles?"

"Good. All seems to be well."

"Excellent. I'll be right back." He clicked his tongue and guided Smudge around the tree and over toward her campsite. After walking the horse around the campsite awhile, Luke dismounted.

He'd come prepared for the duration, with supplies in two bulging saddlebags. Unsaddling Smudge, he put the saddle, blanket and bags over by Naomi's tent. "Welcome to your home away from home, Smudge." He replaced the horse's bridle with a halter and led him down to the stream for a drink.

His promise to "be right back" might have been overly optimistic. Returning to the campsite, he tied Smudge to a tree while he found a good grazing area near the tent. Then he pulled a ground stake out of a saddlebag, along with a mallet, and planted the stake. Finally he transferred Smudge's lead rope from the tree to the stake.

That should take care of the horse until tonight, but he understood why Naomi chose to hike out here instead of riding. A horse was one more thing to deal with. Still, he had limited time to be with her, and even with these few chores, he'd saved valuable minutes by riding instead of hiking.

After scratching Smudge's neck and giving him a handful of carrots from his pocket, Luke walked down the path Naomi's hiking boots had created during her many treks. He couldn't remember the last time he'd been this excited about being with a woman.

He could easily guess why that was. Her interest in wildlife indicated that she was as interested in adventure and exploration as he was. At least she was now. He cautioned himself not to make assumptions of how she'd be in the future.

But he didn't care about the future. At this moment he had the green light to spend quality time with a woman who studied eagles. That would make everything more exciting, including the sex. He had condoms in his saddlebags and in his pocket. Life was good.

He'd look at the eagles first, because he really was interested in them, and because if he didn't look at them first, he might never get around to it. After he'd checked out the eagles, he intended to kiss Naomi until they both couldn't see straight. That dramatic race over here had made him feel like a conquering hero.

"Coming up!" He climbed the ladder and thought of Rapunzel. Naomi was also a blonde, but he appreciated being able to use a ladder instead of her braided hair to reach her tower.

"Hurry!" she said.

"Why?" He hoped it was because she couldn't wait to feel his hands on her.

"Both parents are there for feeding time! It's like a family portrait."

Luke smiled. She really dug those eagles, and he liked that about her. Any woman who was passionate about one thing had the capacity to be passionate about other things, too. He'd sensed that about Naomi from the beginning.

Once he reached the platform, he was struck again by the spectacular view. This platform would be an awesome place to watch the sunset. He'd keep that in mind for later.

She glanced over at him, her color high. "Here." She took off her binoculars. "Take a look."

"Thanks." He accepted the binoculars, but he couldn't resist cupping the back of her head and giving her a quick kiss. "Hi."

"Hi." She sounded breathless.

That was good. She would be even more breathless before long. Adrenaline rushed through his veins. Eagles and a hot woman. What could be better than that?

"I think the nestlings have grown a little." She came to stand next to him. "Tell me what you think."

With her standing so close and radiating warmth and the tantalizing scent of arousal, he couldn't think very well at all. But he made a valiant attempt. Lifting the binoculars, he focused on the nest.

To his surprise, he did notice a difference, even if it was slight. "They're growing, especially the bully. Look at that little sucker, shoving the other one out of the way. C'mon, you. Let the little one have some food."

She chuckled. "So you root for the underdog?"

"Doesn't everybody?" Between having her right beside him and the incredible view of the eagles, he was on sensory overload.

"Humans often do. We're at the top of the food chain, so we can afford to worry about the weak link. Wild animals don't always have that luxury."

"Good point." Luke desperately wanted to slide one arm around her and pull her close, but he knew what that would lead to. Once he touched her, there would be no eagle watching going on.

"Most of the time they're focused on survival." Naomi sighed. "They're so vulnerable."

"You mean the babies?"

"And the parents."

He focused on the sharp beaks and strong talons of the male and female eagles. "They look so powerful."

"I know. But all it takes is a shortage of food, or a car windshield, or an electrical wire, or a gun. We nearly wiped them out."

"Thank God we didn't. Now people are into watching them instead of shooting them."

"Which means I'm employed. That reminds me that I need to make some notes. Can you keep track of the feeding session and report what's happening while I type?"

"Sure." He missed her warmth the second she moved away to sit at her folding table, but he couldn't forget that she had a job to do. That's why he'd planned to stay overnight. She wouldn't be watching the eagles once darkness fell.

He hoped she'd go along with the plan. Now that he thought about it, he wondered if he should have checked with her first. They'd been hot for each other last night, and he was still burning, but she might have cooled down since then.

Well, he'd find out soon enough. In the meantime, he'd act as her research assistant, which wasn't a bad deal. In fact, he considered it a privilege to be involved, even a little bit, in her work.

"After they leave the nest, will you have any way of tracking what happens to them?"

The steady click of the keys stopped for a moment. "No. I won't be banding them. It's too invasive."

"I agree." He went back to describing the movements of the eagles, and she continued to type.

Then she paused again. "I take it you got the afternoon off?"

"Yes, I did. Okay, it looks like the father is getting ready to leave the nest."

She started typing again. "When do you have to go back?" The keys clicked rhythmically.

"Tomorrow morning."

Her typing came to an abrupt halt.

Although his back was to her, he swore he could feel the intensity of her stare. Suddenly it seemed several degrees warmer on the platform. "If that's okay with you."

Behind him, the laptop closed with a soft snap.

"I won't interfere with your work." Lowering the binoculars, he turned around, hoping he hadn't misjudged, hoping he would find… *Yes.* The same emotion sizzling in his veins heated her blue gaze. His pulse hammered as he held that gaze.

Slowly she stood. When she drew in a breath, her body quivered. "Interfere with my work." She stepped out from behind the small table. "Please."

6

EVER SINCE LUKE had come charging toward her across the meadow, Naomi had felt like a shaken bottle of champagne ready to blow at any second. Intellectually she'd known that leaping from his horse and scaling the platform would be silly, but her romantic heart had wanted him to do that all the same. She'd wanted to be taken in a mad rush of passion that gave her no time to think.

But he'd taken freaking *forever* to deal with his horse, which was a good thing but didn't scream eagerness on his part. So she'd concluded he was here as much to see the eagles as to see her, especially after he'd mentioned them before he'd ridden over to the campsite.

But now…now he looked the way she felt. His throat moved in a quick swallow. "How sturdy is this platform, anyway?"

Her heart rate climbed. "Sturdy enough, but—" She

thought of the logistics. Both of them were wearing complicated clothing.

"Right. We're both way overdressed for this."

"We are." She thought longingly of her transparent nightgown and the entrance she could make if they were in a hotel room instead of on a wooden platform twenty feet above the ground. Instead she wore extremely unsexy hiking shorts, a T-shirt and, most problematic of all, hiking boots.

No man should be forced to remove his lover's lace-up hiking boots before they had sex. So that meant she needed to undress herself. Then she thought of what fun it would be to watch Luke strip down right here on her observation platform. Anybody could make a luxury suite seem seductive, but how many people could say they'd had sex in a tree?

She turned and grabbed her camp stool. "I don't know about you, but I'm going to slip into something more comfortable."

A slow smile made him look even more breathtakingly handsome. He took off his hat and laid it brim-side up on the platform. "I knew we were going to get along."

"That's a different hat." She unlaced her boot and pulled it off along with her sock.

"Sarah's going to see what she can do with the other one." He unsnapped his cuffs as he watched her pull off her other boot. "But if you ask me, one ruined hat is a small price to pay."

Her body tingled from the gleam in his eyes. "You don't know that yet."

"Yes, I do." He unsnapped his shirt.

"I might be lousy at sex."

He laughed.

"Really, I might. You know that underdog syndrome we talked about?" She stood and the wood felt warm under her bare feet. "Those are the guys I tend to pick."

"So I'm an underdog? Ouch!" He pulled off his shirt and dropped it to the platform.

"Oh, no." Her gaze traveled lovingly over his broad chest. "You're no underdog."

"That's a relief." He sent her a sizzling glance as his hands went to his belt buckle. "Better get moving, Perkins. You're falling behind."

"No, I'm not." But she'd been caught standing motionless and staring. She'd admit that. "You still have your boots on."

"So I do." He paused, his fingers at the button of his jeans. "After you take off your shirt, how about tossing that stool over here?"

"I can do it now." She reached for it.

"Please pull off your shirt," he said softly. "Your boots seemed to take forever. I thought I'd go crazy."

She paused. Until now she'd been so focused on him that she'd forgotten that he might be as eager to watch her undress. "Don't expect sexy underwear," she said.

"Why would you wear sexy underwear when you're camping?"

With a smile, she echoed his earlier comment. "I knew we'd get along." Then she grabbed her T-shirt and yanked it over her head.

"Mmm."

His murmur of approval sent heat flooding through her, and moisture gathered between her thighs.

"More." His voice sounded husky. "The bra, too."

She trembled as excitement warred with her natural modesty. "I've never stripped for a man in broad daylight."

"I'm honored to be the first." His chest expanded as he dragged in a breath and let it out slowly. His glance was hungry. "Come on, Naomi. I want to see you with sunlight on your breasts."

Pulse hammering, she reached behind her back and unfastened the hooks of her white cotton bra. Then she drew it off and let it fall to the platform.

His gaze held hers for a few seconds before dipping. Then it returned to lock with hers. His voice was tight. "You're incredible. And I want to touch you more than I want to breathe."

Her nipples tightened and she quivered with longing. "Then touch me."

With a groan of surrender, he eliminated the space between them and crushed her in a fierce embrace. Bare skin met the solid wall of his chest, and she gasped at the pleasure of that first contact.

"I need you so much." His mouth found hers as he pulled her in close, letting her feel the hard ridge beneath the fly of his jeans.

The urgency of his kiss drove her wild. No man had ever wanted her like this, as if he couldn't contain the passion gripping him. Keeping her firmly wedged against his crotch, he continued kissing her as he leaned back enough to cup her breast in one large hand. His moan of need vibrated through her.

His hands were calloused from his work, and that only made his touch more erotic. She squirmed against him, aching for relief from the tension that tightened with each thrust of his tongue into her mouth and squeeze of his hand on her breast.

Desperation drove her to shove her hand between them and unfasten the button on his jeans. As she began working the zipper down, he lifted away from her, giving her access. When she slipped her hand inside his briefs and wrapped her fingers around the silky power of his cock, he began to shake.

He lifted his mouth from hers and gulped for air. "I'm going insane."

She moaned as his thumb brushed her nipple. "Me, too."

"We have to… We're not…"

"Condom. Do you…?"

"Yes, but I haven't…my boots are still…"

Her fevered brain searched for the quickest way for them to achieve their goal. "The stool."

"Oh." He let her go long enough to find the stool and grab it.

She used that time to get out of her shorts and soaked panties. When she turned back to him, he was sitting on the stool pulling off his boots, and he held the condom packet in his teeth.

"Forget the boots."

The one he'd been holding fell from his hand with a clatter as she stood before him, trembling with urges stronger than she'd ever had in her life. Those urges made her bold.

"Put on the condom." She braced her hands on his broad shoulders.

His breathing ragged, he quickly did as she asked.

"Now…" She gripped his shoulders. "Help me down."

Hands at her waist, he looked into her eyes as he supported her slow descent.

She felt the nudge of his cock.

Lightning flashed in his brown eyes. He shifted slightly, found her moist entrance. "You're drenched."

"Your fault."

"Hope so." His jaw muscles flexed as he drew her down.

Her fingers dug into his shoulders and she moaned softly.

"Too much?"

She shook her head, unable to speak as he took her deeper and touched off tiny explosions all the way down. So this was what they wrote books and songs about. Now she knew what she'd been missing.

At last she was settled on his lap, her feet on the platform, her body gearing up for what promised to be a spectacular and imminent orgasm. The advance-warning signals rippled through her, making her gulp.

He continued to hold her gaze, but his jaw muscles tensed even more, making the cords of his neck stand out. Sweat glistened on his powerful chest. "Don't move." He shuddered. "I don't want to come yet."

But she couldn't control what her body craved. An involuntary spasm rocked her.

He sucked in a breath and squeezed his eyes shut. "Don't."

"Can't...help it."

Slowly he opened his eyes again, and a wry smile touched his mouth. "You're potent."

"You, too." Another spasm hit.

He swallowed. "Okay, if that's going to keep happening, we might as well go for it."

"Yes, please."

"Oh, Naomi." Laughter and lust sparkled in his eyes. "I had no clue." He drew in a shaky breath. "Ride me, lady. Ride me."

She did, and it was a very short ride. She came almost immediately, gasping with the wonder of it, and he followed two strokes later with a groan wrenched from deep inside him. Quivering in the aftermath, she leaned her forehead against his damp shoulder and listened to the labored rasp of his breathing.

A soft breeze sighed through the pine needles and brushed against her skin. Gradually she became aware of small birds chattering and the rustle of a squirrel in the branches somewhere nearby. She'd always felt a part of nature, but never more so than at this moment.

Luke gently massaged the back of her neck. "That was quite a beginning."

"Uh-huh." She wondered if sex was always this good for him, but she wouldn't ask. "Am I too heavy?"

"Light as a feather." He ran a hand up her back. "Soft as satin."

"I suppose we'll have to move sometime."

"Definitely. Especially if we want to do this again in the near future."

She lifted her head to stare at him. "How near in the future?"

He grinned at her. "That was just a warm-up." He gazed into her eyes. "Am I shocking you, Naomi Perkins?"

She didn't want to admit that she'd never been with a guy who suggested more sex immediately after having it. Apparently she really had been choosing from the shallow end of the gene pool, picking underdogs with a low sex drive.

"We don't have to have sex in the near future," he murmured. "If you need more time, we can wait."

"I don't need more time, but I thought that you, being a guy, would."

"If I weren't starving to death, I'd be ready to go in about ten minutes, but I'm hungry. Are you?"

She hadn't given herself a chance to think about it, but she'd skipped lunch. "Yes, I'm hungry, but I'm all set with my energy drinks and a few munchies. I doubt that you—"

"You've got that right. I brought food enough for both of us, so save your energy drinks for when I'm not here. That way there's no danger of history repeating itself."

"I wouldn't spill it on you again, I promise."

"You never know." He traced the outline of her mouth with the tip of his finger. "You could be drinking one of those green concoctions, be hit with the sudden need to have sex with me and knock the bottle over in your hurry to rip my clothes off."

She laughed. "That's pretty far-fetched." In reality, it wasn't, but she had to be careful not to let him know how powerfully he affected her.

"So you say, but please humor me and don't open one of those while I'm here, okay?"

"Do they carry a bad association for you, then?"

"Actually, no. It's a good association, but even so, I don't care to repeat it. The energy drink served a purpose by bringing us together, so I'm done with it." He gave her a quick kiss. "Let's disengage and I'll head back to the campsite and fetch our lunch."

"Okay." She eased away from him and stood. "FYI, there's a little garbage bag over by the cooler."

"Thanks."

She walked to the far side of the platform to give him some privacy to deal with the condom. How odd that she wasn't embarrassed about strolling around the platform naked. At least she wasn't until she saw a rider at the far edge of the clearing. "Yikes. Someone's coming." She scrambled for her clothes.

"You're kidding." Luke zipped his pants. "Damn it. Where did I set the binoculars?"

"On the table. You'd better put on your shirt." She scurried around getting her clothes back on. Fortunately they always looked rumpled. She used the stool to balance as she put on her socks and hiking boots. That stool would always have the memory of what they'd used it for today.

Luke peered through the binoculars. "It's Jack. And he's got little Archie in the saddle with him."

"Oh." Naomi felt silly for not remembering. "That's my fault. I told him to bring Archie to see the eagles sometime."

"And he picked today. I wonder if that's pure coincidence." Luke put down the binoculars and picked up his shirt. "Emmett's supposed to be the only one who knows I'm out here with you."

"So you talked to him?" She took the elastic out of her hair and redid her ponytail.

"Last night on the way home." Luke buttoned his shirt and tucked it into his jeans. "He reluctantly accepted the idea that you and I would be hanging out together during my time off."

"Then it's probably coincidence that Jack decided to come out today." She was grateful that she hadn't been wearing makeup. She turned toward Luke. "How do I look?"

He smiled. "Like a woman who's been up to no good."

"Really? What's different about me? Is my mouth red?"

"A little, but not much." He rolled back the sleeves of his shirt instead of fastening the cuffs.

"Doggone it."

"Hey." He took her by the shoulders. "I was kidding you. You look fine. I'm probably the only one who would notice a postorgasmic gleam in your eye."

"Luke! I don't want to have a gleam in my eye!"

"Sorry. You probably can't do anything about it.

I'm pretty good at detecting that gleam, but most people aren't."

"I'll bet Jack is. Before he married Josie, he was quite the ladies' man. I wish I had a mirror."

"Trust me, you look fine. That's not what's going to get us in trouble."

She stared at him. "What's going to get us in trouble?"

"I unsaddled my horse and took the time to stake him out in a grazing area. A short visit wouldn't have required all that. I would have left Smudge ground-tied beside this tree."

Naomi groaned. "Then I guess we'll have to see what kind of reaction Jack has to that. He's not a blabbermouth, so maybe this won't get back to my folks."

"Yeah, Emmett said they wouldn't like it."

"Only because they want me to find a guy who's steady. That's not you."

"Nope. Not me."

The sound of hoofbeats grew louder. Naomi glanced at Luke. "We could sit down against the tree and pretend we're not here."

"Like you tried to do with me?"

"Right."

"Forget it. If Jack brought his son all the way out here to see the eagles, he'd haul him up on this platform even if he thought nobody was here. Then he'd find us hiding and looking guilty as hell."

"You're right. That would be embarrassing."

"And because we've stood here debating the issue

for too long, there's no time for me to climb down and disappear into the woods."

That made her laugh. "Hardly. Even if you made it down the ladder, you couldn't get away without Jack hearing you sneaking away through the trees. That would be just as bad as staying here and facing the music."

"At least we're dressed. And we're not actually in the midst of—"

"Oh, God." She put her hands to her hot cheeks. "What if he'd ridden up twenty minutes ago?"

"Little Archie would have gotten an education." Luke shrugged. "He's a ranch kid. He needs to understand the facts of life."

"He's only two," she said in an undertone. "He doesn't need to understand anything yet." She took a calming breath. "This could have been so much worse. I'm grateful that it wasn't."

"Naomi!" Jack's deep baritone drifted upward. "You there?"

She walked to the edge of the platform. "Hi, Jack! I sure am. Hi, Archie!"

The little blond toddler waved wildly. "Hi, hi! Birds! See birds!" He didn't look much like his dark-haired, dark-eyed father. Instead he'd inherited his fair coloring from his mother, Josie.

He was an adorable kid, beloved by his parents, aunts and uncles and grandparents. Naomi's heart did a little flip-flop. No matter what awkwardness the situation produced, this child deserved to see the eagles.

He was very young, but even early memories could have a lasting impression, if only in his subconscious.

"Come on up," she called. "I have a surprise for you. Luke's here."

Jack tipped back his hat and gazed up at her. "Oh, is he, now?"

Archie bounced on the saddle. "Luke! Wanna see Luke!"

Luke joined her at the edge of the platform. "Hey, buddy! How're you doing?"

"Luke!" Archie stretched his arms up. "Wanna see Luke!"

"We'll be right there," Jack said. "Make sure the eagles are ready for their close-up." He dropped his reins, gripped Archie around his chubby middle and dismounted.

"Archie seems excited to see you," Naomi said quietly.

"I've done some babysitting now and then."

She glanced over at him. The drifter babysat for little children? That didn't fit his supposed philosophy of not becoming attached to his surroundings. Little kids like Archie could grab hold of your heart and refuse to let go. "You're a man of many parts."

"I am." He gave her a cocky smile and lowered his voice. "After they leave, I'll show you some of them."

7

FROM THE MOMENT Jack arrived on the platform, Luke knew that he'd come to check out the situation brewing with Naomi. Jack was easing into the role of reigning monarch of the Last Chance, despite the fact he wasn't yet forty. But he considered everyone on the ranch, and most of the people in town, too, as his people—people who required his guidance.

Luke had found it kind of amusing until today. Yes, Jack was his boss, and technically what happened on his property was under his control, but... Okay, maybe Jack had some authority here. Luke didn't have to like it.

Archie, though, was another story. Luke couldn't resist that rosy-cheeked little boy. He dragged the stool over to a spot that would give Archie the best view of the eagles and sat with the kid on his lap and helped him look through the binoculars. It was tricky because Archie didn't quite get the concept of the binoculars.

Luke had a little trouble managing both child and

binoculars. He didn't want to drop either one, with the kid being the more important of the two.

Naomi came to his rescue. "You hold Archie, and I'll hold the binoculars."

"Wanna hold nockles!" Archie stubbornly refused to give up his right to have a hand on them, even if he didn't quite understand how they worked.

"Okay," Naomi said. "We'll all hold them. You, me and Luke."

"'Kay." Archie settled down.

Naomi crouched down next to them. "Archie, can you make your fingers do this?" She created two circles with her thumbs and forefingers and held them up to her eyes.

Archie imitated her, which meant he had to let go of the binoculars, but Luke made sure they didn't drop.

"That's how the binoculars work," Naomi said. "Like your fingers, only better."

Jack observed from the sidelines. "Brilliant."

"We'll see." Naomi had Archie practice with his fingers some more, and then she tried the binoculars again. Eventually Archie caught on.

Once he did, he was very excited. "Birds! I see birds!"

Luke held him as he bounced, but Archie kept his eyes pressed against the twin lenses. Glancing over at Naomi, Luke discovered her looking back at him. They exchanged a smile.

He had a brief flash of what it would be like to be a dad teaching his kid how to use binoculars for the first time. He'd always assumed that whenever he wanted a kid fix, he'd borrow one, like now. But being able to share this kind of moment on a regular basis had its appeal, especially if the other person in the equation happened to be a woman like Naomi.

Then he corrected himself. Not someone *like* Naomi, because he'd already determined that she was one of a kind. It would have to be Naomi herself. He was thinking crazy. He'd been over this ground and knew what he wanted out of life. Absolute and complete freedom.

Being a father came at a stiff price. His own father had made no secret of that. At a young age, Luke had asked for a baby sister or brother. Luke's dad had rolled his eyes and proclaimed that one kid was more than enough to take care of. Luke had never forgotten his father's martyred expression.

Luke could have fun on a temporary basis with other people's kids, like Archie. The little boy had a fairly long attention span for his age, but when the thrill was gone, it was totally gone. Luke handed the binoculars to Naomi and stood up, hoisting Archie into his arms.

Archie wiggled in protest. "Wanna get down!"

"That's my cue," Jack said. "Time to get this guy home. Can't have him running around on a platform twenty feet in the air."

"Great job on the platform," Luke said. "It's plenty sturdy."

"Glad to hear it." Jack continued to eye Luke with suspicion. "How about helping me get Archie down the ladder? Climbing up is much easier. I'd appreciate it if you'd go down and hold it steady at the bottom."

"Will do." It was a reasonable request, but Luke

couldn't help thinking there was an ulterior motive involved.

Sure enough, when Jack reached the bottom safely with Archie on his hip, he turned to Luke and lowered his voice. "What's going on with you and Naomi?"

Luke glanced up toward the platform. He wasn't sure how well sound carried. "We're attracted to each other, and we're both consenting adults."

"I figured something like that."

"Did Emmett say anything?"

"No, he didn't." Jack speared Luke with a glance. "Is he aware of this?"

"He is. I talked to him last night. He said I could ride Smudge over here."

"That reminds me. You were at the Spirits and Spurs with Emmett last night. What was your take on this Clifford Mason guy?"

"Dresses like a rhinestone cowboy, but other than that, I know nothing about him. Emmett's not happy that Pam went to dinner with him."

"She did that because she's the main sponsor of the town's Fourth of July spectacular. Mason is providing the fireworks, and Pam's paying for them."

"Does Emmett know that?"

"He does now, because I told him. I also told him that rumor has it the guy is interested in Pam. He didn't take that well. So FYI, he's not in the best of moods."

"Thanks for the warning. I'll watch myself. He's not totally in favor of my coming out here, so if he's upset about something else besides…" Luke sighed. "I'll just be careful."

"Do that. Look, I don't care what you do on your own time, for the most part, but Naomi is a great person, and you've made it clear you're leaving."

"She knows that. She's fine with it."

"Okay." Jack didn't sound as if he believed it.

"Wanna go home." Archie laid his head on Jack's shoulder.

"I know you have to head back, but I have a question." Luke could see Archie was fading. He needed his nap. "If Emmett didn't say anything about me coming to see Naomi, how did you figure out what was going on?"

"Mom asked me if I had any ideas about cleaning your hat. I know Naomi's big on that green glop, and when I realized that was the liquid that had ruined your hat, I put two and two together."

"My hat's ruined?"

"It's ruined, bro. You can't treat a good hat that way and expect it to survive." Jack looked rather cheerful delivering the news.

"Sorry to hear that." Luke decided not to point out that Naomi had been the one to spill the energy drink on his hat. He'd had nothing to do with the accident. Oh, well. He'd resigned himself to this loss, but that didn't make him happy to hear the hat was DOA.

"Just so you know, if you break Naomi's heart, more than your hat is in jeopardy."

"I've been completely honest with her, Jack. She knows I don't intend to settle down."

Jack gazed at him. "If you say so. But she's one of

ours. And you're not." He touched the brim of his hat. "See you back at the ranch."

As Jack walked away and mounted up, Luke ran a hand over his face. *She's one of ours. And you're not.* That was true, and it was his choice. He'd never been part of any group, and he'd liked it that way.

So why did Jack's words sting? He didn't want to be tied down to this community, or to any community, for that matter. Sure, Jack had a close family, a loving wife and a cute kid, but they all came at the price of his freedom. Jack couldn't pick up and leave whenever he wanted to. He had obligations.

Knowing that, Luke shouldn't be affected by the dire warning Jack had thrown out. The guy's threats were empty and meaningless to someone like Luke. They shouldn't have any effect on him whatsoever.

And they wouldn't. He knew who he was and what he wanted out of life. Many people didn't, and they stumbled along without a plan, allowing circumstances to dictate their future. He wasn't like that.

He waited until Jack and Archie rode away. Then he called up to the platform. "Still want some lunch?"

Naomi came to the top of the ladder. "More than ever. I'm famished." She hesitated. "Did Jack give you a talking-to?"

"Oh, yeah. He and Emmett are both worried that I'm going to break your heart. But Jack was more direct. He promised if I broke your heart, he'd break my legs. Or something to that effect."

"Good grief! Don't these guys realize I can take care of myself?"

"Apparently not."

"I find that rather patronizing…but sort of sweet, too."

Luke took note of that. She might not like being considered a fragile flower in need of protection from men like him, but she didn't mind having representatives from the community watching out for her, either. He'd be wise not to criticize either Emmett or Jack for their behavior. Naomi loved them both and was flattered that they cared enough to stick up for her, even if it wasn't required.

But she'd welcomed Luke to her hideaway, and he'd had one hell of a time with her until Jack had shown up. Despite Jack's obvious scrutiny of their arrangement, Naomi hadn't told Luke to go away. She, at least, didn't think Luke was taking unfair advantage of her. In fact, he'd be shortchanging her if he let Jack's visit cast a pall over the celebration.

He gazed up at her. "I'll be back in a flash with some food."

"Sounds great."

"If you feel like taking off your hiking boots, don't let me stop you."

She laughed, as he'd hoped she would. Then she blew him a kiss and moved away from the edge of the platform. Yeah, they would get their groove back. Jack Chance wasn't going to rain on their parade.

Within fifteen minutes, he had a feast spread out on the platform. He'd even brought a tablecloth, which impressed Naomi to no end.

"Pretty fancy for camping, Griffin." She sat on the

far side of the checkered cloth he'd spread out on the platform. And she was, happy day, barefoot.

"You're camping, but I rode in on a horse, so I can provide more luxuries." He was proud of the cheese, cold cuts and sliced bakery bread he'd brought for making sandwiches. Shoshone's little grocery store wasn't huge, but it carried quality stuff. He'd included only mustard because mayonnaise didn't keep as well.

"This is wonderful." Naomi took one of the paper plates he'd provided and made a sandwich.

Luke waited until she was finished before putting his together. "I considered bringing wine, but I didn't want to sabotage your eagle research, so I brought sparkling water instead. Which reminds me, do you need to check on the birds?"

"After we finish lunch. The webcam does the bulk of the work, but someone should be monitoring the nest on a regular basis and taking some digital still shots. The professor gets the constant webcam feed, but he makes good use of my personal notes and the stills, too."

"How did you hook up with him?"

"He put an ad in the paper, and out of all the people who answered it, he picked me."

"Of course he would." Luke was quickly becoming her biggest fan. "You have the credentials and you're extremely personable. I'm surprised you haven't landed a job with one of the national parks yet."

"Everyone has budget issues, and I'm relatively new to the profession. The parks are struggling to keep their veterans employed, and that's what they should do. I

can wait it out. I don't have lots of bills, and I can stay
with my folks and pay a small amount of rent. I also
have some savings."

He nodded. "You're like me. I don't worry if I don't
have a job right this minute, because I know I'll find
something eventually. Whereas my dad got a job with
an electronics company right out of college and never
left. He thinks if he did, no one else would hire him."

"And you don't want to live in fear like that," she
said.

"God, no. Fear makes you afraid to take risks." He
bit into his sandwich. It was about a thousand times
better than her energy drink.

"Have you ever been engaged?"

Now, there was a question right out of left field.
She should know that he wouldn't do that. "I'm not
into marriage." He glanced at her. "How about you?"

"A guy asked me once, but I couldn't see him as the
father of my children. So I said no, but I did my best
to be gentle about it."

"So that's your criteria? A guy has to pass muster
as the future father of your children?"

"Well, I need to love him passionately, and we need
a good sex life, but yeah, I'd want to be able to picture
him as my future children's dad. Animals in the wild
use that yardstick all the time and it's not a bad one."

She sure wouldn't consider a wanderer like him as
a viable father of her kids, which was a good thing,
really. "I take it you are planning to have kids, then."

She laughed. "I'm planning and my parents are

praying. I'm an only child, so if they're going to have grandchildren to spoil, I'm their only hope."

He was also an only child. His mother had made some noises about grandkids, but his dad had cautioned him to live his life for himself and not worry about providing grandchildren. Luke had heard the unspoken message—*don't make my mistakes.*

Naomi gazed at him. "Did you think I wouldn't want kids?"

"I don't see how you'd manage a family and still be so involved with wild-animal research."

"People do manage it. There's a woman who took her little boy out on the boat while she studied whales. If I could get a job at Yellowstone, then being married and having a family would be no problem at all because it's so close to Shoshone. My folks would help when they could, and I know a bunch of people around here. Child care would be a breeze because I'd have a support system."

He stared at her as a million contradictory thoughts battled in his head. "That kind of thinking is so foreign to me. I've never thought in terms of having a support system." He was both attracted and repelled by the concept.

Something that looked dangerously like pity flickered in her blue eyes. Then it was gone. "If you're a really strong person, I guess you don't need one. When I was in Florida, I had friends, and I cobbled together a loose kind of support system. But it wasn't anything like I have here."

"So does that mean you feel tied to this place?" He was still sorting it out.

"Not at all. In fact, it's the opposite. Let's say I did get a job around here, found the right guy, had a couple of kids. And then I had some fabulous research opportunity for a few weeks. Being here would mean I could consider it, because I'd have backup. Backup in addition to my husband, of course, whoever he might be. I'd have other people I could count on, too."

"I don't know." He shook his head. "It seems a little too cozy for me."

"I'm sure it does. You're a lone wolf. I shouldn't describe this as a one-way street, either. If I expect to count on others to help me, then when they need backup, I have to make myself available."

"Aha." He knew there had to be a catch. "So you could end up being tied down by them."

"For a little while. It's supposed to even out. If I ask my parents to babysit, then I have to be willing to watch their house and feed their dog if they go on vacation. It's a trade-off."

Luke shuddered. "I couldn't deal with that."

"Then it's a good thing you've created the life that you have, isn't it?"

He met her gaze across the tablecloth, littered with the remains of their lunch. "Yes. I like it." He allowed himself a slow perusal of Naomi Perkins, from her bare toes to her golden ponytail. He and Naomi might be headed down different paths, but right now, they occupied the same place and time. "I'll tell you what else I like."

Her skin had turned a sweet shade of pink as he'd studied her. "What's that?"

"The idea of you naked on this tablecloth."

Her breath hitched. "That's quite a change of subject."

"We needed one." He started moving the food off the red checkered cloth. "All this talk about family ties and obligations was playing hell with my sex drive."

"Is that why you're such a sexy guy? You don't get involved in all that cozy family stuff?"

"You tell me." He pulled off his boots.

"Could be. You're a wild guy, Luke." Rising to her knees, she stripped off her T-shirt for the second time today.

And for the second time today, he drank in the sight of her undressing for him. "That must be why you like me." He unsnapped his shirt and took it off. "You're attracted to wild things."

"That's part of it." She gave him the same sort of once-over he'd given her and smiled. "Mostly I just want your body."

Lust shot straight to his groin. "Likewise." He lost track of his own undressing when she arched her back and reached for the clasp of her bra.

Snap, it came undone, and she pulled it off by the straps before tossing it aside. The motion made her breasts quiver. He became completely absorbed in watching them as she moved. When she unfastened her shorts and slid them, along with her panties, down to her knees, he had a visual feast.

He couldn't imagine ever growing tired of this

view—her pale, full breasts tipped with wine-dark nipples, her slender waist and the gentle curve of her hips. She would put an hourglass to shame. His glance traveled lower, to those blond curls covering what was currently his favorite place in the world.

"Now who's falling behind?" She rid herself of her shorts and panties, and her breasts jiggled again, capturing both his attention and his fevered imagination.

"I can't concentrate when you're doing that."

She gave him a saucy look. "I'm only following instructions."

"Then here's another one." He stood and unfastened his jeans. "Take your hair down."

"Okay." She lifted her hands to her ponytail.

"Stop."

"But you said—"

"I know, but I just want to look at you for a minute like that, kneeling on the tablecloth, your hands in your hair. You look like a wood nymph."

"Don't they usually wear clothes?" She pulled the elastic out of her hair and laid it on her pile of clothes.

"Not in my fantasy." He shucked his jeans and briefs while she combed out her shining hair with her fingers. He'd never thought he had a preference for a woman's coloring. But surely nothing was more beautiful than blond hair filled with sunlight.

"And there's my fantasy." She focused on his jutting cock. "Come closer." She ran her tongue over her lips. "I have a taste for something wild."

The blood roared in his ears as he walked toward her. Oh, yes, this was going to be good. Very good.

8

DRIVEN BY URGES she'd never had before, Naomi boldly wrapped both hands around his rigid penis. Until today, she'd never been naked with a man outdoors in broad daylight, and she'd certainly never done *this* out in the open, under a clear blue sky and a warm sun.

Holding him felt like clutching a lightning rod. Energy coursed between them, and her pulse rate skyrocketed. Glancing up, she looked into eyes filled with primitive fire. For this moment, he was truly a wild creature, and so was she.

Slowly she leaned forward. She began with her tongue, and he gasped. She wanted to make him gasp and groan and abandon himself to her questing mouth. Glorying in his salty taste, silky texture and blood-warmed strength, she accepted all he had to offer. The blunt tip brushed the back of her throat, and he trembled.

Then she began to move, applying suction here, a swirl of her tongue there, until his breathing grew labored. He slid his fingers through her hair and pressed them against her head. Another strangled moan was followed by his rapid breathing.

Her heart beat frantically as his excitement fueled hers. She sucked harder, and he cried out. His fingers pressed into her scalp and his body shook. When she was certain he was going to come, he tightened his hold and pulled back, out of reach. "No." He struggled to breathe. "No. I want—"

Quivering, he dropped to his knees. Still holding her head, he gave her an openmouthed kiss. His tongue dived into the warm recesses where his cock had been. But he didn't have the breath to kiss her for long.

He raised his head and looked into her eyes. "Let's do that…again…sometime."

"Anytime."

He smiled and massaged her scalp as his breathing grew steadier. "You may regret that."

"Never." Loving him that way, here on this open platform, had been wonderfully freeing. She vibrated with the power of it. She felt as if she could fly.

"Don't go away."

"Not a chance." She waited while he retrieved a condom from his jeans pocket. "Let me put it on."

He laughed. "Not yet." He tossed the packet next to the tablecloth and met her gaze. "First, I intend to taste the wildness in you, Naomi Perkins."

Ah. The air whooshed right out of her and liquid heat surged right in.

"Lie down," he murmured, his voice as soft and sexy as black velvet. "It's my turn to play."

She wondered if he could simply talk her into a climax with words spoken like that. The man knew his way around a seduction. She didn't care where or how he'd learned to make a woman melt like wax before a flame, as long as he kept that flame burning.

As she stretched out on the smooth cotton, she imagined herself a lioness on the African veld. Nothing covered her but the sky. And now, caressing her with his mouth and tongue, a powerful male was about to make her roar.

That roar began with a whimper as he touched her in secret places, sensitive places, erotic places. She writhed under the teasing lap of his tongue and the urgent tug of his teeth. His mouth was everywhere, exploring her with the thoroughness of a mapmaker.

And then...then came the most intimate touch of all. He tasted her with slow sips at first, but gradually his demanding tongue grew more self-assured. Spreading her thighs, he lifted her, creating the angle that he needed to take her in the most thorough, uncompromising kiss of them all.

His intent was clear, his pursuit of her orgasm relentless. She surrendered, arching against the determined thrust of his tongue and crying out as the spasms rocked her.

She was still riding the crest of that climax when he lowered her gently. Cool air touched her heated body for a moment before he was back, hovering over her, seeking, finding and driving deep.

She gasped and opened her eyes. He was there, gazing down at her, his expression fierce.

Leaning down, he bestowed a flavored kiss on her trembling lips. "You—" he eased back "—are…*magnificent.*" And he shoved home once more.

She looked into his dark eyes, clutched his hips and rose to meet his next stroke. Yes, she was magnificent—magnificently alive. She was bursting with energy and willing to dare…anything, even making love on an open platform twenty feet off the ground in the middle of the day.

"You're going to come again."

Her laughter was breathless. "Is that an order?"

"A promise." He shifted his angle slightly and increased the tempo.

Oh, yes. That would do it. The sweet friction had been wonderful before, but now he'd found the key to unlock her personal treasure chest. Her muted cries grew louder the faster he pumped.

"That's it." He began to pant. "I can feel you squeezing. Let go… There!"

He'd known it a split second before she had, but when her climax arrived, she yelled as she'd never yelled and she hung on tight as the swirling, tumbling force flung her into a brilliant realm of dazzling sensations.

She lost track of where she was, but she never lost track of who was with her. Luke—a god imbued with amazing powers. He'd given her pleasures she'd only dreamed of.

He didn't stop for her, nor would she have wanted him to. His thrusts prolonged the intensity, and when he came, his bellow of satisfaction vibrated through her, too. Then she absorbed his shudders as they blended with the aftershocks of her release. It was perfect sex. She might never have it again, but at least she'd had it once in her life, thanks to Luke Griffin.

She had no idea how long they lay there before he stirred.

Moving slowly, he propped himself on his forearms to gaze at her. "Wow."

She considered making a smart remark to lighten the mood, but he truly did look blown away. "Wow is right."

He smiled. "This was better than the stool."

"Think of what we could accomplish on an actual bed."

"Boggles the mind, doesn't it? I don't know, though. Being up in this tree house gives the whole experience a certain something."

"It's not boring."

"No." He dipped his head and kissed her softly. He added more kisses to her cheeks, her eyes and her nose. "But I have trouble imagining anything being boring with you."

"Coming from a man who treasures variety, that's quite a compliment."

He looked into her eyes again. "I meant it to be. That's probably what brought me out here yesterday. I couldn't imagine how a woman who studies eagles from a platform twenty feet in the air could be boring."

"Thank goodness I didn't disappoint you." But she got a glimpse of how his restless nature might feel confined in a typical relationship. He really wasn't suited for a cottage surrounded by a white picket fence.

"You couldn't if you tried. But I don't want you disappointing that professor who hired you, either. You need to get to work."

"I do."

"And if it's okay, I want to help. I love being your spotter."

"Then you're hired. How much do you charge?"

He laughed. "I've already been paid in full. This has been a great afternoon. Possibly the best of my life. Now let's get moving."

As they dressed and settled in to observe the eagle nest, she kept thinking about that comment. This had been a great afternoon for her, too. Possibly the best afternoon of her life. But she was reluctant to say so because she didn't want him to think she was getting attached.

He was free to say it, though, because he'd already declared his independence. He could rave about their time together, knowing that she wouldn't expect him to stay. It was a lopsided situation.

Somehow she'd set the record straight without being too obvious about it. She had to let him know in no uncertain terms that she didn't *want* him to stay. Then she could relax and make any appreciative remarks she cared to. She simply had to find the right moment.

LUKE HADN'T BEEN kidding. Today had been outstanding, an afternoon he wasn't likely to forget. He had high hopes for tonight, too. Sex in a tent could be a lot of fun. They'd also sleep in that tent, though. Both of them had to work the next day, and all he needed was for Emmett or Jack to catch him dragging around tomorrow.

As the sun started its descent, Luke announced his plan to cook dinner, and Naomi seemed grateful for that. He'd tucked two frozen steaks in his saddlebags, and they would be about ready to put on the grill now. He left her to finish up her work on the platform and walked back to the campsite.

Once there, he gathered firewood and soon had a nice little blaze going in the rock fire pit that he found near the tent. He took a couple of foil-wrapped potatoes and tossed them into the flames. The corncobs, still in their husks, would go on top of the grill once the flames died down a bit.

Next he fed Smudge oats, and because Luke still had a little time, he unrolled his sleeping bag in the tent. Hers was pushed over to one side. It might be the way she normally arranged it, but he'd pretend she'd done that to make room for him in case he showed up. He liked to think she'd hoped for that.

As he smoothed out the sleeping bag and tucked a couple of condoms under it, he found himself whistling. Good sex certainly could make a guy feel like a million bucks. And it wasn't only the good sex. Being with Naomi was a real kick.

He'd already started estimating how often he could make it out here. He wouldn't have another afternoon off for several days, but that didn't mean he couldn't spend some of his nights with her, if she didn't mind sharing her tent.

Normally when he became sexually involved with a woman, they got together only a couple of times a week. That had been plenty. He realized that his thinking was different this time, but he explained it away by the novelty of the situation.

His former girlfriends had lived in apartments, so they'd either spent time at his place or hers, or at a hotel for variety's sake. For some reason he'd never thought to take any of them camping. The professional women he'd dated hadn't seemed like the camping type. Maybe he hadn't given them enough credit, but he couldn't imagine any of them going without makeup and taking a quick bath in a mountain stream.

Today he'd learned something valuable about himself. He *loved* having outdoor sex during the day. He was amazed that he'd never tried it before, but now that he had, he was a real fan. Not every woman would agree with him on that, but he'd been lucky enough to hook up with a woman who was willing to go along.

Having a platform high in a tree helped, too. They weren't as likely to be caught in the act. Actually, if they were going to continue with those episodes, they'd be wise to bring the ladder up. That way they really couldn't be caught in the act. He'd see what Naomi thought about that suggestion.

Before he left the tent, he took off his hat and laid it brim-side up on what he now considered his side. A hat only got in the way when there was a beautiful woman around, so why wear it? He wanted to be free to kiss her any old time he had a chance.

He had the corn and the steak cooking by the time she walked into camp. Even with her clothes and her hiking boots on, she still looked like a wood nymph. She matched the environment, and he liked that about her.

She sniffed appreciatively. "Smells wonderful, Luke. I haven't had steak in ages. You're hired as the camp cook, too."

"I'm happy to accept the job." He crouched down and turned the steak with the long-handled fork he'd brought with him. "I like to make myself useful."

He glanced over his shoulder and caught her eyeing his butt.

"You're *very* useful." She ogled him openly now, hamming it up. "There's something really sexy about a guy slaving over a hot campfire, especially when he can fill out a pair of jeans."

"Watch out." He grinned at her. "I'm liable to start feeling like a sex object."

"I know how you would hate that—having me pester you constantly to strip down so I can worship your body."

"Yeah, that sounds awful. When does the pestering start?"

"If that steak didn't smell like heaven, it would start right away. But I don't want to interfere with this promising meal preparation."

"Tactical mistake on my part." He stood. "I should

have waited to put on the steak until after you'd come back to camp, in case you wanted an appetizer."

"I'll settle for a kiss."

He laid the fork on a rock and walked toward her. "Think we can stop with a kiss?"

"With that steak sizzling on the grill? You bet. Every cowboy and cowgirl knows it's a crime to burn a good steak."

He cupped her face in both hands. "I'll keep that in mind." Then he tilted her head back and brushed the corner of her mouth with his thumb. "Open up, Naomi. I'm coming in."

She moaned softly and met him halfway, parting her lips and welcoming the thrust of his tongue. He delved into her warm mouth with the urgency of a man who'd been denied for weeks, instead of mere hours. She tasted so damned good.

Vaguely he heard a popping sound but didn't realize it was the sound of his shirt being unbuttoned until she slid both hands up his bare chest and pinched his nipples. His cock swelled in response. He lifted his mouth a fraction. "You're not playing fair."

"I didn't say I would."

"Then neither will I." He slipped a hand under the back of her T-shirt and unhooked her bra. Then when he made a frontal assault with that same hand, he discovered that her nipples were as rigid as his.

She moaned deep in her throat.

"You're asking for it," he murmured against her mouth.

"Uh-huh. Make it fast."

Fire licked through his veins. He backed her toward the tent. "Get in there and take off your shorts." He released her, unbuckled his belt and unfastened his jeans.

By the time he crawled in after her, she was in the process of kicking away her shorts and panties. He felt under his sleeping bag, located a condom and knelt at the tent entrance while he quickly took care of that chore.

Then he was on her. With his booted feet sticking out of the tent, he took her with such enthusiasm that he lifted her bottom right off the floor of the tent. She squeaked, but that squeak soon became a whimper as he pumped rapidly.

She came fast, and he followed right after. Then she started laughing, and he did, too. It was crazy to be doing this when it might mean ruining their meal.

But apparently she didn't plan for him to do that. "Go." She kept laughing as she gave him a little push. "Check the meat."

"What if I want some cuddling?"

"I'll cuddle you later! Don't burn the steak."

Grinning like a fool, he backed out of the tent, disposed of the condom and zipped up. He glanced over at the steak, which looked about perfect. Still chuckling, he made a megaphone of his hands. "Dinner's ready!"

God, but she was fun. Yep, best day ever.

9

"THIS STEAK is fabulous." Naomi sat on a flat rock with a tin plate balanced in her lap and a bottle of beer at her feet. Good sex followed by good food was a combination she hadn't had that often, but she'd like to make it a habit.

"I'll bet you say that to all your camp cooks." Luke sat cross-legged on the ground near her. The campsite had one decent sitting rock and he'd insisted she take it.

"I do. You're the first one I've ever had. Are you sure you're okay on the ground? I can go get the camp stool. I didn't even think about seating arrangements. I'm so used to eating alone here."

"Next time we can bring the stool down." He looked up from the ear of corn he was eating. "Assuming I'll get invited back."

"The odds of that are very good."

"I can bring you fresh food each time. I know you're surviving on energy drinks and canned goods, but that must get old."

"I consider it part of the job," she said. "The main focus is the eagles, and I just need to stay reasonably fed and hydrated so I'll be able to keep climbing that ladder."

"Which reminds me. Next time we decide to have sex up there, we—"

"Liked that, did you?" She was amused at his eagerness to continue their adventure. Amused and flattered. Something about this setup had touched a chord, and she wasn't going to argue about that. She reaped the benefits.

"I can't imagine why I've never had sex outside before. Maybe it was the fear of getting caught. That platform gives us a measure of privacy that's not easy to find."

She laughed. "I'm sure that's something Jack and Emmett didn't envision."

"They didn't count on me."

"Neither did I. But I'm so glad you showed up, Luke."

He held her gaze. "Me, too."

Maybe this was her perfect moment. "I've been thinking about something."

"So you had the same idea? Pull up the ladder so we don't get surprised by an unexpected visitor?"

"No, I didn't think of that, but it's a good idea. Yes, it will look suspicious, but better that someone imagines something is going on than that they see it in living color."

"My thought exactly."

"But that wasn't what I was going to say."

"Okay, shoot." He picked up his beer and took a swallow.

She loved looking at him sitting there, his shirt unsnapped at her request, his posture relaxed, happy. He was a gorgeous man. Even watching him drink his beer was a treat.

"What?" He smiled at her.

"You're incredibly good-looking, Luke."

He actually blushed. "That's not what you were going to say."

"No, but it doesn't hurt to tell you."

"You're not afraid it'll go to my head?"

"Actually, no. You're brash, but you're not conceited."

"Thank you." He put down his empty plate. "But you still haven't told me this big revelation."

"Okay. We had a discussion about my potential plans for the future. They're different from yours."

"Yes, they are."

"Just so you know, I realize the difference. When you said this was possibly your best afternoon ever, you could say it because you'd already announced your plans to leave. It was possibly my best afternoon ever, but I was afraid to say so, in case you'd think I was trying to, I don't know…trap you into something."

His expression brightened. "It was possibly your best afternoon ever?"

"Yes. But that doesn't mean that I—"

"I'm glad. I'm really glad. As for being worried that you'd try to trap me, I'm not."

"That's good, but why not? We get along and we

have great sex. Why wouldn't I want to try and change your mind?"

"Because you believe in the principle of live and let live. You're watching those eagles from afar. You're not trying to capture them and band them."

She nodded. Good observation on his part. "So if I'm enthusiastic about something we're doing together, you won't worry that I'm building castles in the air?"

"No. I trust you. If I didn't, I wouldn't be here."

"Fair enough."

"Ready for dessert?"

"You brought dessert?"

"Of course. Hang on." He stood and walked over to his saddlebags. He pulled out a plastic container. "I put them in here so they wouldn't get crushed."

Popping the top on the container, he showed her two chocolate cupcakes.

"Yum."

"Even better, they have cream filling."

"I love that." She reached for one.

"You know what I wish?" He took the other cupcake and returned to his spot on the ground.

"What?"

"That we didn't have to worry about bears. Because if we didn't have to worry about bears, we'd be eating these in the tent."

"You mean like at a slumber party?" She wasn't sure where he was going with this story.

"An X-rated slumber party. Yours would be served on my abs, and mine would be served in your cleavage."

"Mmm." She glanced over at him. "Hold that thought. You can bring cupcakes to the next picnic on the platform."

"Damn. I didn't think of that. We could have—"

"We don't have to do everything at once. I'll be out here until the nestlings fly." *And you leave.*

"You're right. Maybe we should pace ourselves. But you've given me a challenge. It'll be fun to think of all the interesting ways we can have sex between now and then."

"I'll look forward to your boundless creativity." She'd just had another insight. By setting a limit on their time together, he'd ramped up the tension. Lovers faced with a ticking clock always cherished the moments more than those who thought they had forever.

She needed to remember that truism as she joined him on this roller coaster. He was an exciting lover, but he was also a bit of an adrenaline junkie. He didn't know how to relax into a relationship and live it day by day. So she would accept him for the thrill ride that he was and understand that when the ride was over, he'd be gone.

LUKE WASN'T WORRIED that Naomi would let herself get attached to him, but it didn't hurt for her to say that she wouldn't. He let her go into the tent first and undress while he smothered the fire and made sure every trace of food was packed in airtight containers and stored in the sack she hung from a tree.

Someday he'd love to devour a cream-filled chocolate cupcake that was resting in the valley between her breasts, but he wasn't sure when that would be. Even if they met in town, she'd be staying with her parents. There would be no cupcake games under that roof.

But he wasn't about to complain. He stripped down outside the tent in deference to the cramped quarters. Then, holding the battery-operated lantern he'd used for the last stages of the cleanup operation, he crawled into the tent.

Entering a tent where a naked woman lay waiting was arousing enough. But when the light fell on her lounging like Cleopatra on her barge, he was immediately ready for action. His cock twitched with impatience as he zipped the tent closed.

He turned toward her and pretended shock. "My God! There's a stark-naked woman in this tent! What shall I do?"

She crooked a finger. "Come closer and let me whisper some suggestions in your ear."

"Excellent." He moved within range and set the lantern at the end of the tent before bending down to let her murmur sweet nothings. Except they weren't sweet. They were inventive and extremely specific. He proceeded to follow those suggestions, which involved Naomi rising to her hands and knees and Luke, once he'd rolled on a condom, taking her from behind.

Judging from her response, she liked that very much, so much that she climaxed in no time. He wasn't quite there yet, so he proposed the next phase, which involved lying on their sides facing each other with her leg hooked over his thigh. He stroked slowly as he caressed her warm breasts.

How he loved touching her. "I could do this all night."

"It wouldn't be a bad way to while away the hours."

"No, but let's take it up a notch." Reaching between her legs, he found her trigger point and began an easy massage as he continued to rock his hips back and forth.

She drew in a breath. "That's nice."

"I can tell." By the light of the lantern he could see her pupils dilate and her cherry-red lips part. His massage became more insistent. "Still nice?"

"You want me to come again."

"Bingo."

"I don't know if I…oh, Luke…*Luke*." She bucked against him, and that was all he needed. He climaxed with a grateful moan of release. Good. So good.

They lay there breathing hard, gazing at each other.

Reaching over, he stroked her mouth with his forefinger. "Thank you for today."

She sighed. "My pleasure." Her eyes drifted closed.

"Mine, too." He could tell she was tired and ready to sleep. He managed to ease out of her arms without disturbing her. Once he'd dealt with the condom, he switched off the light. "Good night, Naomi."

She was already asleep.

He lay in the dark listening to her breathe. In the distance an owl hooted. A small night creature scurried through the bushes somewhere near the tent. He felt at one with the night and the natural world. His heart filled with gratitude that she'd allowed him to share it with her.

He woke up to hear birds chirping and pale sunlight glowing on the sides of the tent. Naomi was gone. In a sudden panic, he sat up and grabbed his briefs and jeans.

Wherever she'd gone, she'd zipped the tent after leaving it. He took a deep breath. She'd probably left to go to the bathroom or put on coffee. Still, he had a strong urge to know where she was.

He crawled out of the tent wearing only his jeans and his briefs. He thought about pulling on his boots, but that would only slow him down. He needed to see her, needed to know she was okay.

She wasn't within sight. The campfire was still cold. He called her name softly in case she was nearby. No answer. Maybe this was why he'd never gone camping with a woman. You could lose track of them.

Maybe she'd gone to check on the eagles. The soles of his feet weren't used to pine needles and sharp rocks, and he winced as he made his way down the path to the platform. Climbing quickly, he stuck his head over the edge. Nope, not there.

Only one more place to look. He really should have put on his boots, but it was a little late to think about that now. He took the other trail, the one leading to the stream. The rocks seemed even sharper there.

Swearing under his breath, he gingerly picked his way along until he was in sight of the bubbling water. Then he sighed in relief. His wood nymph sat in the middle of the stream, up to her nipples in cold water.

He couldn't imagine how she could tolerate it, but she looked blissful with her hair slicked back and the water swirling around her. He started forward and stepped on a particularly sharp rock. He yelped and she turned to face him.

"Luke! What are you doing walking without your boots?"

"You did it." He saw no evidence of her clothes or her hiking boots on the shore.

"I'm used to being barefoot. Most cowboys aren't."

"That's a fact." But he was nearly there now. "How's the water?"

"Icy when you get in, but you get used to it."

"Really?" He had his doubts.

"After all that sex, I wanted a dip in the stream."

There was a gauntlet thrown down if he'd ever seen one. He'd had as much sex as Naomi, which meant he could use a dip in the stream, too. Or he could eat breakfast with her in his current unwashed state, which didn't seem particularly polite, now that he thought about it.

Hobbling to the edge of the stream, he unbuttoned his jeans and pulled down his fly. "I'm coming in."

"It'll feel really good once you adjust to the temperature."

He wished like hell he believed that. Vaguely he remembered that women had a different tolerance for heat and cold than men. It had to do with some primitive conditioning because they were the ones who had babies, so they needed protective fat layers. Something like that.

But he'd committed himself to this, and backing down would look bad. The very second he put his foot in the water, he regretted his decision. He deeply regretted it. Some people thought the Polar Bear Club was a great idea. He was not one of those people.

"Come on, Luke. Seriously, it feels great once you get past the first few steps."

Damn it. If he turned and went back, she'd think he was a wimp. But if he continued into that water, he might never be able to get it up again in this lifetime. His cock would freeze solid, which would do irreparable damage.

"You're not going to chicken out, are you?" Her laughter was the final straw.

"Absolutely not!" Gritting his teeth, he splashed toward her, and when he reached the spot where she sat chest-deep, he plopped right down. He thought he was going to have a heart attack. "Holy hell! This water's *freezing.*" He would have stood up again, but he wasn't sure his legs would support him now that they were shaking like a willow branch in the wind.

"Wait it out. It gets better."

"No, it doesn't. You're numb by now. You're probably in shock. Can you feel your toes? I can't feel mine."

"You're such a baby. I do this every day."

His teeth started to chatter. "F-first thing in the m-morning?"

"Well, no. I usually wait until the middle of the day."

"Let's do that." He tried to get up, but the rocks were slippery and he was still pretty shaky. "Let's get out and try it again at noon."

She put a hand on his shoulder, so cold it felt like the clutch of death. "You won't be here at noon. Look, you're in the water now, so you might as well relax and enjoy it."

"You realize this could be the end of our sex life."

"How's that?"

"My cock is never going to be the same after this."

"Sure it will." She reached over and cupped his cheek. Her fingers were frigid. "Kiss me."

"The way my teeth are chattering, I might bite you instead."

"Try it."

He figured all was lost anyway, so he might as well go along with this kissing routine. Turning toward her, he tried not to quiver as their lips met. At first it was a chilly proposition, indeed, but then her warmth began to penetrate the frost.

The effect reminded him of a movie where the prince kissed the sleeping princess and she gradually turned from deathly white to pink and glowing. Only he was the deathly white prince and Naomi was the princess reviving him. The longer they kissed, the better he felt.

Soon he had so much feeling in his fingers that he remembered she was naked in this water and he could reach over and play with her breasts. So he did.

She drew away from his kiss. "See? You're starting to enjoy yourself."

"Some. Kiss me again."

"Sure." Sliding around to face him, she held his head and really began to kiss him with enthusiasm.

That helped enormously because now he could fondle both of her plump breasts at once, and as he toyed with her nipples, he felt the most incredible miracle happen. Even in water cold enough to chill a beer keg, his cock began to rise.

She nibbled on his lower lip. "I'm getting hot. How about you?"

"I wouldn't say I'm hot, but I'm hard."

"You are?" She reached under the water, swishing her hand around until she found him. "Oh, my goodness."

"They said it couldn't happen."

"Let's see what else might happen." She began to stroke him.

"Naomi, no." But he didn't pull away.

"Why not? Aren't men more potent in the morning? Let's take the edge off."

"I can't believe you're doing this." Still he didn't stop her. His balls tightened and his breathing grew shallow.

"You want me to. I can tell." Her tongue traced the curve of his lower lip as her hand moved faster. Then she caught his lip in her teeth and fondled the tip of his cock, squeezing, stroking....

He groaned. "Yes...ah...*yes*." He came, spurting into the cold water that no longer felt cold at all.

Her chuckle was rich with triumph. "Wasn't that great?"

He gasped, but not because he was cold. She'd taken care of that in fine fashion. "Great." He wondered if she was spoiling him for anyone else. Now, there was a truly scary thought.

10

NAOMI HAD ENJOYED her first week alone in the forest with the eagle family. But her second week had taught her more about herself than about the nesting habits of eagles. She'd spent her days studying and recording the raptors' behavior, but she'd spent her nights with Luke.

His arrival had depended on his duties. Sometimes he'd show up before sunset and they'd make love on her observation platform, surrounded by fiery hues and the twitter of birds settling in for the night. Other times he'd ride into her camp after dark, when she'd already built a fire in preparation for dinner.

On those nights, he'd swing down from the saddle and pull her into his arms with an impatient oath, as if he'd been gone for days instead of hours. The first time that had happened, he'd been so desperate that he'd backed her up against a tree. Thrilling though that encounter had been, she'd chosen to have a sleeping bag conveniently positioned by the fire the next time he'd arrived after dark.

Sharing her work space and her campsite with Luke was the closest she'd ever come to living with a man. Because she'd fared so well on her own, she'd always wondered how well she'd tolerate such an arrangement. She not only tolerated Luke's presence, she craved it.

With Luke she lost any lingering sexual inhibitions. Having sex with him every night had taught her how responsive she could be. She vowed not to lose that information after he was no longer inspiring her to enjoy her body to the fullest.

Luke had also raised the bar for any guy she would ever become involved with. Although she couldn't dream of a forever-after with Luke, she wouldn't settle for less than someone with his vibrancy. No more underdogs for her.

She was grateful that Luke Griffin had ridden under her tree nearly a week ago. As she swept the meadow with her binoculars around noon, she foolishly wished that he'd appear. He wouldn't, though, not for several hours.

She might have worried about her eagerness to see him, except that she could guarantee he was thinking of her at this very moment, too. Somehow he'd managed to perform his duties to Emmett's satisfaction, even though he'd told her that his thoughts were always on her. He'd described some of those thoughts, and they were all X-rated.

So were hers. Whenever she remembered all they'd shared this past week, she grew moist and achy. Sitting on the camp stool, she took off her hiking boots and socks, even though she knew for a fact he wouldn't be riding out into the clearing until the sun went down.

Standing barefoot on the platform, she still felt restricted by her clothing, so she stripped everything off. She'd love to walk around the platform naked, but after Jack's surprise visit, she wasn't comfortable doing that. She put her shorts and shirt back on, but going without underwear felt risky and fun. No doubt about it, Luke had changed her outlook.

Too bad he wouldn't be here for a sexy picnic. After checking the eagles and typing more notes, she snapped off a few shots with her digital camera. Then she grabbed an energy drink and paced the platform as she sipped it. She pictured what Luke might be doing right now.

He'd mentioned teaching roping tricks to the eight boys who were spending the summer at the ranch as part of Pete Beckett's youth program for troubled kids. Naomi smiled at the thought of Luke working with those boys. He had such an adventurous spirit that he probably had them eating out of his hand. He certainly had her eating out of it.

A movement on the far side of the clearing caught her attention. Quickly setting her energy drink on the folding table, she grabbed her binoculars and her pulse leaped. As if she'd willed him to be there, Luke was riding in her direction on Smudge. What a glorious sight.

Capping her energy drink, she gave in to what was probably a ridiculous impulse. She tugged on her hiking boots, leaving the socks off, climbed down the ladder and started across the meadow to meet him. He'd ridden this path so often that he'd worn a little trail she could follow through the ankle-high grass and wildflowers.

She knew the minute he'd spotted her, because he urged Smudge into a canter. Laughing, she started to run. She couldn't remember the last time she'd run without a bra, and her breasts jiggled under her shirt. This was crazy, but crazy was how he made her feel.

When they were about ten yards apart, she stopped running so she could catch her breath before they met. He slowed Smudge to a trot and then to a walk.

His grin lit up his entire face as he approached her. "I liked that."

"Which part?"

"You being so excited to see me that you had to race out here gave my ego a boost, and the fact that you're not wearing a bra made it even more fun to watch." He tipped back his hat with his thumb. "What's the occasion?"

"I felt like staying loose today."

"That sounds promising. Can I hope it was for my benefit?"

"Let's say it's for our benefit."

"Works for me." He drew alongside her. Sliding his booted foot out of the stirrup, he held out his hand. "Come on up."

"Is there room for me up there?"

"Plenty of room if you sit on my lap."

"Will Smudge be okay with that?"

"Smudge is so well trained you could do a lap dance and he wouldn't spook."

"Is that what you envision? Me doing a lap dance on horseback?"

"Nope. You don't have to do a thing except enjoy the ride." He wiggled his fingers. "Let's go."

She didn't need to be asked again. The sight of him cantering toward her, his body moving in rhythm with the horse, had aroused her beyond belief. She wanted to feel all that manly coordination up close and personal.

Placing her hand in his firm grip, she put her foot in the stirrup and swung up and over the horse's neck so she faced Luke. She marveled at the strength in his arm as he steadied her movements one-handed.

"Hold on to my shoulder."

He circled her waist with his free arm and cinched her in tight against his crotch. "There you go." He clucked his tongue and Smudge started walking down the trail. "How's that? Comfy?"

"You have no idea." She slipped her feet free of the stirrups and hooked her heels behind his knees so she could feel the hard ridge of his erection rocking against her as the horse moved. "I took off my panties, too."

He groaned. "You are rapidly becoming the sexiest woman I've ever had the good fortune to meet."

She wound her arms around his neck and lifted her face to his. "You've always been the sexiest man I've ever had the good fortune to meet."

"Then you won't be surprised if I put my hand up your shirt." He held the reins and focused on the trail ahead, but he slid his free hand under the hem of her shirt and cupped her breast. "I like this decision of yours to ditch the undies." Slowly he rolled her nipple between his thumb and forefinger. "I like it a lot."

Sensation zinged straight to the spot being massaged by the bulge in his jeans. "Mmm." She pressed against his fly and let the steady movement of the horse work its magic. "You can do that some more if you want."

He kept his attention on the trail. "You're trying to come, aren't you?"

"You told me to enjoy the ride."

He glanced down at her and his dark eyes glittered. "You realize what this means, right?"

"Yes." She sucked in a breath as she felt the first twinge. "I'm going to run out to meet you more often."

"It means that the minute we get off this horse, you and I will get very busy."

She moaned softly and rocked a little faster. "Doing what?"

"Take a guess. Now go for it, you loose woman." He pinched her nipple faster. "We're almost there."

"So am...I." When the spasms hit, she pressed her face against his shirt to muffle her cries. She didn't want to scare the horse. But, oh, this was fun. Before meeting Luke, she would never have dreamed of doing such a thing.

True to his word, Luke had her out of the saddle the minute they reached the shade of her pine tree. She was feeling pretty mellow, so she didn't mind when he laid her down on the pine-needle-and-leaf-strewn ground. His expression was so intense that she figured this would be an epic coupling.

He had her shorts off in a flash, but he wasted no time on his clothes. Hooking his hat on the saddle horn, he unbuckled his belt and wrenched down his zipper so he could free his cock and suit up. He didn't bother with foreplay, either. Moving over her, he spread her legs and drove in deep.

She expected him to pump fast and come quickly, but he surprised her. Once they were securely locked together, he propped himself up on his forearms and shifted so he could cradle her head in both hands. They stayed like that as he gazed down at her without moving. He seemed to be studying her.

Wrapping her arms around him, she looked into his eyes. They were still hot, but his expression had lost some of its desperation. "I thought you were in a hurry," she said.

"I was. To get here." Although he'd seemed to be up to the hilt, he managed to slide in a fraction more. "Right here."

"I thought I wouldn't see you until later."

"I switched afternoons with Shorty." He eased back and shoved home again. "I'll work for him tomorrow afternoon."

"Why?"

"I needed this." And he began a slow, steady rhythm as he held her gaze. "I needed...you."

The walls she'd carefully constructed around her heart began to weaken. He shouldn't say things like that. He didn't mean it the way another man might, but...how sweetly he was loving her. How easy to look

into those warm brown eyes and imagine that something more than lust had captured him.

"I'm glad you're here." She grasped his hips and
lifted to meet him. "I needed you, too."

He smiled as he continued the lazy back-and-forth
movement. "Guess so. Running around the place without underwear. What were you thinking?"

"This."

"Yeah? You wanted to have sex on the ground?"

"No. I just…wanted you inside me."

"That's nice to hear, but how about a side order of a
nice juicy orgasm?" He leaned down and brushed his
mouth over hers. "I know you've already indulged,
but…"

"I'll take another, please."

"I thought you might. FYI, don't yell. Smudge is a
calm horse, but let's not push it."

"I won't yell."

"You might want to." Nibbling on her lower lip, he
increased the pace slightly. "How's that feel?"

Tension coiled within her. "Good."

He moved a little bit faster. "And that?"

She gasped. "Better."

"Wrap your legs around me. We're going for best."

Once she did, opening to him completely, he took
command, his rapid thrusts bringing her quickly to the
edge and hurling her over.

As sensations brilliant as diamonds cascaded
through her, she started to cry out. He kissed her hard,
capturing her cries as he continued to pump again

and again. At last, wrenching his mouth from hers, he groaned and plunged once more.

His body shook and he gulped for air. "Hope I didn't…hurt your mouth."

Her words were forced out as she panted. "No… sorry…forgot the horse."

"I'll take that…as a compliment."

"Do."

"Ah, Naomi." He leaned his forehead against hers. "You're every man's fantasy."

"I like the sound of that."

"And I like the feel of you…under me, on top of me, riding in front of me on my saddle while you give yourself a climax…." He lifted his head and smiled down at her. "You know what we should do now?"

"I can't imagine, but whatever it is, I'm up for it."

"See, that's what I'm talking about. You're ready for whatever."

"I am, if I can do it with you."

"Then let's go skinny-dipping in the stream. I'm all sweaty after that little episode. You, of course, are perfect and only a bit moist, but—"

"Liar. My hair's plastered to the back of my neck. But I thought you didn't like cold water."

"I think I'd like it better in the heat of the day than first thing in the morning."

She laughed. "Luke, it's still cold in that water, even at this time of day."

"Not as cold, I'll bet, and I want to prove to you I'm not a wuss. Also, I want to talk to you about something."

"What?"

"Nothing earthshaking, or at least I hope it's not, but I want your opinion. Let's go get in the water and talk. Unless you need to check on the eagles."

"The webcam's babysitting the eagles and I changed the batteries this morning. We can skinny-dip."

"Great."

Twenty minutes later, Luke had staked Smudge to his grazing spot and they stood by the stream like Adam and Eve. Their clothes lay on the bank, along with Naomi's beach towel.

"I'm going first." Luke started down to the water. "To prove I'm a manly man."

"You don't have to prove that to me, cowboy." She drank in the sight of his tight buns, muscled back and strong thighs. Talk about a fantasy.

He stepped into the water and his breath hissed out.

"Want to change your mind?" Naomi couldn't help smiling. He was a baby about cold water. "We could put some water in a saucepan and let it warm in the sun. Then you could take a sponge bath."

"Nope. I'm doing this." Taking a deep breath, he plunged in, sending water splashing as he plowed over to the deepest part, which was still less than three feet. Then he sat down with another loud splash and a strangled groan.

"That was quite a production."

"It's cold as hell."

"I told you."

"Shouldn't it be warmer by now?"

"Did you happen to notice there's still snow on the mountains?"

"Yeah."

"That's where this water comes from. It's snow-melt."

"Oh." He glanced over at her. "You're coming in, right?"

"Of course. I do this every day." She stepped into the water.

"How come you're not shivering?"

"I have this mental trick. As I'm immersing myself in cold water, I visualize it being warm." She made her way over to him and sat down.

"You can do that?"

"Sure. So could you. Don't think about the water as being cold. Tell yourself it's like bathwater."

He gazed at her. "I'm going to visualize having sex with you, instead. That should heat me up really fast."

"If you keep looking at me like that, you'll heat me up, too. And then what?"

His slow smile hinted at watery pleasures. "We'll do something about it."

Despite what they'd already shared today, her body responded. "I thought you wanted to talk. But if you'd rather get friendly instead, you're headed in the right direction."

He sighed. "Right. I do want to talk. It's just that you're so beautiful. I can't seem to get enough of you."

"Then talk fast."

He chuckled. "Okay. It's about my dad."

11

"YOUR DAD?" Naomi stared at him, clearly startled.

He should have led up to it more gradually, but they'd become so close in the past week that he'd forgotten she didn't know anything about his parents. Yet why would she? He'd never told her. But now he needed a friend's advice. He would have gone to Nash, except Nash was involved in wedding and honeymoon plans. And besides, this was the sort of touchy-feely situation that he sensed Naomi would understand. He trusted her.

"Let me back up." He gazed down at the water and trailed his fingers through it. "It's been easier to focus on the fun you and I are having. I'm not into deep analysis of my past anyway."

"So what about your dad?"

Luke looked out across the water tumbling over rocks and gathered his thoughts. "He always claimed he wanted to travel and see the world, but because he married my mother, who hates travel, and he has the responsibilities of a home and his job, he's never gone anywhere."

"That's too bad."

He took a deep breath. "I talked to Emmett about it last week, and he started me thinking. My dad could travel, if he'd allow himself to. If my mom doesn't want to go, that's up to her. But I'm considering calling him and asking him to come out here, maybe even for the Fourth of July. He'd have a little time off then."

Luke had never done anything like this before, and he was surprised he hadn't. Maybe all that his dad needed was someone to say, "Hey, come on, let's go." On the other hand, if Luke invited him and he refused, that rejection would be tough to take. It might also mean his dad's spirit was truly crushed, assuming he'd ever really had a vagabond spirit in the first place.

"I think that sounds wonderful, Luke."

He looked over at her, drawing strength from the certainty in her blue eyes. "So I should do it?"

"Definitely. Where do your parents live?"

"New Jersey. He'd have to fly out, but he could. They have money. Hell, I'd pay for his flight if necessary."

She opened her mouth. Closed it again.

"If you have advice, please give it. That's why I asked you about this before I did anything. I want to make sure I'm not crazy to consider it."

"Okay. I wonder…maybe it would be better if you let him pay."

"You think so?" Luke thought about his mother,

who could raise an objection about the cost of a plane ticket, especially at the last minute.

"It would mean he's making more of a commitment to traveling, which you said he's always wanted to do."

Luke nodded. "You're right. But it could be pricey."

"It probably will be. But if he's been saying all his life that he wants to travel and he never has, then he's saved a lot of money by not traveling."

"That's a good point."

"The biggest thing is whether he can move that fast, but maybe choosing a last-minute vacation is better. Still, this is… My gosh, it's July 1 already, Luke. You should call him right away."

He knew that, too, and he'd wanted her support while he did that, but her location didn't help matters. "I don't know if my cell phone will work out here. It's an older one. Sometimes it gets a signal in this area and sometimes it doesn't."

"Did you bring it?"

"Yes." That was a huge admission because he never brought his phone, first of all because his reception was dicey and second of all because he didn't want to be interrupted when he was with her.

She stood. "We need to go back to camp so you can try to call."

He gave her a rueful smile. "You're right, but we just got here. I'm not sure we've dipped enough skinny."

That made her laugh. He loved it when she laughed, because she seemed to glow with happiness.

"The stream's not going anywhere," she said. "We'll have more chances. The phone call can't be postponed."

No, it couldn't, unless he abandoned the idea. But now that the concept had penetrated his thick skull, he wanted to act on it, especially if Naomi thought he should. He put a lot of faith in her opinion.

So they took turns using her beach towel to dry off. She dressed more quickly than he did now that she'd decided to dispense with underwear. He got such a kick out of that. She was turning out to be quite a seductive woman.

He figured that their week together had something to do with that. Oh, hell, *he* had something to do with that. Might as well admit that he'd coaxed her into becoming less inhibited.

And now what, genius? Will you go off and leave her, so that some other yahoo can reap the rewards? Or does that stick in your craw a little bit?

It did. But unless he planned to stay in Shoshone and make things permanent between them, which he didn't, then he had to live with the fact that she'd bestow her newly discovered sexuality on some other lucky slob. Better not to think about that.

Back in camp, wearing his jeans and boots with his shirt left unbuttoned, he pulled his cell phone out of his saddlebag and turned it on. As he'd feared, the signal was weak. It would be better in town or back at the ranch, but he didn't want to leave Naomi so he could make a damned phone call.

He turned his phone around to show her the bars, or lack of them. "I can call tomorrow."

"Or you can ride back."

"No." He didn't like that scenario at all. He'd always

been able to slip away from the ranch without attracting any notice, but if he went back to make a phone call, someone would see him, and leaving again would be problematic.

Besides, he wanted Naomi's moral support, and he couldn't very well take her back with him. If he had to call tomorrow without her, so be it, but he wasn't leaving her tonight to make that call, no matter what she said.

She slapped her forehead. "Luke, we should try your phone from the observation platform. That might make all the difference. The signal is stronger for my laptop, so it should be stronger for your phone, too."

"Sure, okay. We can climb up there. Let me get the cold fried chicken I brought."

"You brought *chicken?* Why haven't I heard about this before?"

"Sorry. I've been a little preoccupied."

"No kidding. I *love* fried chicken. If I'd known that you brought some, I would have—"

"Wanted that instead of sex? Then I'm glad I didn't mention it." He crouched down and pulled the plastic container out of his saddlebag. "Remind me never to make you choose between sex with me and fried chicken."

She gave him a saucy smile. "Why can't I have both?"

"Oh, you can. I'm just worried about how you order your priorities. I want to be at the top, but I have a feeling that when it comes to fried chicken, I'm not.

And I—oof!" He nearly fell over as she launched herself at him.

"Listen here, my friend." She wound her arms around his neck. "I don't know how many times I have to say this before it makes an impression, but sex with you is the best thing that's ever happened to me in my entire life. Yes, I love fried chicken. And beautiful sunsets and baby eagles and the sound of the wind through the pines. But I would forgo them all for an hour alone with a naked Luke Griffin."

He couldn't have wiped the grin off his face if someone had offered him a million dollars to do it. She'd laid it on pretty thick and he wasn't sure he could believe all of it, but he appreciated the effort more than she'd ever know.

He cleared his throat. "Thank you. I'll probably still be thinking about that speech when I'm a white-haired old geezer who can't get it up anymore."

"You actually think the day will come when you can't get it up anymore?"

He laughed. "No, I don't, but that sounded good, didn't it?"

"It sounded like you're still fishing for compliments about your awesome package." She patted his cheeks. "Bring your chicken and your cell phone and your package up to the platform, okay?"

"Yes, ma'am." Luke followed her down the path to the pine tree that supported her observation platform. He knew she'd been teasing him and acting sexy on purpose to take his mind off the impending conversation, assuming he could make the phone call from her platform.

That was exactly why he'd sought her out once he'd dreamed up this plan. She was the soft landing spot if he should fall and go splat, psychologically speaking. He stood below the ladder and concentrated on the pleasure of watching her climb it. By tilting his head, he could almost see up her shorts. Not quite, but he knew she wasn't wearing anything underneath and that was enough to fuel his imagination.

He wasn't sure if he wanted this phone call to go through or not. He had such mixed emotions about it. But at least, whatever happened, Naomi would be there at the end of it. And he could lose himself in her lush body...if she wasn't too absorbed with eating fried chicken.

NAOMI HAD SENSED all along that Luke's wandering soul had a soft, vulnerable spot somewhere within it. Maybe she'd been afraid to find out what that was because she already cared too much for the guy. Discovering his secret pain could tear down the walls around her heart completely, and those walls were already displaying stress fractures.

But he'd come to her, like a bird with a broken wing, and asked for help. She could no more deny that than she could toss an injured animal out into the elements. Her creed was to live and let live, but when that life hung in the balance, was she supposed to turn away?

She was no psychologist but even she could figure out that Luke had become a wanderer partly by nature but largely so that he could live the life his father had said he wanted. Maybe he'd hoped to please his father and maybe he'd wanted to compete. It didn't matter. He'd come to a crossroads, a place where he wanted to invite his father to share in his adventures.

Luke knew his dad's response to the invitation was important to both father and son. She didn't have to tell him that. Whether it was important to her was another question.

She could no longer deny that she was getting emotionally involved with this drifter who had wandered under her observation platform one bright, sunny day. She knew how much he'd come to mean in her life. She was less convinced how much she meant to him.

Yes, he needed her now, when he was about to make this difficult phone call to his father. But was she only a temporary crutch to get him through this critical time in his life? Or had they made a deeper connection?

She had no answers. But while he stood at a far corner of the deck and dialed the number for his parents' home, she laid out their picnic on the red checkered cloth he'd left there after their first meal on this platform. Regardless of how the call went, she would offer him solace.

If that cost her dearly in the long run because she ended up with a broken heart, she'd deal with that. He'd given her so much in this past week that she couldn't begrudge him whatever he needed. She mentally crossed her fingers and hoped that his father would understand the stakes when he heard Luke's invitation.

She didn't eavesdrop, but she knew when he'd made

a connection because the low murmur of his voice drifted over to her. Sitting beside the picnic tablecloth, she stayed very still, not wanting to disrupt his concentration in any way. This could be one of the most important conversations he'd ever have with his dad.

After what seemed like an eternity but was probably less than five minutes, Luke walked over and sat cross-legged on the far side of the checkered tablecloth. Glancing over at her, he shrugged. "He says he'll think about it and get back to me."

She wanted to scream. Stupid, stupid father! She tried to imagine her own father acting with such indifference. He never would. She thought of the Chance men, devoted fathers, every one of them.

She'd been in Florida when Jonathan Chance had died in a truck rollover, and she'd heard the rumor that he'd been upset with his son Jack at the time. Yes, that had been difficult for Jack to reconcile. But at least Jonathan had been a big part of Jack's life.

All of Jonathan's sons—Jack, Nick and Gabe—were passionately involved with their children. Nick wasn't biologically connected to Lester, the troubled boy he and Dominique had adopted after Lester had spent last summer at the ranch. But Nick was a committed parent.

Naomi searched for the right thing to say. "I'm sure you caught him by surprise. It's hard to make snap decisions."

His dark eyes were bleak. "No, it's not. You and I make them all the time. It's what you do when you're actually living life, instead of hanging on the fringes of it." Anger and disappointment rolled off him in waves.

"Don't give up."

"I won't. But the only way I'll get his call is if I'm up here."

"Then we'll stay up here."

He held her gaze. "Thank you. I…" He looked away and swallowed.

That's when she knew that he needed something more than fried chicken right now. Moving purposefully, she cleared all the food aside. He watched her without moving.

Then she sat on the tablecloth, right in front of him. Cupping his face in both hands, she kissed him as thoroughly as she knew how, putting all her caring, her longing and her passion into that kiss. At first he simply let her kiss him without responding.

That was a new experience for her, and one she didn't care for in the least. Luke had always been eager for her kisses. Once their lips met, he'd usually been the one who had pushed the kiss to the next level.

Not now, and for a brief moment her courage failed her. But she'd told him not to give up, and so she couldn't, either. She kissed his forehead, his eyes, his cheeks and once again his mouth.

With that the floodgates opened. With a groan, he pulled her into his lap. After that she didn't have to worry about how to kiss him. He took care of all the mouth-to-mouth contact, and the mouth-to-body contact, and every form of contact that followed.

Soon she lay sprawled naked on the tablecloth, and he'd covered every inch of her with his mouth and tongue. If she had been an ice-cream cone, she'd be long gone by now.

Standing, he gazed down at her as he took off his clothes with deliberate intent. "I'm going to have you six ways to Sunday," he said. "And then we'll start over and go through the whole damn week again."

"Okay." She watched him pull off his boots with angry motions and shuck his jeans and briefs. But after he'd located the condom in his pocket and put it on, she sat up and reached for his hand. "Lie down here. Lie down and let me love you for a change."

The fierceness left his expression as if a cloud had scudded away from the sun. Without a word, he knelt down and stretched out on the tablecloth. Her heart constricted with the surrender implicit in his reaction. This was what he wanted, what he needed—not to take her six ways to Sunday, but to be loved and cherished by someone who asked nothing in return.

What an easy assignment that was. Straddling him, she began with his beautiful face. She followed the curve of his cheekbones with her tongue and placed butterfly kisses on his eyelids. His mouth became a playground for her lips, his determined jaw a place to nibble and tease until she felt him slowly relax.

With a deep sigh he let his arms fall to his sides, and she traced each vein, each corded muscle in those arms with her fingertips. As his mighty chest rose and fell with his labored breaths, she toyed with his nipples and stroked the silky black hair covering that massive display of strength and power.

She followed the trail of dark hair to his navel, and

as she dipped her tongue into the shallow depression, he quivered. She stroked his cock and wished that nothing prevented her from feeling the velvet-on-steel wonder of it. But she could also fondle what lay beneath and watch as those heavy sacs drew up in tight readiness.

"Take me," he murmured. "Please take me."

She wondered if he'd ever begged a woman in his life. Maybe not. But she wouldn't make him do it more than once. Rising above him, she guided his taut cock into position and began a slow slide downward.

His breathing quickened as she descended, and when she'd taken all of him, he began to tremble. "Go slow," he said. "I don't want to come yet."

Leaning forward, she feathered a kiss over his lips and felt him sigh. Then she lifted her head to look into his eyes. "Tell me," she said softly. "Tell me what you need."

Passion burned in his gaze. His hands found her hips, bracketing them. "Easy strokes." His voice was strained. "Go easy. Let me... I want to wait."

She lifted up only a little and made her way gradually back down.

"Good." He held her gaze. "Again."

She repeated the motion.

He groaned. "So good. Again."

Once more she rose up and came slowly down.

He sucked in a breath. "Good Lord, I want you, Naomi. I want to come. But I don't want to end this."

She smiled. "We can do it again sometime."

A fire ignited in his eyes. He swallowed. "Then ride

me, lady." His words echoed their first time together. His fingers gripped her hips. "Ride me hard."

That was all she'd been waiting for. Yes, he needed the sweet loving, but more than that, he needed heat that would burn away grief, incinerate sadness. She brought the heat, pumping up and down with a frenzy that made her breasts dance and her bottom slap against his thighs.

His first cry was low and intense, his second louder and when he came, his shout of triumph sent the song-birds fluttering and squawking from the branches of the tree. He laughed at that, a breathless, happy sound that resonated in her heart.

She laughed with him, collapsing against his chest and panting from the effort she'd made.

He wrapped her tight in his arms. "Thank you, thank you, thank you. I know you didn't come."

"It doesn't matter."

"It does. I'll make it up to you." He rocked her in his arms. "I will make it up to you a dozen times over. But that…Naomi…that was exactly what I needed."

"I know."

"How did you know?"

"That's my secret." And it would remain her secret. If he ever guessed she was falling in love with him, he'd leave.

12

LUKE WASN'T SURE what he'd done to deserve someone like Naomi, but she was a lifesaver. As the sun went down, she insisted they should haul the sleeping bags up to the platform for the night. Even when he protested that his father was probably in bed by now and wouldn't call, she refused to consider going back down to the campsite, where the phone reception was bad.

"Just don't let me fall off in the middle of the night," she said, laughing.

The thought made his heart stutter and he stopped unrolling the sleeping bags. "Do you think you might? Are you a sleepwalker?"

"No. At least I don't think so."

"Let's forget this." He started bundling up his sleeping bag. "If there's the slightest chance that you'll wake up at night and start wandering around this platform half-asleep, it's not worth the risk."

"I won't. And we're staying." She crossed her arms and planted her feet. "I've always thought it would be fun to sleep up here, but I was a little worried about doing it by myself. This is perfect." She peered at him. "Unless *you're* a sleepwalker."

"Nope. Never been a problem for me." He crouched next to his sleeping bag, thinking. "So spending the night up here would be an adventure for you?"

"Yes. Absolutely."

"You're not just saying that because of the phone thing?"

"That's a good excuse to do it, but from the moment I first climbed onto the platform, I thought of spending the night, pretending I'm Tarzan. I've just been too chicken."

He smiled. "You wouldn't make a very good Tarzan."

"You'd be surprised." She took a deep breath and let out the most Tarzan-like yell he'd ever heard.

He laughed so hard he had to sit down.

"Wait, that wasn't as good as I can do. I'll try again." She sucked in more air.

"No, no, you're great!"

She looked at him. "Yeah?"

"Amazingly good. I wasn't laughing because you were lousy at it. I was laughing at that big Tarzan yell coming out of such a blonde cutie-pie. It's so unexpected."

"My college friends and I taught ourselves to do it. When we backpacked through Europe, we sometimes entertained people in pubs by doing our Tarzan yells. I'm better after a couple of beers."

"I'll bet." He chuckled. "I can just imagine that." He

also felt a pang of longing. Although he'd traveled with friends when he was younger, they'd all settled down with families. They still traveled, but now it involved taking spouses and kids, which was a whole other ball game. Not his deal.

He stood and surveyed the platform. "So if this is something you want to do for the adventure factor, but you're a little scared of falling off, we'll put your sleeping bag next to the tree and mine next to yours so I'm on the outside."

She nodded. "I like that. Thanks."

"You're welcome. It'll be fun." He knew that for sure because everything involving Naomi was fun. He couldn't remember the last time he'd laughed this much.

They ate cold sandwiches for dinner, watched a family of deer graze in the clearing and made love to the sound of wind in the trees. They slept spoon-fashion, with Luke on the outside. He figured if he kept a hand on her at all times, she wouldn't get away from him and risk falling.

That thought made him restless. And then there was the issue of a potential phone call. It didn't come until dawn, and it woke them both.

Luke scrambled to pick it up before the chime disturbed Naomi, but he was too late. She sat up, rubbing her eyes, as he put the phone to his ear.

"Luke, it's Dad."

Luke grimaced. "Hi, Dad." Who else would it be at this hour of the morning? His father had probably forgotten the time difference. Travelers usually thought about that when they made phone calls. Nontravelers, not so much.

"Listen, I thought about your invitation, and it won't work for me."

Luke had prepared himself for that answer, but even so, disappointment sliced through him. Apparently he'd placed more importance on this than he should have. "Okay."

"I checked flights, and it'll cost an arm and a leg."

"So it's the money?"

"Well, that, and your mother has a cookout planned with the Sullivans. She has her heart set on that cookout. You remember the Sullivans, don't you?"

"Yep." They were neighbors whose attitude toward travel was exactly like his mother's. They claimed everything they needed was right there, so why go anywhere else?

"Anyway, thanks for asking. Maybe next time."

"Sure, Dad. Have a nice Fourth. Talk to you later." Luke disconnected and laid down the phone.

"He's not coming."

Naomi put a hand on his shoulder. "Luke, I'm sorry. It was a great idea."

He shrugged. "I should have known better. He'll just keep watching documentaries about places he'll never see."

"His loss."

"I think so, too, but I can't make him get out there and see the world." He gazed at her. "I did think it would be cool, though. I've never been here for Fourth of July, but the town's really gearing up. Are you coming in or staying here?"

She smiled. "Are you inviting me to come and party with you?"

"Hell, yes! We'll have a blast. Although maybe the fireworks will look more spectacular from this platform, come to think of it. We could—"

"Hold on. Did you say *fireworks*?"

"Yeah. Everyone's all excited because Shoshone's never had fireworks before. What's the matter? Don't you like fireworks?"

"That depends. Are we talking about little stuff, close to the ground? Backyard fireworks?"

"Not from what I heard. This Clifford Mason guy, the one we saw having dinner with Pam Mulholland at the Spirits and Spurs, is arranging for a huge spectacular. Tyler Keller...you know Tyler?"

"Yes, she's Josie Chance's sister-in-law. She plans tourist-type events for the town. So she set this up?"

"I believe that's what Emmett said. And Pam's underwriting it. Everybody's happy about it except Emmett, who thinks Clifford's romancing Pam."

"Luke, this is a disaster. I have to stop it."

"I don't think it's our place to interfere in Pam's private life."

"Not that. The fireworks. I know people will be disappointed and I hate that, but we can't have fireworks."

"Why not?"

She gestured toward the eagles' nest. "It's too close. The parents might become terrified and abandon the nest. The babies would die."

"Town's not *that* close."

"I know it doesn't seem like it, because from the ranch road it's about ten miles. But we're out on a far corner of Last Chance land. When I hike in from my folks' place, it's only about five miles straight across. That's way too close to nesting eagles."

He sensed a train wreck coming. "Are you sure the eagles would abandon the nest?"

"Not a hundred percent sure. You can't ever be positive when you're trying to predict the behavior of wild creatures. But I'm sure enough that I don't want to take the risk."

"Okay, but I'm afraid you're going to have some tough sledding. Everyone in town is looking forward to this."

"I'm sure they are. If it weren't for the eagles, *I* would be looking forward to it. But we do have eagles, and fireworks are a bad idea. Tyler's a very compassionate person. When I explain the situation, I'm sure she'll cancel."

He wasn't so sure. "I don't want to be the prophet of doom, but there could be economic repercussions. The fireworks have been paid for and the merchants are expecting to cash in on all the excitement."

"But what about the other activities? They always have a ton of things going on. Won't that be enough?"

"I don't know. Maybe, maybe not. I think you'll get push back. That's all I'm saying."

"I know." Her blue eyes clouded with sadness. "I really hate that, and I hate having people disappointed.

But I can't let them light up the sky only five miles from a nest of eagles."

"No, you can't. I can see that." He picked up his phone and hit a speed-dial number.

"Who are you calling?"

"Reinforcements." He gave her a quick grin. "Hello, Emmett? Listen, I need to take the morning off, if there's any way you can arrange it."

"I probably can," Emmett said. "What's the problem?"

"You might want to take the morning off, too. Naomi needs to shut down the fireworks display and she could use backup. Fireworks are a danger to the eagles. The parents might spook and abandon the nest."

"Is that so?" Emmett sounded pleased. "Never did care much for fireworks, myself."

"Or the guy who sells them?"

"Don't much care for him, either."

"I was thinking we need to have a little chat with the folks involved, but I don't have everybody's numbers."

"I can arrange a meeting," Emmett said. "How soon can you both get to the diner?"

"Thirty minutes to get organized and an hour of travel time, maybe less if Smudge is feeling lively this morning."

"Good. I'll round up the parties involved and meet you both at the diner in an hour and a half."

"Sounds good."

"Thanks for the call, Luke. It made my day."

"I thought it might. See you soon, Emmett." Luke

disconnected the phone and glanced over at Naomi. "Does that work for you?"

Grabbing his face in both hands, she kissed him soundly before releasing him. "Yes, sir, it most certainly does."

RIDING DOUBLE ON a five-mile trip turned out to be an interesting experience. Neither of them thought it would be wise to try it with Naomi sitting on Luke's lap facing him. They couldn't handle the distraction.

So they chose for Luke to sit forward in the saddle, with Naomi perched behind him, hanging on to his waist. Once they were settled, she couldn't see where they were going, but she trusted Luke to get them there safely.

She was, however, concerned about his package. "Are you squished up there?"

He chuckled. "A little. Can't be helped."

"I don't want you to injure yourself."

"I'll be fine unless the conversation turns to sex. Any expansion could jeopardize this entire arrangement."

"Understood. Maybe we shouldn't talk at all."

"We should definitely talk. If we ride along in silence, with your luscious body pressed tight against mine, my imagination will get me into trouble in no time. So think of a topic. Just don't make it anything sexy."

"I know the perfect thing. Tell me about some of your favorite places."

"Well, your mouth, and your—"

"No! In the world!"

"Oh." He laughed. "My mistake."

"You knew what I meant."

"Yeah, I knew what you meant. But sometime, not now, I'll list my favorite places on Naomi Perkins."

"You're not helping your cause, Luke."

"You're right. Okay, favorite places in the world. Jackson Hole is one of them, believe it or not."

"I believe it." She rested her cheek against his broad back. "I've always felt lucky that my parents chose to live here. So, what else?"

He began to list the places he'd seen that had made the biggest impression on him. He'd traveled widely in the United States and had made it to several South American countries. He'd also seen most of Australia and New Zealand. He talked lovingly about his trips, leaving no doubt that being a wanderer was in his blood. It was a good thing he knew that about himself.

About halfway there, he switched the conversation to her and she listed all her favorite spots, although she didn't have nearly as many as Luke. Privately she admitted that his life had some appeal, but she still thought it sounded like a lonely existence.

Thanks to their conversation, the trip went by faster than she'd expected. She didn't stop to think about the message she and Luke would convey with this cozy riding position until they were almost there.

She'd enjoyed resting her cheek on his warm, strong back, but she'd be wise to stop doing that. "I wonder if I should get off here and walk in."

"Why would you—? Oh, I get it. Wagging tongues.

Do you want to walk in? You're the local girl, so you decide. I told Emmett that we'd ride in together, but he probably won't mention it to anyone."

"He won't have to. If we ride down Main Street like this, I can guarantee we'll be noticed. Comments will be made. I may be the local girl, but you'll probably be hit with some personal questions. Assumptions will be made."

"I figure that'll happen anyway if we spend Fourth of July in town together, so I'm okay with it. Your call, though."

She thought about how he'd jumped right in on her side of the argument regarding the eagles. He'd pulled Emmett in, too, which was a brilliant move and something she might not have thought of.

She hadn't been privy to the semicourtship between Emmett and Pam Mulholland, but Luke, having worked at the ranch for nearly a year, knew all about it. Emmett Sterling was respected in Shoshone. If he supported the eagles, that would go a long way toward helping their cause.

"You know what, Luke? If you don't mind having people assume we're a couple, I don't mind, either."

"Good. That makes life less complicated in some ways. But by saying *people,* are you including your parents?"

"Um…" Their opinion wasn't as easy to ignore as everyone else's. She hesitated.

"You're not so sure about them, are you?"

"No."

"Is your father a shotgun-totin' man?"

That made her laugh. "He owns guns, if that's what you're asking. Most people around here do."

"Yes, but would he use a gun to make sure a fellow did right by his daughter?"

"No, he wouldn't. That's an old-fashioned view and I can't believe he'd ever take that kind of stand. Besides, I'm an adult, and I've been on my own for quite a while. But I'd hate for either my mom or my dad to think poorly of you."

"So?"

"So I'll talk to them and explain the situation." She didn't look forward to that, because her parents were eager for her to find the right guy. If she seemed interested in Luke, they would be, too—as a potential son-in-law. She had to nip that concept in the bud.

"Do you want me there for that conversation?"

"Good heavens, no." But she appreciated the courage it took for him to make the offer. "Thanks for your willingness, but I'll handle it."

As they rode down the street toward her parents' diner, she noticed the festive bunting decorating each storefront. Most shops also proudly displayed a poster advertising Shoshone's Fourth of July celebration and the word *fireworks* took center stage on the poster. She felt a little like the Grinch.

But two vulnerable young eagles might die as a result of those fireworks, and she couldn't believe her friends and family would want those nestlings to pay the price for a human celebration they couldn't escape. If she'd known about this sooner, she might have avoided a confrontation two days before the sched-uled event.

She searched her memory. Had the information been out there and she'd simply missed it? Maybe. For the past month she'd been totally engrossed in the eagles, and more recently she'd been focused on Luke, as well. She hadn't needed to make trips to town, because he'd come out every night laden with food. One midweek trip would have told her what was coming down the pike.

When she had hiked in more than a week ago, no one had thought to inform her of the big plans be-cause she hadn't been involved with them. She'd been gone for so many years, first for college and later for her job in Florida. She wasn't hooked into the rumor mill anymore. After this episode, she'd be *fodder* for the rumor mill.

A few businesses in Shoshone still had hitching posts in front of them, and the Shoshone Diner was one of those. It was at the far end of the curbside parking.

Logistics required Naomi to dismount first.

As Luke swung down to stand beside her, he chuckled. "One disadvantage to riding double is that I couldn't help you down from the saddle like a true gentleman."

"People understand that."

"I hope so, because I'm already going to be in trou-ble with your folks. I don't want them to add a lack of manners to my other sins."

"I won't let them blame you for anything."

He smiled. "Good luck. I expect they'll blame me

for everything. But don't worry. I can take it." Then he tied Smudge to the rail.

She supposed that he could take it. For his sake, that was a good thing. But in some ways, she wished that someone would finally pierce his coat of armor and touch the man underneath.

13

BEFORE THEY WALKED into the diner, Luke took Naomi's laptop out of the saddlebag and handed it to her. "Ready?"

"I am. I wish I'd had time to get some of the pictures printed to pass around, but at least we have something to show."

He took her by the shoulders. "You'll do great." Then he gave her a quick kiss, because the way he saw it, he'd already been labeled as her boyfriend. Might as well take advantage of that label.

"Thanks, Luke." She smiled. "I'm glad you're here."

"Wouldn't miss it." He walked to the door and held it open for her. When they stepped into the crowded diner, all conversation stopped. Luke had never been in that situation before. Unfortunately the belligerent stares from people seated at the various tables eating breakfast weren't directed at him. He would have preferred that, but all the glares were focused on Naomi.

He gave her shoulder a squeeze before they started

over to the spot where two tables had been pushed together. Obviously this was the setting for the pow-wow. Emmett was already there, sitting on the far side on Pam Mulholland's right, and the dandified cowboy Clifford Mason had positioned himself on her left. Tyler Keller, a dark Italian beauty, had taken the opposite side of the table, flanked by Nick and Jack Chance.

Luke wasn't sure why the Chance boys had come, but then he remembered Nick was Pam's nephew. He might have come to give his aunt some moral support. As for Jack...well, Jack didn't like to miss out on anything. The mood at the table was decidedly tense.

A red-haired waitress bustled around the table filling coffee mugs, but nobody had food yet. Edgar Perkins, a tall man who wore glasses and was going bald, stood talking to Jack. His wife, Madge, wasn't in evidence.

Then she came out of the kitchen. A trim blonde with her hair in a ponytail and an apron tied over her jeans and Western shirt, she looked like Naomi probably would in twenty-five years. She walked straight over to her daughter and gave her a hug. "Whatever support you need from us," she said, "you've got it. We don't care about the fireworks." Then she flashed a look at Luke. "Thanks for bringing her in."

"You're welcome, Mrs. Perkins." He didn't read any friendliness in her expression. But he didn't see open hostility, either. She'd apparently decided to stay neutral for now. Luke thought that was eminently fair.

They continued to the table on the far side of the diner. Edgar ended his conversation with Jack and walked over to gather Naomi in his arms. "We're on your side, sweetheart," he murmured.

After he released her, he turned to Luke. "So." He stuck out his hand and Luke shook it. "I know we've met before, Luke, but I can't seem to remember where you're from."

"Most recently from Sacramento, Mr. Perkins. I worked with Nash Bledsoe over there."

"Oh, right. I did hear that." From behind his wire-rimmed glasses, Edgar continued to scrutinize Luke as if wanting to ask more personal questions but hesitating to start in, considering the circumstances. "We'll have to talk later," he said finally.

"I look forward to that." What a whopper that was. Luke doubted that a heart-to-heart with Naomi's dad would go well.

By the time Edgar headed back into the kitchen, Naomi had already taken one of the two remaining chairs, which were at opposite ends of the table. She'd chosen to sit with Emmett on one side of her and Nick Chance on the other.

Luke didn't blame her. He'd gladly take the other end and be the one closest to Clifford Mason, who was dressed in a bloodred shirt with silver piping.

Mason spoke first. "I know who you are, young lady, but I don't believe I know the person you came with. Or why he's here."

Luke's jaw tightened. He didn't care for the tone or the implication. The guy had better watch himself.

"Luke's my research assistant," Naomi said smoothly. "He's here on behalf of the eagles."

Clifford glanced over at Luke, and Luke gave a nod of acknowledgment. He *was* a research assistant...sort of.

Pam Mulholland leaned forward. "Naomi, Emmett has related some very disturbing news regarding our fireworks display. Could you clarify the situation?"

"Certainly." Naomi switched on her laptop. "These pictures were taken yesterday, so the nestlings haven't changed much in twenty-four hours. I wanted you all to see them." She handed the laptop to Emmett. "If you'll pass that around, everyone can get a look at what we need to protect."

Luke had seen the picture. Naomi hadn't had much time to choose one, but she'd found a charmer. The baby eagles looked bright-eyed but vulnerable while their mother perched on the edge of the gigantic nest and gazed down at them. Luke would have liked to say she gazed at them fondly, but an eagle couldn't look fond if it tried. She was imposing, though, and a preview of what those babies could become if allowed to grow up.

Everyone else's food arrived as the laptop circled the table, so there was some juggling involved. Luke didn't have food yet, so he was free to watch all the reactions to the picture.

Emmett chuckled and Pam's expression softened. Mason looked pissed—no surprise there. Jack grinned as if he were personally responsible for those nestlings looking so adorable. Tyler studied them closely, and she too seemed caught by the winsome image.

Nick studied them even more closely than Tyler. "They look healthy to me. Perfectly viable."

Then Luke realized that Nick might be here in his capacity as a vet more than for his aunt Pam. In practical terms, if the nestlings hadn't seemed healthy, then protecting them from fireworks wouldn't have made economic sense.

A waitress came for Naomi's order and she shook her head. Luke caught that and decided he wouldn't get any food, either. He probably couldn't stomach a meal right now anyway. They could eat a late breakfast at the campsite before he went back to work.

Once the laptop had made the rounds, Naomi described the proximity of the nest to the town. "A constant barrage of explosions at close range could easily scare away those parents, leaving the babies to starve. There have been documented cases of that happening, and I can supply that evidence before the end of the day, if you need it."

Mason leaned back in his chair. "Please do. We need a lot more evidence. I find this hard to believe, frankly. Aren't wild creatures supposed to defend their young fiercely? Why abandon them at the first hint of trouble?"

"Not all wild creatures respond the same to a perceived threat," Naomi said. "Some parents defend their young, and others abandon them. Eagles tend to leave."

"You say they *tend* to leave." Mason glared at her. "And you're proposing we cancel a major civic event, one that will bring much-needed revenue into this community, on the *supposition* that two little eagles *might* be harmed. That's a lot of variables. I don't buy the argument."

"I'll have statistics available later today," Naomi said. "Personally, I can't imagine going ahead with a fireworks display if there's even a slight chance that two of our valuable eagles will die as a result."

Mason sent Tyler a challenging glance. "How about you, Mrs. Keller? Are you ready to have all your hard work go down the drain on the slight chance it will cause harm to a couple of eagle chicks?"

"Naturally I would rather we go ahead as planned," Tyler said. "We've put in a lot of work. But this area is dedicated to honoring and protecting its wildlife. To ignore that doesn't feel right."

Jack cleared his throat. "Mr. Mason, have you considered the potential PR nightmare if word gets out that a fireworks display provided by your company caused the death of baby eagles?"

Luke was impressed. Maybe Jack deserved to be in charge of the world after all. The guy had come up with a killer argument.

"Most likely the eagles will be fine," Mason said. "Even if they're not, who will know?"

"Me," Naomi said. "And I will report my findings to Professor Scranton, who's funding this study."

Emmett leaned around Pam, obviously wanting more eye contact with Mason. "I can't say how a college professor might influence the situation, but I can guarantee the influence the Chance family will have. The Last Chance gave permission for the study, and we support Naomi's work. Right, Jack?"

"Yes." Jack's face was like granite. "We certainly do."

Emmett's blue eyes grew very cold. "Just some friendly advice, Mason. When in Jackson Hole, don't mess with the Chances."

Mason laughed. "What do we have here, a gunfight at the O.K. Corral? Give me a break. I have a contract that says I'm supplying fireworks to this event. Cancel the contract and I'll have you all in court."

Pam Mulholland turned to him. "That's enough, Clifford."

He blinked. "Pam? Surely you're not going to let some silly eagles' nest spoil the town's Fourth of July celebration. We're going to put Shoshone on the map, you and I. The townspeople won't be happy about this." He stood and addressed the rest of the diners. "Help me out here, folks. You want your fireworks, right?"

"My kids are counting on it," said one man.

"It'll be good for business," piped up a woman.

Naomi stood, too. "I'm sorry about the last-minute notification, but I've been out at the observation site and just found out about the fireworks. Yes, I'm sure kids will be disappointed, but we're preserving those eagles for their generation. I'll bet if you explained the situation to them, they'd understand. Kids have an affinity for baby creatures."

"So do I." Tyler stood and turned toward the group. "And had I known that fireworks could be a problem for those nesting eagles, I never would have accepted Mr. Mason's offer to provide them."

"I wouldn't have, either." Pam also rose from her

chair. "I own a business, and my guests may be disappointed initially, but not once I explain. Anyone who comes to Shoshone knows it's a haven for wildlife. That's one of the main reasons they visit. Not for fireworks."

Mason glanced at her. "You're missing the point, Pam. There's only a possibility that the eagles will be harmed. To cancel all our careful plans for the *potential* harm to a couple of eagles isn't good business. It's not smart."

Emmett unfolded his lean body from his chair. "Excuse me, Mason." His voice was dangerously low. "But I won't have you taking that tone with the woman I love."

Pam gasped. "Emmett!"

Mason's mouth twisted into a dismissive sneer. "This isn't any of your concern, Sterling. You had your chance. Now it's my turn. Pam and I have a business arrangement. Her emotional response to the eagles is understandable. She's a woman. But once she has a chance to think logically, she'll—"

"Shut up, Mason." Emmett moved Pam gently aside. "Sorry. I know how you hate to make a scene." Then he grabbed Mason by his gaudy red shirt. "I didn't like you when I first laid eyes on you, but I tolerated you because you were a guest in Pam's establishment. Now that you've insulted her by implying that her gender has affected her good judgment, I don't have to tolerate you any longer."

"Pam!" Mason's eyes bulged. "Are you going to let him talk this way?"

"Yes, Clifford, I am. Because you are a horse's ass."

Luke felt like applauding but decided that wasn't appropriate. He did note that both Nick and Jack were smiling.

Emmett continued to hold Mason by his shirtfront. "I'll tell you this once, and once only. Get out of our town. And leave my woman alone." He released his hold, and Mason had to scramble to keep from falling down.

Pam sighed. "Oh, Emmett."

"I'll leave, all right." Mason backed away from the table. "Because you're all *crazy*. Your little town is going to amount to *nothing*. I hope you all rot!" And he ran out of the diner.

Emmett stood there breathing hard, but he didn't seem to know what to do next. Luke considered whether or not to tell him. Emmett had asked him to offer suggestions regarding Pam at any time. This was a critical moment. Even Luke, who avoided entanglements at all costs, recognized it.

He leaned toward Emmett. "Propose, man," he said in an undertone. "Now's the time."

Emmett gulped. Then he squared his shoulders and turned to Pam. "I think you'd better marry me before some other damned fool comes along and thinks you're available, because you're not!"

Pam laughed and threw her arms around his neck. "Finally!" Then, still holding on to a very red Emmett, she glanced at the other customers. "I have witnesses, right? He asked me, and I accepted!"

"We'll back you up, Pam!" shouted someone in the far corner of the room.

"You waited long enough!" cried another.

"This is better than fireworks!" yelled a third person.

Pam gave Emmett a quick kiss before grabbing his hand. "Let's get out of here."

"Hell, yes. This is a nightmare." Blushing furiously, Emmett allowed himself to be led from the diner amid laughter and cheers.

Luke sought Naomi's gaze and they exchanged smiles of triumph. But he detected something else in her expression, an emotion that put him on alert. She seemed...wistful.

He shouldn't be surprised. She wanted a happily-ever-after someday, too. She'd admitted as much. So naturally, when she watched a man declare his love for a woman, she had to start thinking about when that might happen for her.

And here he was, enjoying all the privileges of a potential life mate, without any intention of filling that role. He felt like a poseur, a selfish bastard who was taking the place of someone who could promise to love and cherish her forever.

Then she looked away with an abruptness that made him wonder if she'd been able to guess his thoughts. They'd been together so much lately she might be capable of doing that. He didn't want to hurt her, but he had the horrible suspicion that he wouldn't be able to stop that from happening.

NAOMI TRIED TO talk Luke out of taking her back to the observation site, but he insisted. Arguing with him about it while everyone filed out of the diner wouldn't have been classy, especially because so many people stopped to thank her for protecting the eagles.

So she climbed on behind him as she had before, attracting more attention in the process. She ended up introducing Luke to several people who'd never met him, so getting out of Shoshone took some time.

Finally they reached the outskirts of town. "Thank you for being there," she said.

"I didn't do much. You handled everything beautifully."

"I didn't have to do much, either. Mostly I let Clifford Mason dig himself into a hole. I think if Emmett hadn't grabbed him by the shirt, someone else would have."

"Like one of the Chance brothers?"

"Or others sitting in the diner. Pam is well liked. She runs a quality bed-and-breakfast that's a credit to the town, and she's generous with her money. People don't forget things like someone buying new Christmas decorations for Main Street or having the Shoshone welcome sign repainted. Any man insulting her is creating a problem for himself."

Luke chuckled. "I think he figured that out. His talk about lawsuits faded fast."

"I spoke briefly with Jack, and they've had the guy investigated. He's a shady character, so I think the lawsuit was an empty threat. He might have thought he was dealing with a bunch of hicks who wouldn't know any better."

"Then he didn't do his research."

"Obviously not." She gave in to the temptation to lay her cheek against his back again. But she couldn't shake the nagging feeling that things had changed between them in some subtle way. Emmett's proposal had touched her, and then she'd made the mistake of gazing at Luke. He'd probably thought she was dreaming about the proposal she'd like to receive someday.

Well, she had been, but that didn't mean she expected Luke to do the honors. Luke had said something to Emmett before that proposal, though, and she was curious. "You made a comment to Emmett after Mason left. What was that all about?"

"I told Emmett to propose."

"I wondered. I could sort of read your lips, and then he turned around and did exactly that, as if he might be following orders."

"If he was ever gonna do it, that was the time."

"Oh, Luke." She allowed herself to hug him just a little bit. "Do you realize how long that proposal has been dangling between them, waiting to be said?"

"Awhile, I guess."

"My mother said it's been years. Pam desperately wanted him, but he couldn't get past her wealth, when he doesn't have a whole lot of money. Your nudge was a good thing, Luke."

"You talked to your mom? When?"

"As everyone was leaving, we grabbed a few minutes." She'd noticed Luke having a conversation with

Nick and Jack, so she'd ducked into the kitchen to say goodbye.

"How about your dad? Did you talk to him, too?"

She heard the note of anxiety. "Briefly. He's glad the eagles are safe." In reality, she hadn't invited a deeper discussion with either of her parents. Earlier today she'd thought that speaking to them about Luke was important. Now she wasn't sure.

Luke was pulling away. She couldn't explain how she knew, but she did. To confess everything to her parents made no sense if her special time with Luke was coming to an end soon.

"So you just talked about the eagles."

"Yes. If you're asking whether I explained our situation to them, the answer is no, I didn't."

"Okay." He didn't ask why, and that was telling.

She fell silent for a while and just soaked up being close to him as Smudge walked along the path with a slow and steady gait. She had the distinct feeling she wouldn't ride like this with him again, so she wanted to get all the pleasure from it that she could. He was such an enigma, this man she'd known so intimately yet in some ways knew not at all.

"Tell me something," she said at last. "If you're convinced that marriage ties a person down, why urge Emmett to propose? It seems as if you'd be the least likely one to do that."

"Because I think it would work for him. He's not a traveler. He likes it fine right here, and he's already tied to the ranch. Being tied to Pam, a woman he clearly loves, isn't adding much to his obligations. He was letting her money get in the way, which was only making both of them more miserable."

"I agree, but I'm still surprised you made the suggestion."

He laughed. "You mean because it's none of my business?"

"Well, yeah."

"The night we came home from the Spirits and Spurs, after he'd danced with Pam, he told me that if I ever had another bright idea about how to deal with her, to let him know. So I had a bright idea today, and I let him know."

Naomi smiled and hugged him again. "Then all I can say is well done. Pam looked as if she was lit from within. And I don't suppose she'll ever know that she has you to thank."

"She won't hear it from me, and unless Emmett's completely clueless, he won't tell her. She needs to believe it was Emmett's idea."

"Yes, she does. No woman wants to think a man had to get cues from the sidelines when he was proposing."

"He probably would have thought of it himself anyway."

"I don't know, Luke. He's been shilly-shallying around for a long time, according to my mother. I'm glad you gave him a push."

"Yeah, me, too. They'll be happy."

Luke was such a puzzle to her. He sat on the sidelines—matchmaking, babysitting other people's children, having brief affairs with women—but he never really got in the game. He saw amazing places, but he made no permanent connections with them. He truly was a drifter in the old-fashioned sense of the word.

And yet she felt the tug of strong emotion whenever they had… She couldn't even say they just had sex, because it was more than that. At least it was for her. In her biased opinion, they made love.

They might not be *in* love, but they made love. They cherished each other in a way that lifted the act above the simple joining of bodies for mutual satisfaction. At least she thought so.

But maybe he didn't think so. No, he did. She'd seen it in his eyes. And after watching that special tenderness in his expression while he loved her, she wondered if he'd be able to walk away without regret this time around.

"You're awfully quiet back there."

"It's peaceful riding along like this." She wasn't about to admit that she'd been wondering whether he would miss her when he left.

"So are you hungry?"

She lifted her head in surprise. "Yes, come to think of it, I am. I wasn't the least bit hungry when we were at the diner, but now I'm starving."

"Me, too. So here's my plan. When we get back to the campsite, we cook up some breakfast."

"I'd like that." She wanted to recapture the cozy atmosphere they'd created when it was just the two of them. He didn't seem threatened by that. But when they were in town, surrounded by people who had conventional expectations of what their relationship might become, that was when she felt him starting to leave her.

"You know what else we need?"

"What?" She hoped he was thinking the same thing she was.

"A victory romp."

"Is that what I think it is?"

"Well, you do it naked."

She hugged him tight. "Then it's exactly what I think it is. And yes, we need that." She had him back again. Maybe not for long, but for now.

14

In town Luke had begun to feel trapped, especially after seeing Naomi's reaction to Emmett's proposal, but the closer they came to Naomi's campsite, the more he relaxed. And the fact was, he loved being with her. It wasn't only the sex, which was fantastic. He just plain liked her.

He'd never met a woman who was so at one with nature that she could completely abandon makeup, skinny-dip in a cold stream and walk around a camp without underwear. He admired her devotion to the eagles and her ability to be alone for long periods of time without freaking out.

As if all that weren't enough, she could imitate Tarzan's yell perfectly. He almost asked her to do it again on the way home, because he had loved hearing it. But Smudge might not appreciate that, so he didn't ask.

Then he realized how he had just thought of the campsite: *home*. He had pictured where they were heading, and in his head he'd called it *home*. Oh, boy. That wasn't good.

Maybe leaving the campsite together and returning together had created that sense of coming home. If so, he wished he hadn't brought up the idea of going into town for the Fourth of July celebration. He'd invited her to the celebration, so he should escort her there, right? That would set up another leaving-and-coming-back scenario, as if they lived together.

He'd never lived with a woman, because he'd wanted to avoid that feeling of domesticity, which could lead to marriage, which could lead to the end of life as he knew it. Apparently he'd kidded himself that coming out to her campsite night after night was different from moving in with someone, because, hey, it was camping. She didn't exactly *live* here. Except she did.

And in a sense, so did he. He'd left his sleeping bag, a personal possession, with her. No, it wasn't the same as if he'd brought clothes and toiletries and his collection of DVDs. But it was more than he'd ever done with any woman.

He had a problem, but it wasn't too late to fix it. It wouldn't be too late until he was so firmly tied down that he didn't feel he could leave. He wasn't to that point yet, so he needed to start planning his exit strategy.

He couldn't leave now, with the Fourth of July celebration coming up, especially since he'd asked her to go with him. But afterward he might just as well go. Better to leave while she was still involved with the eagles so she'd have something to take her mind off him. Maybe she wouldn't miss him all that much, but he had a feeling she might.

He had a feeling he was going to miss her, too, and that was all the more reason to get out of town. Staying would only make things worse for both of them. And summer was a good time to travel and find another great place.

Riding into camp after making that decision was a bittersweet experience, because he really had grown to love spending his nights beside her campfire and in her little tent. He and Naomi had fallen into a routine that seemed to suit them both. That also should have been a warning to him. He was becoming entirely too comfortable here.

"I need to check the eagles before we eat," she said as she dismounted.

"You bet." He gave her a smile and swung down from the saddle. "I'll start the fire and get things going." Then he kissed her, because very soon he wouldn't be able to do that anymore. She tasted so damned good.

He forced himself to end the kiss, resisting the temptation to drag her into the tent for the activity he'd planned for after breakfast. He had to keep his eye on the time. Emmett had given him the morning off, not the whole day.

"Get going, lady." He turned her around and gave her a little push. "Before I forget the plan."

"Okay." She blew him a kiss and jogged down the path to the observation platform.

Fool that he was, he watched her go and felt a lump

form in his throat. Wow, he was in way more trouble than he'd thought if he could get choked up over this woman. Clearing his throat, he turned back to Smudge.

The paint stared at him with his warm brown eyes, and Luke realized he was also going to miss the horse, for God's sake. He'd let himself get attached there, too. For a guy who was supposed to have his head screwed on straight, he seemed to have it right up his own butt.

"Come on, Smudge." He led the paint over to his little plot of grass and dropped the reins to the ground. No point in unsaddling him when Luke would be leaving in an hour or so.

First he unzipped the tent flap and double-checked that there was a condom under his sleeping bag. Soon after that, he had the fire going, coffee brewing and bacon sizzling in a pan. That was the other thing. He'd done more cooking this week than he had in the previous six months. At the Last Chance bunkhouse, the cowhands took turns cooking breakfast and dinner. Lunch took place in the ranch house's big dining room, a tradition that allowed the Chances and their hands to mingle and exchange ranch-related information.

Luke had rotated through bunkhouse kitchen duty with the rest of the guys, but he hadn't put much thought into it. Nothing like the planning he'd done for breakfast and dinner with Naomi. He couldn't complain, though, because he'd enjoyed making meals the old-fashioned way, over a campfire. Naomi's gratitude didn't hurt the situation, either. She'd acted as if he were doing her some huge favor when in reality he was simply having fun.

By the time she returned to the campsite, he'd put the finishing touches on the scrambled eggs by adding a little salsa. Naomi liked them that way. He'd piled a few fresh blueberries on each of their tin plates because he knew she liked those, too.

She walked into camp carrying the stool. That had become part of the routine, too. Now he took the flat rock and she took the stool.

"This looks so good!" She gave him a quick kiss on the cheek as she accepted her full plate and a tin mug of coffee. "I was way too nervous to eat anything at the diner, but that's over and we won!"

"We did." He touched his coffee mug to hers. "Or rather, you did. Congratulations."

"No, *we* did. If you hadn't mentioned the fireworks, I hate to think what would have happened." She sat down on the stool.

"That was dumb luck. I didn't know it was important." He settled on the flat rock. "Jack mentioned the fireworks to me the day he came out with little Archie. I didn't have sense enough to realize you needed to know about them." He dug into his food, which tasted better this morning than it ever had, probably because he knew he might only have one more breakfast with her.

"You couldn't have known the fireworks were an issue unless you'd spent a lot of time studying eagles like I have. Clifford Mason is a jerk, but his attitude is common. Why would anyone assume eagles would abandon their young if they felt threatened?"

"I didn't. I had no idea how fragile the situation is.

They build this big-ass nest, and they're such fierce-looking birds. You'd think they'd hold their ground. Or their sticks."

"Well, they might." She gazed at him. "I screwed up part of the celebration without knowing for sure that they'd abandon the nest. I do feel sad about that."

"Don't." He looked into those blue eyes and wondered how in hell he was going to leave. "Mason wasn't exactly a crook, but he wasn't totally legit, either. No telling whether he would have substituted crummy fireworks for the ones he promised."

"True."

"And you gave Emmett a reason to object to the guy on grounds other than jealousy, which led to a proposal. I'll bet Pam is happy about the way things turned out, and knowing her, she'll figure out a way to make up for the lack of fireworks."

"You're right." She smiled at him. "I thought of something else, too. We know about this nest, but there could be others within range of those fireworks. More than two eagle babies might have been at risk."

"There you go." Luke polished off the last of his breakfast. "You might have saved a bunch of little eagles. The Shoshone eagle population may boom as a result of this day." He sipped his coffee and in the process managed to check out her plate to see if she'd finished her meal.

He'd thought he'd been sneaky about it, but her laughter told him different.

She stood and dumped her plate in the kettle of water they always had available for that purpose. Another routine. They'd created them so effortlessly together that he hadn't seen the net of routine and connection being woven until today.

"Yes, I'm finished," she said. "I take it you're ready to move on to our victory romp?"

"I'm more than ready." He got to his feet and dropped his dishes in the same kettle. He needed to hold her, yearned for it in a way that was also a warning. Sure, he was eager for the sex. But he wanted the closeness more.

She pulled her shirt over her head and tossed it on the stool. "Whoops. Hiking boots." She sat down to take them off.

"Let me." Crossing to her, he dropped to his knees.

"I can do it." She grabbed his hands. "Unlacing and removing hiking boots has got to be the least sexy part of undressing a woman."

"Unless it's me taking off your hiking boots." He shoved his hat back and looked at her. "Let me."

Her voice softened. "All right."

As he leaned over her and untied the laces, his hat kept bumping her knees. Finally he took it off and handed it to her. "Hold this a minute."

"I'll just wear it."

"Be my guest." He glanced up at her just to check it out. He was curious, nothing more. She'd never worn his hat and he wondered how she'd look in it.

Then he went very still. He couldn't explain why, but seeing her looking so cute while wearing his hat flooded his chest with warmth. He had a pretty good idea what that indicated, and it wasn't good news.

"Do I look bad?"

"No." He swallowed. "You look so good it hurts." He didn't know why he'd said that and wasn't even sure he knew what he'd meant by it.

But she seemed to. Cupping his face in both hands, she gazed into his eyes. "I know."

That blasted lump formed in his throat again and he broke eye contact. "Let's get these things off." He'd intended to do it slow and sexy, but that didn't matter anymore. He needed her too much to play seductive games.

Pulling the boots off, he tossed them aside. Then he scooped her up and carried her over to the tent as he kissed everywhere he could reach. They'd established another routine—taking off their clothes before they climbed into the small tent—but he ignored it. He didn't have time for that, either.

Their entrance into the tent wasn't elegant, but he got her in there without landing on top of her and squashing her flat. Then he continued kissing her as he worked her out of her bra, shorts and panties.

There. At last he had her the way he wanted her—all creamy, soft skin exposed; all fascinating dips and crevices, mounds and deliciously slippery places available to his hands, lips and tongue. He covered every last inch of her as she moaned and thrashed beneath him.

He made her come twice and would have gone for a third time, but she clutched his head and dragged him up her moist body until she could look into his eyes.

"You," she said, panting. *"Inside me. Now."*

He was still completely dressed, but a man didn't ignore a command like that. He got his pants pulled down and a condom on in less than twenty seconds. It was as close to "now" as he could manage.

He'd prepared his way quite well. One quick thrust and he was right where she'd asked him to be. Bracing himself above her, he looked into her blue eyes. "Like that?"

"Exactly like that." Breathing hard, she pulled at his shirt and the snaps gave way, popping wildly. "This was supposed to be a two-person victory romp, remember?" She stroked his damp chest.

He rocked forward, cinching them up even tighter. "I've been fully present."

She slid her hands upward and cupped his face again as she'd done before. Her gaze probed his as she drew in a ragged breath. "What's going on with you, Luke?"

He was afraid she saw too much, saw through him. "I just…needed to…touch you, kiss you…" He couldn't explain.

"You're leaving, aren't you?"

His pulse leaped. "I always said that I—"

"Yes, I know. But you're going soon. I can feel it."

No, he couldn't tell her like this. Not when he'd plunged into her warmth, when she'd opened herself to him with such trust. Agony sliced through him and he groaned. "Naomi."

"It's okay, Luke." She laid her finger over his lips. "Don't say anything. Just make love to me."

There was that damned lump again, blocking his throat. He couldn't have spoken if he'd wanted to. So he spoke with his body, instead. Holding her gaze, he began to move.

With deep, steady strokes he told her how much she meant to him. He told her that there would never be another woman like her in his life. She would hold a unique and precious place in his memory. And if he were a different sort of man, he would stay and fulfill all those dreams she kept close to her heart.

Her body responded, as it always had. He doubted she could help it, just as he couldn't. They communicated on a different level when they were locked together like this.

And so she arched beneath him as an orgasm claimed her, but this time she didn't cry out. Instead her eyes welled with tears.

The sight of those tears filled him with despair, but he was no less driven by the pulsing of their bodies than she was. He came because he had no choice. Her response demanded his. His surrender was not much of a gift, but it was all he had to offer.

When the shudders lessened, he lowered his head and kissed away her tears. He'd vowed that he wouldn't hurt her, and he'd failed to keep that vow. He might never forgive himself for that.

He left the tent quietly. She'd told him not to say anything—there wasn't anything he *could* say. He'd intended to stay long enough to be her date for the Fourth of July celebration, but he hadn't even been able to accomplish that. She'd guessed his decision, and he'd never lied to her. He wouldn't lie to her now.

Putting himself to rights didn't take very long. His

hat had fallen to the ground when he'd swept her up in his arms. He picked it up, dusted it off and put it on.

Sometime soon he'd give the hat away and get a new one. He'd never be able to wear it after today, transfixed as he'd been by the sight of her wearing his hat. He'd leave it for her, but she wouldn't want the thing, either. She'd have reminders enough without something like that hanging around.

Thank God he hadn't unsaddled Smudge. He climbed aboard the patient horse and rode away from the campsite. About ten minutes into the ride he remembered his sleeping bag, which was still in her tent. Screw it. He'd never be able to use that sleeping bag without thinking of her, either. She'd probably burn the damned thing, and he couldn't blame her if she did.

The ride back to the ranch seemed to take an eternity, and at every turn in the path, he asked himself if he should ride back and talk to her, comfort her in some way. But what good would that do? The only thing that would comfort her was if he stayed, if he changed his entire way of life and became what she needed.

He knew how that could turn out—attending cookouts with stodgy neighbors instead of heading off on adventures to parts unknown. Maybe his father had done him a favor by rejecting his invitation this morning. Luke had probably needed a reminder as to why he'd chosen this life.

When he reached the ranch at last, he felt as if he'd been traveling for days. The place looked familiar, but strange, too, as if he'd already left it in his mind. No one was around, and he realized they were all up at the main dining room for lunch.

Just as well. He gazed at the huge log house that the Chances had built. The grandfather, Archie, had started with a boxy two-story structure. Over the years, two-story wings had been added on either side, canted out like arms ready to welcome visitors.

Or ensnare them. This Chance family was about as tied to one place as anybody could be. Luke had found a few travelers on the fringes of the clan. Tyler Keller used to be an activities director for a cruise line. She and her husband, Alex, traveled quite a bit because Tyler loved doing that.

And to Luke's surprise, he'd found a couple of fellow travelers in Mary Lou Simms, the ranch cook, and her new husband, a ranch hand who went by the single name of Watkins. Gabe Chance competed in cutting-horse events, so he occasionally went out of state for that.

But other than those folks, nobody at the Last Chance had a burning desire to explore the world. They were content to enjoy what they had right here. Luke agreed it was beautiful, but for him it wouldn't be enough. There were too many other beautiful places, and he couldn't ignore the urge to see them.

Because of that, he'd quite likely broken Naomi's heart, and once Emmett and Jack found out, Luke wouldn't be welcome here anymore. With that concept in mind, he quickly took care of Smudge and turned the brown-and-white paint into the pasture. He didn't linger over the horse any more than he'd lingered in

Naomi's camp. Prolonging the moment of separation was never a good idea.

Packing up the belongings he'd stashed in the bunkhouse took no time at all. He had everything loaded in his old truck before the hands started trickling back from lunch. He accepted their good-natured ribbing about his absence this morning as he waited for Emmett to show up.

Eventually he realized Emmett wasn't coming. When he asked someone, he discovered that Jack had given Emmett the rest of the day off so that he could spend it with Pam. They had a wedding to plan.

That meant Luke would have to deal with Jack. Emmett might have been easier to break the news to, especially after Luke had helped the foreman out during the scene at the diner. However, as a result of that event, Emmett wasn't here.

With a resigned sigh, Luke headed up to the main house. He wasn't sure whether to hope that Jack was or wasn't in. If he was out, Luke could talk to Sarah, who held equal power with her sons in anything to do with the ranch.

But Jack had been the one who'd taken Nash's recommendation and hired Luke. If Emmett, Luke's immediate boss, wasn't available, then Jack was the next logical person to accept his resignation. He was also the one most likely to want to clean Luke's clock for hurting Naomi.

Luke mounted the porch steps. He had to admit the long porch, which stretched the entire front of the house, was a good feature. Rocking chairs lined the porch, but Luke had never sat in one. He supposed it would be a nice enough experience.

Sarah came to the door. Tall and silver-haired, with the regal bearing she'd inherited from her New York model mother, she commanded respect with a glance. "Hi, Luke." She opened the door with a friendly smile and stood back so he could walk in. "I'll bet Naomi's a happy lady now that Clifford Mason has left town and taken his fireworks with him."

"She's very glad about that." Luke could say that much without stretching the truth. "Is Jack around?"

"He's in the office. You know your way." She gestured to an open door on the far right side of the living room area. "Go on in. He's handling some paperwork, so he'll welcome an interruption."

"Thanks." Luke touched the brim of his hat before proceeding through the living room. The massive stone fireplace and leather furniture gave the room an air of permanence. No doubt about it, this house was an anchor—that could be seen as a plus or a minus, depending on a person's viewpoint.

Jack sat behind a battered wooden desk that Luke had heard once belonged to his dad. His hat rested brim up on the edge of the desk, and his hair looked as if he'd been running his fingers through it.

He glanced up when Luke came through the door. "Hi. Have a seat."

Luke decided it was best to do that, so he lowered himself into one of the wooden armchairs positioned in front of the desk. He'd sat in this same chair when he'd interviewed for the job last October.

Jack made some notes on a pad of paper before tossing down the pen. He studied Luke for a moment. "I heard what you said to Emmett at the diner. That was good. I appreciate you stepping in."

"He'd mentioned something a few days ago about being open to suggestions when it came to Pam. So I made one."

"We're all in your debt. The guy needed a push in the right direction. Thanks to Mason and you, he got it."

"I hope they'll be very happy."

"Oh, they will. My mom is one of Pam's best friends, and she'll see to it that everything goes smooth as silk." He leaned back in his chair. "But that's not what you came here to talk about, is it?"

"No." Luke cleared his throat. "I hate to do this on short notice, but—"

"Damn it. You're cutting out, aren't you?"

"Yeah. I'm sorry, Jack. I know you could use more notice than this, but it's time. If you don't want to give me a recommendation as a result, I understand."

"You're a good hand and you'll be missed, but we can manage until we find somebody. I'll give you a recommendation. But all that's beside the point. Does Naomi know you're leaving?"

"Yes."

"How's she taking it?"

Luke just looked at him. There was no good answer to that question.

Jack steepled his fingers. "I see."

"You and Emmett were right all along. I shouldn't

have… Well, she would have been better off if I'd left her alone. But I didn't, so the best I can do now is let her start forgetting about me."

"There's a lot of truth to that. If you're not sticking around, then you might as well leave." Jack stood and held out his hand. "When you get settled, send me your address and I'll mail that recommendation."

"Thanks, Jack." Luke shook his hand. "I thought you'd be ready to take me apart."

Jack's eyes glittered. "I haven't talked to Naomi yet. If she's a basket case, I reserve the right to do just that."

"Then maybe I won't send you my new address." Luke touched the brim of his hat. "Thanks for taking me on last year."

"Yeah, well, I'll say one thing for you."

"What's that?"

"You're one hell of a roper. Now get out of here and don't come back unless you have a ring in your pocket for our mutual friend."

"That's not going to happen. I'm not the marrying kind."

"Then I guess we won't be seeing you around these parts."

"No, you won't. Goodbye, Jack." Luke walked out of the office, through the living room and out to the porch. There he paused to catch his breath. Sometimes leaving a place was easy, and sometimes it was hard. Until now it hadn't been gut-wrenching.

But standing around wouldn't make it easier. Hurrying down the porch steps, he climbed into his truck, closed the door and started the engine. As he drove away, he glanced in the rearview mirror. Yep, that house was definitely an anchor.

15

NAOMI HAD ZERO interest in hiking into town for the Fourth of July celebration, but she'd promised her folks she'd be there. Besides, if she hid out in the woods, everyone would assume that she was devastated by Luke's departure.

Jack had come out to check on her and had confirmed that Luke was gone. She'd put on a brave face then, and she'd do the same today. Even though she ached as she'd never ached before, she'd keep that fact to herself.

She'd hiked in very early so she'd be able to shower and change clothes at her parents' house before the parade. She walked in through the kitchen door, as she usually did, and came face-to-face with the one person in the world who could always see right through her.

Her mother stood in front of the stove frying up eggs and bacon, but she put down her spatula and turned when Naomi came in.

"Hi, Mom!" Naomi pasted on the biggest, fakest smile she could manage. "Did you make enough for me?"

"Of course." Her gaze met Naomi's.

And just like that, the charade was over. Naomi's resolve to be tough was no match for the warmth and understanding in her mother's blue eyes. Leaving the backpack by the kitchen table, Naomi went straight into those comforting arms.

"I'm so sorry." Madge Perkins was a small woman, but she had the biggest hug in the world. "I know you cared for him."

Naomi sniffed. "Yeah, I did. But he wasn't right for me."

"No, he wasn't."

"And I'm well rid of him." Naomi didn't believe that, but maybe saying it would start the healing process.

"You most certainly are. You can do much better than him."

"Right." Naomi gave her a quick squeeze and stepped back. "He's last week's news. We have a Fourth of July to celebrate."

Her mom's smile was filled with pride and encouragement. "That's my girl."

"Is everybody okay with not having fireworks?" That was the other reason Naomi hadn't been eager to show up today, in case some folks continued to be upset.

"Absolutely. Pam's subsidizing Lucy over at Lickity Split so Lucy can give away free ice cream all day."

"Oh, good." Some of the tension eased from her

shoulders. "Everyone will love that, and Lucy gets the revenue instead of that creep Mason. I—"

"Hey, has my favorite wildlife expert arrived?" Her father walked into the kitchen wearing a Western shirt with pinstripes of red, white and blue.

"Hey, Dad!" She gave him a hug. "Love the shirt. You're stylin'."

He glanced down at his shirt and smoothed the front pockets. "Just so I don't look too much like that Mason fellow."

"Not a chance. This is way too subtle to be in the Clifford Mason category."

"Well, good, because your mother bought it at some fancy-dancy store in Jackson and wouldn't tell me what she paid for it, which means it's probably the most expensive shirt I've ever owned."

Naomi gave him a thumbs-up. "It looks great on you."

"Thanks." He peered at her through his wire-rimmed glasses. "Are you okay?"

"I'm fine, Dad." It was a forgivable lie. She wasn't going to tell him how much she hurt, because there wasn't a damned thing he could do about it. "All set for the watermelon-eating contest?"

"You know it." He seemed relieved at the change of subject. The contest was the Shoshone Diner's traditional contribution to the festivities, and her father loved it. So did the participants. The Chance boys had multiple wins to their credit.

"I think you should enter this year," her father said.

"Nope." They'd had this discussion in years past,

so she was surprised he'd bring it up again. "Not when you're the judge. It would look bad if I won, and I might. I'm pretty good at eating watermelon."

"So I'll get somebody else to judge."

Both Naomi and her mother stared at him. He'd never offered to give up his cherished role as judge. Then Naomi figured out why he would now.

He wanted her to be so immersed in the activities that she forgot her broken heart. In his mind, a watermelon-eating contest served that purpose like no other. That was both touching and incredibly cute.

Resting her hands on his shoulders, she stood on tiptoes to kiss his cheek. "That's the sweetest thing you've ever offered to do for me. But I'm not robbing you of something you love so much."

"Seriously, I could get Ronald Hutchinson to judge. He'd do it. He knows my watermelon-eating contest is way more fun than his sack race."

"No, Dad." She patted his shoulder. "But if you want to partner up with me and reclaim our title in the sack race, I'm your girl."

"Hey, that sounds great." He grinned at her. "It's good to have you back, kiddo, at least for the summer."

"I love it here. It's my favorite place in the world." The words created an unwelcome reminder of Luke and their recent discussion about favorite places. As she thought about that discussion, her feelings toward him began to shift. Slowly, the deep sorrow that had threatened to drown her began to evaporate in the heat of her growing anger.

Two days ago Luke had claimed that the Jackson

Hole area ranked as one of his favorite places. Yet he'd left. Working at the Last Chance was a dream job for any cowboy, and through Nash, Luke had been lucky enough to land a position there. Yet he'd left.

More than once he'd said how much he enjoyed being with her. Even without the words, she'd known just by looking in his eyes. He had strong feelings for her, perhaps stronger than he'd had for any other woman. Yet he'd left.

Well, good riddance! If he couldn't appreciate that both she and this place were wonderful beyond belief, she was glad that he was gone. He was officially an idiot.

LUKE WAS A certified moron. He surveyed a panorama of snowy peaks, shadowed valleys and a denim-blue lake in the fading light of evening. He'd always wanted to visit Glacier National Park but had never made it. So here he was atop Apgar Mountain with a bucket list–worthy view of the park—its North Fork, to be more precise—but could he enjoy the splendor of the scenery? No, he could not. Oh, he'd tried. He'd told himself that this landscape was spectacular, that it rivaled the Grand Tetons. Even better, he was once more on his own, free to stay here until he grew tired of the place or until his money ran out, whichever came first.

He'd been in the park for three days, hoping that he'd snap out of the funk he was in and get back to his normal travel routine. He'd hiked the impressive trails, all the while congratulating himself on what a great life he had because he was so free of entanglements.

So far he hadn't been able to swallow a single line of that bullshit. In his heart, a place he'd avoided going for years, he knew why he wasn't having any fun. Naomi wasn't here.

And she needed to be here, damn it. There were critters *everywhere*. Deer, bears, raccoons, wolves, birds galore—specifically eagles. Oh, my God, she'd go nuts over the eagles.

Finally, here on this mountain, he faced facts. When he'd met Naomi Perkins, his life had changed forever, and it was never changing back. He'd only put about five hundred miles between them, but even five thousand wouldn't matter. He'd still feel that magnetic pull, still see her face in his dreams, still...love her.

Because he was a moron, he hadn't figured out that he loved her until now, after he'd broken her heart. He knew for a fact he'd smashed it to smithereens. He'd seen it in her eyes when she realized he'd moved up his departure by a couple of months.

He'd seen the misery he was inflicting and he'd left anyway. If he were in her shoes, he wouldn't take him back under any circumstances. A guy who could walk away from Naomi Perkins didn't deserve her.

That was the crux of his dilemma. He didn't deserve her, but if he couldn't have her, he was doomed. She'd shown him that being connected to someone didn't mean being tied down if she was the right someone.

Naomi was the right someone for him. So basically he had no choice but to head back to Shoshone and grovel. It might not work. But it was the only strategy that he'd come up with.

Shoshone was approximately eight hours away, which meant he could be there before dawn the next day. He decided to start driving and hope that a more imaginative approach to winning her back would come to him before he arrived. It didn't. After hours behind the wheel, he still saw groveling as his only option.

He couldn't expect her to respond to that right away, so he could be in for days, weeks, maybe even months of waiting her out and hoping she'd forgive him. That meant he needed his job back, but he'd have to grovel to get that, too. Jack was none too pleased with him.

Then he remembered Jack's final words. Luke wasn't supposed to show his face without a ring in his pocket. Okay, so he'd stop in Jackson and buy a ring. He pulled into town long before the shops opened, so he cruised around the square, located a jewelry store and parked his truck.

He must have dozed off, because the next thing he knew, the sun was out and the square was no longer silent. Shops were open, cars drove past and people walked along the sidewalk in front of him.

He got a better look at the jewelry store and decided it looked pricey. Well, okay. He had quite a bit of room on his credit card.

The brunette woman behind the counter gave him a friendly smile, but he didn't miss the quick once-over that told him he probably looked like hell. That made sense. He hadn't shaved since yesterday morning or changed his clothes—he wore rumpled jeans, hiking boots and a faded plaid shirt.

"May I help you with something?" she asked in a pleasant voice.

"I need a ring." Then he realized that wasn't specific enough. The glass cases glittered with what might be hundreds of rings. "An engagement ring."

Her gaze softened. "Are you interested in a diamond ring or something less traditional?"

"I don't know." He thought about it. "A diamond," he said finally. He figured he couldn't go wrong with a diamond, but if he ventured into that "something less traditional" area, he could get into trouble fast.

"That narrows it down a little. We have solitaires, of course, and then there are the clusters, with a central diamond in the center and smaller ones arranged around it."

"A solitaire. She's not a fussy woman. She'd appreciate simplicity."

"Then let me show you a few and see what you think she might like." The saleswoman laid a couple of trays on top of the case.

The diamonds sparkled under the high-intensity lamps and Luke blinked. He should have had a cup of coffee before coming in here. And maybe some food. He couldn't remember the last time he'd eaten.

"Do you think she'd prefer an emerald cut? Or perhaps a pear shape. Then we have—"

"That one." Luke pointed to a ring with a roundish stone that seemed to shoot fire. "She'd like that."

"You have very good taste." The woman plucked the ring from its slot and held it out.

Luke took the ring between his thumb and forefinger, and his heart began to pound. He was buying a diamond engagement ring. He also was buying it for someone who might never accept it. "Do you have a return policy?"

"Of course." She didn't hesitate. "The choice of a ring is so personal. Couples often come in together. After all, this is something she plans to wear for the rest of her life. You want her to love it."

Luke began to hyperventilate. Until now he'd only thought about getting back in Naomi's good graces. Jack had been the one who'd said a ring was necessary to the process.

"Do you want to think about this?" The woman sounded sympathetic.

"Just for a minute."

"Take your time."

Luke stared at the ring. Soft music played in the background. He hadn't been aware of it before now, but as he listened, he wondered what kind of tunes Naomi liked. Country-and-western probably, but what else?

Did she like to sing? He knew she could yell like Tarzan, but he didn't know if she could sing. Or whistle. He yearned to know every detail about her, big or small.

That would take a long time…years. A lifetime. And when he thought of growing old with Naomi, warmth filled him.

He cleared his throat. "I'll take it."

"All right."

He started to hand it back, and that was the moment he noticed the little white tag fluttering from the band.

He glanced at it and gasped. He'd had no idea. Not a clue. But why would he? He'd never shopped for a diamond ring before.

"Is there a problem?"

He took a shaky breath and handed over the ring. "No. This is the one I want." Reaching in his back pocket, he pulled out his wallet and extracted his credit card. He needed to get his old job back. Immediately.

NAOMI PULLED AN energy drink out of her cooler and unscrewed the cap. The eagle parents had finished feeding their growing nestlings, so she could take a lunch break. Moving the camp stool next to the tree trunk, she sat down and leaned back while she sipped her drink.

Moments like this were dangerous because it was way too easy to think about Luke. If she'd known he'd leave so abruptly, she might not have allowed him to invade her observation post, because now it was filled with vivid memories she couldn't seem to stamp out.

But she hadn't known, and to be fair, neither had he. He hadn't realized their relationship would get so hot so fast. She'd scared him to death, no doubt. She closed her eyes and gave in to the temptation to remember.

She replayed it all—the first day when she'd spilled this green drink all over him, the day when he'd galloped toward her like a Hollywood cowboy and all the days and nights after that. She thought about the way he'd complained about the cold water in the stream, and how much fun they'd had cooking meals together, and sharing the tent, and…

The sound of hoofbeats roused her. Damn. Both Jack and Emmett were worried about her. It would be just like one of them to come up with an excuse to ride out here and see how she was doing.

Sighing, she stood and walked over to the edge of the platform. And there, about a hundred yards away and riding toward her at a brisk trot, was none other than Luke Griffin. Setting down her energy drink, she rubbed her eyes and looked again.

Nope, still seemed like him. Same horse, same broad shoulders and narrow hips. Same tilt of the hat and casual grace in the saddle.

Her heart began to race, and she forced herself to take deep, calming breaths. If he thought he could come out here and make up with her, then leave again when he felt threatened by his feelings, he could forget that noise. She didn't plan to go through that ever again.

Frankly, she was disappointed in whoever had loaned him Smudge after the way he'd left everybody in the lurch, including her. Was he that charming? Could he really make them forget his past sins? Well, *she* wasn't going to forget.

She didn't care if he'd wangled his old job back and planned to spend a few more months here after all. He wouldn't get the time of day from her. She almost wished she had a shotgun so she could point it at him and tell him to back off. Bear spray wouldn't have the same dramatic effect; besides, she'd left it in her tent.

Because she didn't have a shotgun, and because she had no intention of letting him come up on this platform, she ran over to the ladder and pulled the whole thing up. Now she was protected from whatever scheme he had in mind.

Then she returned to the front of the platform and waited, arms crossed. She could tell when he spotted her there, because she slowed Smudge to a walk. About ten yards out, he stopped completely and gazed up at her.

She wished he didn't look so damned gorgeous with his manly physique and freshly shaven jaw. He always had looked like a fantasy and probably always would. That was what he did—traveled around making women salivate. He was very good at it.

She waited for him to speak first. He knew why he was here. She could only suspect, and what she suspected didn't bode well for him.

He rested his hands on the saddle horn. "You seem upset."

"I'm not upset. Just determined."

"About what?"

"That you aren't going to run me around the mulberry bush the way you did before. I've pulled up the ladder."

The irritating man actually laughed. "Good for you. I deserve that, and more."

"What are you doing here?"

"I came to see you."

"That's obvious. But if you came here expecting me to be the same willing wench you left, think again, cowboy."

"I came expecting exactly what I've found, a woman who's furious with me because I ran out on her."

She shrugged and tried for nonchalance. "Don't flatter yourself. I'm over you."

He sighed. "I can't say the same."

"Sweet-talk me all you want. It won't do you a damned bit of good."

Pushing his hat back with his thumb, he gazed up at her. "I haven't treated you the way you should be treated, Naomi, and I readily admit that. But have I ever lied to you?"

She thought about it. No, he hadn't lied. Instead he'd been brutally honest about his drifter lifestyle. She'd known he would leave. She just hadn't expected him to leave so soon.

"No," she said. "I suppose you haven't lied to me."

"In that case, you should be able to take me at my word."

She wasn't sure where this was leading. "I suppose."

"Then here's the deal. I've discovered that life without you is not much fun."

"What?" She stared at him, not comprehending.

"I came back because for the first time I can remember, I'd rather be with someone, with *you,* than be alone. After the way I've treated you, I don't deserve to be welcomed with open arms. But I...I'm planning to stick around and see if I can change that."

She had difficulty forming words. She wondered if this was some sort of hallucination brought about by too many days out here by herself. But the horse snorted and pawed the ground. Birds chirped in the trees, and not far away the stream gurgled over a bed of rocks.

Then a shadow passed overhead, and she looked up as the female eagle returned to the nest. This was real. She was standing on the platform and Luke had just claimed that he preferred being with her to traveling through life alone.

"She's returned to the nest," he said. "So you need to go back to work. I'll leave you to it. See you around." He wheeled Smudge around and started back the way he'd come.

"Wait! You can't make a speech like that and then leave!"

He turned Smudge to face her. "I figure you need time to think about what I've said. I don't want to push you."

Her breath caught. "Push me toward what?"

"Me," he said simply. "I've hurt you. I can't expect to come waltzing back into your life and have you believe that I want to stay."

"Do you?" She began to tremble.

"Yes. I do. Here in this place, but if you have to move for your job, then I'll go there. I want to be with you, Naomi."

As she held his gaze, Smudge walked steadily closer. She gulped in air. "What are you saying, Luke?"

"I love you."

She thought her heart would beat itself right out of her chest. "You…love me?"

"With all my heart. My wild, crazy heart."

"I'll let down the ladder." She whirled around but her foot caught something solid. In that moment she knew what it was. "Watch out!"

But it was too late.

"Aah, shit!" Luke sputtered and cursed.

"I'm coming down!" She dropped the ladder and scrambled to the bottom as fast as she could. By the time she rounded the tree, Luke had dismounted. He'd taken off his hat and was wiping his dripping face with his sleeve.

"I'm so sorry." She ran over to him. "I'm so, so— oof!" The breath left her lungs as he grabbed her and pulled her hard against his chest.

"Don't be sorry." He held her tight. "Just kiss me."

So she did, until both of them were so sticky that she wondered if they'd be glued together for eternity. And that was fine with her.

At last he got them unstuck so he could look into her eyes. "Naomi, I've been a complete fool, but I'll make it up to you, I swear."

She smiled. "You've made a good start."

"I have more than a start. I have a ring in my pocket. I know that was extremely optimistic of me, but I—"

"A *ring?*" She stared at him. "Who are you and what have you done with Luke Griffin?"

His dark eyes clouded. "You don't want it."

"I didn't say that. It's just…you're not the type— and you said…"

"I wasn't the type. But that's because I believed a bunch of junk that wasn't true, and I'd never met you. I'm probably doing this wrong, and I can't get the ring out now because I'm all sticky, but…will you marry me?"

She looked into his eyes and realized he actually

wasn't sure how she'd answer. That was touching. "I'd love to."

The air whooshed out of his lungs. "Oh, thank God. I thought this would take weeks."

"You were prepared to wait weeks for my answer?" She was stunned.

"I was prepared to wait for as long as I had to, but I was determined to make you love me."

"And here I've loved you all along. But I couldn't let you know until…"

"Until I stopped being a damned fool?"

She laughed. "Exactly." And she pulled him into another very sticky kiss. It was the sort of kiss that could last a long, long time…maybe even an eternity.

Epilogue

MICHAEL JAMES HARTFORD was screwed. Putting down his cell phone, he wandered to the window and stared out at the green swath of Central Park five stories below. As Western writer Jim Ford, he'd portrayed himself as a genuine, gold-plated cowboy. His readers believed it, his agent believed it and his editor believed it.

For some reason they'd never questioned why a real cowboy would choose to live in New York City. His books were so authentic that everyone had assumed he owned a secluded ranch where he spent a great deal of time. They'd assumed he could ride and rope and shoot.

He'd let them make those assumptions because the truth—that he belonged to a wealthy New York family and had never been on a horse in his life—wouldn't sell books. Although he didn't need the money from those sales, he needed the satisfaction of being read. He also needed the joy of living in the fantasy world he created every time he wrote a new story.

He'd been caught in a web of his own making. The

books had done so well that he'd become a minor celebrity, which had aroused the interest of his publisher's PR department. They wanted to push him to the next level.

As part of that campaign, they'd scheduled a video of Jim Ford doing all those cowboy things he wrote about. All those things he couldn't do. And they wanted to shoot the video at the end of the month.

Michael had to think of a solution, and he had to think fast. He could fake an injury, but that seemed like the cowardly way out. He'd always meant to visit a dude ranch and learn some of those skills, but deadlines had kept him busy.

The dude ranch still seemed like a good solution, but he'd become so well-known that he couldn't book a week just anywhere and admit that he didn't know how to ride. He required discretion. As he racked his brain for people who might have a ranching connection, he remembered Bethany Grace.

He'd appeared with the motivational author on Opal Knightly's talk show a few months ago, and while they'd hung out in the greenroom, she'd mentioned growing up in Jackson Hole, Wyoming. They'd hit it off so well that they'd exchanged phone numbers. On impulse he scrolled through his contact list and dialed her number.

She answered on the second ring. "Jim! Wow, it's lucky that you called! I'm going to deactivate this number next week."

"How come?" Last he'd heard, she was on the fast

track to becoming a permanent guest on Opal's show, which was a terrific career move.

"I'm getting married and moving to Jackson Hole."

"No kidding? Hey, congratulations. But what about—?"

"I know. Opal's show. I'm not cut out for that, and thanks to various circumstances, I've realized it. So what's up with you? Your books are doing great!"

"They are, and that's why I called you. My publisher wants a video of me being a cowboy, and my skills are…rusty." He winced at that whopper. "I wondered if you know anyone out in Wyoming who would help me on the QT."

"I sure do. I'd work with you myself, but between the televised wedding and leaving on a honeymoon afterward, I'm going crazy."

Michael chuckled. "Opal's making you get hitched on TV?"

"She is, but I can't begrudge her that after the gracious way she's let me out of my contractual obligations. Listen, call Jack Chance at the Last Chance Ranch. Tell him what you need and that I recommended him for the job."

"And he'll be discreet?"

"I guarantee it. The Chance family is a classy bunch. You'll love them all. Let me give you the number."

Michael grabbed a notepad and jotted down Jack Chance's contact info. "Thanks, Bethany. This could save my life—my writing life, at least."

"I just thought of something, though. Jack's mother, Sarah, is getting married soon. Call right away so you can sneak in there and get the job done before the festivities start."

"Don't worry. I'll call the minute I hang up. But back to your marriage. Who's the lucky guy?"

"Nash Bledsoe. He owns a ranch that borders the Last Chance."

Michael heard the love vibrating in her voice as she said that. "He must be special."

"He is."

"I wish you the best, Bethany. I'll admit I'm a little envious." Living a double life, he was caught between two realities—his family's glittery world of charity balls and gallery openings, and the writing community he loved but didn't allow himself to embrace. He didn't belong in either group, which meant he was sometimes lonely.

"You sound a little wistful, Jim. Is everything okay?"

"Sure. I'm fine."

"Well, the Last Chance will do you good. Take it from me, that place has a way of reordering your priorities."

"Right now my priority is getting comfortable on a horse."

Bethany laughed. "I thought I knew what I wanted when I went out there, too. And now look at me. My life is taking off in a totally different direction."

"I doubt that will happen. In fact, I don't want that to happen."

"If you say so. But let's keep in touch. I'm curious to know how this turns out."

"I'll fill you in when you get back from your honeymoon."

"You'd better, or I'll have to rely on Jack's version."

"Then I'll definitely be in touch. And congratulations." As Michael disconnected the call and keyed in Jack Chance's number, he remembered what she'd said about how the Jackson Hole area had affected her. But he didn't need his priorities rearranged. All he needed was riding lessons.

* * * * *

FROM THIS MOMENT ON

BY
DEBBI RAWLINS

Debbi Rawlins grew up in the country with no fast-food drive-throughs or nearby neighbors, so one might think as a kid she'd be dazzled by the bright lights of the city, the allure of the unfamiliar. Not so. She loved Westerns in movies and books, and her first crush was on a cowboy— okay, he was an actor in the role of a cowboy, but she was only eleven, so it counts. It was in Houston, Texas, where she first started writing for Mills & Boon, and now, more than fifty books later, she has her own ranch. . .of sorts. Instead of horses, she has four dogs, five cats, a trio of goats and free-range cattle keeping her on her toes on a few acres in gorgeous rural Utah. And of course, the deer and elk are always welcome.

1

"YOU HIT THAT YET?"

Trace McAllister didn't wait to watch the six ball sink into the corner pocket. He stepped back from the pool table, and with a bad feeling he knew who Sam meant, turned to follow his gaze.

Of course it was Nikki.

After delivering a pitcher of beer to the men waiting their turn to play, she was walking toward the bar. The close-fitting pink T-shirt tucked into her tight worn jeans showed off her small waist and curvy hips. She'd left her shiny dark hair loose tonight, falling halfway down her back. Hard for a man not to take a second, even a third look. Trace understood, but making a remark like that…

Nope. No way he'd let it slide.

The Watering Hole was crowded for a Thursday, though it was warm even for June, and every cowboy in the place had either a frosty mug of beer or a bottle in his hand. Two of the handful of Sundance guests, a pair of blondes whose names Trace couldn't recall, hovered near the end of the bar talking to a wrangler from the Double R. A tall brunette in a short skirt leaned over the jukebox, studying the selections.

So just to make sure he wasn't getting worked up for nothing, Trace asked, "You don't mean Nikki…"

"Hell, yeah. Look at her." Sam tipped back his beer bottle, draining it while his eyes stayed on Nikki's rear end. He wiped the back of his arm across his mouth. "That's what you call U.S.A. prime. Give it to me straight, McAllister. You do her yet, or what?"

"Are you serious?" Another remark and Trace wouldn't be able to hang on to his temper. He didn't know Sam all that well. He worked as a hired hand at the Circle K and had a reputation for being popular with the ladies, not so much their fathers. Trace had done his share of getting around, but he knew how to be respectful and discreet. "You know she's Matt Gunderson's sister."

"So?"

"So lay off." Instead of lining up his next shot, Trace looked Sam dead in the eye. "That's not a suggestion."

Sam leaned against the wall, chalking the tip of his pool cue, and giving Trace an amused look that aggravated him further. "Must be nice to have a rich family and the second biggest ranch around. Guess you figure that entitles you to speak down to the rest of us."

If he wasn't so pissed, Trace would've laughed. Man, Sam had it wrong. The Sundance had once been a nice spread. still was, with over three-thousand acres of choice land and a nice healthy herd. But they hadn't escaped fallout from the economic downturn. Most folks around Blackfoot Falls knew the McAllisters had converted part of the Sundance to a dude ranch in order to weather the storm. But then Sam wasn't the sharpest tool in the shed.

"Look, Sam, I've enjoyed shooting pool with you this week. And I don't wanna have to butt heads with you, but if you make another remark about Nikki, you and I are gonna have a big problem."

A short stocky kid who worked at the Lone Wolf moved closer to the far wall. Another guy left the back room. Trace had to motion for Lucas and Josh, two Sundance hands who looked as if they were itching to jump in, to stay out of it. Sadie owned the bar, and she had zero tolerance for fighting and foolish men in general.

"I knew you had it bad for her." Sam abruptly moved his hand. Trace tensed, ready to block a punch, but Sam only shoved his fingers through his long blond hair and grinned. "I wondered why you been coming to town to play when I heard you got a real nice table out at the Sundance."

Trace kept his face blank. Nikki had returned to Montana three weeks ago and had started at the bar a week later. He knew people were bound to put two and two together but most of the guys wouldn't say anything. Except for Sam, the pain in the ass.

"Admit it, McAllister, and I'll back off. Let you have her all to yourself."

That made Trace smile. The guy was dreaming if he thought he could get anywhere near her. Maybe he should let Sam find out what Nikki would do to a hound dog like him. The woman was small and beautiful, but she was tough. Get her mad enough and she had a mouth that could make a sailor blush. She also knew how to swing a two-by-four. Trace had seen it for himself.

"What the hell you grinning at?" Frowning, Sam glanced around, saw that the boys from the Sundance hadn't made a move. He seemed to relax and said, "You don't stake your claim, then I'm gonna have me a taste of that honey."

Trace really wanted to plant a fist in his face but he saw Nikki coming toward the back. No time to smooth things over, and he sure didn't want to start a fight, not in here. Sadie would probably ban him from the place. Knowing he was taking a risk, he waited until Nikki reached them, then he leaned his cue against the wall. What the hell…he could keep a straight face and the odds were in his favor.

"Go ahead, tell her what you just said." Trace folded his arms across his chest and smiled a little, just enough to make Sam second-guess himself.

He squinted at Trace, trying to gauge whether he was bluffing or really did know something Sam didn't. The fact was since his sister and Nikki's brother had gotten cozy, Trace knew Nikki better than anyone in the bar, which wasn't saying much, but made for a hell of a bluff.

"What?" Nikki held her empty tray against her hip and looked expectantly at Sam. "You wanted something?"

He shot her a glance but didn't answer. The other hands were still hanging around, waiting to see Sam turn tail. They all knew him, and had probably arrived at the same conclusion as Trace. Sam couldn't afford to bring on Sadie's wrath. The Watering Hole was his hunting ground. He'd already gone through the eligible local women, been threatened with an angry father's shotgun—twice—so that left him with the Sundance guests. And this was the best place to meet the new batch of single women who checked in each week.

"I don't have all night, Sam," Nikki said, impatience flashing in her brown eyes.

They looked darker in the dim bar lighting. Normally, if he looked closely, Trace could see gold flecks. That is, when he wasn't fascinated by the shape of her wide generous mouth. He liked the way her lips turned up slightly at the corners.

"Another beer," Sam said, moving closer to her, and when her eyes narrowed in warning, he stopped and set his empty bottle on her tray. "Please, darlin'."

"I hope you're not driving." Her gaze slid over the front of his Western-cut shirt to the sloppy untucked hem. "Are you?"

"Ah, you worried about me?"

"No," she said with a short laugh. "I don't want you running into anyone."

Trace smiled. The other guys chuckled.

Sam had to be about six-one because Trace was only taller by an inch or so. And Nikki was on the petite side, maybe five-four. So when Sam leaned toward her, it was hard to guess his intention, but he was asking for trouble no matter what he had in mind.

She tensed, and so did Trace.

Sam whispered something in her ear, then slowly drew back, a stupid grin on his face.

Nikki shook her head. "You keep on dreaming," she said in a dry tone. "See how that works out for you." She turned to Josh and Lucas. "Y'all want another beer?"

Her slight Southern drawl came out when she was irritated or excited or caught off guard. Trace didn't have to guess at how she was feeling right now. She didn't care for Sam, which seemed hard for the idiot to believe so he'd continued to make a jackass out of himself.

Trace watched her finish taking drink orders, collect empties and then start to leave. "What about me?"

She arched her brows at him. "What about you?"

"I need another beer."

"You still have half a bottle left."

"It's warm."

Eyeing him with suspicion, she made room on her tray as he walked over to give her the bottle. "You do this all the time."

"Do what?" He reached for his Stetson before he remembered it wasn't sitting on his head but on a wall peg in the corner. To cover the gaffe, he plowed his fingers through his hair. It was too long, hugging the back of his neck and curling at his collar.

"Tell you what," Nikki said, her gaze fixed on his hand

before slowly moving to his face. "Switch to tap. I'll give
you half a mug at a time and ask Sadie to charge you for a
kiddie portion."

Sam laughed, and so did the rest of the guys. But Trace
didn't care. Nikki hadn't looked at any of them the way she'd
just looked at him. The heat had lasted only a moment. If
he'd blinked he would've missed the flicker of awareness in
her eyes, the brief parting of her lips as she tipped her head
back to meet his gaze.

"I'll stick to bottles, and don't worry about me leaving
some behind." He leaned in just like Sam had and whispered
so only she could hear, "I do have to drive."

She reared back and looked at him as if he'd lost his mind,
then let out a startled laugh. "Maybe I should cut you off now."

Better she thought he was being weird or tipsy than figure
out he was trying to outdo Sam. Everyone was quiet, stepping aside to clear a path for her, though any minute Josh and
the other hands were gonna bust from curiosity. Same with
Sam, even if he was trying to appear cool.

Fighting a smile and shaking her head, Nikki left to fill
their orders. He wished she'd laid one of her rare but dazzling smiles on him. He could've gotten a lot of mileage out
of that, but Trace figured her answer was vague enough that
he'd be able to mess with Sam a while longer.

Already Trace was paying for his mischief. She was halfway across the bar yet he could still smell her. Just like her
sexy almond-shaped eyes and lightly golden skin, her scent
was exotic, kind of mysterious. It seemed to cling to his shirt,
the walls, the air around him. No wonder his pool game had
been crap lately. His concentration was shot. Sure didn't help
that he couldn't seem to drag his gaze away from the sway
of her hips.

He'd finally convinced himself to return to the game when
he saw a Sundance guest call Nikki over to her table. The

woman's name was Karina, which he hadn't known until to-night, and only because she'd been hanging around the pool room earlier. She'd arrived yesterday and was blonde like so many of the guests, but easy to distinguish since she towered over all of them.

She wasn't just tall, but close to six feet kind of tall. Behind her back Sam called her The Amazon, but mainly, Trace sus-pected, because he'd made a play for her and she hadn't been interested. Trace liked her fine. It was refreshing to have a guest who actually wanted to watch a game of pool and not breathe down a guy's neck.

Nobody in the family had wanted to go the dude ranch route. Both his brothers had hated the idea. They were all cattlemen, just like every McAllister man before them. Swal-lowing their pride left a bitter taste, though Cole and Jesse got off easier than him.

Cole ran the cattle operation. He'd barely turned twenty-one when the reins were passed to him the day after their father's funeral. Jesse had been in college at the time, and Trace and Rachel still in high school. The sorry state of the Sundance had nothing to do with Cole's management and everything to do with the economy. In the end, Rachel had been right to push the dude ranch idea to bring in cash. But that didn't mean Trace liked being her flunky when it came to entertaining the guests. All of them female, because that's who Rachel targeted.

When they'd first opened and the women had come pour-ing in, Trace had a blast. Women of every shape and size lit-erally landing on his doorstep? It was heaven on earth. Now, ten months later, he was jumping at his own shadow and hid-ing in the stables like a skittish colt.

Karina said something to Nikki, who nodded and glanced over her shoulder. At him.

He could've kicked himself into next week for getting

caught staring. Leo, who owned the filling station at the south end of town, was sitting at a table behind the women, and Trace lifted a hand to him. The older guy frowned, then grudgingly lifted a hand in return, probably wondering if Trace was drunk.

"You gonna play or what?" Sam sounded irritable. "Plenty other guys are waiting to take your place."

"Yeah, I mean, no, go ahead." He nodded at the cue he'd left leaning against the wall. His mind wouldn't be on the game. No sense going through the motions and holding up the others.

"We're not finished," Sam said. "Afraid I'm gonna whip your ass?"

"That's right." Trace snorted. "I bet you still believe in Santa Claus, too."

Sam cursed under his breath. His mood had gone south fast and no one would want to play him. "Who's up?" he asked, looking around the room.

"I'm just watching," Josh said, and Lucas shook his head.

The guy from the Lone Wolf didn't say a word, just sipped his beer. Trace didn't know his name but nodded to him, and he gave him a friendly nod back. Matt Gunderson had returned to run the ranch since his father had been confined to bed, and Trace wondered if Matt had sent the man to keep an eye on his sister. Probably not. Nikki would catch on and be mad. Then again, it wasn't likely she'd recognize one of the hands.

Although she'd been living at the Lone Wolf since her return, according to Matt she wanted nothing to do with the place. Or their father, for which no one in town would fault her. Wallace Gunderson was a despicable human being. But as his illegitimate daughter she was a Gunderson by blood, if not in name, and entitled to half the large ranching operation upon Wallace's death. Which apparently was fast approaching.

Trace chanced a look and saw that she'd slipped behind the bar to fill mugs of beer while Sadie was busy pouring shots. Almost as if she sensed he was watching, Nikki swung a look at him. Neither of them broke eye contact right away, but then she had to stop the mugs from overflowing.

She did a good job of acting indifferent toward him, but it was mostly pretense. He might've thought it was his ego overriding his brain but his sister had confirmed Nikki had a soft spot for him. Though Rachel hadn't meant to give him hope. In truth, she'd been warning him that if he played fast and loose with her boyfriend's sister, she'd wring his neck.

He supposed she had some cause for concern. He'd always been lucky with women, and a number of them considered him a big flirt, but usually because they flirted back or initiated the dance. And Rachel sure hadn't been shy about exploiting his so-called easy charm to help her keep the guests happy.

But with Nikki he'd been careful from the moment he'd met her in February. At first because she was Matt's sister, and then because Trace had seen the cracks in her cool facade. They'd sat right here in the Watering Hole after a drunken idiot had accosted her outside. Matt had arrived in time to stop the guy, but the idiot's friend had joined the party and Matt ended up with bruised ribs, a swollen face and lucky to still have teeth.

Nikki had been quick to accept the blame for her brother's beatdown. So quick, it had stunned Trace. She'd been a victim as much as Matt, but all she'd been able to see was that she'd brought him trouble and that was all she'd ever do. She hadn't come out and said it like that, but in those few unguarded moments, Trace had listened well. And he'd learned three things about her that night: she was fiercely loyal to people she cared about, didn't trust easily and liked to keep her emotions tightly wrapped.

He knew she'd had a rough life growing up in Houston. Being raised by a single mother who'd worked two jobs to support them wasn't a tragedy in itself, but Nikki had hinted that as a teenager she'd gotten into some trouble in her gang-infested neighborhood. She hadn't elaborated, and it was pretty clear she'd regretted being so open.

Other than that night when he'd looked after her while Matt got patched up, Trace hadn't spent any time alone with her. She'd come to Blackfoot Falls because her brother had wanted her to meet Wallace and get closure before he died. Matt also hoped she would like Montana and move to the Lone Wolf. They'd stayed two weeks and then Matt had to return to the rodeo circuit and Nikki to her waitressing job in Houston.

And in those three months they were gone, Trace had thought about her every single day. He'd never been that dogged over a woman before. His last new truck, yeah, and technically it hadn't been new. But he'd thought about that honey every day for over five months before he had enough cash to bring the Ram home with him.

"Hey."

Trace snapped out of his preoccupation the same time Nikki touched him. He looked at her small hand resting on his forearm, at the neatly trimmed nails that had a light sheen but no color. Then he looked into her pretty brown eyes that had seen too much. They got to him every time.

"You were daydreaming." She drew back her hand. "If you had knocked this tray over I would've strangled you. Here."

He took the bottle from her. "Thanks."

"Don't thank me." She motioned with her chin. "Thank your friend sitting near the jukebox. The beer's from her."

His stomach turned. "Karina?"

"Yep."

"I don't want anyone buying my beer. Tell her I said thanks anyway."

"Tell her yourself." A small smile tugging at her lips, Nikki turned to pass a mug to Josh.

"I'm serious. Add this to my tab and then I'm cashing out."

"You're leaving?" Disappointment flickered in her eyes, and then she blinked and it was gone. "I can give you a total now," she said, all business. "You've had, what…two beers?"

"This one makes three." He waited for her to meet his gaze but she was being stubborn. He really didn't want to leave yet, and if she gave him the slightest indication she'd like him to stay, he'd wait for her to get off work. But no, she seemed determined to treat him like he was any other customer. Which he supposed he was, but sure didn't like it.

He set the bottle down and dug in his pocket. For over a week he'd had the same thing every night so he knew his tab came to $9.75. He pulled out two bills and laid them on her tray. "Keep the change."

"Isn't Karina a guest at the Sundance? You really want to turn her down?"

"Yeah, I do." He wasn't about to let that bronc out of the chute. Bad enough he had to socialize with the women crawling all over the Sundance. He didn't need to owe any of them.

"It's just a drink, Trace."

He smiled. No, it wasn't, not with these women. "Your next day off, how about you and me take a drive to Kalispell?"

"Why?" She glanced around, but no one had heard. He'd made sure he kept his voice low, and Sam was busy racking balls for the next game. "Isn't that forty-five minutes away?"

"You haven't been, right? It's nice. Lots of restaurants, bars, department stores, movie theaters. I think there might even be a bowling alley."

"So…you're asking me to go because…?"

"I don't know." Man, she didn't make it easy. "I have

business there, anyway," he said, lying through his teeth. "I thought you'd like to check out what's available…stuff we don't have in Blackfoot Falls."

"I appreciate the thought." She picked up two empty mugs off the shelf that ran along the wall. "But I have a bunch of things to do when I have time off." Now she was lying. She wasn't any better at it than him.

"Okay." He saw Sam eyeing them, curiosity coming off him like steam. "If you change your mind let me know." Trace grabbed his Stetson off the peg and returned his nearly full beer to her tray. "And don't worry, Nikki. It's just a drive."

2

NIKKI FLORES WATCHED one of the blondes who'd been sitting at the end of the old mahogany bar run for the door that had barely closed behind Trace. Another woman had stopped him before he'd even made it that far. Whatever she'd said had him shaking his head, but he'd flashed her that movie star smile of his, the kind that had silly women forgiving and forgetting when they should be slamming doors shut.

"You gonna sulk the rest of the night because he went home early?" Sadie set a pitcher of beer on Nikki's tray.

"Me?" She rolled her eyes. "No, but his fan club might. If we're lucky they'll drown their disappointment in expensive cocktails. I say we raise the price of those stupid appletinis."

Sadie chuckled, sounding much better without the rusty wheeze she'd had a few months earlier when Nikki had first met the older woman. A lot of Nikki's traumatic first visit to Blackfoot Falls had blurred once she'd returned to Houston. She'd only remembered a few things…the beauty of Montana wasn't something easily forgotten, and the air, so clean and clear that taking a deep breath actually made her head light.

And the McAllisters…Nikki had never met a family like them. Their warmth and kindness was part of the reason she'd agreed to come back with Matt. At first she'd been wary. How could all three brothers and a sister be that well-adjusted? But then she'd met their mother. An hour spent with Barbara was all it had taken for Nikki to understand them. Oh, they weren't perfect, not even close, but it was their unconditional love for one another and how they had each other's back that impressed her.

Sadie had also made the short list. Nikki had only talked with her a couple times, but the woman sure seemed to know when to speak up and when to keep her opinion to herself. Nikki had been a wreck the night Matt had gotten into a fight protecting her. Every instinct had screamed for her to find the guys and get even, show them they couldn't mess around with her or her family. Growing up, she'd learned to protect her own because no one else would.

But Matt had brought her to Montana so she could have a new life. Leave her troubled past behind. Sadie hadn't known her circumstances, yet she'd seen the thirst for payback in Nikki's eyes and in a few well-chosen words, convinced her it wasn't worth it. When Nikki thought about it now, she had to hold back a shudder. The people here didn't understand what she was capable of. Not even Matt got it. He hadn't known her as a teenager.

That same night Trace had come into the bar with her, and to be fair, he'd played a big part in calming her down. He'd sat and listened and told her he wouldn't blame her one bit for wanting to slap those guys into the next zip code. And then he'd reminded her that it wasn't over—the men would be fired and the pleasure should be Matt's.

God, it still bothered her that she'd told Trace little things about her past she wished she'd kept to herself. She'd known him less than a week, had never spoken to him one-on-one before that night. At the last minute he'd shown up to help Matt and ended up with a split lip. Not a big cut, just a small nick near the corner of his mouth. It had stopped bleeding pretty quickly, but every time she looked at him, she was reminded he'd been hurt because of her.

That was the only reason she'd opened up to him. Why she'd confessed that she hated Wallace more than she thought humanly possible, that he deserved to be sick, and how she was glad he was dying. She hadn't censored her vile thoughts. They'd tumbled out of her mouth, and Trace had just sat there, without a hint of judgment.

Of course some of it wasn't news to him. The McAllisters knew quite a lot from Matt because he trusted them. The scary part was, for those two rocky hours she'd sat with Trace, she'd actually trusted him, too.

That was enough to rattle her. She just didn't put that kind of faith in people. She trusted Matt, but getting there had taken nearly a year of ups and downs. The only other person she completely believed in was her mother, who loved her no matter what. Her mom was the main reason Nikki was giving Blackfoot Falls a try. She'd met a businessman from Mexico City who wanted to marry her. But it wouldn't happen, she'd never leave Houston as long as Nikki was there.

No, trust didn't come easy for Nikki. Especially with men. They always disappointed her. And a guy like Trace with his looks, his family's clout, money and a bright future... He was the worst kind of man to count on. Good-looking smooth guys like him couldn't seem to help themselves. They had charm to spare and felt they owed it to the female population to spread it around.

She'd fallen for a man like that before, and she'd been burned. Badly. Just like her mom had been crushed by Wallace all those years ago. If nothing else, Nikki had learned a lesson from the experience. Or so she'd thought until that night she'd blabbed to Trace.

"You need anything else besides those tequila shots?" Sadie asked, with a glance at Nikki's loaded tray.

"No, this is it. Thanks."

"I wouldn't worry about Trace."

Nikki hefted the tray at the same time Sadie spoke and almost let the pitcher slide off. "Where did that come from?"

"You've been staring at the door the last five minutes. I figured you were worried about him."

"Why would I be? That's crazy."

Sadie smiled. "My mistake."

Nikki dropped off the pitcher first. She'd been carrying heavy trays and serving drinks since she was old enough to work. But something in Sadie's smug expression had thrown her off and all she needed was for the entire order to crash to the wooden floor.

Her tips weren't so good that she could afford to hand half over to Sadie.

She delivered the tequila shots to the two cowboys sitting in the corner and managed to give them a smile. They were nice laid-back guys whose names she really should remember. Both were good tippers and patient when she got slammed. She hated that all the other customers seemed to fade when Trace was in the bar. But what she hated even more was that he hung out with Sam.

Sometimes Sam was okay. He'd come in nearly every night since she'd started working for Sadie. He liked to flirt and tease, not just with her but with the Sundance guests. She knew that at least one of the women had gone off with him last week. For her part, Sam was the kind of guy she'd go a mile out of her way to avoid. He was good-looking, but too cocky and full of himself. Definitely a one-night stand guy. After checking on her customers, she stowed her tray and slipped behind the bar to wash glasses. The dishwasher had conked out three years ago and Sadie had gone without since. Last week she'd admitted to Nikki that she'd almost closed the bar a month before the Sundance opened their doors to guests. Business had gotten slow with so many layoffs in the area. The hired hands who were left had started going to Kalispell for their entertainment. Until all the young single women began arriving each week.

At the end of the bar Sadie made jukebox change for a customer and then grabbed a clean towel and joined Nikki. "I was gonna get to those glasses next, but thanks for pitching in. You're a good worker, Nikki. And God bless you, you showed up at the right time. I would've been up a creek without anyone reliable to fill in for Gretchen."

"She's ready to have her baby anytime now, right?"

"Next Tuesday is her due date." Sadie picked up a mug and dried it. "Claims she'll come back to work in two months but I've got my doubts. Even if she does I can still use you two nights a week if you're willing."

Nikki nodded, though she'd been hoping for something more full-time. But then again anything could happen in two months. Her mother planned on relocating to Mexico City in three weeks. As soon as she was settled Nikki could start thinking about where she wanted to end up.

Cole's girlfriend, Jamie, loved San Francisco, claimed it was one of her favorite cities, and she was a travel blogger who'd been around the world more than once. Maybe Nikki would go have a look for herself, see if she could find a decent job there. Although she was hoping to save more money before she left.

If she left. She really was trying to keep an open mind, but she couldn't seem to imagine the Lone Wolf ever feeling like home. The huge two-story house was beautiful, nicer than any place she'd ever lived or most likely ever would. And the guest bedroom, which was now hers according to Matt, was almost as big as the apartment she'd had in Houston.

Most of the time the ranch was quiet, too. So still and quiet that at first it had creeped her out. In her old neighborhood it wasn't unusual to hear gunshots in the middle of the night. Sometimes at the Lone Wolf if she kept a window open she'd hear a calf bawling or a rooster crowing. She hadn't gotten used to that yet.

"Do you think Marge might need help at the diner?" she asked, and Sadie frowned. "I'd still work here whenever you needed me, but after Gretchen comes back, I wouldn't mind picking up a few shifts over there."

"I don't think she needs anyone but it wouldn't hurt to ask. Frankly, though, I think the tips are better here." Sadie dried two more mugs before she said, "Of course I'd never refuse to take Gretchen back, but it wouldn't surprise me none if she wanted to stay home with that new baby and only work a couple nights a week. If that happens, the other shifts are all yours."

"Thanks. I appreciate it." She watched Sadie brace a hand on the back counter while she stretched up to stow the clean mugs on the upper shelf.

Her diabetes was under control, and she'd lost some weight, which allowed her to get around more, but she still had a few health issues. She'd been divorced a while and her only daughter lived in Oregon. For whatever reason, they rarely spoke and hadn't seen each other in years. Sadie only had the Watering Hole. Leaving her would be hard. Nikki hadn't expected that, especially not after working for her only two weeks. She'd miss the small rustic bar, too, with its warped tables and mismatched chairs.

"You look a little sad tonight, honey." Sadie took the soapy mug from her and rinsed it. "You missing your mama?"

"A little. Mostly I'm happy she's found someone who really cares about her." Nikki couldn't say the words without thinking about Wallace and how horribly he'd wronged her mother. She'd been young, hopeful and in love with the handsome older man who'd used her until she and Nikki had become an inconvenience.

"She have any family in Mexico City?"

"Some cousins and an uncle. I've never met them, but she's stayed in contact."

"I imagine you'll be visiting her soon enough."

Nikki nodded, though she worried she couldn't scrape together the money to make the trip. No way she'd accept the fare from Matt even though he'd offered. She still planned on repaying him for the money he'd secretly sent her mother for a year. He just didn't know it. Good thing, because it was going to take her forever.

"I hope I'm not opening a can of worms here," Sadie said, "but how's Wallace doing?"

Nikki shrugged. "He has a few weeks. He's not even seeing the doctor anymore. A nurse from the clinic stops by now and then. Matt and Lucy are taking care of him."

"Well, I sure give Matt credit. I doubt that boy ever heard a kind word from Wallace."

"I think in Matt's mind he's doing this for his mom."

Not anxious to talk anymore about Wallace, Nikki finished washing the last glass and then rinsed and dried her hands. "I'd better go check to see if anyone's thirsty," she said, her gaze going to the door. It had been a while since Trace left and the woman who'd chased after him hadn't returned. Nikki had no business wondering what they were doing. They could be making out in his truck for all she cared.

"I bet she asked him for a ride back to the Sundance just to get him alone." Sadie moved closer and lowered her voice. "Some of these city gals are downright shameless."

Nikki didn't bother denying her thoughts had drifted to Trace. Sadie saw too damn much. "Yes, sometimes we are."

"I didn't mean you."

"Sure you didn't."

Sadie gave her a long look and laughed. "Don't you start getting sassy with me."

"Well, I am a city girl. Before coming here, I'd only left Houston once." For a quick trip over the border to Mexico when she was sixteen and what a disaster that had been. Too late she wished the memory had stayed buried along with the other stupid rebellious things she'd done.

"Yes, but you aren't like them." Sadie's gaze flickered toward the tall brunette talking to Sam. "That one, Sam Miller, he's like a hound in heat. I'm not complaining, mind you. He's good for business."

"So is Trace."

Sadie didn't appreciate the remark, judging by her narrowed eyes. It was clear she liked Trace, maybe simply because he was a McAllister, no telling. "Those two names don't belong in the same sentence."

Nikki had to put her opinion on hold when a customer signaled for her. She'd meant to check to see who needed refills, not start thinking about Trace. Or trying to figure out how she could get information about him from Sadie without being obvious. Really stupid because she'd had him figured out the first night she met him at the Sundance. He'd been surrounded by fawning guests, eating up the attention. She'd promised herself right then she'd stay away from him. If she decided to hang around Blackfoot Falls for a while, she didn't want to be the subject of gossip and embarrass Matt.

While collecting drink orders she had the feeling of being watched and looked over to find Sam staring. He gave her a sly wink that made her want to smack him. She pretended she hadn't seen it. After working in bars for five years, she'd found it was best to ignore men like him when they were on the hunt.

"Four more tequila shots and three beers," she told Sadie, then slid her tray onto the bar.

"I think Sam was trying to get your attention."

"Sam can kiss my—" Nikki pressed her lips together.

Sadie chuckled. "I hate to tell you, honey, but I think that's exactly what Sam wants to do."

"Sorry," Nikki muttered. "He's a customer. I'll play nice."

"Not if he gets out of line, you won't. I'll take a switch to him myself. Though I reckon Trace would beat me to it."

She sighed at the woman's teasing smile. "Why would Trace care? They're friends."

Grunting, Sadie grabbed the bottle of tequila. "That'll be the day. That pool table is about the only thing those two fellas have in common."

"And being good for business."

"That, too." Sadie moved the shots she'd poured onto Nikki's tray. "Although I think poor Trace has been coming to town to get away from those city gals." Sadie didn't even try to hide her amusement. "More likely, though, he has his eye on a certain pretty new waitress."

"You're delusional and a troublemaker." Shaking her head, Nikki grabbed a stack of cocktail napkins. "Why does anyone want to work for you?" She ignored Sadie's laughter and picked up the tray. "Don't forget to check your blood sugar."

Sadie glanced at the round clock on the wall behind her. "Thanks, honey."

Nikki heard the soft gratitude in the older woman's voice and hurried off to deliver the drinks. Letting herself care too much about Sadie would be a foolish move. So would letting Sadie think she could depend on her. Right now she was so lost and confused she was no good to anyone.

NIKKI WAS FINALLY getting the hang of driving a pickup and she wasn't even grinding the gears so much anymore. No sooner had the thought formed than she shifted to make the turn onto the gravel drive and cringed at the awful sound she made. The truck Matt had given her to use was old and smaller than the other two big four-door, extended cab models that belonged to the Lone Wolf. He'd tried to convince her to take Wallace's Escalade, which was an automatic, but driving the luxury SUV scared the crap out of her. Even though she'd gotten her license at eighteen, she'd never owned her own car. In Houston she'd used buses to get to work, then always managed to find a ride home.

The Watering Hole didn't stay open late. Most of the customers were either hired hands or ranchers who woke up at an ungodly hour to take care of their animals. By eleven the bar was usually pretty dead. A few of the men stuck around if they had the next day off or were close to hooking up with a Sundance guest. No matter who was there, Sadie shooed them out and locked the door by midnight.

Something else for Nikki to get used to. Since she was eighteen she'd worked until the wee hours of the morning. Even while she'd attended community college for two years she'd worked late, and then studied when she got home. This going to sleep early crap wasn't easy.

Driving slowly toward the Lone Wolf she saw that the bunkhouse was completely dark. Only the low-watt security lights were on in the barns and stable. The house was a different story. Lights blazed from the foyer and Wallace's office, even the kitchen was lit up.

She saw Rachel's small white car parked next to Matt's black truck on the side of the house. No other strange cars were there, like one that could belong to the doctor, so she figured Wallace hadn't died. It still seemed weird living in his house. She never saw him…only twice in the three weeks since she'd come back with Matt. God only knew what Lucy, the housekeeper, or Rachel thought of Nikki for refusing to help with his care. She knew Matt understood why she'd have nothing to do with the bastard, and that was good enough for her.

The promise her mother had forced her to make still irritated Nikki. Why the hell did her mom care when Wallace finally passed on? He'd caused her nothing but misery. For two years before Nikki was born and three years after, he'd gone to Houston pretending it was business while he cheated on his wife. The arrangement might've lasted forever if her mom hadn't given him an ultimatum—divorce Matt's mother and acknowledge Nikki as his daughter. That was the last time they'd seen him.

Of course Nikki didn't remember him very well because she'd been too young. But it wasn't easy to forget the violent crying jags and gloomy weeks her mom had been too depressed to go to work. Nikki loved her with all her heart, but she would never be that weak. She'd die before she gave a man that much power over her.

3

NIKKI BURIED HER FACE deeper into the pillow. The windows were closed and she'd shut the blinds tight before she'd crawled into bed at four this morning. So where was the light coming from? And the noise… Outside men were talking while horses were doing whatever annoying things horses did…besides terrify her. How was a person supposed to get any sleep?

She blindly felt around the other side of the queen bed, found the extra pillow and plopped it on her head. It helped to mute the sounds but not enough. Oh, man, maybe she hadn't closed the windows. Her bedroom was too chilly. Even in June, at this altitude, the nights and early mornings had a nip in the air that had her thinking twice about staying for the week much less indefinitely.

With a groan, she flopped onto her back and stared at the digital clock on the oak nightstand—10:16 a.m. Okay, this was a ranch and she knew people had work to do but really, did they have to be so loud?

Her problem could be solved if she just got up and checked the windows. It seemed a simple fix until she tried to swing her legs off the side of the bed. They felt as if they weighed a hundred pounds each. So did her head. She wasn't the least hungover, even though it felt that way. After work she and Sadie'd had one lousy shot. That was it. And Nikki doubted she would've had anything to drink if Trace had come to the bar last night.

That got her heart pumping faster and her eyes fully open. Okay, maybe she was coming out of a blackout because that was the stupidest thought ever. She glanced around her room, spotted her phone where she'd left it to charge on the massive dresser and forced her feet to the floor. She had to squint at the screen in order to focus on the date. Yep, it was Saturday. Last time she'd seen Trace was Thursday when the blonde had chased after him.

Come to think of it, Nikki hadn't seen the woman last night, either. Only the friend she'd come with two nights earlier. Which probably meant that she and Trace were…

No. She didn't care what Trace was doing. She didn't. Thinking about him at all would make her a fool. Or maybe it was a form of therapy…or avoidance…transference…something like that. She couldn't think about Trace and Wallace at the same time. If she tried, Trace won.

Sometimes she missed the rinky-dink Houston community college that had been close enough to work that she could walk.

She'd loved studying psychology until she learned how much schooling it took to actually get a useful degree. It could've been fun and challenging but she was nothing if not realistic. Higher education required money. And that was something she'd never have to spare.

She set the phone down, lingering to touch the smooth oak.

Matt said the hand-carved dresser had been in the family for over a hundred years. She wondered if that meant it was an antique. Or just old. She never could figure out the difference. One thing she knew for sure, the obnoxiously big mir-

ror mounted on the back was newer and really had to go if
she stayed much longer.

Staring at the dark smudges under her eyes because she'd
been too lazy to remove her makeup was not how she wanted
to wake up. Her hair was a mess. She'd worn it in a ponytail last night rather than iron out the two stubborn kinks
that had appeared as it dried on its own. And oh, yeah, they
were still there.

Hearing voices, she turned to the window. She'd meant
to close it when she got up. Now she could swear she heard
Trace.

But he wouldn't be here. He had too much to do at the Sundance, and besides, she doubted he'd step foot on Lone Wolf
property. Not as long as Wallace owned it.

She shoved the curtain aside and yanked the cord to raise
the closed blinds. Matt and Trace stood near the walkway
below, talking, but her impatience with the blinds drew their
attention.

Trace tipped his head back, and with his forefinger, pushed
up the brim of his Stetson. With the sun shining on his tanned
face, his green eyes seemed to sparkle. "Morning, sunshine,"
he said, his mouth curving in a grin.

Nikki knew exactly what she looked like and her first instinct was to jump back and jerk the curtain closed. But giving in would only tell him she cared how he saw her. And
that was so much worse. "God, can you be any louder? Some
of us have to work at night."

"Have to?" Matt lifted an eyebrow at her. Apparently he
wasn't in the best mood. He hated that she worked at the Watering Hole instead of adjusting to the ranch, though lately
he hadn't said much. "I'm pretty sure you could've gone to
sleep earlier than four."

Her heart sank. If he knew when she'd turned off her lamp,
that probably meant he'd been up with Wallace. In fact, Matt

looked drawn and tired. She was the worst sister in the whole world. How did he put up with her?

"Would y'all like some coffee?" Her neckline had slipped down her shoulder and she pulled the nightshirt back in place. "I'll bring it out to you."

"Sure." Matt rubbed his eyes, then frowned. "No, that's okay. I wasn't thinking... Go back to bed."

"I'm up. It's no trouble."

"I wouldn't mind a cup." Trace wasn't smiling anymore but he was staring up at her.

Her nightshirt was made of thin yellow T-shirt fabric and she wasn't wearing a bra. No, he wasn't being obvious or horrible but he'd noticed all right. "Cream and sugar?" she asked, stepping backward.

"I like my women sweet, my coffee not so much."

Nikki rolled her eyes and noticed Matt trying not to smile. "Is that your oh-so-charming way of saying no sugar?"

"You got it, darlin'."

She hated when he called her that, and he knew it. The smile was back, and he might've winked, she wasn't sure with the sun in his face. Very tempting to renege on the offer, go back to bed and let them get their own coffee. Oh, who was she kidding? She'd never go back to sleep knowing he was just outside. She only wished she knew why he was here.

"Okay, give me a few minutes." She pulled the curtain closed and grabbed a pair of jeans she'd tossed on the blue upholstered chair last night.

It took her a minute to sift through her underwear drawer before she realized he wouldn't actually see that her bra and panties matched. Sighing, she plucked a black thong from the pile along with the most unflattering white bra she owned. She found a clean red T-shirt, washed her face, brushed her teeth, then twisted her hair up and clipped it.

She hurried to the kitchen, still wondering what Trace was

doing here. All she needed was for him to flirt with her like he did at the bar. She didn't know how Matt would react. He liked Trace but Matt was protective of her and he'd seen how Trace behaved around the Sundance guests.

But then Trace already had kind of flirted with her earlier. Or maybe that was just how a guy teased his friend's kid sister. In many ways, having a brother was still new to her. Little things surprised her, like how Matt worried that she drove home alone at midnight. It was that sort of reaction that made her realize Matt didn't truly understand how she and her mom had lived. Because Nikki would feel a whole lot safer with a pack of coyotes than she'd felt in her old neighborhood.

Holding three mugs made it hard to open the front door. She managed, but pulling it closed was trickier. If only she had someplace to set down…

In seconds Trace was at her side. "I figured you went back to bed," he said, closing the door and reaching for a mug. "Which one's mine?"

"The blue." She held it out to him.

He wrapped his hand around the cup, his warm fingers brushing against her knuckles. It had to be deliberate, the way he let the tips trail along the backs of her own fingers before he took the mug from her.

She stared down at his hand. "You have calluses."

"What?" He gave her a funny look. "I work on a ranch, you know. Here, I'll take Matt's."

"I didn't mean anything. I was just—" She let go of the coffee with cream and sugar, and this time, he was careful not to touch her. "Trace?"

He'd already started walking toward Matt and acknowledged her with a quick glance over his shoulder.

It was too awkward to talk with all that space between them. Plus Matt would hear her fumbling to explain that the calluses had surprised her and she had no idea why. She followed him in mute frustration wishing Matt wasn't standing so close to the corral where two mean-looking horses had been kept yesterday. No sign of them now, but Nikki was already edgy and she preferred a vast distance between her and where any animal the size of a horse might be. Dogs and cats were fine. She'd always wanted a cocker spaniel or a cute little poodle. But people's fascination with horses? She didn't get it. Those beasts were huge and dangerous.

"You said something back there." Trace had already given Matt his coffee, and he was leaning against the railing watching her as she joined them. Well, sort of joined them…by stopping a good six feet away. "Sorry, I didn't catch it."

"Oh, it was nothing." She cradled her mug with both hands and sipped from it, sweeping a gaze toward the barn and stable.

"You haven't been out here before, have you?" Matt asked, and Trace laughed.

She could see why he thought it was a joke. They weren't *that* far from the walkway, but still farther than she'd ever ventured. The area between the front door and where she parked the truck on the side of the house, now that was her turf.

"No," she said, and had to clear her throat and try again. "I haven't."

A pair of hired hands left the barn on noisy ATVs so no one bothered to say anything. Trace drank his coffee, watching her, his brows puckered in a slight frown. She hoped he wouldn't ask why she hadn't been to the corral, because she didn't really want to answer in front of Matt. He didn't know about her fear of large animals. It had only started after she'd watched him compete in the Houston rodeo last year.

He was a professional bull rider, with fancy belt buckles and millions in prize money. Nothing intimidated him. He'd been calm and cool sitting on top of that fifteen-hundred-

pound bull. She was pretty sure his eight-second ride had
knocked a year off her life. That had been the first and last
time she'd gone to a rodeo.

Matt kept glancing toward the stable as if he were waiting for someone. Trace apparently preferred to stare at her. It
made her nervous, and she pretended not to notice, but what
annoyed her most was that she would've liked the chance to
check him out.

He wasn't dressed all that differently from when he
came into the bar. If he owned more than one pair of pants
that weren't jeans she'd be shocked. And he seemed to like
T-shirts. He wore them all the time, even in this chilly morning air. Twice he'd come into the Watering Hole wearing cool
Western-cut shirts. But the other guys gave him so much crap
about it she knew it wasn't a normal thing. The cowboy boots
and Stetson seemed to be daily requirements.

When the ATV engines had faded and they could be heard
again, Matt spoke first. "Do you know if Wallace is awake?"

Nikki shrugged, feeling a bit defensive. No reason for it
because Matt never criticized or pushed. He accepted her re-
fusal to have anything to do with the man.

"How's he doing?" Trace asked.

Matt shrugged. "Depressed. Not even interested in drinking, if you can believe that."

"I believe it," Trace murmured.

"Yeah." Matt sighed. "Right." He knew Trace understood
because his own father had died of cancer years ago. And
Nikki knew this only because Matt had told her.

It got quiet after that. She wondered if Trace was thinking about his father. The McAllisters were a close family, but
she didn't know anything about Trace's relationship with the
man. Or much about Trace, really.

The night Matt had gotten beaten up was the only time
she'd spent alone with Trace. She'd had a bit too much to

drink and he'd driven her home. He'd been a perfect gentleman, not even trying for a good-night kiss, though she knew he really wanted to.

She wasn't used to guys like him. He'd kind of rattled her at the time. But when she thought about it, all he'd really done was show restraint. And only because she was Matt's sister.

Trace's mouth curved into a slow, sexy smile.

She blinked, her insides fluttering with the realization that she'd been staring at him as if he were a hot fudge sundae. And he was loving it.

"What are you doing here anyway?" she asked, wishing she could just disappear. "Don't I see enough of you at the Watering Hole? You have to come sniffing around here?"

"Jesus, Nikki." Matt frowned at her. "You need more sleep. I phoned Trace. He's here to help me."

She looked from her brother to Trace, who was still smiling.

"It's true," he said, touching the brim of his hat. "Though I'm always happy to see you, Nikki."

"Oh." She took another sip, sorry she'd gotten out of bed. "So I'm interrupting."

"Nope." Trace casually glanced over his shoulder. "We're just waiting."

"For who?"

"Petey," Matt said. "He's our best man, been here for over twenty years. You met him yet?"

"Is he the really big guy with the shaggy beard?" she asked, and when Matt nodded, she said, "I've seen him around but I haven't actually met him. He always seems to be working with the horses."

"That's what a wrangler does, though we can count on Petey for just about anything."

"Nowadays we use ATVs a lot," Trace said. "Back when I was a kid, everything was done on horseback and the horses had to know how to work around the cattle. You needed a good wrangler so you didn't spend half your time with your ass planted in the dirt."

Matt nodded, grinning. "Now they even use helicopters for roundups and drives. The job's gotten too cushy."

"Hey, as soon as we start seeing profits again, we need to chip in, start a co-op and buy a chopper," Trace said. He put his mug on the corral post, then flexed his shoulders as if trying to get the stiffness out. "We've already got ourselves a pilot. That's half the battle, right?"

She knew he meant his brother Jesse, but she didn't understand the remark about profits. According to Matt the Lone Wolf was doing great. The Sundance seemed to be doing well, too. But watching Trace arch his back and stretch his arms in that snug black T-shirt, she couldn't concentrate on anything but his broad chest and muscular biceps. She'd never thought of him as the type to work out but he had to be lifting weights or something to account for the flat belly and ridges of muscle.

Trace straightened and let his arms fall to his sides, so she could finally relax. If he'd caught her staring she didn't know it because her gaze never made it higher than his chest.

She forced herself to look toward the barn where someone was moving out bales of hay. "What's that equipment called?"

They both looked, but Trace answered first. "It's just a Toolcat," he said. "Good for small jobs and tight places." Nikki felt a little guilty when she caught Matt's pleased expression. He thought she was finally showing interest in the place when all she really wanted was a distraction.

"Okay, here he comes." Matt's tone was all business, even his posture had changed as he peered toward the stable.

Trace turned his attention to Petey. He wasn't alone. The big grizzly looking man was leading the brown horse—the mean one from yesterday—toward them. As big as the wrangler was he seemed to be having trouble holding on to the animal when it reared up.

"He's a beauty," Trace murmured, slowly bending to slip between the wood railings into the corral.

Nikki tried to grab his arm and missed. "What are you doing?"

"Hey." Matt drew her back. "You have to be quiet."

After a brief struggle, Petey got the horse through the open gate. She watched in horror as Trace approached them from the opposite side. The horse put its head down low, arched its back and leaped into the air. Both men stepped clear as the animal came down on stiff legs.

Trace reached for the lead. "I got him," he said in a calm voice.

"God, Matt, don't let him do this," she whispered, her throat tight and raw. "Please."

"Trace knows what he's doing. Nobody's better with mustangs. But he doesn't need to be distracted. Understand?"

No, she didn't. How could she comprehend any of it? The horse's nostrils were flared and his eyes wild… He looked as if his mission was to kill Trace. She couldn't watch. If she'd had it in her power to make Trace leave the corral she would have.

She backed up slowly, covering her mouth because she didn't trust herself not to scream or do something equally stupid. All eyes were on the mustang, so she turned and ran to the house.

4

SHE'D BEEN SCARED to death. Trace had seen it in Nikki's flushed face and unfocused eyes, even the way her body had stiffened. What he didn't know was whether she was afraid of horses in general or this particular mustang. Trace had to admit, the stallion could be a mean-looking son of a bitch. But only because he'd been afraid, just like Nikki.

"You're feeling better now, aren't you, boy?" He wiped the powerful flank, lathered with sweat, and used the back of his free arm to blot his own wet forehead.

Stupid not to wear long sleeves. He should've known better.

The T-shirt was sticking to his sweaty body, so he pulled it off and used a dry spot to mop his face. He had a spare in his truck that probably ought to be tossed in the rag bin but it would serve the purpose until he got home.

After three hours, the mustang was exhausted, and so was Trace. Diablo was the most fiercely stubborn horse he'd gone up against in a long time. Since the stallion had been purchased only two days earlier, he hadn't actually been named yet. But Trace figured why not go for the obvious, the Spanish word for devil.

Matt walked out of the barn with a young hand and more

bottles of water. Trace had lost track of how many he'd gulped down just in the past hour alone. A drop of sweat trickled into his eye. He squeezed it closed and used the T-shirt to stop the sting. When he could open his eye again he looked toward the house and saw Nikki standing at her window.

She moved back, and he pretended he hadn't seen her. He wondered if Matt knew about her fear of horses. Trace didn't think so. If he did, it wouldn't be like Matt to let his sister come anywhere near an untamed mustang. It didn't matter that she hadn't been in danger. Seeing the stallion's wild-eyed look wouldn't win her over.

And her living on a ranch of all places? Man, no wonder she hightailed it off the Lone Wolf every chance she got. Matt had mentioned he thought her skittishness was about Wallace. Since she obviously hadn't spoken up about her phobia, Trace wouldn't say a word, either. Not to Matt, anyway. But he fully intended on having a talk with Nikki. She'd never give the Lone Wolf a shot if she didn't figure out that a horse was harmless if you treated it right. And Matt really wanted his sister to stay.

Truthfully, Trace wouldn't mind, either. Hell, if he really wanted to be honest, he'd outright admit he wanted her to stick around. Admit it to himself, anyway. No one else needed to know he was getting a little soft.

Diablo sure knew. Reading Trace's sudden energy shift like a book, the stallion tossed his head and stamped the ground. Rotten timing. Matt and the hand had just reached them, and the poor kid looked as if he might pee his jeans.

"He's okay," Trace said, stroking the mustang's neck. "It was me. I got him a little jumpy. I'll take him back to the stable and give him a good brushing. All will be forgiven."

"No, you won't," Matt said. "You've worked hard enough. Lester is gonna take him." Matt passed Trace a water. "I got beer inside if you want."

Holding on to the lead, Trace eyed the young man. "You're Morgan's boy, aren't you?"

"Yes, sir. I'm the oldest."

"I thought you were still in high school."

"Graduated last month."

"Sorry," Matt said. "I figured you guys knew each other. Things have changed in the ten years since I moved away."

"Not so much." Trace held out the lead, which Lester seemed reluctant to take. "I doubt he'll give you trouble. Just stay calm, keep your voice low." Trace let go once he saw the boy had him. To Matt, he said, "By the way, I think this one needs to be called Diablo."

Lester groaned. "Great."

Matt and Trace both laughed.

Trace clapped the kid on the shoulder as he turned slowly toward the stable. "Son, I wouldn't let you take him if I thought he'd be too rowdy for you." He watched Lester and Diablo move toward the stable, then caught Matt staring at him. "What?"

"Son?" Matt chuckled. "He's what…seventeen? You've got only ten years on that kid."

"You have been away too long. Hell, I call Jesse son and he's five years older than me." Trace downed more water but kept his gaze on the boy and the mustang. He wasn't necessarily worried, but it didn't hurt to be cautious. If he had to make a dash, he was ready. "You remember Lester's father, right?"

"You said Morgan?" Matt frowned, shaking his head. "To tell you the truth, I've been so busy with Wallace and straightening out payroll, I don't even know all the men who live in the bunkhouse, much less the day hands. Duke is still the foreman. He's been running things."

"Morgan Dunn was a year ahead of Cole in school. He stepped in as quarterback at the last minute and took us to finals."

Matt swung a stunned look at Lester's retreating back. "That Morgan? He has a son that age?"

"He knocked up his girlfriend senior year. They're still married and running her dad's ranch. It's a small operation but they haven't gone under and that's something." Trace rolled his left shoulder. It was getting stiff again and he was tired of the sun beating down on him. He often worked without a shirt when he was mending fences but not at this time of day. He started for the gate, and Matt walked along with him.

"Man, do I feel old."

"You are old."

"Thanks." Matt snorted. "Tell your sister she'd better hurry and marry me while I can still get it up."

"Nah, she's gotta wait for Cole to tie the knot with Jamie, then Jesse has to marry Shea. It's a McAllister tradition. Oldest to youngest. Everyone's gotta wait their turn."

Matt stopped and gave him a panicked look.

Trace laughed, scooped up the mug he'd left on the railing and looked at Matt. His expression hadn't changed. "Tell me you aren't that damn gullible."

"You're older than Rachel," Matt said with a straight face. "That's gonna be a long wait. Who the hell would marry you?"

Trace automatically glanced up at Nikki's window. He didn't know why. She wasn't there, but that didn't matter. That he'd looked was stupid.

Matt started them walking again. "Yeah, good luck with that."

"What?"

Matt just smiled, then nodded at the T-shirt Trace had balled in his hand. "I owe you a shirt."

"I'm not messing around with your sister." Trace kept his eyes on the ground. He'd never been more confused over a woman in his life. No matter what he tried, he couldn't seem to get her out of his head. Staying away from the Watering Hole hadn't helped. The only thing he knew for sure was that if he made a move, he'd better be serious about her. Matt was a friend and soon he'd be family. "I know better."

"Hey, not my business. Nikki's a big girl, and she knows her own mind. If she doesn't want you messing with her, she won't be shy about letting you know." Matt grinned. "If I need to worry, it should be about you. Cross her and she'll chew you up and spit you out."

"Yeah. I can see that." Trace laughed, because that's what Matt expected, but he wondered if Matt really believed his own words. Nikki might not be as tough as he thought.

But then Trace was starting to get the feeling she was a little mixed up about how tough she was, too. It wasn't just about her being afraid of horses. She'd told him about the gang violence in her old neighborhood, so he understood she'd needed to come off hard as nails. That didn't mean she hadn't been scared a time or two. She liked to pretend nothing bothered her. But he'd seen her feeling defenseless and uncertain, and trying her damnedest to hide it.

Maybe that tug-of-war between vulnerability and bravery had gotten to him, because something sure was preventing him from keeping his distance. He wasn't the kind of guy who needed to ride to the rescue, either. Still, for her to live on a ranch and fear horses? That was unnecessary grief. Maybe he could help her with that.

They were approaching the house. Trace's truck was parked over on the right. "You want to come in for that beer?" Matt asked. "I just need to check on Wallace first."

"No, I got a lot to do at the Sundance yet. I'm just gonna give this mug to Nikki."

"I can take it..." Matt's voice trailed off. "Sure, come on in."

"I'm too grimy. Mind asking her to meet me at the door?"

"Just wipe your boots so Lucy won't take a broom to both of us, but otherwise you're fine to come inside." Matt opened the door while scraping off his own boots. "I'll call her. She's probably in her room." He stuck out his hand and they shook. "Thanks. I appreciate what you did with Diablo."

"Anytime." Trace looked around. "It was good seeing how well kept the place is."

A loud kitchen noise had Matt frowning over his shoulder. "I'll go get her. See you soon, huh?"

Trace nodded, waited until Matt left and then used the rest of the water and his T-shirt to wipe his face and upper body. He figured he had time to run to his truck for the other shirt, but he'd taken only one step off the porch when he heard Nikki.

"Everything okay?" she asked, her voice at a nervous pitch.

"Sure." He turned to her. "Just fine," he said, smiling. But she didn't see because her gaze was aimed at his bare chest. "Sorry. I was just about to get a clean shirt out of my truck."

"Huh?" Her eyes slowly lifted to meet his. "Oh, no problem. Matt said you wanted to see me?"

Trace had to quietly clear his throat. No mistaking the look on her face. She liked what she saw. "I wanted to give you this." He stepped back up onto the porch, holding out the mug.

"Oh." She took it from him. "Did you want more coffee?"

"No, but I'd like you to come for a short walk with me."

"Where?"

"To the stable."

Her eyes widened. "Why?"

"You don't have to get close to the horses." Trace made sure his hand was clean, then held it out to her. He'd been sensitive about the calluses earlier but he got it. Nikki had only seen him as goodwill ambassador to the guests. Maybe it was time for her to see that he worked on the ranch just like any other man. She might not like it but he was a cowboy.

She stared at his palm, then up at him. "You didn't answer me."

"I want to show off Diablo. He's much better behaved now."

She let out a laugh. "Diablo?"

Trace smiled. "I don't know what Matt's going to call him. Until an hour ago the name seemed appropriate. Are you gonna leave me standing here with my hand out?"

Sighing, her gaze slid to his outstretched palm, then to his chest.

"Don't worry. I'll put a shirt on first."

"I'm not worried about that." She clutched the mug so tightly he hoped she didn't break it.

Maybe he was wrong to push her. Maybe he needed to let her take more time to get used to the Lone Wolf. He withdrew his hand and stuffed it in his front pocket. "That's okay, Nikki," he said, stepping back. "I should get going, anyway."

"Are all the horses in their stalls?" she asked in a rush.

"They are." He paused, knowing he had no business making that assumption. Lester could've brought one out to groom. "I'll make sure they are before you go inside."

She studied his face, as if trying to decide if she should trust him. "Let me get rid of this," she said, waving the mug. "Want me to take that water bottle, too?"

"Thanks." He passed it to her. "Seems you're always waiting on me. We ever get over to Kalispell, I'll have to buy you dinner."

Her lips parted and she darted another look at his chest.

For a second he got excited that she might be interested in going on that drive, then just as quickly regretted mentioning Kalispell again so soon. Though she didn't tell him to get lost, just went back into the house with the mug and bottle, even left the door open a little so that was a good sign she'd come back.

Skipping the steps, he jumped off the porch and hurried to his truck. If he remembered correctly, the white T-shirt had a small stain and the hem was frayed but it would do. He found it wadded up on the backseat, shook it out and sniffed the armpit area just to be sure. Yeah, it was clean enough.

He pulled the shirt over his head, stuck his arms in the sleeves, tugged down the hem and heard the seam tear. He looked down. It wasn't just the seam but a large hole in the front. "Well, shit."

Muffled laughter brought his head up. Watching him from the porch, Nikki tilted her head to the side. "I hadn't seen that style yet. It's a good look for you."

"Hell, I don't care. I'd wear it like this if I were headed home."

She shrugged. "Wear it now. I don't care, either." She frowned slightly. "Or go without a shirt," she said, and averted her eyes.

He hid his smile by yanking the T-shirt off. She could shrug and toss her hair as though she was indifferent all she wanted. Right now she was so easy to read it almost felt as if he was cheating. "I bet Matt would lend me one."

She turned so sharply to him, her ponytail whipped to the side. "Can we just go and get this over with?"

"We can." He got rid of the shirt and closed the truck door. "Try not to be jumpy. Animals can sense your mood."

"Well, great because—" She shoved her hands deep into the pockets of her jeans and stared down at her track shoes. "You know, don't you?"

They started to walk. "I'm not sure what you mean," he said, his gaze snagging on her slender neck.

"That I'm afraid."

"I suspected. Is it only horses?"

She kept her head down. "Bulls. I hate bulls, too. I saw

Matt ride once… Never again. I wish he'd quit the circuit and stay here."

"That's the plan, isn't it?"

"No, I mean, quit right now. He's scheduled for five or six more events this year."

"I'm pretty sure Rachel feels like you do. Bull riding can be a dangerous—" Trace cut himself off. It was too late. He saw her shoulders tense. What the hell was wrong with him? "Matt is good. And he's careful. He's got you and Rachel in his life now. He'll finish his career in one piece."

"I hope so," she murmured, hunching her shoulders forward and sounding small and fretful.

Trace slipped his hand around her nape. She shot him a startled look, but he just smiled, left his hand right there and massaged her tense muscles as they continued to walk.

She moved a little closer to him, which kicked his heart rate up. He kept kneading and rubbing her soft warm skin and by the time they reached the stable, she'd started to relax. They hadn't made it inside yet when one of the horses whickered and she went stiff again. She stopped, probably would've jerked away if he hadn't been caressing the back of her neck. The pulse below her jaw beat wildly.

"Wait right here, okay?" Trace moved his hand to her chin and urged her to look up at him. "I'm going to make sure Lester is done brushing Diablo."

"Who?"

"He's a kid who works here."

She stayed motionless, only her eyes moved to sweep a gaze inside the dim stable.

Trace didn't want to let go. He'd give just about anything to let his fingers trail down to her collarbone, slip beneath the scooped neckline. Just a little…he only wanted to feel more skin. Hell, he wanted more than that, but for now, what he cared about most was for her not to be afraid.

"Nikki?" He waited for her to look at him. Her eyes were black and filled with so much fear it sliced into his confidence. Maybe this wasn't the right thing to do. He was good with horses. Everyone assumed he was good with women. And mostly he was…flirting was easy. But he'd never been tested when it really counted. "Can you trust me? I'm not going to let anything happen to you."

She stared into his eyes and moistened her lips. Taking in a deep breath, she lifted her hand, and he expected her to push him away. She held on to his wrist. "No offense. I don't trust anyone."

Trace smiled. That wasn't entirely true but if that's what she wanted to believe…

Her grip on his wrist tightened. "Does Matt know?"

"Not from me."

"Whatever happens in there, don't tell him."

Now he knew he'd screwed up. Lester was inside. The kid might talk. "I won't say a word. Will you wait here? I'll be right back."

She nodded, her gaze still locked with his, and he wanted to kiss her. Right here, where the sunlight glistened off those soft full lips and glowed from her golden skin. Fear slowly faded from her eyes replaced by something that looked suspiciously like it could be trust. Whatever it was it stopped his foolish thoughts and he let her go before his good sense ended up in the dust.

NIKKI WATCHED TRACE disappear into the cavernous stable. Along with him went her short-lived confidence. That she couldn't fully appreciate the breadth of his shoulders or the muscular definition of his back told her how out of control her fear had grown. Back at the porch when she couldn't smell and hear the animals, she'd been real clear that she wanted him with his shirt off. Now all she could think about was whether or not to run.

He wouldn't force her to get too close to the horses, and even if he tried she'd refuse. But what if being in a stable made everything worse? Oh, she really did believe Trace wouldn't let any harm come to her, but she also believed that the horses could sense she was terrified. If facing her terror head-on didn't work, it would be murder living on the Lone Wolf. Maybe she could find an apartment in town. Sadie would know...

From deep inside the stable someone was walking toward her. Not Trace, but a shorter, huskier guy. He was young, she saw when he stepped out of the shadows, his hair lighter. Had to be the guy Trace mentioned. Already she'd forgotten his name.

"Hi," he said as he got closer, eyeing her with curiosity.

"Hey." She hugged herself, doing her share of sizing him up as he passed, checking for signs of evil-horse attack.

She casually angled to her left to inspect him from the back. His clothes weren't torn and there was no blood. He wasn't limping. All good to know.

"Nikki?"

She must've jumped three feet in the air before she spun toward Trace. "God, scare the hell out of me, why don't you?"

He raised both hands, palms out. "Sorry."

Okay, for the moment she could appreciate his chest. It was mostly smooth, just a faint dusting of hair between his brown nipples.

"You ready?"

"I guess." She sucked in as much air as she could manage and wiped her damp palms down the front of her jeans.

"Good. Keep taking deep breaths."

"If I tell you I have to leave then I'm leaving. Period."

"Got it."

"It does not mean I'm opening the subject for negotiation."

"Glad you cleared that up."

She swung a look at him. "I'm serious."

"Me, too. You women seem to think everything requires a discussion."

Nikki gaped at him, then noticed they'd advanced several feet inside. Bales of hay were stacked in the corner. On a railing three saddles sat in a row. The scent of leather and weirdly, soap, was strong. "Are you purposely being an ass to distract me?"

"Think about it. You ask a guy if he wants to stop for a drink, and he says yes or no. A man asks a woman the same question and what does he get?— 'Oh, I don't know, isn't it too late? What do you think?'" He'd raised his pitch to mimic a feminine voice and Nikki almost laughed.

"That's not true," she said. "And it's sexist."

He finger-combed back his dark hair, and frowned as if giving the matter serious thought. "You're probably right about it being sexist, but I swear to God it's true."

"Really? Ask me again about going to Kalispell and see what I have to say."

Trace grinned and caught her hand. "I wish we were at the Sundance. Then I'd know all the horses' names."

She slowly looked to her left. They were standing in front of the first stall, but she didn't remember walking this far in.

The horse looked at her with its ears pricked forward.

Nikki moved closer to Trace. "Is it male or female?"

"She's a mare. You might hear someone refer to her as a roan. That's for the color. The paint over there might be referred to as a pinto."

"I won't touch her," Nikki said, watching the mare's nose strain over the stall door. "Any of them."

"I wouldn't let you. I don't know these horses. We're just

having a look." He slid his arm around her shoulders and she leaned into him as they kept walking.

Despite the fact that he'd been working in the sun and sweating, he smelled nice. Very masculine. Very different. Whatever combination made up his scent it was a turn-on. She almost forgot they were surrounded by horses. For a second she considered sliding her arm around his waist but didn't. It would be crazy to let this turn into something else. This was perfect. She had an excuse for the clammy palms and racing heart. No need for Trace to know he was partly responsible. The fiery tingle low in her belly was all him.

He rubbed her arm. "Maybe some day when you're at the Sundance helping Rachel and Jamie I'll take you to our stable."

"You're never there when I am." She bit her lip, wishing she hadn't admitted she'd noticed his absence.

"I figured you were trying to avoid me."

"I only go over to cover for Rachel when she's busy with Matt or if Jamie calls."

"Ah. I won't take it personally then."

She didn't have to look to know he was grinning. She much preferred keeping her eye on the stalls as they walked by. A horse at the back made an angry sound. "Gee, don't tell me…that's Diablo."

"He's still getting used to being penned in."

"Maybe we should turn around."

"You've trusted me this far. Give me five minutes. You can stand as far back as you want."

"The next county?" She sighed. "Five minutes." Neither of them wore a watch. So what? She'd know when it was time to make a run for it.

They got to the last stall, and Trace took his arm from around her shoulders. She moved back as he stood at the stall and stroked the horse's neck.

"Mustangs have a reputation for being harder to tame and train than other breeds. They're innately suspicious of humans."

"So he was wild when Matt bought him?"

"Someone else had him for a short while, but they couldn't handle him."

It had taken Trace about three hours. She'd watched him from her window, awed by his patience, never speaking above a whisper. The horse had responded fairly quickly all things considered.

"See this black hair rimming his ear? We call them black points." Trace stayed focused on the stallion, murmuring things she couldn't hear. She was beginning to think he'd forgotten about her when he said, "I have a proposition for you, Nikki."

"What's that?" she asked, suspicious when his gaze remained on the horse.

"Let me teach you to ride."

"Diablo?"

"No." The corners of his mouth quirked, but he kept the smile in check. "I have a Sundance mare in mind."

She didn't care if it was a pony. "Why? What's the point?"

"You live on a ranch. It'll be easier when you see you have nothing to fear."

"I've been doing just fine by staying in my own corner."

"You're also missing out. Horses are terrific animals." Trace met her eyes. "Come on, Nikki, give me a shot."

Breathing in deeply, she turned her gaze to the stallion, and watched Trace stroke its velvety neck. "Okay," she said, the word nearly sticking in her throat. She hated feeling afraid... of anything.

5

THE NEXT DAY Trace waited for Nikki at the agreed upon spot, a grassy field between the Lone Wolf and the Sundance. It was the perfect place because she could easily access it by truck, and yet they'd have privacy.

He'd brought Gypsy, a sweet bay mare that was a guest favorite because of her gentle disposition. She rarely spooked and she was also on the small side, a good size for Nikki to control. Not that he expected her to climb in the saddle right away. She had to get to know Gypsy first and let confidence squeeze out some of the fear.

Damn, he hoped she hadn't changed her mind. He glanced at his watch. She was only five minutes late. Nothing to sweat over. He thought he'd given her good directions but he might've taken a turn or two for granted. There weren't many landmarks out here.

He checked his phone to make sure she hadn't called him to cancel, relieved to see he didn't have a voice mail. I wouldn't have shocked him if she'd had second thoughts, but she wouldn't leave him dangling. A moment later he heard the truck, and through the aspens and spruces, saw flashes of chrome reflecting the sunlight.

Gypsy barely reacted. The mare was used to the sound o

vehicles around the Sundance, but he stroked her neck, passing his calm energy to her. Then Nikki parked and climbed out of the truck in tight jeans and there went his composure. He was still fine on the outside, it was just his pulse that seemed to be headed for a finish line. Gypsy danced a bit to the side, but he held on to the reins and hoped Nikki hadn't seen the nervous step.

She walked toward him, her gaze fixed on the mare, her hands restless until she buried them in her front pockets. "Hey."

"You have any trouble finding the road?"

"Only one wrong turn." She finally met his eyes. "FYI, it's not a road."

He smiled. "It's gotten overgrown since I was here last. Gypsy and I rode over the grass a few times to make a trail for you."

"She's a bay," Nikki said, stopping a fair distance away and eyeing the mare as if she were an opponent in a boxing match. "I did some checking online so I'd know what I was getting myself into."

"Good for you doing your own research. The more you know what to expect, the better." He could stare at her sexy pink mouth and almond-shaped eyes all day, so he turned back to Gypsy before he forgot what he was supposed to be doing. "She's about the best tempered horse I know. Josh and I use her to give riding lessons to the guests. Come closer. She wants to meet you."

Nikki seemed to favor close-fitting stretchy shirts with necklines that dipped just low enough to make a man itch. He'd seen her wear four different colors. Today's was yellow. And with the deep breaths she was taking, he'd have to watch himself. It didn't help that he'd spent too long in the shower wondering how those lips would feel....

"I have to admit, she does have a sweet face." Nikk
stepped closer. "You're holding on to her, right?"

"I am. Honestly I don't need to, but we're gonna take ou
time, let you two get acquainted for a while."

She nodded, eyes only for Gypsy. "I'm not sure what I'r
supposed to do."

"As soon as you're comfortable, you keep moving close
Remember what I told you yesterday about a horse's ears?"

"Yes, forward means friendly or curious. And I'm tryin
to keep my voice quiet and even."

Trace smiled. "You're doing fine."

"Oh, the other thing I read was that quarter horses ar
good horses to use to teach someone to ride."

"That's partly true, I suppose, but more important, th
horse should be used to beginners. Also important is that
know the horse well." He pulled off his right glove. "You ca
get online and read for hours, but it comes down to wheth
you trust me or not."

Her lips parted and she tore her gaze away from the ma
to look at him. "I do," she said softly.

They were only talking about a horse and riding lesson
for Christ's sake. No reason for his chest to tighten. "Good
Obviously he'd been looking into those pretty brown ey
too long. He switched his focus to Gypsy. "Makes it easi
all the way around."

"I'm coming closer now."

He didn't want to make her more nervous by watching h
inch forward, but he'd never met anyone this scared of a hor
before. She wasn't faking like some of the guests had done
get his attention. Her face was pale and if he touched her han
he'd bet it would be ice-cold. She stopped after three steps

"Nikki?" He moved away from Gypsy to get closer
Nikki, but the mare went with him making her retreat. "Sorr
My fault." He tethered Gypsy to a shrub, then went to Nikk

Her eyes locked on the loose tie. "Will that hold her?"

"She'll stay right where she is. That really was my fault." He pulled off his other glove before he reached for her. "What re you afraid will happen?"

"I—I'm not sure." She frowned at his fingers wrapping round her upper arm. His thumb almost touched his middle inger. The sassy mouth and tempting curves made him foret how small she really was.

"I'm not going to force you to do anything, so you can elax."

She smiled a little. "You're treating me like Diablo. Letng me get used to your touch."

"Something like that."

Her lashes lifted and her eyes looked every bit as enticing s her body. "Why?"

"So we can approach Gypsy together." He put an arm round her shoulders, and held her against his side. And then rdered himself to calm the hell down. Finding out he was etting hard wouldn't ease her mind.

"Okay," she said, her body stiff.

"You're short. I think you're afraid the horse might lunge rward and overpower you."

"Maybe. Yeah."

"I still have a free hand to block her, but it won't be necssary. Think this might help?" he asked, feeling her start to elax. "Two to one, plus I'm taller than Gypsy."

"I was thinking a stool, but yes, this—"

The mare stepped closer. Nikki grabbed his hand and ulled his arm across her middle like a shield. Leaning into is side she tried to move them backward.

"You're okay," he said, his arms circling her protectively. ot wanting to lose ground, he slipped behind her, holding er against his chest, ignoring her death grip on his forearm. Gypsy was probably curious, that's all."

She nodded, her gaze trained on the mare, her fingers digging deeper into his muscle. Her hair smelled like a beach drink, something with coconut and vanilla in it. The soft shiny strands caught on his roughened chin, though he's shaved early this morning. He should've been more thoughtful and waited until just before he came to meet her. Taking another pleasant whiff, he vaguely reasoned that needing a razor didn't play into any part of today's—

Shit.

He froze in sheer panic, though he obviously wasn't panicked enough. She was too short for her ass to be a strategic hit to his fly, but her lower back was doing a fine job. He had an erection the size of a national monument.

"Hey, you know…" He moved so that they weren't touching, caught her shoulders when she lost her footing. "A stool is a good idea." He couldn't let her turn around and see him like this, let her think his motives for bringing her out here were anything but aboveboard. "I'll get one and you can keep it in your truck for next time."

Dammit all to hell. He rushed past her, afraid there wasn't enough cold water in the whole state of Montana to cool him down.

"TRACE." NIKKI UNDERSTOOD the problem. What she didn't know was whether she should admit it or try to act as if she hadn't noticed. If she came clean, she risked the chance that this innocent and very sweet overture on Trace's part would turn into something that couldn't be undone. Because she was turned on, too. How could she not be?

She knew what was under that brown T-shirt. And he had strong muscled arms that made her feel protected and safe—which was juvenile, because she knew better, from personal experience. A man could use his good looks and charm to make a woman believe promises he had no intention of honoring.

To be fair to Trace, he was slowly proving that maybe she'd been too quick to judge him. He had sides to him she hadn't expected. In his own subtle way, Matt had tried to tell her there was more to Trace. But as much as she had grown to love her brother, when it came to men, she trusted her own instincts over anyone else's. Right now, though, she was a little shaky in that department.

"Trace."

"Yep." He was keeping his back to her and stroking Gypsy's neck.

Nikki had no desire to get in the mare's space or to embarrass him, so she stayed back a few feet. "Thank you for taking time away from your work to do this for me. Gypsy, I want to thank you, too."

He smiled at her over his shoulder, then frowned and leaned into the mare, his ear close to her muzzle. "What's that?" He drew back, looking annoyed and glaring at poor Gypsy. "I've warned you about your manners."

Nikki laughed. "Okay... What did she say?"

"'Talk is cheap. Where's my damn apple.'"

"You're nuts."

"Yeah, Gypsy said that, too." He was still smiling when he moved to unfasten the saddlebag.

She knew he couldn't still be hard or he'd be turned away, but she had to look. Not quite normal yet, though not nearly as impressive as five minutes ago. She almost sighed. Such a waste.

Gypsy had to know what was coming. Stretching her neck, she turned to watch him pull out her treat.

"I'm not sure why, but I'm surprised you feed her apples."

"I don't usually." He shrugged. "Sometimes I let a guest give her one. I thought you might like to."

"Um, I—I—" She ended in a soft whimper.

"Not now. I'd hoped we'd get a little further." He gave the glossy red apple to Gypsy, who chomped down on it. Wow, she had big teeth. "Maybe next time," he said. "You still game to try again?"

"Tomorrow?"

He shook his head. "Maybe the day after. I've got some thing going on in the morning and can't predict when I'll b done."

She'd bet it had something to do with the guests, which shouldn't matter to her. And it didn't...not at all...

Now that she thought about it, he hadn't flirted with her once. Not like he did at the bar. The hard-on didn't count. I was a natural physical reaction and he'd run from it.

Huh.

"You know I don't have to leave yet," she said. "Unless you do."

"No, I planned on us spending a couple hours out here. What time do you have to be at Sadie's?"

"Around five."

"You going straight there?"

She nodded. "I'm not hot and sweaty so I don't need t go home first."

He gazed up at the passing cloud cover, adjusting his ha to protect his eyes. "It feels nice in the shade."

"Yes, it does."

Silence stretched, and she didn't understand why it sud denly seemed awkward between them. They'd moved past th embarrassing hard-on thing easily. Was he disappointed tha she hadn't made much progress with Gypsy? She really had she thought, staring at the mare who seemed to be looking fo another snack. Standing here with no wall separating her an the horse was progress. And she hadn't had a single momer of pure dread, imagining evil lurking behind Gypsy's soft chocolate-brown eyes. Maybe she should explain that to him.

"I meant to—"

"This is the—"

They looked at each other, not smiling, just staring. It figured they'd both speak at once. And now nothing.

"I'll go first," Trace said. "I want to get it off my chest. If I overstepped earlier, I'm sorry."

"You didn't. It never crossed my mind that you had. Here I'm worrying that I disappointed you."

"What?" His brows rose in disbelief. "You're doing great. Ever think you'd get this close to a horse outside of a stall or corral?"

Nikki smiled. "I was going to point that out to you."

"Don't you worry, darlin', I'm paying attention."

Her mood deflated. "I really don't like you calling me that." She watched him frown and fidget with the brim of his Stetson. He called guests darlin' all the time. Especially if he'd forgotten the woman's name. She wouldn't explain why it bothered her. But she refused to be part of the herd. He could figure it out for himself. Or not. As long as he stopped.

"I won't do it anymore."

"Okay, then we're good." She patted her pockets for her keys, then remembered she'd left them in the ignition.

"If you're feeling edgy because of Wallace, we can wait on your lessons."

"I don't give a damn about the man, and you know it." That he would say something so stupid pissed her off. Why was everyone trying to make her feel guilty for not caring? She had no reason to feel anything but contempt.

"Doesn't matter if you care or not. He's sick and dying right there in the house. The atmosphere changes. For everyone." He kept looking at her, even when she glared back. "I

bet the hands living in the bunkhouse who can't stand him
are affected. That's the way it goes."

"What do you know about it?"

"It's been twelve years but I damn well remember what it
was like when my dad died."

"No, you don't understand. Everyone loved your dad."
Nikki regretted her childish tone the second she heard her
own voice. But Trace didn't get it. People spoke Gavin McAllister's name with reverence.

"He was a great man. The best man I've ever known,"
Trace said, turning to pet Gypsy. "He was a fair employer.
And a good father, though I might've argued that point a
few times when I was fourteen and getting grounded every
month." He smiled a little. "But to say everyone loved him?
That's stretching it. Dad had some zero-tolerance rules about
conduct on the ranch and if the line got crossed, there were
no exceptions. Some guys didn't see that as being fair. He'd
had his share of getting flipped off behind his back. But once
my dad was too sick to get out and work alongside the men,
the whole mood around the place changed.

"Even my friends didn't want to come over and play pool.
For months Dad was confined to his bed, so nobody saw him.
Just the family and the nurse who'd come out to check on him
and bring pain meds. It's not only about knowing he's upstairs
suffering, but looking around while you do everyday things
and recognizing his absence. Lucy's feeling it, so is Matt, I
guarantee you. And that's bound to affect you."

Nikki hadn't realized he'd switched from talking about
his father to Wallace. She'd been too unsettled by the raw-
ness in his voice and how his face had changed. Usually she
was good at reading people. For all the gang-related funer-
als she'd attended, maybe she'd never seen loss up close, because right now, it felt as if she were staring it in the face.
But after twelve years?

She was lucky she hated Wallace. If this is what loving and losing someone did to a person…

"Hey, I didn't mean to freak you out." Trace was back to being himself, but with a concerned frown aimed at her.

"You didn't."

"I'm trying to tell you that you don't have to act tough around me, Nikki. I get it."

"Act tough?" She scoffed. "I am tough. I've had to be. And no, you don't get it." She felt badly he'd spent those past few moments reliving his father's illness. She did. But their situations were different and she didn't like him thinking she was weak and needy.

"For the sake of argument, how about we agree that you can use me as a sounding board or a shoulder to cry on if the need arises."

"Look, I'm sorry about your dad. You have such a great family and he was too young, but I'm fine. I am. I—" She totally lost her train of thought when she saw tenderness soften the lines bracketing his mouth. Why did she find it so hard to accept kindness? She didn't doubt Trace's sincerity, so why was she always unprepared for it? Looking past him, she stared at the cloudless blue sky, the snowcapped peaks of the Rockies. So much beauty. She should be finding peace inside, not panic, certainly not fear that her legs would give out. Oh, God…

Trace was quick, startling both the mare and her. He reached Nikki, and put his arms around her before she could tell him to stop. She was tempted to sag against his broad chest until the shakiness passed. For that same reason, she struggled to get away from him. Maybe that was the trouble with him. He made her weak. His kindness, the concerned looks and gentle touches chipped away at her defenses. Somehow he seemed to see past her facade and that was dangerous for her. How had he even known about her horse phobia? Matt hadn't seen it.

"Come on, now. I'm not hurting you." Trace loosened his hold. "I'm not even gonna kiss you." He had that damn smile in his voice. "Of course if you want me to…"

She'd quit fighting him when he mentioned the kiss, but realized it only now. And then told herself it was better that she stay where she was so he couldn't see her face. "Trace, I swear—"

"I'm just teasing you." His short husky laugh skipped along her nerve endings. He began gently stroking her back, she imagined, much like how he'd been stroking Gypsy's neck. "I have something to say but not while we're looking at each other." He rested his chin on top of her head. His heart pounded against the palm she laid on his chest. "Okay?"

It was probably a trick to spark her curiosity. "I don't like my hands and arms trapped like this."

"Put them around my waist. I don't mind."

She laughed. "Oh, Trace."

"What?" He leaned back to look at her. "I'm serious. I have something to tell you."

"All right. I'm listening." She couldn't seem to stay mad at him, which was irritating in itself. Another reason she should stay away from him, not be meeting him in secret. If there was another guy like him on the planet, she sure hadn't met him.

His chest expanded on a sigh. "I've never told anyone this so I'd appreciate you not repeating it."

"I won't." She slipped her arms free and slid them around him, pressing her cheek to his chest, feeling his strong steady heartbeat.

"One day my father and I were mending fences in the north pasture. I was pissed off that I had to work that particular afternoon because we were having a dance at school later, and any one of the hands could've been doing the work.

But my dad, he had this thing about doing different projects with each son. Cole had had lots of one-on-one time with him when he was in high school and so had Jesse. Dad wanted to make sure we boys knew how to do everything on the ranch and felt it was a good way to spend individual time with us.

"Well, I bitched and moaned that I wouldn't be ready in time to pick up my date, it was my first dance and I'd be too tired to enjoy it and on and on. Normally he would've let me go and we would've rescheduled. But I'd done that to him twice before so I could try out for varsity football. Then once he'd had to cancel." Trace paused. "I reminded him of that and accused him of never having been that stubborn with Cole and Jesse. Not the day of their first dance. Why poor me?"

His sudden slide to sarcasm jolted her. She tried not to tense, especially since he was already holding her kind of tight, but she knew something bad was coming.

"He smiled at me, said 'you're right, son, this can wait for another time.' He looked tired and there was no reason for him to work alone. I told him he should ride back to the house with me. He shook his head, told me to go, and I was still mad, checking my watch and my phone, too anxious to jump in the shower to care what he did.

"The next day, he and my mom sat all of us kids down. Jesse was home for the weekend from college. And they told us Dad had cancer. He'd taken too long to go see the doc. The late diagnosis meant he didn't have much time left." Trace swallowed. "We never did finish the fence line together. That afternoon in the north pasture was the last day he got his hands dirty. When he'd said there'd be another time, he'd lied. He knew he was too weak. He'd wanted to give me that last day and I was a total friggin' self-centered asshole."

"Oh, God, Trace, don't—" She tried to look at him but he wouldn't let her. Unsure what emotion she'd find in his face, she let him have his dignity and just hugged him. "I hope you're not still holding on to that argument. From what I've heard about your dad, he would never want that for you."

"Wanna know what I regret the most? I never brought it up. It ate at me yet I pretended the argument never happened. Hell, it wasn't an argument, it was me mouthing off. I was so ashamed and stupid. That damn McAllister pride that kept him from seeing the doctor kept me from telling him I—" His voice broke. "Talk about stupid. I don't know why I'm telling you this."

Nikki knew why. He'd given her a piece of himself so she'd feel comfortable confiding in him. What an incredible gift. Her eyes were moist, and she blinked like crazy when he leaned back, threading his fingers through her hair. She finally looked up at him, and found his tender smile almost more than she could take.

"Thank you," she whispered.

"I didn't do anything."

She just smiled back, amazed at how familiar his face had become. His green eyes had darkened and his mouth looked firm and soft at the same time. "I don't suppose one kiss would hurt," she said, her heart pounding. "Do you?"

His brief hesitation surprised her, then he slowly lowered his head, and she pushed up onto her toes to meet him halfway.

6

HE SLANTED HIS MOUTH to fit hers better, and flipped the hat off his head when it got in the way. A soft kiss, a few nibbles, teasing her lips before he ran his tongue along the lower one. She opened for him, eager to taste him, anxious for him to give her more. She smiled a little against his mouth. If he didn't want to be hurried, it wouldn't happen.

Trace's lips moved in a faint smile in return, his warm moist breath gliding over her tongue and melding with her own. His fingers tightened in her hair and she wasn't sure whose heart pounded faster when he slipped his tongue inside her mouth.

She'd thought about this moment...what it would be like. Back in Houston right after she and Matt had returned. For a few nights she'd lain awake in bed wondering what kind of kisser Trace would be. In the end, she'd decided that while he might be a flirt, he'd be considerate. Trace would want to leave a woman satisfied.

Too soon he withdrew, but before she could object, he trailed his lips to the side of her neck. He nipped at her earlobe as he ran a hand down her back, stopping at the curve of her ass. His soft moan against her sensitized skin flooded her with longing. He found her lips again, the urgency clear, his tongue thrusting against hers. She tasted his desire and passion, and fisted her hands, torn between pushing him away and pulling him to the ground with her.

But it was Trace who ended up gentling the kiss. Then drew back so he could see her eyes. His seemed troubled. "What are we doing?"

Looking at him made it hard to answer. "I don't know," she said, burying her face in his shoulder. He held her against the warmth and strength of his chest, and while part of her wanted nothing more but to be right where she was it also scared her to feel so safe, even for these few fleeting moments. "Maybe we should stop until we do."

"I reckon that's wise," he muttered, sounding as confused and miserable as she was.

Neither of them moved. Then Nikki finally took the initiative. She was smarter than to travel this dangerous road only to satisfy a physical urge. Her options were so few already. If she left Blackfoot Falls, she wanted the decision to be hers. Not made for her because of a weak moment.

As she moved farther back, Trace seemed to have trouble letting go of her hand. She seriously flirted with the thought of just saying screw it. Even if they had sex just this one time. Only they would know. That alone told her she'd been right to stop before impulse replaced good sense. The old Nikki had taken that route and look how much trouble that had landed her.

"You don't need to worry about next time," Trace said, scooping his hat off the ground and studying her face. "This doesn't have to happen again."

"It won't."

His jaw tightened. "I was kind of hoping we'd leave that open."

"Oh." She lifted a hand to block the sun. His lips were still damp, and his eyes dilated and dark. Something fluttered in her belly. "Well, it probably wasn't a good idea."

"Says you." With a wry smile, he set his Stetson on her head. It was too big, but it did the job of keeping the sun off her face. "You need one of these."

"A cowboy hat?"

"Excuse me, but this is a Stetson."

"And the difference would be?"

He shook his head in mock disgust, then scratched the side of his neck. "Were you serious? You think it was a bad idea?"

She breathed in slowly and evenly. "I don't know what I think." She could barely stand the disappointment on his face, mostly because of her own frustration. It would be too easy to give in and worry about regrets later. She pulled her phone out of her pocket and made a show of checking the time. "I need to get going. I thought of something I forgot to do."

He didn't look as if he believed her, but then she hadn't expected him to. "You remember your way back to the main road?"

"Yes, and thanks." She backed toward the truck. "Oh, here." She took off the hat and gave it to him, then rushed to retrace her backward steps so they wouldn't start kissing again. "I know I don't have to tell you this, but I'll say it anyway. The kiss should stay secret along with the lessons."

"Understood," he said, settling the Stetson on his dark hair. He hadn't indicated if he agreed, but that didn't matter. "You drive safely now."

"Like a nun."

He might as well have touched her with the way his throaty chuckle shimmied down her spine. "That's an image I'm having some difficulty with."

She grinned and climbed into the truck. It took all her concentration to reverse without hitting a tree or shrub. When she finally got herself pointed toward the road, she checked the rearview mirror.

Trace hadn't moved. He stood with his arms crossed, his long jean-clad legs spread, his boots planted hip-distance apart, and stared after her. The Stetson hid his expression. She could see the shape of his mouth, though, that very clever, sexy mouth of his. And wasn't that a terribly stupid thing to notice because now she was getting all tingly.

The grassy trail he'd made was a bit dicey so she was forced to give up the mirror. Five minutes later she was safely on the road that led to town and the Lone Wolf turnoff. Only then did she realize she'd forgotten to ask if he'd be at the Watering Hole later.

"I'M SURPRISED HE'S not here since he didn't show last night." Sadie transferred the pitcher of beer from the tap to the space Nikki had left on her tray.

For a long-drawn-out moment, she debated whether to respond.

Naturally she knew her boss meant Trace because she'd seen Nikki eye the door every time it opened.

"I assume you're talking about Trace?" Nikki's dry smile matched Sadie's. "He was helping Matt at the Lone Wolf for a few hours yesterday. Maybe he's still playing catch-up at the Sundance, or playing with the guests."

Sadie snorted a laugh. "I like the way you say it as if you don't give a hoot. You practice long and hard with that line?"

Nikki nearly told her to shut up, though it wasn't a term she cared to repeat since she'd literally had her mouth washed out with soap when she was seven. Despite her mother's long work hours, she'd been strict enough to keep Nikki in line most of the time. Instead, she picked up the tray, noticed that the blonde with the serious bling sitting nearby seemed to perk up at overhearing Trace's name. Nikki was tempted to ask her if she'd seen him at the Sundance tonight. But what purpose would that serve? If he was MIA, Nikki would only assume he was out with the guest who'd chased after him three nights ago.

Nikki really wished she hadn't remembered that. He'd kissed her. She'd kissed him back. Not that it mattered. They'd agreed not to do it again. Sort of.

"Who needed a fresh mug?" she asked the group of men waiting for their turns to play pool.

Josh smiled and shook his head. She'd liked him even before she found out he was Trace's friend. He was a hand from the Sundance and the kind of guy she could count on if a customer ever got too rowdy. It hadn't happened while she'd been waitressing here, but she'd had to fend guys off twice back in Houston. After that she'd thought about carrying a knife, then decided she'd find a new job before going that far.

"Where's your buddy?" she asked, real casual-like as she set down mugs.

"Lucas?"

"The other one."

"She means Trace." Sam took his shot, cursed when he missed, then straightened and grinned at her. "Don't you, sweet cheeks?"

"Was I talking to you?" Nikki seriously reconsidered the whole knife thing...if only to see the look on Sam's face when she pulled it out. "And keep calling me sweet cheeks if you like your beer warm."

Josh laughed. "He worked late vaccinating the last of the calves. I don't know that he has the energy to come to town."

She blinked. It was because of her that he'd fallen behind on his normal duties. "You mean he actually does real work?" she said, since they'd all expect a wisecrack and not the guilt needling her.

"Trace works harder than any man on that ranch," Josh

said, his tone defensive. "Cole, Jesse, everyone works hard."
He shrugged, almost in apology for being sharp. "But they
don't have double duty like Trace. Rachel relies on him to
handle the guest activities." He glanced sideways to check
for eavesdroppers. "The dude ranch business is a lot more
trouble than you'd think."

He would know. Cole had assigned Josh and Lucas, another hand, to help Rachel run the dude ranch side of the
operation. Nikki was well aware how much the men had to
juggle because in February she'd helped Rachel and Jamie
scramble to make lunches or do whatever when the weather
had forced everyone indoors. She'd seen the annoyed looks
on the men's faces when the women opted out of snow activities and hung out in the barn instead. Not Trace, though,
he always had a smile. He ate up the attention.

She set down the last mug. "Y'all okay? Need anything
else before I go?"

Most of the guys shook their heads and made room to let
her pass. Sam leaned over directly in front of her to grab
some chalk and block her escape route. She reared back,
locking gazes with him, silently daring him to push her one
more time.

"See, this is what I don't get," he said, a grin tugging at
his mouth. He was cute sometimes, when he wasn't being
a smug jerk. "Why pine away for Trace when you can have
me? I'd always have enough energy for you, Nikki. Hell, I'd
even switch from beer to Red Bull if I had to."

That made her laugh. "Pine away? I don't even know what
that means."

"Withering on the vine, honey, as my grandma used to say.
Just waiting and hoping and praying your little heart out he'll
come through that door."

"Oh, God." She waved for him to get out of the way. "I'd
bet your grandma sold snake oil."

He swept his long blond hair back from his face, the grin still there. "A team of wild horses on steroids couldn't keep me away if you were mine."

Okay, he wasn't even mildly amusing now. "I'm not anybody's anything. Now move. I mean it."

"Trace thinks otherwise."

She froze, aware that the rest of the men had quieted.

"All right, Sam, that's enough," Josh said. "You shoulda quit while you were still funny."

Sam didn't even blink. He kept smiling at her.

She had the feeling he was going to wink, and then she'd have to smack him. "You're either delusional or drunk, and now you're cut off." She grabbed the bottle out of his hand.

He only laughed, which made her angrier. She wanted to know why he'd said that about Trace, but she couldn't ask. Sam worked at the Circle something-or-other ranch. It wasn't located anywhere near where she and Trace met today, but on the other side of town. So he couldn't have seen them.

Briefly she glanced at Josh. He'd been quick to stop Sam. Did that mean Josh knew Trace had said something? Or was he just being nice helping get Sam off her back?

"You wanna know what I mean, don't you?" Sam moved to give her a clear path. His faint smirk challenged her to stuff her curiosity and go on to other customers. He was about to find out she was too stubborn to lose that dare.

"Settle up with Sadie before you leave," she said, pushing past him.

"Trace warned all of us to keep away," Sam said. "Made it plain you were off-limits. To everyone but Mr. McAllister himself. Those McAllisters...you know those boys get what they want. Especially Trace."

Nikki told herself to ignore him. It was the smart thing to do. She stopped under the dividing arch to the front of the bar, and turned. "What?"

Sam chuckled. He picked up the beer left on the ledge by the other pool player, and took a swig. "It's true."

"Don't listen to him." Josh snorted with disgust. "Trace never told *me* that."

"Hell, why would he?" Sam cast a dismissive glance at him. "You're a kid. She's so far out of your league you'd need one of those bullet trains to catch up."

Josh turned red.

"Are you kidding?" Nikki's abrupt laugh held no amusement. "I'd go out with Josh before I'd cross the room for you." The other guys seemed to think that was funny, and she decided it was a good time to disappear. "And, you jerk, the 'kid' is my age."

"I'm talking experience, honey," Sam called after her. "We both know you've been around the—"

He cut himself short, and she'd almost made it to the jukebox, but stopped and slowly turned to face him. Sam wore the expression of a man who knew he'd gone too far and wasn't sure how to get out of the mess he'd made. But then, there was no way out. The words couldn't be taken back. People sitting at nearby tables either weren't paying attention or were politely ignoring what had been said. The guys hanging around the pool table, though, they'd all heard.

Watching Sam try not to squirm did little to appease her. She wouldn't let him get away with being a prick, but causing a scene wouldn't help. Dammit. She couldn't decide. Keep walking or make him spell out what he meant. He'd backpedal and apologize before he'd say anything else stupid. Nikki wasn't the only one pissed, and he knew it.

"Sam." Josh stepped in, his jaw tight, a vein popping along the side of his neck. "You don't know when to keep that big mouth shut, do you?"

"I'm just teasing." He tried to shoulder past Josh, who

wouldn't budge. "I don't know anything about Nikki. We were baiting each other and it got out of hand."

"Josh?" Just before he'd spoken up, she'd decided it was better to walk away, but now she moved closer, hoping to keep things contained. "Let it go. Sam's right, he doesn't know me," Nikki said, looking him directly in the eyes. "Because if he did, he'd be sweating and tripping over himself to apologize. I am this close—" she drew her thumb and forefinger together, leaving a hair-thin space between them "—to making sure you're not allowed in here as long as I'm waiting tables. How would that work for you?"

"Shit." Sam scrubbed at his flushed face. "I'm sorry. I really am. Not because you'd get me kicked out. It was a dumb-ass thing to say."

She caught Josh's sleeve when he started to jump in, her gaze staying on Sam. "It was disrespectful," she said, "and I won't have it."

Sam pushed a hand through his hair and briefly looked away. All the guys in back were staring at him, the tension so thick she could stick a straw in the air. "You're right. I was a jerk. The thing is, I like you. I really do, and if it makes you happy to know, I feel like hell."

She sighed. "No, Sam, that doesn't make me happy."

"You leaving might," Josh muttered.

Sam gave him a dirty look. To Nikki he said, "I will, if you want. Leave."

"It's over. Do what you want." She moved a shoulder, truly feeling indifferent and turning back toward the bar where Sadie was probably getting antsy for her to check on other customers.

The whole thing would've gone better if Nikki wasn't feeling off balance. Nothing major, but wow, who was that person who'd confronted Sam? Yet another glimpse of her trying out her new skin. The old Nikki would never have been so calm, refrained from cussing or, sadly, considered that she'd been disrespected. Not that she'd have assumed she deserved the poor treatment, but anger and revenge would've been on her mind.

Had to be Matt's influence, and even partly Rachel's. Or maybe Blackfoot Falls in general. Who knew? Not her. She seemed confused about everything lately.

"How are y'all doing?" She smiled at the three young cowboys getting low on beer. Their table was closest to her but luckily they'd missed the pool room drama. They had prime seats near the jukebox and were busy watching sly women lean over to study the song selections.

One guy smiled back. So did the other two…after they dragged their gaze away from the redhead. "I'll take another longneck."

"Tap for me, and a tequila shot this time, please." The second man had a boyish grin that lightened her mood. "I'm Jerry, in case you forgot."

"How could I?" The little white lie seemed worth it when his smile widened. She'd remember him from now on. "You have perfect manners every time you come in."

His slightly older friend with the narrow face and shaggy brown hair elbowed him. "Guess I'll be switching to soda water. It's my turn to drive." He sighed, then quickly added, "I'm Chip."

"Way to go being responsible, Chip." She held up a hand for a high five. It took a second for him to get it. He wasn't much younger than her but he was so cute the way his eyes lit up as if he'd won the lottery. He started out with gusto, drawing back his hand, then seemed to remember she wasn't one of the guys, and very gently touched his palm to hers.

He had calluses like Trace.

The thought ambushed her. God, she could not let every little thing make her think of Trace. Today had been nice, but hadn't changed anything between them. And this dreamy thinking crap was why she couldn't allow that to happen. You know what, your soda's on me."

"You don't have to do that, ma'am."

"It's Nikki."

The three of them grinned, and Jerry said, "We know who you are."

"I'm still learning names," she admitted. "But I'll get there. Y'all need quarters?" She slid a pointed look at the jukebox, where the redhead had been joined by a short dimpled brunette who was eyeing Chip.

He glanced at the woman, then quickly brought his gaze back to Nikki. "You think so?"

"I do." She wanted to laugh at his bewildered expression. Of course she didn't dare. "Here," she said, reaching into her pocket and pulling out change. She only had three quarters, and laid them on the table. "Until I get back."

He passed her a ten. "Will that be enough?"

"Um, I doubt you'll need that many quarters," she said, and left him grinning.

The Watering Hole really was a nice place to work. She liked these customers, and she liked Sadie. Even Sam was okay, or at least manageable. If he hadn't apologized or looked as if he wanted the floor to swallow him whole, she might've felt differently.

She stopped at another table, glancing around to make sure everyone had drinks, then headed for Sadie. Nikki's breath caught. Trace sat on a stool at the end of the bar with a beer in front of him. Part of the bottle was already gone so she knew he hadn't just walked in. What she didn't know was what he'd heard.

7

TRACE'S PATIENCE HAD gotten pretty thin by the time he spot ted Nikki out of the corner of his eye. She stopped at Jerry' table and was joking with him and his friends, and Trace ha to remind himself this was where she worked and socializing with the customers was her job. It wasn't that he was jealous Never been the type. But he was beat, and he'd had no busi ness driving all the way to town just to see her.

Hell, they'd been together not more than eight hours ago and they planned to meet day after tomorrow. He could've waited until then, and stayed home tonight, gotten some sleep Obviously he couldn't, and that was the problem. It was the damn kiss that had messed everything up. He should've known better.

Nah, knowing what was right and acting accordingly were two different things. That's where he went wrong, he thought letting his gaze drift toward her. She was wearing her hair down, the way he liked it best.

"I heard you were out at the Lone Wolf yesterday." Sadi wiped the rings off the bar, then leaned a hip against it.

"Yeah, I was helping Matt with a mustang." Trace picke up his beer and took a halfhearted sip. "The place looks good I hadn't been out there in years."

"How's Wallace doing?"

The concern in her eyes didn't surprise him. Whether she liked the man or not, she'd known him forever. He slid a look toward Nikki.

"Ah, you know her," Sadie said. "She won't talk about him. I quit asking."

Trace smiled. Yeah, he knew. "Matt doesn't think he'll last the week."

"Tell you the truth, I'm shocked he's held on this long. Must be that stubborn streak in him. How's Matt holding up?"

"Seems okay."

"Tore him up bad when Catherine died. I didn't expect he'd get too sad over the old man going, but you never know until the time comes."

Trace studied Sadie for a moment. She was strong, independent, and as far as he knew, never repeated anything that didn't need repeating. He'd always liked her. "I'm thinking that about Nikki. What's your take?"

"Not to say she's cold or unfeeling, but my guess is she'll just be glad when it's over."

He nodded, though he'd been hoping she might've opened up to Sadie a little. Sure didn't sound like it.

"You want coffee instead of that?" Sadie glanced at the bottle he'd barely touched, except to pick it up and put it down.

"I look tired?"

"Half-dead."

Trace chuckled. "That about sums it up. I'll pass on the coffee, though."

"You know you can come in and see her without ordering anything."

He frowned, thought about a denial…

"Don't give me that scowl. I'm old, not stupid." Sadie snorted. "She's coming. Look sharp."

"You're not old. And I always look sharp."

"That grin of yours should be illegal," she said, slowly shaking her head, then wandering toward the other end of the bar.

Unable to help himself, he tipped back in his seat, pretending to stretch, and angled for a better view of Nikki.

She sure didn't look happy to see him. She almost stopped in her tracks. What was that about? The kiss? He thought they'd figured that out.

"What are you doing here?" The brief frown she sent him held an accusation he didn't get. "Josh said you worked late."

"I did."

"So? Should you be drinking beer and then driving?" She leaned over the bar searching for something or other.

It nearly killed him keeping his eyes from going straight to her nice round behind. His mind flashed back to earlier. His hand had rested right there at the curve when he'd kissed her. The temptation to fill his palms had damn near crippled him.

"How long have you been here?"

"What?" he asked, having trouble switching gears. "Ah, ten, maybe fifteen minutes."

"Why aren't you playing pool? Have you been back there yet?" She was acting peculiar, kind of nervous, glancing toward Sadie, then finally slipping behind the bar and setting up shot glasses.

"I don't feel like playing tonight. Who's back there?" He didn't really care. He wanted her to finally look at him, or at least figure out why she wouldn't.

"The regulars."

He watched her make busywork out of pouring two tequila shots and filling three mugs. "You mad at me?"

"No." She looked at him then and sighed. "Why would be mad?"

"I can't think of a reason. Nothing we hadn't already ironed out, anyway," he said, lowering his voice as if anyone who heard would know what he meant.

She smiled down at the lime she was cutting up, and he was pretty sure she was remembering the kiss. Good. It didn't seem fair for him to be doing all the thinking on it. Lord knew he'd done plenty of that the whole time he'd helped five guests saddle up for their trail ride with Lucas, and then finished vaccinating the rest of the calves. A couple of the women commented on his exceptionally pleasant mood. Probably had something to do with the sappy grin Josh had been quick to point out.

Trace turned to look toward the pool room. Feeling this tired, he wouldn't play if someone paid him. He couldn't take a humiliating loss from Sam, or in front of him. The guy was getting on Trace's nerves. Maybe he'd stick to sitting at the bar. He'd see more of Nikki... The downside was the guests. Harder for the women to get to him around the crowded pool table.

"What?" Nikki asked. "Why are you staring back there?"

"No reason." So that's what finally got her full attention? She was studying his face close enough to see which spots he'd missed with the razor. "Is Josh playing?"

"He was, but I don't know about now. Want me to check?"

"You're jumpy."

"Am I?" She moved a shoulder. "I don't think so." After loading her tray, she came back around to his side. "I have to deliver these drinks. Be right back."

"Okay."

She'd taken a few steps, then backed up. "Don't go anywhere."

"I won't move a muscle." A whole lot more than his muscles were twitching. This was new, her acting as if she cared whether he stayed or left.

Watching her go from table to table did a better job of get-

ting him revved than caffeine. A second wind was coming on
worthy of a high gust warning, and if she wanted him to wait
until she got off work, he'd be ready for anything.

"Hi, Trace."

He recognized Karina's voice behind him, too close behind, and he did everything in his power not to cringe as he
turned his head. "Evening."

"I didn't know you were coming to town or I would've
bummed a ride." She slid onto the stool beside him. Her heavy
floral perfume almost knocked him off his seat. "Will you
let me buy you a drink this time?"

"Thanks, but I'm done." He patted his belly…out of habit…
and could've done without the lingering gaze. "Not one of
my better ideas," he said with a smile. "Coming to town. I'm
too tired to be out this late." He faked a yawn, covered it and
murmured an apology.

"Maybe I should drive you home."

His almost-choke was genuine enough. "I have my truck."

Karina smiled. "I assumed you did. Is it a manual? I can
handle a stick shift."

"You stay here and enjoy yourself. I'm good to drive."
He watched Nikki set down drinks and shoot glances back.
"Or else she would've cut me off," he said, with a nudge of
his chin.

Karina didn't bother looking. "Is Nikki your girlfriend?"

He laughed, thought what the hell and leaned a little closer.
"I'm working on it."

The woman didn't seem the least put off. She nodded, widened her smile. "Does she know?"

"Kind of hard to judge." He was busy tracking Nikki, but
Karina's soft laugh brought him back.

"I pity you."

"Why?" He frowned. "She say something?"

"No. Nothing like that." She tilted her head slightly to

the side, studying him as if he was a lab rat. "You're a good-looking charismatic guy and all these pushy city women must drive you crazy."

He drew back, shaking his head and avoiding her gaze. Grabbing the bottle he'd pushed aside, he took a sip of luke-warm beer. "Hey, I'm just a simple cowboy."

"Maybe you were before your sister started the dude ranch, but I doubt it."

"You think differently, you'll be disappointed."

"Would you like to prove it?"

No ignoring the urge to look at her face. She sounded weird, not flirty, sort of like she was conducting business. Her eyes were brown, he noticed for the first time, though not warm and pretty like Nikki's. Karina's eyes were too shrewd. "Are you sitting at a table or would you like me to get Sadie's attention for you?" he asked.

"I just got here." The woman still hadn't broken eye contact. She kept staring at him, and smiling, as if that would make it less rude. "But I can wait for a drink. Let me ask you something…think it would help if you made Nikki jealous?"

"No," he said abruptly. "No, ma'am, I do not." That was it. He'd have to leave. Man, he'd been hoping to talk Nikki into taking a five-minute break and going outside with him. He dug in his pocket for money. "I need to get home."

"I'm sorry. It seems I've given you the wrong impression." Karina laughed and touched his arm. "Though I do have a proposition for you."

Nikki walked up at that exact moment. Even if she'd pretended not to hear, it would've been impossible to believe. No worries there. She didn't bother playacting. Later if he mentioned the annoyed hair flip over her shoulder, or the firm set of her lips that was half pout, half screw-you, she'd deny she ever did those things.

No, she wasn't happy. But she slid behind the bar and plastered on a smile for Karina. "Has Sadie taken your order?"

The blonde shook her head. "I'd love an appletini." She glanced at Trace. "I'm still offering to buy you a beer."

"Pass. Thanks." He tried in vain to catch Nikki's eye. "I'm cashing out."

"You know how much, just leave it." She focused on lining up liquor bottles and finding a suitable glass.

"I'll see you day after tomorrow, right? Same time?"

Her head came up. She frowned. "Oh, right." Their eyes met for a split second, then she swept a gaze over Karina that ended on the drink fixings. "Drive carefully," Nikki murmured.

Unfortunately, at the exact moment Karina said, "I still want to talk to you, Trace."

Nikki kept her eyes downcast and her expression completely blank.

"Good night, ladies." He pushed in his stool. If Karina thought him rude for not answering, so be it. The woman knew she was causing trouble for him. So what that she was a Sundance guest? That didn't excuse her. Partly his fault for opening his big mouth, but enough was enough.

He wasn't going to get Nikki's attention again, and he sure wasn't up to listening to Karina. Halfway to the door, Eli Roscoe from the Circle K stopped him to ask if he'd heard about the next mustang roundup. Since Trace was straddling the fence on the issue, and still doing some reading on the timing viability, he wasn't keen on entering into a hot discussion.

In fact, he wanted to get the hell out of there. Unless Karina had moved to a table and he could have a minute alone with Nikki. He took a chance and looked in that direction. Nikki was leaning toward Karina, intently listening to the woman. Blinking, she drew back, her lips parted in surprise. She glanced at him and burst out laughing.

NIKKI STARED AT HER reflection in the mirror as she brushed her teeth and checked for puffiness around her eyes. Last night she'd managed to get to sleep by two and woke up by nine this morning on her own. Not bad. She was really trying hard to adopt a better schedule. Partly to be a team player, though mostly in self-defense. When these country people said rise and shine, they meant before sunrise. Never gonna happen for her, but she could learn to compromise.

Today she was going to see Trace at their secret spot. It had been her first thought when she woke up feeling like a kid on Halloween morning. Her classmates had all loved Christmas best. Not her. She liked dressing up as someone else. With the right costume, no one could tell she was one of the poor kids. If you weren't riding a shiny new bike by Christmas afternoon, everyone knew you belonged in *that* neighborhood... As if everyone west of Dairy Ashford had the damn plague.

She'd had it easier than most because the boys thought she was hot. Even the private school guys had sniffed around her at the mall, tried to buy her things, asked her to go on dates. The Galleria Mall was where she'd first met Garret Livingston when he was seventeen and she was an easily impressed fifteen-year-old.

Oh, God, she didn't want to think about him now. Or the stupid prom. The dress, no, she refused to think about the dress. That's what always got to her the worst. If she could've changed anything about that day...anything at all...

But that was impossible and she sure knew that by now. She just wished the memories would stop sneaking in. Though they came less often now, and only when she was feeling down. She'd never been able to completely let go of the shame of being needy and foolish and horrible to her mom. So why today? Was her subconscious trying to tell her something? Like she had no business missing Trace. They'd kissed, big deal, and now she couldn't stand not seeing him for one crummy day? It wasn't as if they suddenly had a thing.

Or maybe the problem went deeper. Would getting involved with Trace be repeating the mistake she'd made with Garrett? No, they were two different guys. Sure there was some common ground, like looks, good family, the right name, but lumping Trace in with Garrett was just plain ridiculous. And insulting to Trace. Anyway, her subconscious could just chill. She had no intention of hooking up with anyone in the near future.

She left her room, closing the door behind her. As always, it was quiet in the hall. Deathly quiet. She glanced at Wallace's closed door and shivered. Quickly she shifted her thoughts to the other night and hurried toward the stairs. Thinking about what Karina had to ask Trace had Nikki biting her lip. She'd given her word she'd keep mum, in exchange for the woman's promise Nikki could be there when the bomb was dropped. It sure wouldn't be easy.

With a grin, she swung off the last step and nearly knocked Lucy over. The frail housekeeper lost her grip on the laundry basket she was carrying and it fell to the floor. Amazingly the orderly stacks of folded clothes stayed intact. Lucy bent to retrieve the basket but Nikki grabbed it first.

"I'm so sorry. I wasn't paying attention." Nikki balanced the basket against her hip and touched Lucy's bony arm. As short as Nikki was, she felt tall next to the woman. "Are you okay?"

"I'm fine." Lucy smiled. "I'm not used to having kids around the house again. It's nice."

"I'm twenty-five."

"You and Matt are still kids to me. I just made a fresh pot of coffee. I assume you're headed for the kitchen." Lucy tried to take the basket but Nikki wouldn't have it.

The guilt for not chipping in more was finally getting to her. "Where do you want me to take this?"

Hesitating, Lucy studied her. "Wallace's room."

Nikki's mind started spinning excuses to back out. She didn't want to see Wallace. Even if he was sound asleep and didn't know she was there. It would depress her. Probably make her feel even guiltier for not helping Matt more. "Fine." She'd hand over the basket at the door. "Lead and I'll follow."

Lucy nodded, then held on to the railing as she slowly climbed the stairs. She had to be over seventy, and according to Matt, had known the Gundersons forever. There were no secrets hidden from her. She'd seen Wallace at his worst, breaking family heirlooms in drunken rages and verbally abusing Matt and his mother. But Lucy had stayed loyal long after Matt's mom died, cleaning up after Wallace, making sure he had home-cooked meals and never gossiping behind his back. Matt didn't understand it. He thought the woman was a saint.

Nikki had a different take. To her, the women in Wallace's life, including her own mother, had been spineless fools. Not Barbara McAllister...she'd had the good sense to stay away from Wallace. And still she'd been dragged through the mud that awful February day when the bastard had gotten toasted and called her a whore in front of her sons.

The same day it had finally struck Nikki that she'd been unfair to Matt. Yes, she'd suffered from abandonment issues, but she'd been too self-centered to see that Matt's childhood had been worse. He'd had to live under Wallace's thumb. Four months later she clearly hadn't made much headway. And that wouldn't change at this particular moment. But for her brother's sake she was trying.

She stopped outside Wallace's door and handed the basket over to Lucy. "I'll let you take it from here."

The woman's lined face remained expressionless, though her eyes slowly filled with disappointment. "You should see him. Just for a couple minutes. He doesn't talk much, only stares at the wall when he isn't asleep."

"Another time."

"Wait."

Nikki had already turned away. She didn't want to have this conversation, and she sure didn't want to feel crappy for sticking to her principles. Seeing Wallace wouldn't help Matt. "Look, I know you mean well. And I appreciate all you do for us." She sighed, searching for the right words. "Wallace has never been a father to me. I don't feel anything for him, and I sure don't owe him."

"You're right," Lucy said. "The man's lived here his whole life, yet you don't see folks lining up outside the door for a visit. He's got a foul temper even when he's not drinking. Truth be told, Wallace is getting exactly what he deserves. It's you and Matthew I worry about. Regret can follow a person around like a dark cloud."

"So I've been told." She left out "too many times." "That won't be an issue for me. I promise."

"You claim you don't feel anything for him, but you do." A sad smile touched the woman's thin lips. "You hate him. I see it in your eyes, and I can't say that I blame you. Trouble is, hate can fog a person's thinking."

Nikki silently watched her reach for the doorknob. "Can I ask you something?" she said before Lucy opened the door.

"I'm listening."

"Why stick around? After Catherine died, it was only Wallace. And you continued to clean up after him, cook, bring groceries. I don't get it."

"No reason you should." Her gaze narrowed and her mouth tightened. "My family has owed the Gundersons for a long spell. And that's all I'll say on the subject." Then she went through the door to Wallace's room, closing it behind her.

Much as Nikki was relieved to be off the hook, now she was curious. Matt would've told her if he knew anything about Lucy's family owing the Gundersons. He'd chalked up her loyalty to his mother's talent for convincing people to make difficult promises.

Cinnamon-laced Columbian brew scented the air from the foyer into the kitchen. Lucy always added a heaping spoonful of the spice to the dry grounds, and Nikki was totally hooked. A plate of poppy seed muffins sat near the coffeepot. Homemade, naturally, and after sampling one last week, she was a fan. It was way too early to eat, but she grabbed one anyway, and carried it with her mug of coffee to the front windows.

She was hoping to spot Matt working outside. She hadn't expected to see him in Wallace's office, looking grim and sitting at the massive old desk. Ledgers and stacks of paper sat. on the rawhide couch to his right. Since the door was open she didn't hesitate to poke her head inside.

"Hey."

Matt lifted his gaze. "You're up early."

"I'm a country girl now."

"Right." Despite his smile, he looked tired. "I'm glad you're here. I wanted to talk to you."

Something was wrong. She thought of her room with longing, then braced herself and entered the office. "What's up?"

"First, no need to panic. This isn't a request, strictly information." He slowly exhaled. "Wallace is refusing liquids. If you wanna say goodbye, now might be the time."

"Thanks for letting me know," she said calmly, tamping down the sudden denial swelling inside her and making her chest ache. She managed to keep her expression blank. "Anything else?"

Matt shook his head. His eyes searched her face, probably looking for a sign she was human, before lowering to her hand.

She'd squeezed the muffin into a misshapen lump.

8

NIKKI KNEW BETTER. Nothing good came of waking up before noon. She should've stayed in bed. But it was too late for that, now that she was already at the Sundance.

"Hey." She found Rachel and Hilda making lunch in the big modern kitchen with its stainless-steel appliances and gleaming pearl-gray granite countertops. "I came by to see if you needed help today."

"Oh." Rachel seemed surprised, which she would since Nikki never dropped by without being asked or calling first. "That's nice of you. But I think we're okay. Most of the guests are out kayaking."

"With Trace?" God, Nikki hoped she didn't sound as desperate and panicked as she did to herself. They were still supposed to meet since she hadn't heard otherwise. And she wanted to see him. Needed to see him. She didn't know why. She just did.

"No, he had them yesterday. It was Josh's turn. Grab something to drink and sit down."

"Have you eaten yet?" Hilda asked, studying Nikki from head to toe. The housekeeper's round face darkened. "You've lost weight, *chica*."

Odd remark considering Nikki wore tight jeans and an old

tank top that had shrunk from too many washings. In fact, had she been thinking, she would've changed before leaving the house.

"I've eaten," she lied, and slapped the side of her thigh. "This baby fat hasn't gone anywhere, I'm afraid."

Rachel opened the fridge to return a jar of mayo, but stopped to give her the stink eye. "Don't think I won't hurt you because you're Matt's sister."

Nikki managed a smile. "Have you talked to him today?"

"Early this morning. Why?"

"He say anything about Wallace?"

"It's sort of a given." Rachel's eyes narrowed. "He normally ends up part of the conversation. Tell me what's going on."

Taking a deep breath, Nikki pulled a chair out from the table and sat down. "Matt said if I want to say goodbye, I should do it today." She glanced at Hilda, who was making the sign of the cross. The woman had been with the McAllisters forever. She knew Wallace was worthless, but she still acted human. Why couldn't Nikki find that kind of compassion?

Rachel sat at the table with her. "So, did you?"

"See Wallace?" Nikki frowned. "No. I came here to cover for you in case you want to be with Matt."

Rachel's expression held no censure, simply concern and kindness. "Maybe you should be with him."

Nikki sighed and stared out the window over the sink. All she could see was the sky, so clear and blue. "I think I might make things worse."

"Come on, you can't really think that." Rachel reached over and rubbed her arm. "Your brother loves you, and he understands."

"I don't want to disappoint him, but I can't fake that I care. Because I don't. I—I—" Nikki looked at Hilda. "I saw you

ay a brief prayer and I thought, why can't I be that charita-
le? What's wrong with me?"

"Oh, Nikki." Rachel scooted her chair closer. "You barely
now the man, and he's been nothing but horrible to you, to
our mom, everyone."

"What I hate most is how he treated Matt. I can't forgive
im for that."

Rachel shrugged. "Neither can I."

"But then I'm not hurting Wallace. It's Matt who's suffered
ecause I've been selfish, and now it's too late." Nikki rarely
ried, but she was starting to choke. Kindness did that to her.

"This is my honest opinion," Rachel said, her gaze steady.
'Both of you were better off with you keeping your distance.
Two extra hands might've helped, but not the tension. Know-
ng how you feel, Matt never wanted you waiting on Wallace
r taking care of him. He'd rather you make a clean start here,
reate good memories."

In a way this was making Nikki feel worse. Rachel was
varm, supportive and perfect for Matt. And Nikki adored her.
So how could she feel jealous at the same time? She strug-
led daily with her petty thoughts. Her relationship with her
rother was still new but already changing since he'd hooked
p with Rachel. They were great, both trying to keep her from
eeling like the odd person out. Nikki's contribution was to
disappear as much as possible.

"I have a confession." Hilda put a glass of orange juice in
ront of Nikki. It was understood she'd better drink it, or else.
'Yes, you saw me making the sign of the cross. You know
vhy? Because I know Mr. Gunderson is not going up there,"
he said solemnly, pointing at the ceiling.

With a straight face, Rachel asked, "You mean upstairs?"

Nikki was able to hold back a grin. Until Hilda glared at
Rachel, who started laughing and turning as red as a tomato.

"I wouldn't even expect that from your brothers." Hilda turned to the stove, no amusement in her face.

"I'm sorry," Rachel said. "I shouldn't have joked. I'm tired, though that's no excuse." She stood. "If you don't need me, I'll go see Matt."

Nikki didn't dare look at her again. If she did, she'd start laughing and not stop. It was one of those weird inappropriate reactions you couldn't explain. And she'd hate to upset Hilda. She reminded Nikki of her grandmother, and she'd been just as kind, throwing in Spanish words here and there, trying to make Nikki feel at home. She didn't have the heart to admit her Spanish vocabulary consisted mostly of cusswords.

"I can help," Nikki said, once Rachel was gone. "I'll wash sheets, towels, do whatever you need." She picked up the glass and gulped down some juice before Hilda turned to her.

With amusement dancing in her dark eyes, Hilda waved a wooden spoon in the direction Rachel had disappeared. "Lucky for that one she doesn't get into more trouble." Hilda looked at Nikki. "How about a bean and cheese burrito, *chica?*"

Nikki blinked. Her go-to comfort food. Of course Hilda would know...she was from a poor Texas border town and had grown up much like Nikki. "I would love one," she said.

"Red hot sauce?"

Nikki nodded, saw Hilda shake her head again at Rachel, and started to laugh. The short break she'd taken to compose herself meant nothing. She couldn't stop laughing.

Until her eyes filled with tears.

TRACE HAD SEEN Nikki's truck so he knew she was at the Sundance. He figured she'd be in the kitchen with Rachel. He entered the house through the mudroom and found her sitting at the table.

Her head was bowed, her long dark hair loose and hiding

her face. Her shoulders shook, and it kind of sounded as if she was laughing. But he prepared himself to be wrong. Pulling off his work gloves, he lifted a brow at Hilda. She shrugged, then gestured for him to stay back. Bad sign.

He liked being around women, no secret there, but one who was crying made him want to pack a tent and stock a cooler. But then Nikki wasn't just any woman, and he had offered her a shoulder to cry on.

"Hey." He moved closer. "Nikki?"

She looked up with wide watery eyes. "What are you doing here?"

He smiled and pulled out a chair.

"I know you live here. I just thought you'd be out in a pasture somewhere." She wiped her cheek and sat straighter.

Damn, but he still couldn't tell if she'd been crying-crying or laughing-crying. Either way he wanted to pull her into his lap and put his arms around her. He didn't care that Hilda was watching, but Nikki might. "You okay?"

"Yeah, fine." She shoved her hair back, wincing when her fingers pushed through a tangle. "You missed Rachel by a few minutes."

"She lives here, too. I'll see her." He leaned over and used his thumb to wipe a dark smudge from her cheek.

She jerked away. "What are you doing?"

He held up the evidence on the pad of his thumb. Makeup, probably, and he didn't know why that made him think those were real tears but that's what he concluded.

"Better not be here to cancel on me," he said, and her gaze darted to Hilda. But he'd been careful how he worded it so no harm.

"No." She dabbed under her eyes. "I know Jamie's away for a few days so I stopped by to see if I could cover for Rachel so she can go see Matt."

He wiped his hand on his jeans, not sure what to do. With Hilda there it was hard to talk. "Is that where she went?"

Nikki frowned. "Oh, Rachel. Yes, but she may not have left yet."

Trace shrugged. "I was just wondering…"

"Did you have lunch?" Hilda asked.

"An hour ago. In the bunkhouse with the boys."

"So now you like Chester's cooking better than mine?"

"Come on…" He grinned. "You don't believe that, Hilda. You know you've ruined me for any other woman. Or I should say cook."

Chuckling, she washed and dried her hands. "I'm making bean and cheese burritos if you want one. But first I have to check the clothes in the dryer."

He might've believed her had she gone in the right direction. "What's going on, Nikki?"

"Nothing." Her brows lifted, and her eyes widened just enough to fake surprise, but he wasn't buying it.

Leaning forward, he slid a hand behind her neck and pulled her face toward him. Her stunned expression looked real enough now. "Were you crying?" he asked, and brushed his lips across hers.

"You must've been out in the sun too long," she murmured, but didn't retreat. "You can't do this here in the kitchen."

"If Hilda or Rachel or my mom walked in right now, think they'd be shocked?"

"Yes, I do. *I'm* shocked."

Trace smiled and used the tip of his tongue to dampen her lower lip. "Tell me the truth."

"About?"

"Everything."

Nikki's warm sweet breath slipped out, tempting him to do more exploring. "Dream on," she whispered, her lips lightly moving over his.

He applied more pressure, making it a real kiss, until it started getting out of hand. "I'd settle for the reason you were crying."

She pulled back, sighing. "I wasn't crying, really. I was a little...tense...and Rachel made me laugh, and then I couldn't stop. You know how that is.... Sometimes laughing and crying sort of blur together."

"Is it about Wallace?"

"Jesus, it wasn't about him." She jumped up, and he caught her arm.

"Wait. Don't get all bent. I just wanna make sure you're okay." He held on to her while he got to his feet.

"I'm fine. I'm always fine."

"You don't have to stand on your own all the time, Nikki." He ran his palms down her bare arms. "You're not alone anymore."

She stiffened. "What does that mean?"

"People here care about you."

Her chin came up, and her gaze locked on his face. A hint of challenge glinted in her eyes. "Who?"

Trace hadn't expected the question and it stopped him. "Matt, for one," he said. "Rachel. Hilda. Jamie." Nikki kept staring at him. "Sadie." He touched her cheek, wondering why he was having trouble including himself. It wasn't as if the *L* word would come into play or that she was asking for a commitment. And he did have feelings for Nikki. Her small sad smile got to him. "And me. I care about you."

"You don't have to say that."

"I know I don't." He finger-combed her hair, massaging her scalp and watched her lashes flutter, then droop. "If I hesitated it was only because I figured how I felt was understood."

"That's lame."

He smiled. "I know that, too."

"You're forgiven as long as you keep this up." She let her

chin drop as he worked his fingers toward the back, all the way down to the top of her spine.

Her small-boned frame felt fragile, and even though he was careful not to rub too hard, her whole body rocked under the pressure of his fingers. But he kept kneading out the tension, feeling her relax until her forehead rested against his chest and she let out soft moans.

When he couldn't stand it anymore, he tightened his arms around her and cradled her to his chest.

Slowly she brought her chin up, tilting her head back to look at him. "I thought we were supposed to cool it until we figured out what we're doing."

"I'm not starting anything, just letting you know I'm here."

"So that's what you call this."

"Why?" He dipped down for a quick kiss. "What do you call it?"

"Trouble."

"Ah. You've got me there." He stared down at her lips, fascinated with their silky smooth texture, at how they plumped into a perfect pout. When he met her dazed eyes, his jaw clenched. "You," he whispered, his whole body tensing, "give trouble a new meaning."

She pressed her breasts against him, peeling off another layer of his control. The little imp knew exactly what she was doing. A few more minutes and he wouldn't be interested in any more talking.

Nikki clutched his shoulders and arched her back, just a little, enough to expose more of her slender neck and throat. "You realize Hilda could walk in at any moment."

"Hell, she's probably listening at the door to see if it's safe to come back."

"God no."

She froze when his answer was to kiss the tip of her chin. He traced her lips with his tongue, getting too heated for his own good. But Nikki wasn't responding. Not in a way he'd hoped, anyway. Her body had stiffened and now she was trying to evade his mouth.

He stumbled back a step but held on to her. "What?"

"Hilda."

"I was joking."

"No, you weren't."

"You'd really care if she caught us?"

"Yes." She swung a gaze toward the dividing door to the dining room.

"You keep surprising me."

She shrugged a shoulder as if she wasn't happy with her reaction but there it was. "You'd be embarrassed, too. And don't deny it."

He didn't, even though she was wrong. After being with the family for over thirty years, Hilda was as much a part of the Sundance as any of them. She'd waded through the hormone-driven teen years of her own son, Ben, as well as Trace and his brothers. Not much left that could embarrass him or Hilda.

Tightening his arms around Nikki, he brushed his lips over her ear. "I get you moaning loud enough she'll never come in."

Nikki let out a startled laugh. "You're that sure of yourself?"

He grabbed a handful of hair and tilted her head back again. The curve of a woman's throat had never been a turn-on for him, not like this. He kissed the soft silken skin, knowing damn well he was only torturing himself. This had to end soon. Before it got out of hand. Before he couldn't remember the reason they'd stopped the other day. Matt. Rachel. Nikki's fresh start. She didn't need a complication right off. Or to have folks gossiping about her. They all knew he wasn't the type to take on a relationship. He hadn't been serious about a girl since high school. He just hadn't met anyone who made him want to put on blinders.

She made a muted purring sound that vibrated against his mouth. It might as well have zipped straight to his cock. Not much separated common sense from a wild need to drag her up to his room. He had to calm down.

"And the guests?" she asked, letting her head fall back even more. Eyes closed, lips parted, ready for him to slip his tongue inside. Taste the sweetness he'd already sampled.

"What about them?" He breathed in her dizzying scent, warned himself again to back off. The argument was already fading in his mind.

"One of them could walk in on us."

"So?"

She smiled, swaying enough that he had to tighten his arm around her waist. "This is crazy."

"Maybe we should start your lesson early."

"My—?" She opened her eyes. "Oh, right," she murmured, blinking away the confusion. "What time is it?"

The big round clock hung on the wall to his left. He strained to see it without losing ground, fearing if he let her go, the moment would be lost.

Nikki pushed on his arm, trying to look for herself. He relaxed his hold and she broke away. The sensible side of his brain told him it was for the best. His body strongly disagreed.

He turned to the clock, so worked up inside that he had to squint to focus. No way that much time had gone by since he'd come inside. He cut off a curse at the last second. Cole wanted to meet him in the east barn, and Trace had agreed to be there five minutes ago.

"What's wrong?" Nikki touched his arm, then quickly withdrew.

She shouldn't have to worry about a casual touch, that was the kind of thing he'd been trying to avoid. If he hadn't pushed, she might not have given it a second thought. He lightly squeezed her shoulder, then went to the window and looked outside for Cole. If he were on time, he'd be waiting at the entrance.

"I forgot I was supposed to meet Cole. I'll come look for you when I'm done and we can talk about later." When he saw his brother standing outside the stable talking to Karina, Trace grinned. He knew by the look on Cole's face he'd been caught off guard and would do anything to escape. That gave Trace a couple more minutes with Nikki.

She joined him at the window, and the instant she spotted them she broke out in a huge smile.

"What's that for?"

"Nothing."

"Yeah, sure looks like nothing." It reminded him to ask her about the other night. "You and Karina, at the Watering Hole, what were you laughing about?"

She turned away, shaking her head. "I can't tell you. I promised."

"Well, that's a fine thing." He caught her arm, spun her back to face him. "You trust her more than you do me?"

"You want me to break a promise?"

Hard to argue when she put it that way. "Give me a hint. Did it have anything to do with what I told her about you and me?"

Nikki lost the smile. "What did you say?"

Trace cringed. He should've thought before putting himself on the hot seat. "She asked if you were my girlfriend and I sorta said I was working on it."

"Sorta said?"

"Yeah, okay, I said it, but it was in self-defense...not to mention your fault."

She folded her arms across her chest. "I can't wait to hear this."

"I was getting a group ready for a ride and thinking abou us kissing and…well…I might've looked a little sappy whe I helped Karina into the saddle and I worried she'd gotte the wrong idea."

"Oh." Nikki's lips again curved into a smile, but a strang one. "What she told me had nothing to do with that."

Well, hell, that didn't tell him squat. "I didn't know yo two were so chummy."

"That was the first time we'd really talked." She lifted shoulder. "I like her." She moved closer, lowering her voic to a teasing whisper. "If you can't keep your mind on work then no more getting down and dirty."

"We haven't even gotten dusty yet." Trace tried to snea an arm around her waist but she danced out of reach. "Com on now, I only have a minute before I have to go save Cole."

Nikki suddenly got serious. "What if Karina repeats wha you told her and it spreads?"

"About me working on you?" He dismissed it with a shrug "No one will think anything of it. You're in the clear, an people will figure that's just me being me."

Regret hit him instantly. Even before her expression fel and her body tensed. A lot of people considered him a player and Nikki didn't have evidence to the contrary. He neede to explain….

Hilda reentered the kitchen.

Too late. He had to let it go for now. At least he still ha later when they could talk in private. "I gotta go get Cole," he said, looking directly at Nikki. "I'll see you soon. Sam time?"

She hesitated, and he tried to hold her gaze, tried to si lently communicate that he needed to see her. But he kne he'd lost her the second her lips lifted in a faint smile. "An other day, okay?"

Dammit. He glanced at Hilda. She'd busied herself wit

tirring a pot on the stove, but she could still hear. Saying anything more would only make Nikki uncomfortable. He et out a frustrated sigh and headed for the door. Maybe he ad been that guy, but meeting Nikki had changed his ways. He just wished he could convince her of that.

9

"Nikki?"

She turned at Sadie's voice rising above the boisterous laughter from the back room crowd, and saw her boss motioning that she needed her. Nikki had been idly chatting with Chip and another cowboy while she cleared off a table, so she grabbed the last two dirty glasses and headed to the far end of the bar where Sadie waited for her.

"I can't figure out why it's so slow tonight," Sadie said, glancing around the room.

"It's not that bad."

"Huh. Most of the hands got paid two days ago. Can't tell me they've already gone through their paychecks."

Nikki leaned on the bar, studying Sadie. Her comment was odd enough, but to call Nikki over for that? Maybe the phone call she'd gotten a while ago had something to do with her strange mood. On the first ring Sadie started grumbling like she always did, swearing to disconnect service because it was a waste of money and she was tired of passing on messages from angry wives. But she hadn't yelled for anyone to get home before they had to sleep in the barn.

Maybe she'd heard from her daughter. They didn't speak often, but the one time Mariah had called while Nikki was working, Sadie had gotten depressed after hanging up. Part of her wanted to ask if Sadie needed to talk, but the gesture didn't come naturally. Nikki hated people butting into her life so she tried to stay out of theirs.

And today probably wasn't the time to change her ways.

Turned out everything had sucked, from getting up early to the reminder that Trace was exactly the kind of guy she'd feared. He was a player. Guys like him used to be exciting to her, a challenge she couldn't resist. No more.

Okay, the thrill hadn't disappeared, but she needed to work at tamping down her attraction. She'd been bitten twice already by hooking up with guys who had more charm than substance. That was enough. At least she'd had the sense to cancel her riding lesson. The consolation was so tiny she wanted to scream.

"Um, Sadie, did you want something?" she asked when it seemed as if nothing more would be said. "You know, when you called me over?"

"Oh, right." Sadie waved an acknowledgment when a customer yelled they needed beer in the back. "Why don't you go on home? No need to stick around when it's this slow."

"It's really not that bad. Everyone's drinking steady." Nikki didn't get it. What was going on? They'd been less busy quite a few nights and Sadie had never suggested she go home. "Did I do something wrong?"

"No." Sadie reached over and squeezed her hand. "You've been a godsend. Don't go thinking that way. I just don't see the point in us both hanging around on a night when it's a one-person job."

"But I don't mind. I—"

"I don't wanna hear any more about it," Sadie said, shaking her head and coming out from behind the bar.

"I can check the back first, see who needs beer."

"Would you just go on?" Sadie could be impatient and

irritable with customers, but she'd never used that annoyed tone with Nikki.

"I have five open tabs sitting beside the register. I can close them out before I leave if you—"

"We're getting thirsty back here," one of the pool players yelled loud enough to be heard at Abe's Variety down the street.

Sadie craned her neck to see who it was, then hollered, "Keep your pants on, Leo." She turned back to Nikki. "I've been doing this a long time, honey, I'll figure it out. And don't worry, I'll make sure to set aside your tips."

"I'm not worried about that." Feeling like a kid who'd just been suspended from school, Nikki watched her amble toward the back. Except she hadn't done anything bad. If there had been a complaint about her...

A sudden thought struck as Nikki crouched to grab her keys from the shelf under the cash register. Maybe Sadie needed the money. The tips weren't great tonight, but working alone could amount to a nice chunk of change. If that was the case, Nikki was glad to leave the business to Sadie. She dug into her pocket for the tips she'd collected earlier. It was only twenty bucks or so, but it could help. She made sure Sadie wasn't in view, then stuffed the bills into the older woman's tip jar sitting on the rear counter.

On the way out, customers ragged on her about leaving, asking if she had a hot date. She sent wisecracks back at them, but she couldn't deny feeling at loose ends. If it was about money, she would've worked for free, she didn't care. The Watering Hole was as much home to her as the Lone Wolf.

She stopped on the sidewalk and sucked in a deep breath. Directly in front of her, Trace's truck was parked at the curb. He was leaning back against the door with his arms folded and the brim of his hat pulled down low. As if he were waiting for someone. For her?

"Hey," he said, pushing off the truck.

"What are you doing?" She hadn't seen him inside. Unless he'd slipped in and out while she and Sadie were talking. "Were you in the Watering Hole?"

"Nope. Just got here. Come sit in the truck with me for a minute."

"What is this?" She wished she could see his eyes better. "How did you know I'd be out here?"

"Come here and I'll explain."

"No." She squeezed the set of keys until it dug into her palm, then pulled her arm back when he reached for her. "I'm staying right here until you tell me what's going on."

Main Street almost always quieted down after six-thirty. At nine, with the Food Mart and Abe's Variety closed, the town was dead. Two trucks and a blue sedan were parked in front of the diner. Other than a pair of headlights coming toward them from the south, nothing moved on the street.

She wouldn't even have noticed the headlights except Trace seemed weirdly interested. He stood silently watching the vehicle's approach, his mouth a grim line as the car passed.

"Dammit, Trace, you're scaring me."

"I don't mean to." He caught her this time, tightening his grip on her wrist when she tried to shake him off. "Would you settle down?"

"No, I won't. First Sadie sends me home like I'm a kid who's disobeyed, then I come out here and—" She gasped at the feel of her breasts being crushed against his chest. His rough treatment stunned her.

"I'm sorry if I pulled too hard." He put his free arm around her before he released her wrist. Apparently he wasn't contrite enough to let her go.

"What is wrong with you?" With the light from the bar's sign shining in his face, she could see his eyes now. They were dark and serious, and she knew something bad had happened. "Is it Matt?" Her heart nearly exploded from merely voicing the question. "Tell me he's okay, Trace. You tell me right now."

"Matt is fine." His genuine look of surprise reassured her more than the words. "It's Wallace."

"He's dead?"

Trace nodded. "He passed away about forty minutes ago."

"Why did you scare me like that?" She punched his shoulder. "Damn you." Pausing, she struggled to take a breath, and shivered in the warm summer air. It was finally over... the waiting and having to watch her brother care for the man who'd shown him nothing but contempt. She should feel relief. Still she felt nothing. "I thought it was Matt. God."

"Now will you get in my truck?"

"Why? I drove—" She stared at him as things started falling into place. "Is that why Sadie told me to go home? She knew about Wallace?"

"I called her after Rachel phoned me. She and Matt, we all thought it was best that I come get you before you heard the news from someone else. Doc Heaton gets summoned this late it means either he'll be delivering a baby or certifying a death."

"Was that him in the blue car?"

"Yep. Somehow his comings and goings seem to spread fast around here."

Nikki sighed. She couldn't be mad at everyone for caring, no matter how misguided. When Trace hooked a finger under her chin and gently tipped her head back, she said, "If you're looking for tears there aren't any."

A faint smile curved his mouth. "I want you to be okay, that's all."

She twisted away from him, lifted her hands, palms up. "Look, I'm fine. Just like always." She twirled all the way around. "See?"

"Yes, good." He gestured to his truck. "We should go."

Screw his patronizing tone. She sidestepped him and headed for her own truck. No, not hers, the pickup belonged to the Lone Wolf. She didn't have anything of value. Never had, probably never would. The hell with the Gunderson trust fund. Matt considered half the ranch hers, she didn't.

"Nikki…what are you doing?"

"Going home like a good girl. Isn't that what everyone wants?"

She kept walking without glancing back, wanting to run. But that would only convince Trace she was upset and needed a babysitter. The stupid door was locked so she readied her key. Everyone in Blackfoot Falls left their vehicles open, windows half-down, everyone but her. She hadn't broken the habit yet, and damn she wished she had because her hand shook too hard to get her key inserted. Of course she'd chosen the only truck at the Lone Wolf that didn't have a remote.

Sneaking a peek to locate Trace, she saw him standing right where she'd left him. She didn't have to see his watchful eyes to know they tracked her every move. On the third try she got the door open and climbed in, quickly checking the rearview mirror to see him slip behind the wheel of his own truck. She knew he'd follow her, but there was nothing she could do about it.

Cursing her unsteady hand, she missed the ignition twice before pushing the key home. After she'd pulled away from the curb she realized she hadn't checked for oncoming traffic. So what? No traffic except for her and Trace. If she passed a single car in the next fifteen minutes to the Lone Wolf she'd be surprised.

Her hands were freezing, and she rolled down a window instead of using the heat. The warm air rushed in. She glanced at the speedometer, saw how fast she was driving and eased her foot off the accelerator. She hadn't even left the town limits yet. All she needed was to get stopped and ticketed. Though she was pretty sure Roy was on duty, and the deputy would probably let her skate with only a warning.

Forcing herself to breathe in deeply shouldn't have been hard. But she couldn't seem to draw in enough air and panicked for a moment. Trace was the problem. He followed close behind and, God, she didn't want him seeing her fall apart.

No, no, that wasn't it. She didn't even understand where the thought had come from. Even after what Matt had told her this morning, she hadn't truly believed Wallace would die soon. She figured the bastard was too stubborn and mean… he'd hang on just to make everyone else miserable. Her worry wasn't that she'd fall apart, but that she wasn't prepared. Her emotional bank was empty, void, not even a hint of compassion had surfaced. How was she supposed to react appropriately?

She knew Rachel was with Matt, and Lucy had to be there, too. Maybe Petey was at the house. The wrangler knew the family well. And the doctor, of course, he'd still be there when she got home. Or maybe not…if she slowed down. What if she waited a couple of hours? She'd call so Matt wouldn't worry.…

No, she'd feel like shit if she ditched him. As if that wasn't exactly what she'd been doing for weeks. He'd given her a chance to help even things out by asking her to see Wallace a final time. Oh, Matt had claimed he meant only to give her the facts this morning, but she'd understood the subtle suggestion that she step up and say goodbye, and she'd walked out anyway. She'd been too stubborn and defiant to give so much as an inch, and now… Oh, God, she didn't know.

All she wanted was to stop thinking.

It was too quiet. Listening to music would help. She turned on the radio, knowing the signal sucked this far north. Her CDs were tucked in between the passenger seat and the console. She fumbled trying to find one, momentarily lost control of the wheel and weaved into the other lane.

She checked the rearview mirror, half expecting Trace to overtake her and force her to pull over. But he continued to stay at a sensible distance behind, and somehow the knowledge that he hadn't overreacted calmed her. Deciding against risking her neck over a CD, she clutched the steering wheel with both hands and stared at the dark highway ahead. And the stars. Lots of them twinkled in the clear inky sky. So different from Houston with its pricey high-rise condos and gleaming skyscrapers blazing with lights. Not exactly a star-friendly place.

So Wallace was dead.

Okay, Nikki had known his end was coming, but she hadn't seriously considered what life would look and feel like after he was gone. Matt planned on easing out of the rodeo circuit and running the Lone Wolf. He insisted half the ranch was hers, but she didn't give a crap about inheritance. The place belonged to Matt, period. She had no interest, no investment in the Lone Wolf, emotional or otherwise. She was only here in Montana because…

Her breathing stalled again, and she forced herself to pay attention to what her body was telling her. She was in major stress mode.

With Wallace alive, she'd been coasting. Any decision regarding her future she'd easily shelved for later. Matt had been busy with his care, and she'd scrambled to make herself unavailable. A tiny part of her had hoped by the time Wallace was gone she'd have grown attached to the ranch and Blackfoot Falls. She liked her job and most of the people she'd met, but enough to make this her home? She couldn't say. So where did that leave her? Aside from feeling utterly confused.

Startled, she saw the turnoff to the Lone Wolf up ahead. Of all the nights for the drive to seem short… She slowed to make the turn and, yep, Trace was still right behind her. Maybe it was best he'd be there with her. He'd be a distraction and Matt wouldn't fuss over her so much in front of Trace.

She forced herself to concentrate on the narrow private road, looking out for deer that liked to come bounding out of nowhere and dash in front of the truck this time of night. Her hands were cold again, actually freezing and stiff, and she let go of the wheel to shake the circulation back into her fingers.

She hadn't made it far when the lights became visible. Normally she wouldn't see the Lone Wolf for another half a mile. But tonight, God, so many lights were ablaze they lit the sky. Had someone flipped every single switch on the property? How many people were there? And why? Had they come to see her father in his last hour?

The thought stopped her, the truth hitting her so hard it was impossible to breathe.

Wallace was…or had been…her father. It didn't matter how much she hated him. Or that they'd never bonded, and she'd resented him as far back as she could remember. Her father, the man who'd given her life, had died tonight. And she had the horrible, horrible suspicion that she had wanted something from him after all.

Just once she'd wanted him to look at her, really see her as his daughter. Give her that special smile fathers reserved for their little girls. Let her believe that in his heart he was happy she existed.

God, how could she have been such a fool?

In spite of herself, in spite of all the nasty things of which she'd known he was capable, she'd secretly been hoping Wallace would tell her he regretted abandoning her and her mother. People changed. She had, so why not give him the benefit of the doubt? But she'd never gone to see him at the end, so how could he have told her?

In her heart she knew he hadn't changed, and he hadn't

cared about anyone, not even Matt. To think she'd pitied her brother for yearning for Wallace's approval. She was no better. And the really sad thing was, she'd prided herself in being too smart to buy into such emotional nonsense.

Her foot slammed on the brakes before she knew what she was doing. Not much room for her to pull over, but she managed to park halfway off the road in case anyone had to squeeze by. She cut the engine and jumped out, knowing Trace would've stopped, as well.

She couldn't go inside. Or be anywhere near the house. Funny, how only minutes ago she'd worried people expected tears she couldn't shed. Now she feared the flood gates wouldn't hold.

"Hey, honey, you okay?" Trace had gotten out of his truck and was walking toward her. The night was black except for the pickup's headlights, and she focused on his long legs closing the distance between them.

She flung herself at him, knowing he'd catch her, confident he wouldn't let her fall no matter what.

His arms came up around her, and she burrowed against him, burying her face in his chest, hugging him around the waist, holding on as tight as she could.

"Nikki," he whispered when she shuddered. "It's okay, honey, I've got you."

What was it about Trace that made her want to trust him? She couldn't figure it out, and right now she didn't care. "Take me someplace," she said, finding comfort in the sure steady beat of his heart against her cheek. "Anywhere we can be alone."

He stroked her back. "Matt's expecting you."

"It's fine. I'll call him."

"I know it'll be hard to—"

She cut him off by gripping the back of his neck and pulling him into a kiss. He resisted at first, and then she didn't have to stretch so high because he lowered his head and kissed her back. His breath was warm, laced with mint and coffee. She parted her lips for him, offering only panic and desperation in return.

He touched his tongue to hers, teasing and tempting her to join the dance. She clung to his neck, tugging him closer, willing him to kiss her harder and deeper and help her forget what she had to do.

Instead, Trace gently peeled her hand from the back of his neck. "Nikki," he whispered. "This isn't the time."

"Make love to me, Trace. Please. Take me away from here. Anywhere." She heard his sharp intake of breath and pressed her advantage by moving his hand over her breast.

"Sex isn't the answer."

She yanked her blouse from her jeans, then started unfastening buttons. He caught her hand on the third one. "I know you want me," she said, jerking his shirt hem loose. She slid her palm underneath the fabric, over his flat belly, up to his bare chest, knowing she was turning him on. "Deny it if you want, but I'll know it's a lie."

"I'd never deny it."

"So? Come on. You must know someplace private around here. Your truck has a backseat, let's go park somewhere."

"Ah, Nikki." He moved his hand away from her breast to touch her face. She sucked his forefinger into her mouth and rubbed her body against his. What he said didn't matter, he was hard, really hard. "I know you're hurting," he said huskily. "But do you really want to worry Matt? Or Rachel and Lucy?"

She almost bit him. She hadn't asked anyone to care about her. Wrong thing to do. If anyone got too close they'd see how cowardly and selfish she really was, and what then? Would they still think she was worth their concern?

Pulling up his T-shirt, she pressed her mouth against his

warm skin. He smelled strong and masculine, and she had no doubt he could make her forget a whole lot. With the tip of her tongue she tempted his resolve and sampled the slight saltiness of his skin. His breath came out harsh and raspy, and she knew he was on the verge of giving in to her.

"Come on, Trace," she murmured against his chest. "Last chance." She cupped his erection through the thick denim fly, pressing against his cock with her palm, using just enough pressure to make him moan.

He jerked. Stilled. Then pushed her hand aside. "Nikki, stop. I mean it."

She froze, not sure what to do next. She could've sworn she had him. "Goddamn you, Trace," she said, and shoved him back. "Damn you."

"Wait." He tried to capture her hand, but she dodged him and ran for her truck.

She was too angry, hurt and embarrassed to hear anything more. He probably assumed she'd make a beeline for the highway. Good. Let him waste time blocking the road. Exhaustion had dug in to every pore and was slowly leveling her. She wanted to crawl into bed, pull the quilt over her head and sleep for three days. Maybe she'd find that today had only been part of a bad dream.

Her name carried on the breeze, and she muffled his voice by starting the noisy engine. By the time she pulled into her normal parking spot near the house, she saw Trace's headlights right behind her. Taking the flagstone walk, she counted four extra cars, two of them unfamiliar. Trace met her at the front door.

"You didn't have to follow me," she said. "I'm a big girl."

He smiled. "I came to pay my respects to Matt."

Nikki swallowed, briefly closed her eyes and breathed in

deeply. She put her hand on the doorknob and told herself she could do this. But she only believed it when Trace touched the small of her back.

10

"THIS IS WAY TOO MUCH food." Nikki eyed the huge bowl of cubed potatoes, then frowned at the whole ones she had yet to cut up. "Everyone's going to be eating potato salad for a month."

"Don't bet on it." Rachel used the back of her wrist to dab at her tears. "Any time you want to trade is okay with me. We don't need as many onions."

"No, thanks." Nikki started to smile, then sighed.

She probably should show more gratitude. Here Rachel, Hilda and Mrs. McAllister were doing all this work to feed people after Wallace's funeral tomorrow. Plus they were dirtying their own kitchen. All because Lucy insisted on a proper church service and burial.

Matt hadn't argued with her, though Nikki doubted he cared one way or the other. She'd stayed completely neutral. What mattered most to her was that this whole thing be over and done with. Let everyone get back to normal. Including her. Last night Sadie had refused to let her work again. It had really pissed Nikki off. She'd already done her dutiful best the night Wallace died.

So what she'd remained in the corner praying for a shot of tequila until Wallace's body was taken away and everyone left. At least she'd been present, and that was more than anyone should've expected. Rachel hadn't batted an eye, and that was one of the things Nikki liked about Matt's girlfriend. She was totally nonjudgmental and supportive at the same time. Must be a McAllister trait. Trace was the same way.

Nikki hadn't seen him since that night…. Actually, it had been after midnight when he left. She'd gone up to her room five minutes later, feeling no less embarrassed than she had when he'd turned down her offer.

God, the humiliation still hadn't disappeared. If things had gone differently and they'd had sex? Hard to even imagine how she'd be feeling. He'd been right to refuse. She kind of owed him, though she was happy to ignore the incident.

"Will there be booze served at this thing?" she asked.

"Huh. I don't recall it coming up." Rachel turned away from the cutting board, making a face and sniffling. "I am so over dicing onions. This has to be enough."

"No." Hilda kept stirring the refried beans on the stove but frowned at the small mound in front of Rachel. "We need at least three more."

"Seriously?"

Hilda gave her a look that said she was quite serious.

"I'll do it," Nikki said. "This is for my fa—" She almost choked on the word. Where had *that* come from? "For Matt and me," she muttered, focusing her attention on laying down the knife. "Let's trade."

"No, it's okay." Rachel gave an exaggerated sniff. "Really."

Hilda shook her head and went back to humming while she stirred.

Nikki sighed. The onion-dicing job would be better for her. Every now and then, she got a little teary-eyed. She couldn't explain it, other than a general feeling of sadness. But if the waterworks started, at least she could blame the onions.

"I want to do it, honest." She tried to elbow Rachel aside.

"No, go call Matt. Ask him if we should offer beer and/ or liquor tomorrow."

"You know him," Nikki said. "He won't care."

"Yeah, maybe we should ask Lucy."

"She's not home," Mrs. McAllister said, carrying in bags of beef and vegetables she'd gone to get from the freezer. "She's delivering the clothes Wallace is to be buried in."

Nikki stared down at the potatoes. His death hadn't completely sunk in yet. His bedroom door remained closed. Every time she went upstairs it was a jolt to realize he wasn't there.

"Thank you for doing all of this," she said quietly. "I can't say I understand…I know how horrible he was to your family."

"Wallace wasn't always difficult." Mrs. McAllister dropped the packages on the counter and patted her arm. "As a young man he could be quite charming. Besides, this really isn't for him."

Charming.

The word alone was like an intolerable high-pitched scream to her ears. Nikki's mother had used the same description. He'd charmed his way right into her bed and made promises he never intended to keep. But then Wallace had made a daughter, too, and hadn't kept her, either.

Dammit, she'd also made a promise, one she had yet to honor. Why was she finding it so hard to call her mom? Why did her mother even care that he was gone?

She smiled at Mrs. McAllister, who'd moved to the sink. "We're trying to decide whether to serve booze tomorrow. I can pick some up after I leave here."

"That's your call. Some people do, some don't." She narrowed her eyes at something outside the window. "What in the world is that woman thinking? That stallion was still rearing not ten minutes ago. Trace doesn't need to be distracted."

Nikki and Rachel hurried to the window. He was in the

corral with a horse, holding a lead, trying to calm the animal down. A blonde Nikki recognized from the bar had slipped between the railings. Dividing his attention between her and the now bucking stallion, Trace waved frantically for the woman to get out.

Rachel cursed under her breath. "I'll go get her."

It was too late.

Trace lost the lead, fell hard and rolled clear of the horse's hooves by a scary few inches. The blonde scrambled to safety outside the corral. A cowboy ran from the barn to help Trace regain control of the stallion.

"It seems we need to have another talk with the guests after dinner." Mrs. McAllister's hand was at her throat, her face pale.

"I'm going to have one with Eve right now," Rachel said, steam practically coming out of her ears.

"No, don't. Trace is going to talk to her."

Watching him walk over to the guest, Nikki knew he was hurt. He subtly probed his left shoulder and winced. After speaking with the woman for a minute, he gave her the usual killer smile. But as soon as he started walking toward the house putting her behind him, the smile abruptly vanished as if a switch had been flipped.

"My poor brother," Rachel said. "I've been overloading him with guest stuff and with all his other duties he's exhausted." She sighed. "These women have been driving him nuts lately. He's so sick of them. I'll have to figure something out."

"Other than his shoulder he seems okay," his mother murmured. "He reminds me of your father more and more each day. Same mannerisms, same temperament. Of all your brothers he's most— Oops, he's headed for the mudroom. I doubt he'll appreciate us standing around watching him. I have to run upstairs, anyway."

As soon as she left, Nikki looked at Rachel. "Trace is like your dad?"

Rachel blinked. "Yeah, I guess he is."

Quite a compliment considering what she'd heard about Gavin McAllister. "Does he know that?"

Rachel shrugged. "Beats me." Her gaze returned to the window. "I hadn't really thought about it before."

Nikki saw that he was close to the house. "I need to talk to him."

"Go," Rachel said, with a nod at the mudroom door.

"Thanks." It would be private in there, at least for a few minutes. Trouble was, she didn't know what she wanted to say except to apologize for the other night.

He entered from outside just as she came in from the kitchen. His brows lifted in surprise. "Hey, I didn't know you were here."

"Are you all right?" She stopped when he did, standing a few feet away and feeling awkward, unnerved that her first instinct had been to touch him.

"Fine. Why?"

"I saw you fall."

Disgust transformed his expression. Flushing, he squeezed his eyes shut and muttered a mild curse.

"Don't be embarrassed. It wasn't your fault."

He yanked his gloves off and squinted at her. "Who said I'm embarrassed?"

"Okay," she said, trying not to smile. "Forget I said that." She cleared her throat. "And while we're at it, can we forget about the other night?"

"Why?" He shrugged, doing a better job than her of controlling a smile. "What happened?"

She fixed her gaze on his shoulder because she was still worried about him, but also to avoid his eyes. "Thank you for not taking advantage of my stupidity."

"Told you. It's forgotten." He reached for her hand and drew her closer. "How are you holding up?"

"Numb, confused, overwhelmed…" She sighed. "Anxious to get back to work. Sadie wouldn't let me go back last night."

"She was right not to," he said, rubbing her arm.

"I'm better off keeping busy."

"Yeah, but you never know what bonehead thing a customer will say that could set you off. I'm not naming names, mind you."

Nikki smiled. "What else hurts besides your shoulder?"

"Ah, Jesus." He let her go and plowed his hand through his hair. "Nothing. Nothing hurts."

"Well, I see your ego is in working order."

One side of his mouth lifted and he caught her chin. "Lucky for you I hear people in the kitchen," he whispered.

"Yes, they're waiting to fawn all over you."

"Well, hell." He lowered his hand and yanked a glove back on. "Thanks for the warning."

"Wait." She laughed. "Where are you going?"

"Where there aren't females trying to either get me hurt or patch me up." He stopped with his hand on the doorknob. "How long you gonna be around?"

"Until we're done preparing food for tomorrow." She shook her head. "We're making a ton of stuff. Way too much. I keep telling everyone— Go, before it's too late."

Trace smiled. "I'll see you later, huh?"

Nikki nodded, amazed how much better she felt just talking to him. "You'll be there tomorrow, right? At the funeral."

"Of course I will." He gave her a long gentle look that stirred a whole new batch of strange emotions inside her. "Standing right beside you."

TRACE HADN'T PULLED close enough to the curb to be legal. But that was just too damn bad. Main Street wasn't exactly bustling at suppertime and he didn't plan on staying long anyway. He opened the heavy oak door to the Watering Hole and backed up onto the sidewalk when Nikki stormed toward him.

"Oh." Frowning, she stopped, leaving enough room for him to close the door. "What are you doing here this early?"

"What am *I* doing here? Just this afternoon we talked about you not coming back to work too soon."

"Actually, no, we didn't." Shoving her fingers through her hair, she dislodged her ponytail and ripped off the elastic band. "You agree with Sadie. I don't."

"So, are you working or not?"

"Sheila's in there," she said. "Sadie asked her to cover for me tonight." Nikki growled and groaned at the same time, her restless gaze sweeping the street. "I'm so pissed I can't see straight. Why does everyone think they can make decisions for me?" She exhaled a harsh breath, then eyed him with a frown. "I assume you came for a beer. I'll have one with you."

"I didn't come here to drink. I came to talk some sense into you."

Her lips parted and she just stared at him for a long drawn-out moment. "Seriously?"

"Yeah, seriously." He tugged on a lock of her hair. So soft and shiny, he wanted to grab a whole handful. "You gonna stand out here and argue with me?"

She sighed, her shoulders sagging as if the fight had suddenly left her. "I haven't called my mom yet."

He took her arm and guided her the few feet to his truck. "Are you saying this is cosmic justice? I doubt you're being punished for procrastinating."

"What?" She looked at him and laughed, then sighed again. "Oh, Trace, I want life to be normal. I need normal."

"You might want to look up the definition." He opened the passenger door, feeling that familiar tug in his chest when she looked up at him with those wide trusting eyes. "You waiting for me to lift you up?"

"I'm kinda normal. You just aren't used to city women."

"Right." He snorted a laugh. "Because I haven't had my fill in the past year."

"Hey, what about me? Had enough of me?"

"Sometimes I can't decide if I wanna kiss you or strangle you." He had her trapped between the door and the seat, his body blocking her escape. "Does that answer your question?" He leaned close enough to kiss her, close enough to see the gold flecks of excitement dancing in her warm brown eyes.

"I get that," she said with a small grin. "Where are we going?"

"For a ride…maybe find a place to park on one of the ridges."

Her brows lifted.

He smiled, draping one arm over the door and letting his weight bring him even closer to her. "And watch the stars."

Nikki laughed and pushed him back so she had room to climb up by herself. But she caught the sore spot on his shoulder, and he winced before he could stop himself.

She got in and turned in time to see it. "Oh, no. I'm sorry. God, Trace, are you bruised? Let me see."

"It's fine. I'm fine. Everything's fine," he muttered, made sure she was clear, shut the door and rounded the hood.

"Why don't I drive us in my truck?" she asked, eyeing his shoulder as he slid in behind the wheel.

"No, thanks. I saw how you drive."

"Hey." She drew her knees up and hugged them to her chest. "That was different."

"You want to call your mom now?"

She shot him a startled look. "Yeah, I guess."

"Want me with you when you call?"

After taking a deep breath, she nodded, which shocked

him. He hadn't expected her to let him listen. If she changed her mind before they found someplace private, he'd understand.

He pulled a U-turn and drove toward the Sundance. She stretched out her legs, dug into her pocket and brought out her cell phone. All she did was stare at it, though, then turn her head to watch the scenery.

It was still light. Usually he liked the longer June days, but not this evening. He would've preferred a nice dusky glow. The upside was they'd probably be able to catch a decent sunset.

"You're not taking me home, are you?" she asked ten minutes into the ride. "Because I won't—"

"Nope."

She twisted around to check the mile marker they were passing. "I don't want to go to the Sundance, either."

"Good."

Settling back, she stared at her phone again. "Wherever we're going, will I have cell service?"

"Yep."

"Can you manage more than one syllable while you drive? Because if not I can take over."

Grinning at her, he lifted his boot off the accelerator, then slowly made the turn.

Sitting taller, she peered out the windshield. "Oh. I know where we are. I think."

Trace didn't correct her. She'd see soon enough she hadn't been up to this particular meadow. He shifted to four-wheel drive and took them up as far as the eroded trail would allow. The last of the yellow and purple wildflowers dotted the mountainside. Another week and they'd fade.

"Wow, this isn't where I thought we were. It's pretty, but why are there flowers up here and nowhere else?"

"It's cooler because of the elevation so they hang on lon-

ger. A month ago there were three times as many. Wait until
next spring. You'll see all kinds of wildflowers in back of
the Lone Wolf." He cut the engine and suddenly her attention went straight to her phone.

"Okay, I'm ready to do this."

"Want me to take a walk?"

"No." She grabbed his arm, surprising both of them. "I
don't understand why she wants to know," Nikki said, letting him go to press speed dial. "I mean, she hasn't even seen
Wallace in over twenty years. What difference does it make
that he's dead?" She held the phone to her ear with an unsteady hand. "She's finally getting married to a decent man
and moving to— Mom? It's me."

Nikki turned away from him, her back stiff and tense. He
lifted the center console out of the way and angled his body,
sliding closer to her so he could reach her shoulders.

She jumped, but when he started to massage and work out
the knots, she relaxed. "How are you? Getting packed?" She
paused. "No, everything is fine." Another pause. "How did
you know?" she asked, her voice softer. "Yes, he died in his
own bed. Last night. No, actually the night before but I've
been kinda busy helping make food for after the funeral.
Fine. I promise."

Letting her chin fall forward, she quietly listened to whatever her mother had to say as he continued to carefully work
his fingers into the layer of muscle above her shoulder blades.

"No," she said after a minute. "I'm with a friend. No. No.
Why does it matter?" Nikki sighed, and Trace smiled, wondering if she realized she sounded like an annoyed teen being
interrogated. "Rachel's brother, okay?" She stiffened again.
"Yes, it's Trace."

So she'd spoken of him to her mother. Well, wasn't that
something? He splayed his hand and ran it down her back,

giving her the bonus rubdown. She gave a tiny shiver and sent a glare over her shoulder.

He winked at her.

Rolling her eyes, she faced the passenger door again but made it obvious by leaning back that he was to return to his slave duty. "You sound good. I expected you to be upset." Nikki got quiet, listening for a while and really starting to relax.

"Oh, Mom, I'm sorry. Though I should've known, because I couldn't figure out why you'd want the details." She laughed. "If you knew how much I was dreading this call—" Nikki went perfectly still. "What? Say that again."

All the tension he'd managed to work out returned full force. She leaned forward as if she wanted him to stop touching her. So he lowered his hands, feeling as though he'd caught some of her anxiety.

"What did you tell him?" She chewed her thumbnail, something he hadn't seen her do before. "No, no, I understand. How was he? No, I meant…could you tell if he'd been using?"

Her voice had lowered but of course he was still able to hear everything, and she had to know.

"Good for him." She started to rock, a slow small motion that might be giving her comfort but made him edgy as hell.

It was crazy how much this woman continued to get to him. How many nights had he lain awake trying to figure out what it was about her that had him feeling as if he was running a race without a finish line. He'd tried taking small time-outs since she'd come back. Staying away from the bar, away from her, hoping to get his head straight.

He'd even tried convincing himself to call the pretty blonde he'd met at the Billings auction. She'd given him the green light and two phone numbers. Might've been smart to take her out to dinner, see what happened. Right now, he couldn't even remember her damn name. Hanging around Nikki did that sort of thing to him. Made no sense. Until he'd met her, he even preferred blondes. What was that about?

Clenching his jaw, he noticed the way her shoulders had slumped. She was still rocking, and he wanted to grab the phone from her and stop whatever was making her unhappy. The riding in on a white horse crap wasn't his style, either. He liked things nice and easy. More than once he'd been accused of hiding behind his "trademark smile." Not that he gave a damn. Why mess with something that worked just fine?

"No, Mom, really…I swear you did exactly right. I've got to go, though. Say hi to Edward for me, and I'll talk to you before you leave for Mexico City." She disconnected the call and with a sigh, dropped the phone onto the seat beside her.

"You okay?"

She scooted back, found his arms and pulled them around her as she leaned against his chest. "The clouds are pretty with those streaks of pinkish-orange."

Closing his eyes, he inhaled the floral scent of her hair. His arms rested loosely just below her breasts. She only wanted comfort, and he wanted to give her that but, damn, she wasn't making it easy.

"Trace?"

"Hmm?"

"Thanks for being a friend," she said softly.

He smiled, feeling more than a little deflated, and kissed her hair. Okay, so maybe he'd grown bored of nice and easy. Besides being gutsy, loyal, independent and sweetly vulnerable, Nikki was by far the most complicated woman he'd ever met.

11

Nikki crossed the threshold into the small stone church and froze. God help her, why were there so many people? Most of the pews were filled. Up front was the dark cherry casket Matt had chosen. She'd gone with him to be supportive and agreed on the style while barely sparing a glance. Vases of flowers had been set on either side and in front of a podium.

Lucy, Matt and Rachel had driven together and were already seated in the first pew. Nikki took a deep breath and pulled her shoulders back, ready to make her way down the aisle when she saw the portrait of Wallace. Taken when he was a much younger man, the blown-up head shot sat on an easel to the right of the casket.

That was it for her. She couldn't seem to make her feet move. Vaguely she recalled Matt and Lucy discussing which picture to use, but Nikki hadn't seen it. Not this one, anyway. Her mom had once had a similar photo. She'd kept it in a silver frame she polished every day, sitting on a nightstand in the shabby bedroom she'd shared with Nikki. Right after Nikki started kindergarten the photo had disappeared. Just like the man himself had vanished two years prior.

"Nikki?" Trace touched the small of her back. She looked up at him and he smiled. "Let's find our seats."

She nodded, took the arm he offered, and then leaned on him the whole way to the front pew. Matt stood, kissed her cheek and indicated the seat next to him. She saw the rest of the McAllisters and Hilda sitting directly behind and gave them a shaky smile before sinking down to the hard wooden bench. A moment of panic nearly set her off, but she relaxed when Trace sat on the other side of her and squeezed her hand.

The minister took his place behind the podium and started with a prayer. Nikki had no idea what he was saying. Her goal was to avoid looking at the picture of Wallace. It stirred up too many bad memories. Of course the stupid easel stood only a few feet away. She couldn't even look straight ahead without being aware of Wallace's image. But each time she felt her chest tighten, she squeezed Trace's hand and he squeezed right back. That's all it took to calm her, which in itself should've terrified her.

That, and how since Wallace's death she'd been thinking of him as her father. Before it had been easier to think of him as Matt's father and not hers, or the dying man down the hall. Mostly she realized she'd been better off without Wallace in her life. Matt had been the unlucky one. But somehow she had to get through the service, so she decided to focus her thoughts on Trace...thoughtful, dependable, handsome Trace with his killer smile and big heart. Had she ever encountered someone so unexpected? She didn't think so. She turned her head a little to look at his profile, and met his watchful green eyes. This time he rubbed his palm against hers, creating a pleasant warm friction. Much better than the squeeze.

God, she wanted to feel his arms around her like yesterday when they'd sat quietly watching the clouds turn pink and orange. He'd known exactly what she needed.

The sudden awkward silence might as well have been a gunshot in the dark. Lost in her own thoughts, she had no idea what was going on, or where they were in the service.

Okay, now she was nervous again. She glanced at Trace and saw that he was looking past her and Matt. She turned her head and watched Lucy walk stiffly to the podium. Her hands were as white as the handkerchief she was wringing.

Trace lowered his head and spoke close to Nikki's ear. "No one volunteered to give the eulogy."

Oh. Poor Lucy.

The woman was so small you could see only her face over the podium. Nikki imagined that was fine with Lucy, who noisily cleared her throat, started to speak, then cleared her throat again. After about a minute she mumbled something about knowing Wallace his whole life, then gave in to tears. Matt got up and returned her to the pew.

Nikki bit at her thumbnail, a habit she'd kicked long ago. She didn't want her brother to feel as if he had to say something. It wouldn't be fair. Everyone would know he was lying if he said anything nice. How awful would that be…?

Rachel seemed worried, too, twisting in her seat to look at her family. Probably giving Cole or Jesse the eye.

Trace released her hand and slowly got to his feet. She hadn't noticed the black jeans or that he was wearing a long-sleeved black shirt and his new boots. None of it mattered. But she wasn't thinking very clearly.

He looked nervous standing behind the podium trying to loosen his collar and keeping his gaze high. "You folks out there who went to school with me know how much I *love* being up here," he said, and people laughed. Eyes downcast, he took a deep breath. "Most everyone knows there was bad blood between Wallace and my family, and I'm not going to stand up here and pretend otherwise. We had our differences." He shrugged. "But I'm truly sorry Wallace has passed on. He was too young to die and it's a shame he didn't have more time to get to know the man his son had become or the fine daughter he brought into this world."

Nikki held her breath. Trace was looking at her, and she suspected so was everyone else. She would've died herself right on the spot if not for the affection on Trace's face. Somehow she managed to give him a shaky smile.

"Wallace could be mean when he was drinking, though I heard it from people who knew him back in the day that he wasn't always so ornery. No matter what, the one thing nobody can take away from him is that he produced two exceptional children who will do the Lone Wolf proud and who make our community a better place." He tugged at his collar again. "I guess that's all I got to say."

On his way back to his seat, Matt shook his hand. Then Nikki grabbed it. She didn't say anything since she didn't trust her voice, but the rest of the service seemed to go fast. Half the people showed up at the cemetery. She only went because she felt she had to, though she would've preferred going to the Lone Wolf with Hilda, Rachel and Mrs. McAllister to handle the food.

Trace stuck by her side, then followed her back to the house. She headed straight for the bar that she'd personally stocked yesterday and poured them each a drink. Screw anyone who didn't like it. They were welcome to help themselves.

"What is this?" Trace asked, squinting at the glass.

"Tequila." She held hers up to the light. "I hope."

"Now, that doesn't sound good." He smiled. "You okay?"

"I am now. I can finally breathe again." She took a sip. "You don't drink hard liquor, do you? I can get you a beer."

"This is all right."

Nikki hadn't even gone to the kitchen yet. But she saw the casseroles, roasted chicken and salads already spread out on the dining room table and figured she'd get cleanup duty. Several people she didn't know came up and introduced themselves. Others officially welcomed her to town and extended a blanket invitation to Sunday suppers. Trace was included as if they were a couple. She hoped that hadn't upset him, though if it had, he didn't let on.

She smiled and nodded a lot, even when she didn't understand some of the older people, and just hoped her responses were appropriate.

"Hey, McAllister." A guy walked toward them holding a plate heaped with food and grinning. He was about Trace's age but thick around the middle. "I thought you were gonna shit a brick up there talking in front of everybody."

"I tell you what, Buck. I did just like Mrs. Wilson told us in the ninth grade. Pretend everyone in the audience is naked. If I looked queasy it's because I got to your ugly ass."

Buck laughed. "Hi, Nikki. I met you once at the Watering Hole. You probably don't remember. But I am sorry about your pa."

"Thank you," she murmured, wishing she was better at faking a smile. As soon as Buck left to find a chair, she told Trace, "We're too close to the food. That's why so many people are stopping. Let's move."

He didn't seem to mind the suggestion and hustled them into the empty living room. "There are a lot of folks here. I doubt we'll be alone for long." He brushed the hair off her face. "You look good. I'm glad you're holding up."

"Thanks to you," she said, and he shook his head. "Yes, you. What you did…back at the church…" She swallowed. "Thank you. For all of it. Even though it's not quite over," she said, glancing out the window at the cars coming down the driveway. "I feel as though a big weight has been lifted."

"I'm glad." The tenderness in his smile reached his eyes. "You seem relaxed." Something behind her drew his attention. "There's Sadie. When is she letting you back to work?"

"Oh." Nikki groaned, turning to glare. Not that Sadie noticed. "I'm so mad at her. She's making me wait until day after tomorrow and she won't budge."

"Good."

"Gee, thanks."

"Tomorrow night. You and me, we're going to Kalispell for dinner." Trace snuck in a quick kiss. "And I'm not budging, either."

"Wow, ALL THIS TRAFFIC is making me nervous." Nikki turned to catch the movie listing being flashed on a monitor outside a theater. She didn't recognize the titles, but then she hadn't kept track of new releases since moving to Blackfoot Falls.

Trace was shooting looks at her with one raised eyebrow. "Yeah, okay, so this isn't Houston but a year from now let's see how itchy you get to come get your ya-yas out."

"Ooh, so touchy." She sat back, checking out restaurant signs and the people crowding the sidewalks. "I was kidding. This is fun. Looks like a lot of tourists, though, what's that about?"

"We're close to Glacier National Park, which brings in the summer tourists. In the winter they come to ski Big Mountain. Whitefish Mountain Resort isn't far from here. Neither is Blacktail Mountain Ski Area. I know you didn't get to see enough snow in February. We'll go up there once the resorts open and you'll have your fill."

That was a few months off. Would she even still be in Montana? "Do you ski?"

"No," he said, a hint of regret in his voice. "I thought I'd learn but life seemed to get in the way. Why? You wanna try?"

"Oh, no. Not me. Watching from indoors with a cup of hot chocolate is more my speed." They stopped for a red light, giving Nikki the chance to read a banner strung to a corner post. "They sure have a lot of festivals here. I wouldn't mind coming to one. Have you been?" She watched a couple hurrying to cross the street against the light, then turned to Trace when he hadn't answered.

He was staring at her, a faint smile on his handsome face. His dark hair was as long as she'd seen it, curling at his collar and occasionally falling across his forehead. She was glad he hadn't cut it.

Reaching for her hand, he intertwined their fingers, his callused palm feeling warm and right against hers. His hunter-green Western shirt was brand-new, probably just out of the packaging. She knew for sure because he hadn't ironed out the creases from where it had been folded. The thought made her smile.

Trace brought her hand to his lips and kissed it, lingering to inhale the vanilla-scented body cream she'd rubbed everywhere.

"Have I told you how beautiful you look?"

"Once when you picked me up and twice at dinner." She tried to ignore the heat surging to her cheeks. It had been quite an eye-opener to discover she was more comfortable with Trace teasing and flirting than she was when he got serious and looked dangerously sexy. "But don't let that stop you."

His mouth curved in that same slow patient smile he'd given her across their candlelit table an hour ago. She'd had a glass of wine, something she did only on special occasions. His concession was to drink his beer from a wineglass. That had made her laugh, which she suspected had been the point.

Of all the ridiculous things, her nerves were getting the better of her. She couldn't explain it. She was supposed to be more worldly, more sophisticated and…what was the word… *blasé?* Yeah, that was it. Anyone may have assumed tonight was something she'd done a thousand times. Not give a second thought to having a really hot guy come to her door, take off his hat, kiss her and tell her she looked beautiful. Oh, not just say the words but really mean it, so that she'd see the truth in his eyes.

She'd certainly tried to give the impression of a woman

who'd seen it all when she started at the Watering Hole. And it was partly true. Her fast life in Houston was so different from anything here in Montana, people here wouldn't get it. But right now she was out of her element, and she had the feeling he knew it. The shift in power would've bothered her more if it was anyone but Trace.

He released her hand, slid his arm across the back of her seat and leaned in to her. Their lips barely touched when a horn honked behind them. The light had turned green.

Trace cussed under his breath and hit the accelerator.

Nikki laughed. "What are we doing after the driving tour? Not that I'm not enjoying this."

"I'd planned on checking out what movies are playing, but I don't know..." His gaze started at her exposed shoulders then slid down the front of her strappy sundress. "I should be showing you off."

"Oh, God, there you go being sexist again."

"I know, and I don't care."

She shook her head, faking disgust. The thrilling way he'd practically devoured her with that look trumped political correctness. "Then we should go dancing."

"Um..."

"Relax. I'm kidding." She twisted around for a second look at the fancy hotel they'd passed. So much nicer than the motels she'd seen closer to the highway.

Nikki turned back and faced straight ahead. She couldn't tell if Trace had noticed the hotel or her interest in it. Of course sex was on her mind. And she'd bet her savings he'd been thinking about how tonight they had the perfect opportunity. The heated looks were hint enough. But after throwing herself at him the other night, the subject was still touchy for her.

"You seem restless," he said. "Is there somewhere you wanted to stop?"

Suspicious that he *had* seen her check out the hotel and was teasing her, she studied his profile. He wasn't trying to hold back a smile or anything. "No. Just getting the lay of the land as they say." She sighed, wishing the horn hadn't interrupted their almost kiss. "I haven't had many dates."

He frowned, darted her a glance. "What's that?"

She sighed again. The thought had passed through her mind so many times she wasn't sure she'd meant to say it out loud. "I haven't had many dates. Not the real kind. Like tonight with you picking me up at the house."

"Why not?"

"It wasn't like that in high school." She shrugged. "My friends and I did group things and then sometimes paired off. After graduation I worked nights, even when I went to community college, so I didn't have time for a social life."

"We went out in groups, too. Mostly to football games or rodeos, so I get that. But what about proms or dances or just dinner and a movie?"

Nikki bit her lip. Ten years later and she still cringed just hearing the word *prom*.

"Obviously you think I'm an old-fashioned country boy, and you go right ahead—"

"I don't think that at all. Don't put words in my mouth."

"I see you trying not to laugh." He caught her hand again. "A woman accepts an invitation from me and she's gonna get picked up at her house, and seen to her door at the end of the night."

"Oh, boy, if you ever have daughters their teen years won't be pretty."

He let out a short laugh. "Probably not."

"I like that you're all gentlemanly and chivalrous." She saw the corner of his mouth quirk. "I do. It's nice. I wasn't laughing." She braced herself. "I had a bad prom experience," she said, hoping she was right, that telling Trace would ease the tightness in her chest. "I'd met this boy at the mall when I was fifteen. Garrett was seventeen, a private school kid. His family was loaded. Obviously he didn't live in *my* neighborhood.

"Anyway, he followed me and a girlfriend around, asked for my cell number, tried to buy me lunch. I kept saying no and—" She smiled sadly. "And probably giggled a lot. Garrett was hot and funny and smart, and not what I was used to, so of course I was flattered. Every day for a week he showed up at the food court where we hung out. I have to admit, I looked forward to seeing him. Finally I gave him my number and agreed to go to a movie. The next weekend it was a party and then another party after that. It went on for three months.

"My friend was convinced he was using me, but he'd never pushed me into sex. We made out a lot but nothing too hot and heavy. I mean, I think Garrett really did like me. He even asked me to go to his prom." Taking a breather, she studied the familiar storefronts they were passing. Were they headed back to the highway?

Trace squeezed her hand, then released it to use the turn signal. "I'm still listening," he said quietly.

"His friend heard him ask me and I should've gotten a clue from his shocked face. But I was too excited. I'd seen a dress at the mall, a very expensive dress, and I was already planning the argument I'd give my mom. We couldn't afford it, but I begged and pleaded so I wouldn't feel out of place with all the rich girls. She gave in, then two days before the prom, Garrett called it off. He was still going, but he had to take someone else."

She saw that he was pulling the truck over to the curb. "What are you doing? Don't stop." Part of the reason she was able to talk about it was the situation. Trace had to divide his attention, and somehow that made it easier. "Please."

The helpless uncertainty in his eyes touched her. "All right," he said finally, and returned to the flow of traffic.

"Garrett said he felt terrible. His parents had hired a limo for him, and a photographer to take pictures, and he said he was sorry but they wouldn't understand him taking someone like me to the prom. He had college to consider and didn't want to piss them off." She refused to look for Trace's reaction. "He said nothing had to change between us. He wanted to continue seeing me."

"What a bastard." He spat the words with so much anger she had to look at him. The veins stuck out on his neck.

"It's okay. Jeez, it was so long ago. Anyway, I should've known better. My friends tried to tell me."

"Tell you what?" Now he sounded angry with her friends.

"That I should stick to my own kind, and that Garrett was too class conscious and would eventually kick me to the curb." She laid a hand on his thigh. "I don't think about him anymore. Honestly, I don't. Of course it crushed me at the time. I was only fifteen. In my head Garrett was like Wallace and I was mad at myself for being as stupid and weak as my mother."

Trace shot her a confused look.

"Like I said, I was fifteen. One week my mom was the enemy, the next she was my BFF. I took so much crap out on her." Nikki shuddered at the memories. "What still bothers me is the dress. She busted her butt working overtime to buy it for me. And I couldn't return it because—" Oh, God.

She laid her head back against the headrest watching the thinning crowd. No use admitting she'd been the worst possible self-centered idiot. It wouldn't change anything. Already she'd said too much. Trace was probably disgusted with this new glimpse of her. She was pretty sure they were about to reach the highway that would take them back to Blackfoot Falls.

Her hand still rested on his thigh. She could feel the muscle bunch when he applied the brake. "I wanted you to know how special tonight was for me," she said. "That's why I told you all that. I wish I hadn't gone overboard— I don't know, it felt good to let it out. It's the first time I've told anyone."

"I'm glad it was me." He caught her hand when she tried to pull it away and put it back on his thigh. "Garrett's a damn fool but I can't say I'm sorry he blew it with you," he said as they passed the last two motels on the outskirts of town.

If he had planned on a more intimate night, she'd screwed that up. She'd treated him like a friend, not a lover, and she'd never had a man play both roles in her life. And, dammit, Trace made a really great friend. Although she still wanted to find out if she was right about what kind of lover he'd be. She'd sure thought about it often enough.

She held back a sigh. "Hey, can we listen to some music? Matt said they have radio stations here."

"Yep." Trace turned the knob and a country song blasted from the speakers. He lowered the volume. "We'll have reception for about thirty minutes. Go ahead, find something you like."

Thank God. She was sick of all the country music people played at the bar. After a few seconds of button pushing, she settled on a classic rock station. "This okay with you?" She looked over to find him smiling. "What?"

"I do enjoy your enthusiasm."

She thought for a moment and laughed. "Matt wanted to kill me by the time we reached Blackfoot Falls. On the trip back we had rules about how many times I was allowed to change stations."

Trace's grin widened. "No rules in this truck. Go for it."

"Ah, you really know how to sweet-talk a girl." She turned to face him and curled up in the seat. She wasn't the type to daydream or replay events over and over in her head, not since she was a teenager, anyway. But tonight would live in her memory for a very long time.

They'd been driving awhile when Trace flipped on the interior light and looked over at her.

She blinked. "What are you doing?"

"Getting another eyeful of that dress. Kind of a shame it has to come off," he said, watching her carefully.

Her breath caught. "And that would be…when?"

12

"This isn't how I planned tonight." He shook his head at himself. She was staring at him, looking as confused as he felt. "I want you, Nikki. That's not news, I know. But I swear I had every intention of taking the evening nice and slow…have dinner, show you around…return you to the Lone Wolf…"

"You do realize we left Kalispell a while ago." A small smile lifted her lips and made her eyes sparkle.

"Of course I know." He tried not to sound irritable. "I had to get us out of town before we passed one more damn motel and I did something stupid."

Laughing softly, she scooted closer. "I was really hoping for stupid."

His heart worked overtime. "Yeah?"

Nodding, she slid her palm up his thigh.

He checked the rearview mirror, saw there were no other cars and slowed to make a U-turn.

"Wait."

No way he'd misread her. But he brought the truck to a complete stop and met her eyes.

"Are we closer to Kalispell or Blackfoot Falls?"

"About the same. Maybe five minutes less to get home." He saw where she was headed with this. "No privacy, though."

She stroked his thigh, her heat penetrating the thick denim. The side of her hand brushed his fly, and he gritted his teeth. "Five minutes will seem like forever," she said, leaning over and kissing him. "And I bet we find lots of privacy."

"Not if you want a bed," he said, but he'd already released the brakes and was picking up speed toward Blackfoot Falls.

"You have a blanket in that big cargo box you keep in the back?" She reached up to flip off the light, letting her breast graze his arm.

Trace's laugh came out hoarse. "You're killing me."

"Sorry." Sighing, she laid her head on his shoulder. "Can't this truck go any faster?"

Later he'd be pissed at himself for stepping on the gas and ignoring caution. But right now he was thinking like her. The sooner they got to Blackfoot Falls the better, and he knew the perfect place. Pretty sad that at twenty-seven he'd resort to his high school make-out spot. Though no sense wasting a full moon.

He blasted the radio for a distraction. Then alternated between five and fifteen miles over the speed limit. By the time he turned off the highway and parked the truck, Nikki was pulling his shirt out of his jeans. She attacked the buttons, and man, he thought for sure she'd end up ripping the shirt open. But when he held her face in his hands and kissed her long and slow, her feverish pace settled to a sexy caress.

"You can wait here while I get the blanket and a flashlight from the back." He'd meant to pull away and go do what he said he'd do, but her eagerness was contagious. Barely had he dragged his lips from hers when his craving for more pulled him back for another sweep of her mouth.

She clung to his right shoulder, the tips of her fingers digging into him, her mouth soft and yielding, her exotic scent seeking a permanent nook inside his head. Damned if he knew how he could make himself leave her even for a minute. He cupped a hand over her breast. She wasn't wearing a bra and he felt her hard beaded nipple through the thin fabric.

Her fingers went back to the buttons and she continued where she'd left off, tugging with impatience, her breaths coming fast and hard in his mouth. Fear that he'd end up coming before he peeled off his jeans motivated him to make the break.

"Nikki, wait. Let me get us set up."

"I can't wait," she whispered, pushing his shirt off one shoulder and pressing her lips against his skin.

"I'm in the same boat, honey," he murmured, his body so tense he thought he might have to physically remove her to a safe distance. Her hand lowered to his fly. "Dammit, Nikki."

"Okay." She slumped back. "Hurry."

Leaving on the headlights, he fumbled with the door handle, cussing while she laughed. He waited until he was outside the truck before he looked at her. Nikki stared back, her moist lips glistening, her face flushed with need. "Your dress…don't take it off yet." He couldn't decide if he wanted to do the honors, or lie back and watch her strip down in the moonlight.

Her lips moved in a teasing smile. "You sure?"

"No." Barely intelligible, the strangled sound seemed to come from his throat. "Just…just leave it on for now."

He found the blanket, then remembered the flashlight was in his glove box. It didn't matter. The moon was bright and the sky cloudless. He inspected the tall grass, kicked away a couple rocks, then shook out the blanket. Crouching, he ran his palm over the wool to make sure nothing hard lay underneath, wishing he were about to make love to her on a soft bed with silk sheets.

Maybe he should've insisted they return to Kalispell. He should've taken a minute to make sure it was his brain doing the thinking. He didn't want to get this wrong. Nikki deserved to feel special. She'd nearly torn his heart out telling him about the prom incident and that prick Garrett.

He was straightening when he heard the car door. She stepped out and walked over to him. "I thought you'd started without me," she said, grinning and kicking her strappy black high heels onto the blanket.

"I like those." Nodding at the sandals, he loosened his buckle. "I like them a lot."

"You would. They're ridiculously high and pinch my feet."

"So why wear 'em?"

Nikki wrinkled her nose. "I knew you'd like them," she said, looking small and fragile in her bare feet. Her sudden burst of laughter had a nice sound to it, lusty and full of humor, and she wasn't the least self-conscious.

So far that's what he'd liked most about the night. Their relationship had reached a new level. Knowing she was comfortable enough with him to share a part of herself gave him a quiet pleasure he scarcely understood. It wasn't easy for a woman like her to let her guard down and trust she wouldn't be burned.

"What's that expression for?" Her smile slipped. "I was loud, I know." She shivered, her dark eyes sweeping a gaze toward the trees that flanked them on the right. "I hope I didn't attract a bunch of critters."

"Just one." He reached for her and tugged her close.

A warm gentle breeze stirred her hair as she tipped her head back to look up at him. "I love tonight. I love everything about it." She wound her arms around him. "And as much as I'm beginning to like Gypsy, I'm glad she stayed home."

"I wondered if you recognized the place."

"Of course I do. We kissed here for the first time."

Trace smiled. Damn sentimental coming from her. "We have a lot more to do than kissing." He skimmed his hand down her back, molded his palm and fingers over her firm round bottom. "After tonight, I suspect this place will deserve its own monument."

"Wow, that's pretty cocky."

"Hell no, I'm counting on you to do your part."

Her throaty laugh had him searching for her zipper. He found the tab and carefully drew it down her back. She did a little shimmy that helped him pull the snug-fitting dress up to her waist, then she raised her arms. His heart raced and his pulse was going nuts as he lifted the dress over her head. She stood there in nothing but tiny black panties.

He rearranged the long dark hair swirling around her shoulders so that he could see all of her. She had amazing skin, the slight golden color, the silky texture, her dusky rose nipples flushed with arousal... She was so beautiful he couldn't breathe. "God, Nikki."

"Come on, Trace," she said, putting her hands on his chest where his shirt hung open. She slid them up over his ribs and pecs and shoved the fabric off his shoulders.

He shrugged out of the shirt while she unzipped his fly, his short jerky movements hindering rather than speeding things along. "Wait," he said when she started tugging down his jeans. "I gotta get rid of the boots first."

"I'm not waiting." Her impatient hands were everywhere. But it was the one she was trying to slide into his boxers that would be his undoing.

"Okay, if that's how you want to play it." He took her shoulders and turned her around, ignoring her gasp, and forcing her to lean back against his chest and thighs. Banding an arm across her ribs, he held her in place and slipped his free hand inside her panties.

A FIERCE JOLT of longing rocked Nikki against his probing fingers. "What are you doing?" A moan punctuated her protest. His mouth was near her ear, his warm breath gliding over her sensitive skin. She clutched his forearm, intending to force him to let go, but all she did was hang on.

"You're so wet," he murmured, his voice a gravelly whisper, and then he was kissing the side of her neck and if he said anything else she couldn't hear, not when his fingers circled and plunged and made it hard for her to breathe.

She had the vague thought that she should make him stop. Need burned too hot inside her and it had been so long since she'd been with a man. And to make things worse and better at the same time, this was Trace.

God, he had great hands. She leaned back against his strong chest and closed her eyes, moaning when he cupped the weight of her breast. It took her a moment to realize that with both hands busy he was no longer trapping her body against his. But as soon as she tried to move, he released her breast and again banded his arm across her ribs. His fingers between her thighs hadn't let up even a little.

"Let me take your jeans off," she said, her voice a notch above a whisper.

In answer he intensified the pressure of his circling thumb on just the right spot to keep her submissive. The strength to argue was slipping away, replaced with an overwhelming need to let him take her to that surreal place where she couldn't think. Only feel the amazing things he was doing to her body. And knowing that if her weakened knees gave out, Trace was a man she could count on. He would never let her fall.

His sure and unrelenting fingers hit a new plateau, and the sound that escaped her lips was more whimper than moan. Heat surged through her, melting her bones and willpower and the last of her resistance.

"Come on, baby, let go," Trace whispered. "I've got you." His warm lips moved over her skin, down the side of her neck and brushed her shoulder.

She quivered, knowing it was coming, any second…any second…any…

Her climax hit with such force she rocked back against him. Still he wouldn't let up on the pressure. He tightened his hold around her middle, his other hand anchored between her thighs, his fingers steady and determined as the most breathtaking sensation rippled through her. Each new wave of pleasure pulled her in deeper, surrounding her in a soft sensual fog and threatening to rob her of air.

His breathing came as fast as hers, racing over her fevered skin, making her want more and more. Wanting him to share the same dizzying experience. She was still weak but able to stand on her own. He didn't fight her when she pried his arm away from her body, then moved her hips to disengage his fingers. She spun to face him and saw the desire burning hot in his eyes. She had the distinct feeling her stamina would be tested tonight. Well, she planned on testing his right back.

She went for his jeans again, but Trace seemed set on kissing her. He used his tongue to part her lips, then slipped inside her mouth and palmed her left breast. Nikki managed to shove his jeans down to the lower section of his thighs, and then she remembered his boots. That's what had tripped them up the first time.

Her patience was gone. She broke away. "Sit down."

"In a minute," he murmured, trying to capture her mouth again.

She turned her head, but that didn't stop him. He settled for kissing her jaw. "Now," she ordered, then gasped when he sucked in her nipple. She let him have his way for a few more seconds because, God, it felt so good. Then she lowered herself to the blanket and he followed her down.

"Boots," she said, shoving him away when he tried to lay her back. She grabbed one, and he tugged off the other boot.

After that it was easy to strip him of his jeans. She reached for his black boxers at the same time he tried to pull off her panties. They got tangled up for a second and started laughing, though neither of them would give in and let go. Finally they were both naked, and Nikki just stared at him.

How could he be so perfect? From the breadth of his shoulders to the thickness and length of his erection, to the ridges of muscle in his thighs and calves. She wanted him to stand up so she could get a better look. And his ass…she'd already felt it through the denim and knew it was perfect, too. She still wanted to see.

"I don't suppose you'd want to get up and twirl around for me?" she said, grinning at how his brows shot up.

"Not as long as you're willing to reciprocate." His slow sexy smile distracted her.

She jerked at the feel of his hand sliding between her thighs. Clamping her legs together she stopped him from going any further. "Condoms? We should be ready."

"Right here." He reached behind to his jeans and produced a packet.

"Wow, you're good. I didn't even see you—" She'd forgotten about his hand. The startling invasion of his fingers made her tremble. She bit down on her lip, too hard, but at least it brought her to her senses. "No," she said, wiggling backward. "Not yet."

She came up on her knees and pushed on his shoulders, forcing him to lie back. He wouldn't go down all the way, but braced himself on his elbows and watched her. She didn't care. She had what she wanted. With the tip of her finger she lightly traced the hard silken length of his cock, then circled the crown. It leaped at her touch.

"This isn't gonna work." His voice was hoarse and his expression strained. His body had tightened, so that it seemed every muscle across his belly and down his thighs was clearly defined.

"Seems to be working just fine." Nikki gave him a light squeeze then stroked upward.

His laugh turned into a groan. He briefly closed his eyes and clenched his jaw. Then he let out a slow exhale. "I'm serious."

"About?" She took her time exploring, grateful for the bright moonlight, and ignoring his low moans, the occasional hiss. She already knew from the day he was at the Lone Wolf that his belly, shoulders and back were as tan as his forearms and face. He obviously worked a lot without a shirt. But now she also knew exactly how low he wore his jeans. The tan stopped two inches below his belly button. Still, he wasn't lily-white, and she wondered if the McAllisters had Native American blood in them.

"Nikki." He grabbed her wrist and moved her hand away while raising himself to a sitting position.

"I'm not done."

Curling his fingers around her nape, he pulled her face toward his until he'd claimed her lips. The kiss wasn't rough but neither was it anywhere close to gentle. It felt to Nikki as if a fair amount of restraint was required for him to keep himself in check.

With his other hand, he found her breast and toyed with the nipple. She was sensitive there, always had been, but Trace doing the touching made her tremble like a butterfly caught in a windstorm. He switched to her other breast, then kissed his way down from her chin to her collarbone to the nipple he'd abandoned. She watched him take the pearled tip into his mouth, sucking greedily for a few seconds, then lightly flicking it with his tongue.

She let her eyes drift closed and arched against him. "I want you inside me," she whispered.

His fingers tightened on her neck, the slight pressure an amazing turn-on, even as his mouth stilled. She could feel his breath, though, warm and moist and seductive, skimming her hypersensitive flesh. He pressed a final kiss to her breast, released her neck and urged her to lie back.

He knelt beside her to tear open the packet, recoiling when she touched his erection. "Not a good idea."

"Really?"

His laugh came out shaky. "Really." He sheathed himself, then spread her legs farther apart.

She wanted to touch him so very badly but the desperate need to feel him hot and throbbing inside her won out. He positioned himself between her thighs, running his hands along the outside all the way to her calves, catching an ankle and bending her leg. He paused to kiss the tender skin just above her knee, and her impatience flared.

Yes, it felt good, but she wanted him pushing inside and filling her to the hilt. The need was so great it was crazy, completely irrational, igniting sparks of both longing and panic she didn't understand.

He pulled her legs around his waist, and she lifted her hips and clutched two fistfuls of the wool blanket. The big bright moon was behind him so she couldn't see his face. It didn't seem fair that he could see hers.

"God, look at you," he murmured, and teased her opening with his cock. He'd barely dipped inside when he leaned back again.

"Dammit, Trace."

"Don't you want this to last?"

"No. Later, yes." She probably wasn't making any sense. Too bad. "Now, no. Come on. Please."

He moaned her name and plunged inside her. The force behind his entry shocked her even though it was exactly what she wanted. She couldn't catch her breath. Couldn't form the words to tell him to keep going when he slid partway out. But he knew and pushed back in, slower now, but just as deep.

She tightened her legs around him, clenched his cock, daring him to withdraw.

Trace shuddered. "I can't hold back."

"I don't want you to."

He surprised her by pulling out. The next thrust nearly rocked her senseless. She let go of the blanket. It wouldn't help her. Instead she clung to him, lifting her hips to meet each thrust, the fire raging inside her growing out of control.

"Open your eyes, Nikki," he whispered, still gripping her hips, but the pressure of his fingertips easing.

She lifted her lashes. Even though his face was in shadow, she sensed he was staring into her eyes. The thrusts had subsided, too, but he was still moving inside her as he lowered his head and kissed her parted lips. At this new angle, his erection sent a jolt of sensation that shimmered through her entire body.

Trace stopped moving. The earthy cry that exploded from his throat raced along her nerve endings. It seemed impossible that she could be triggered by a sound, but the climax that washed over her was stunningly real. So was the hot openmouthed kiss consuming her.

It struck her as funny that he could be kissing her with this much hunger, as if she was the first woman he'd encountered after being celibate for a year. She knew that wasn't true.

He lifted his head. "You're laughing?"

"No. Uh-uh." She bit her lip. "Just a little."

After a long silence, he said, "I'm gonna need some serious therapy."

"No, you don't." Nikki giggled and hugged him. "I'm not laughing at *that* part."

Bracing himself on one elbow, he tenderly brushed aside the strands of hair that clung to her cheek. "Will I hate myself for asking?"

She heard the smile in his voice and decided she needed to see his face. "Roll over," she said, giving him a gentle shove.

He did, and took her with him.

Soft moonlight lit his features. Much better. Sighing happily, she stacked her hands on his chest, rested her chin on them and stared into his darkened eyes. "Am I too heavy?"

"Not even a tiny bit."

"Good answer." She shivered when he cupped her backside with his large calloused hands. He looked serious. "What are you thinking about?"

A faint smile curved his mouth. "I knew from the get-go that you, Nikki Flores, were gonna be a heap of trouble."

13

"WHAT DID YOU DREAM about, Nikki?" Trace asked out of the blue. He shifted his gaze from the glowing moon and stars shining against the dark sky to her face. "When you were a kid, what did you want to be or do?"

She lay beside him on the blanket, both of them looking up at the stars, completely naked. Her left palm was pressed to his right palm, their fingers intertwined. "When I was really little, like second or third grade, I wanted to be an astronaut."

"A what?"

"Hey. It could've happened."

"I'm sure you could be anything you set your mind to. It just wasn't what I expected, is all."

"Remember I lived in Houston. NASA wasn't far and was always in the news. Turns out I didn't really want to be an astronaut," she admitted. "I thought if I had a big important job, then my father would love me."

Trace touched her cheek. "He didn't even deserve you."

She smiled, shrugging. "I guess every kid with divorced parents or who was abandoned has an 'if only' version floating around in their heads. It's no big deal."

"I reckon you're right. Even after my dad died I kept thinking if only I hadn't argued with him over that stupid dance…"

"You don't still go there, do you?"

"No, not for a long time. We had a great relationship and I focus on that."

She squeezed his hand. "Look at my poor brother. After all he went through he never completely let go of wanting to please Wallace. In February Matt found a stack of articles going back to the beginning of his rodeo career. They were hidden in Wallace's desk, but did he have the decency to say a word to Matt?"

Nikki breathed in the fresh Montana air, unwilling to let the old man ruin her night. He was gone and couldn't hurt them anymore. Unless she allowed it.

Trace shifted so that he could put an arm around her, providing a nice comfy spot for her head to lay on his shoulder.

"You know what, though…? I scored because I ended up with having Matt for a brother. I'd trade a father for him any day."

"Matt's a good guy. I'm glad for both you and my sister." He kissed her hair, then smiled at her. "I'm not doing too badly, either."

He did look happy.

But for how long?

The unwelcome thought sneaked in before she could block it. Tonight was about tonight, and that was it. One brief moment in the whole scheme of things. They'd had sex, so what? She'd only hurt herself if she started confusing hormones and unjustified feelings for Trace with a future that would magically fall into place.

"So," he said, "once you nixed the rocketing into space thing, what then? What did little Nikki have a hankering for?"

She sighed. "Little naive Nikki woke up and figured out dreaming was for fools or people who had time and money to spend."

"Come on now, you don't mean that."

"I do," she said with a laugh, mainly to tone down her pessimistic words. "What about you? What haunted your dreams?"

"Haunted, huh?" He rested a cupped hand on her breast. Somehow instead of being suggestive, it was a casual, comfortable touch. Still, it made her pulse race. "In eighth grade," he said, "I decided I wanted to go to college and study modern ranching techniques."

"Did you?" she asked, and he shook his head. "Why not? Rachel and Jesse went."

"Lack of money and bad timing."

She pulled back to look at him, then found a position lying on her side that made it easier to watch his face. The Sundance was the second largest ranch in the county. The Lone Wolf beat them by only a hundred acres. She'd figured the new dude ranch operation was helping to bring in cash, but mostly to avoid layoffs while times were tough. At least that had been her assumption. It was hard to imagine the McAllister family having serious money problems. Severe enough that Trace couldn't afford school.

"What do you mean by bad timing?" She decided to lead with the less touchy issue.

"After Jesse finished college he joined the air force. None of us expected that. My father had passed away two years earlier and Cole was running the ranch. He did a hell of a job. I helped as much as I could but I was still wet behind the ears. Man, I would've felt like shit taking off for college and leaving him to shoulder everything. I figured I still had time, even if I had to wait until Jesse got out of the military." He lifted a thick lock of her hair, then watched it sift through his fingers and fall behind her shoulder.

She thought the gesture sweet until she realized he was simply preserving his view of her bare breast. It made her smile.

"What?"

"Nothing." She scooted closer and rested her hand on his waist. "And?"

"Rachel was coming up behind me and I knew she was itching to go to that fancy college in Dallas. Tuition wasn't cheap, although we didn't have money problems back then. Several years later, yeah, big hurdle. But nearly everyone around here was in the same fix, and we're still meeting payroll so no complaints from me."

"Except Jesse is home now and you should be able to go to school if you want."

"Money is still tight. Anyway, no point in learning about a bunch of new techniques we don't have the financial resources to implement. Maybe someday." He shrugged a shoulder. "I read a lot and try to keep up on what's out there or what might be coming down the chute. Let everybody else be guinea pigs."

She hated that he'd been held back, and was stunned to learn the McAllisters weren't the family of power and means she'd imagined. They'd compromised and worked their butts off so their hired hands could keep their jobs. She liked them all the more.

"By the way…" Trace let the backs of his fingers trail over her breast. Her nipple's instant response made his mouth curve in a smile. "Don't say anything about my wanting to go to college to anybody. No need kicking up dust for nothing."

"Doesn't your mom or any of your family know?"

"Nope. I was a pretty decent student. I got mostly B's, though, not like Rachel and Jesse. My mom was still mourning my dad, and I think she figured I was more like Cole and didn't have a head for school."

"You must've mentioned it at some point."

He leaned closer and tongued her nipple. They'd already made love twice in the three hours since returning from Kalispell. Trace had been quick to inform her he had a third condom in his glove box. She knew he wanted to distract her, but he also wanted her, period. No hiding that fact with his hard-on swelling hot and thick between them.

She touched him, hadn't yet wrapped her fingers around his penis when he jerked back.

"Careful now, honey, or we'll be heading for that finish line too soon again."

"We?" Nikki laughed. "You're like a teenager. You can't hold back for one—" She gasped at the speed with which he spread her legs and positioned himself between them.

He pressed soft warm kisses just under her belly button, down to the narrow strip of hair left from her Brazilian wax.

"Hey." Ordering herself not to react, she arched off the blanket anyway. "We were talking."

"Go right ahead." He slid a hand under her butt and lightly squeezed.

She tried to grab a fistful of hair but missed. He'd moved out of reach, trailing his lips lower, inserting a finger to test how slick she'd grown. He lifted his head, and her groan turned into a laugh at his self-satisfied smirk. "What are you doing?"

His gaze moved to her breasts. Looking like a kid who'd been told not to touch the hot stove but couldn't seem to help himself, he rubbed his thumb over her nipple. "You haven't figured it out yet?"

"I know *what* you're doing. What I want to know is— Oh." She jumped at the intimate swipe of his tongue.

Trace licked his way back up to her lower belly and smiled. "I'm gonna go so slow you'll be begging me to hurry."

It was after four by the time Trace drove her to the house. The foyer lamp had been left on, as well as the porch light. Matt's room was completely dark. He normally didn't stay up too late, though she doubted he ever fell asleep before she got home from the Watering Hole. She wondered if he'd been listening for her tonight.

Trace surprised her by cutting the engine. She'd been ready to jump out and dash inside before the hands' two Border collies started barking.

"I'm not making out with you in front of the house," she said, barely able to keep a straight face.

"You don't think I could get you to do that if I wanted?"

Her startled laugh came out much too loud and she covered her mouth. "You cocky bastard."

"Come here." He reached for her, catching an arm and pulling her toward him.

"Oh, no. You don't even get a good-night kiss for that."

He settled for holding her hand. "We should talk."

Her heart nose-dived. "About?"

"How we should handle our relationship."

Relationship. She turned the word over in her mind. They'd had sex, and yes, it was really great sex. The best she'd ever had, and she hoped for more of it. But that didn't mean anything had changed between them.

"I'm not sure how open you want to be about us," he said. "There are things to consider."

"I'm not going to take out an ad in the *Salina Gazette* and announce I had sex with you, if that's what you're worried about."

"Nikki." He looked shocked, his hand tightening around hers. "Did I really give you that impression?"

"No. I'm sorry." She sighed. "I promise we aren't pulling anything over on Matt. I doubt he thinks we've been playing checkers all night. Personally, I don't care that he knows we've had sex."

For a moment she thought Trace might've flinched slightly. He continued to study her, his expression troubled. The silence kept growing, and she didn't know how to fill it. He hadn't released her hand but whether he did or not, in a second she was getting out of the truck.

"I'll talk to Matt later," he said, finally. "Tell him it was my fault…that I kept you out late."

"You will not. I can't believe you—Matt is my brother, not my guardian. For God's sake, Trace, I'm twenty-five." She really wanted to throw something. "I can handle my own life. God," she said through gritted teeth.

Trace just sat there as the furrow in his brow deepened. "That came out wrong. I only meant that I don't want him thinking that anyone saw us, or— Look, this is a small town, people talk. He should know we were careful. That's all I'm saying."

"Careful about what? Are you worried about my reputation?"

"Well, yeah. You know how bad the gossip can be."

She breathed in deeply. First, he talked about a relationship, and now he cared if anyone had seen them? That didn't even make sense. She might be Matt's sister, but everyone knew she wasn't like him.

Though she *would* prefer not to be thought of as just another notch on Trace's belt once he moved on, but if that happened… "If there's gossip, I'll deal with it."

"Just you? On your own?"

She nodded. "Seriously. Don't worry about it. I can take the heat."

"Honey, do you regret what we did tonight?"

"No. Not at all." Nikki sighed. "I really don't. I just hope things don't change between us."

Trace stayed silent for a long time. He'd turned his head so that he could stare out the windshield and into the darkness.

"Hey," she said, and he turned back. "If we hook up again,

we hook up again. If we don't, that's okay." She shrugged. "That's all."

If he'd seemed confused before, now he looked pissed. "What?"

"Nothing. You seem to have figured it all out." He pushed his hand through his hair. "Look, you're strong and independent and I admire that about you. I have no doubt you can handle your life just fine. But that doesn't mean I'll sit on my thumbs and not want to have your back. If it makes it easier letting Matt know what's what, then I want to be there."

Again, she didn't know what to say. With the exception of her mother and now Matt, no one had ever had her back. Not in the way Trace meant. It seemed hard to believe he was sincere, but everything from the way he looked at her to the care he took when he held her said he was.

That didn't mean she thought he'd still be knocking on her door next week. "Fine."

"Damn right it's fine." He cupped her chin and looked into her eyes. "Tell me you wouldn't be there for me."

"Of course I would," she murmured, still not sure how to take this. She'd expected him to be the one to make it clear there were no strings attached. In her experience guys tended to do that after they got what they wanted. Maybe their friendship made things different.

She'd never been friends with a guy before. Garret had been concerned with his own reputation, not hers. And the others? She doubted if they'd ever given it one thought. All Trace did was confuse her. "I'd better get inside before the dogs start barking." She lifted the handle, but before she could get out, Trace had come around to her side.

"What?"

"You couldn't wait and let me get the door for you?"

Nikki grinned. "First you say sexist things about showing me off and then you want to open the door for me."

"At least I'm consistent." That damn smile of his. He slid his arms around her, apparently unconcerned that the porch light was shining on them. "I want that good-night kiss."

She glanced at the dark bunkhouse. "So much for not sparking any gossip."

"Yeah," he said, pulling away a bit. He rubbed her back, brushed a quick kiss on the tip of her nose. "About that…I sure can try to keep us low-key, but it means I'd have to stay away from the Watering Hole." His gaze dropped to her mouth. "Although I don't see me pulling it off for more than an hour."

"A whole hour, huh?" Nikki was getting pretty good at appearing cool, except for her traitorous sprinting pulse. "You better not be using me to discourage all those women from chasing after you."

"Using you? You know better." He tipped her chin up. "Gotta admit, though, that's a nice bonus." He looked at her as if kissing her this very instant was the most important thing in his whole life. But he held back. For her. When he let go of her hand to step away, she grabbed on to his shirtsleeve.

"Wait." Why she had the sudden urge to confess, she didn't know. But she had to tell him about the prom dress. She had to say it out loud because remembering had triggered old shame that started eating at her on the way home. And Trace was her friend, right? She hoped he wouldn't judge. If he did, well, still better to let him see her for who she was. "I have something to tell you."

He nodded, his gaze narrowing slightly.

"That dress…the one my mom bought me for the prom. It cost so much, I had no business asking for it in the first place." She paused to swallow. "I'd picked it up from the store just before Garrett cancelled on me. I should've turned around right then and gotten a refund. But I was furious and hurt and I wasn't thinking."

She shook her head, amazed that the pain of that day felt

so fresh. Almost as crippling as her shame. "I missed the bus and had to walk home. The dress was wrapped in plastic but I'd dragged it a mile before I saw that the hem had been completely ruined. My mother had worked so many hours so she could get me that dress."

Staring at him, she let out a pent-up breath. Well crap, confessing hadn't felt as freeing as she'd hoped. Probably because he didn't really understand what it had been like for her and her mother back then. Which was made more clear by his helpless shrug.

"Hey, fifteen. That's a tough age. Everybody messes up when they're fifteen."

"But I hurt my mom, the only one who's always been there for me. What kind of person does that?"

"A teenager." He'd gone back to rubbing her back. "Feel better getting it off your chest?"

"I'm not sure," she said, still off balance and mentally scrambling to pull herself back on track.

Trace talked as if what she'd done was nothing. Like skipping a class or not returning a library book. He'd implied there would be more between them. He'd used the word *relationship,* although she'd have to ask him what he meant by that. Later. Because she wasn't certain she wanted to know yet. There was a part of her that wanted to pretend that the look in his eyes was full of promises he'd keep. But that couldn't be true. She wasn't some delicate flower. She'd never be that. No matter where she lived, or how clean her slate was supposed to be.

"Come on," he said. "Let's get you to the door. I've kept you out way past your bedtime." His arm was around her back as he led her up the steps. "Besides, if we get close enough to the door, I don't think anyone could see me steal one more kiss."

She didn't object. And when he kissed her in the shadows,

she kissed him back. But instead of getting swept away by the kiss, an unpleasant thought occurred to her. Had she really needed to tell him about the dress? Or was she trying to sabotage the best thing that had ever happened to her? It didn't matter, though.

Whatever this was between them would come to an end sooner or later. Given her experiences, she'd bet on sooner.

TRYING TO WAKE UP, Nikki stared at the coffee carafe, watching the brew drip, and yawning as if she hadn't slept in a month. The clock taunted her, claiming it was one-thirty in the afternoon, but her poor tired body and pounding head swore it was the middle of the night. That was more accurate since she hadn't fallen asleep until after seven.

As soon as there was enough coffee brewed, she filled a mug before returning the carafe to the fancy chrome station so it could finish the job. She savored the first sip, convinced there wasn't enough caffeine in the house to get her moving faster.

Naturally tonight she had to work. With it being her first day back since Wallace had died, she hoped people gave her space. She didn't need it because of his death, but she was bound to be cranky from too little sleep.

"Hey, you made coffee." Matt entered the kitchen from outside. She hadn't even heard the door. "You just get up? Late night?" He tried to look innocent, but she saw the corners of his mouth quirk up.

"Not particularly." She wasn't volunteering a damn thing.

He brought a mug out from the upper cabinet, then opened the fridge. "We have to talk about Lucy."

"What about her?"

"Did she say anything to you about staying on here?"

"Oh." Nikki saw why he'd brought up the subject. The refrigerator shelves were sparse. "No, but I think she would've talked to you before me."

"The past few days seemed to fly by. I don't know if she needs the money or would rather quit working."

"I can run to town and pick up groceries." She noticed the wood floor needed sweeping. God, she hoped Lucy stayed on. It was a big house. "I'll sweep and dust later. Right now coffee isn't optional."

"I won't be surprised if she wants out. She's getting up there in years and I wouldn't want her doing too much. If she's ready to retire we'll find someone to come in a couple times a week."

Nikki leaned a hip against the counter. "I'll chip in to cover the cost."

"No, you won't. A housekeeper's salary comes out of the ranch fund. It's half yours, anyway."

"I'm not arguing with you over the Lone Wolf again. I don't want anything from Wallace."

"Don't be so damn hardheaded." Matt set down his mug with a thud. "This place was never Wallace's to give. How many more times do I have to explain the Gunderson trust fund to you?"

"None." Nikki topped off her coffee. She was going to the living room to drink it in peace.

"Fine. I'll let the attorney spell out the terms for you. Maybe he can get through that thick skull of yours."

"Good luck with that." She had no intention of being railroaded into going to an attorney's office.

"Tomorrow morning I'm flying to Dallas. Just overnight. I'll be back by noon the following day. Mr. Kessler will meet us here at 4:00 p.m. to read the will."

She sighed. So much for refusing to go to the attorney's office. "Wait." She stopped at the door and turned. "Did you say Dallas?" she asked, and he nodded. "For a rodeo?"

"No. Not until next month. I'm meeting with a guy who breeds champion bulls. The Lone Wolf is doing fine for now but we have to keep our eye on the future."

Ranch business wasn't on her mind. Having the house to herself overnight? Different story. "Sounds like a short trip. Are you sure you won't need to stay longer?"

"You're not afraid to stay here alone, are you?" Matt didn't bother to hide his grin. "I'm sure Trace wouldn't mind baby-sitting."

"Oh, shut up." She left the kitchen smiling, too, thinking how it would've been just like this ten years ago had they known each other. He would've teased her all the time, and she wouldn't have liked it. She did now.

She headed for the privacy of the living room, one hand searching her jeans' pocket for her phone. This was awesome. If she could get Sheila or Gretchen to work for her tomorrow night, it would be even more perfect.

"Nikki?" Matt had followed her as far as the foyer. "Don't forget our appointment with Mr. Kessler. He's driving in from Kalispell."

"No reason for me to be here."

"You're specifically named in his will."

She fisted her hand around the cell phone. "I already told you…I don't want anything from that man."

"Fine. Whatever he's left you, give it to charity. I don't care." He raked a hand through his hair and heaved a tired sigh. "Just be here on Wednesday."

14

TRACE OPENED HIS EYES, stretched out his arms while arching his back, then rolled over and cussed a blue streak when he saw the digital clock. How could it be 1:40 in the morning?

"Son of a bitch."

He jumped out of bed and grabbed the clean pair of jeans he'd left on his dresser. Before he pulled them on he figured he'd better make a pit stop and ducked into his attached bathroom. He'd showered and changed his boxers earlier after quitting work for the day. Dark stubble covered his jaw and chin but he'd purposely left shaving for the last minute.

His razor wasn't where it should be. That's right. He'd abandoned it where he stood this morning the instant he remembered to replace the condoms in his wallet, just before he'd had to haul his ass to work. He found the razor next to the tube of hand lotion he'd bought to help with his calluses. Then grabbed the can of shaving cream and was about to lather up when it finally hit him. He was rushing for nothing. The Watering Hole was closed and Nikki would've driven home by now. She could be sound asleep at this point.

Part of him hoped she was since she'd told him she hadn't gone to bed until seven this—well, yesterday—morning. The selfish part still wanted to curse and punch walls. How could he have overslept? He'd even set the alarm. Yeah, right, getting only three hours after dropping her off had nothing to do with it.

After supper he'd lain down for a two-hour nap, mostly because Nikki had made him promise. Her concern hadn't been misplaced. He'd spent a good portion of the day branding, a job he disliked when he wasn't tired. Today had been a mother, chasing and wrestling calves until he couldn't tell where one ache in his back ended and the next one started. It would've been irresponsible of him to drive to town that exhausted. But he'd wanted to see her. He still did, but he wouldn't be a jerk about it.

Maybe he could at least call her. If she was asleep her phone would be off or charging. If not, he could explain why he hadn't shown up. Though she'd practically begged him to stay home and hit the sack early. Tomorrow Matt would be in Dallas and they had the whole house to themselves. He grinned just thinking about how excited she'd sounded when she told him. It had been kind of a relief. Nikki wasn't always easy to read.

That conversation in the car when he'd dropped her off had played and replayed every minute he'd had a breather. He hated her casual talk of hooking up, how she'd been so determined he knew she didn't want anything serious.

He'd been hoping for more. It still bothered him that he hadn't said as much. But damn, how could he when he wasn't certain what he meant by *more*?

Oh, in his head he was real clear he didn't want her seeing anyone else, and that he only had eyes for Nikki. But coming right out and asking her to be his girlfriend? That was tricky. Especially when so much was going on in her life.

Then there were his own doubts. She wasn't like anyone he'd ever known. Feisty as a wild colt, cagey about her feelings, and so damn beautiful it made him ache. She intrigued him as much as she rattled him. The combination had never been on his wish list, but now that he'd met her, other women had started fading into the background.

Maybe he should be more worried about himself and all the weird feelings he was experiencing but couldn't understand. And maybe he wasn't anxious to look too closely, either. Hell, he was only twenty-seven. Too young to be getting serious about a woman. Cole and Jesse had waited until they were in their thirties...

Screw it. He grabbed his phone off the dresser and hit speed dial. He had to try. Even if only to hear her voice. He'd lost track of the number of rings but was prepared to leave a message when she answered.

"Hey," she said. "You should be asleep."

"I was. I even set the alarm, then slept through it."

"Good."

"Thanks." He smiled at her sigh, then used his free hand to stack the pillows against the headboard of his king bed.

"You know what I meant so stop it."

"Sounds like you had a pleasant night at work."

"It was okay. A few customers mentioned the funeral or apologized for not coming, but overall it wasn't bad. I'm feeling icky about tomorrow night. I called Sheila, but she has plans and can't cover for me. I even called Gretchen, totally forgetting that she's pregnant. Can you believe that? I felt like an ass."

"Yeah, I believe it." Still in his boxers, he crawled into bed and lay back against the stacked pillows. "Today I almost branded Josh instead of a calf. He'll be telling that story for a while."

Nikki laughed. "I can't wait for tomorrow. I wish you were here now."

"Me, too. Want me to try climbing up to your bedroom window?"

"Um, you have experience doing that sort of thing?"

"No," he drawled out the word. "Not me. I'd rather charm my way in." His teasing was met with a long stretch of silence. "You know I'm joking, right?"

"Yes." She tried to brush it off with a laugh, but he knew he'd hit a nerve.

Trace scrubbed at his face. She'd seen him casually flirting with the guests, or more like humoring them when they flirted because lately he hadn't been into that whole thing. And God only knew what kind of stories she'd heard about him from Sam or any of the other guys who hung out at the Watering Hole. They could've said something jokingly not knowing it mattered. "You haven't told me what Matt said about our late night. He seem cool with it?"

She let out an exasperated sigh, which oddly made her sound more relaxed. "He asked if I needed you to babysit me while he's in Dallas."

Trace chuckled, relieved Matt could joke about it. "I guess we can assume Rachel knows, too. Unless you asked him to keep it quiet."

"I didn't say anything." She hesitated. "You could come over right now and spend the night and I wouldn't care who saw you. Rachel does it all the time. The only reason I won't let you is that you need your sleep."

He swung his legs out of bed, glancing at the clock, knowing he could be there by 2:10 a.m., five minutes later if he shaved first. "I got lots of sleep. Almost six hours."

"Not enough. I plan on totally wearing you out tomorrow night, or technically it's tonight. Hey, what are you doing? Sounds like you're—" Nikki's soft laugh was pure disbelief. "You are not driving over here."

"Come on now, you just said—"

"God, you can't be that horny. I'm sure you can wait a few more hours."

He entered the bathroom, his enthusiasm waning. Man, she really did think he was only in this for the sex. This was pretty messed up. He thought about how that boy Garrett had treated her and the strange *Salina Gazette* remark. Maybe it was time for him to man up, publicly claim her.

"Trace? You still there?"

"Yeah, sorry."

"I figured you fell asleep on me."

"Nah, just thinking." He rubbed his chest. "You're probably right, though. We should both get some rest. You said Matt's going to be in Dallas only one night?"

"He has to be back in time for the reading of Wallace's will," she muttered.

"I take it you have to be present."

"According to Matt, I do."

Trace decided to drop the subject. No use getting her riled. "Are you in bed now?"

"Yes. You?"

"I'll be crawling in between the sheets in two seconds." He turned off the bathroom light, picturing how she'd look with her silky dark hair spread out over a pillow. "Just so you know...I wasn't coming over for a booty call." He hesitated. Oh, hell, it wouldn't kill him to say the words. "I miss you, Nikki."

CUSTOMERS KEPT POURING in to the Watering Hole, which made the night go by quickly. But no way would Nikki be able to leave early. She might've been in a more pleasant mood if Trace had come to the bar to wait for her, but she was still glad she talked him into meeting her at the Lone Wolf. It turned out he was working late, anyway. He'd traded an early morning chore with one of the Sundance hands who wanted to play poker. That meant they could sleep in. He was going to need the rest, she thought, smiling. She hoped they both would.

"Glad to see you won't be a sourpuss again tonight." Sadie glanced at the order ticket Nikki set down along with her tray. "After being such a delight when you'd nagged me to let you come back to work."

"I haven't bitten off a single head yet, now have I?"

Grinning, Sadie grabbed bottles of tequila and whiskey and started pouring. "Heck, I just figured you being grouchy was on account of your trip to Kalispell, but I didn't want to say anything for fear of my life."

Nikki stared in astonishment. "How do you— No, you can't know."

Sadie laughed.

Nikki groaned. "This town is unreal…half the time I swear I'm being punked."

"Being what?"

The door opened, and Nikki turned to see who was coming to torment her now. Tall, lean, mid-to-late thirties, wearing faded jeans and boots like every other cowboy in the place… She didn't recognize him.

"Hell, look what the cat dragged in." Staring at the man, Sadie cocked her head to the side. "What are you doing around these parts? It can't be roundup time again."

His lazy smile disappeared in a flash. "Christ, Sadie, now you're gonna give me shit about that. And here I came in for a beer and a sympathetic ear."

"Since I don't know what on earth you're talking about, I have no response."

"Something slipped past you?" Nikki pretended to be shocked. "Wow. This has to be some kind of record."

Sadie narrowed her eyes. "Watch yourself, missy."

"Don't have to." Nikki smiled sweetly and picked up her tray. "It seems everyone else around here does it for me."

Sadie shook her head. "Aaron, this is Nikki, Matt Gunderson's sister. You know Matt, don't you?"

"Know of him, that's it." Touching the rim of his hat, Aaron gave Nikki a quick smile. "I was hoping I'd find Trace here," he said, glancing around. "Either of you seen him?"

"Not tonight." Sadie nodded at Nikki. "You must know where he is."

"Home."

Aaron gave her a closer look. "You expecting him here later?"

"No, he's working. Sorry, but I have drinks to deliver." She left with her tray, her mind racing. Whoever this guy was if he did anything to screw up their night she would just scream.

"What's Aaron doing here?" Eli Roscoe asked, when she dropped off his beer.

"I have no idea. Who is he?"

"A government guy…works for the Bureau of Land Management." The older man squinted under his bushy graying eyebrows. "He has something to do with rounding up mustangs living on public land. About the only time we see him around here is when he's looking for the McAllister boys to help."

Sitting across from Jerry at the next table, Chip said, "Too soon for another roundup, isn't it?"

"I ain't got an opinion on the matter," Eli said, "but I know Jesse McAllister thinks so, and I believe Trace is still straddling the fence on the issue. Says he's got more reading to do but my feeling is that he's got the same notion as Jesse. If Aaron's looking for their help, he's not gonna get it this time."

Nikki delivered more beers and shots, swinging around so she could keep an eye on Aaron. He was leaning on the bar, drinking from a mug and talking to Sadie.

"Just last week Trace told me he didn't think they've given the sterilization program enough time," Jerry said. "Infertility treatments were given to the Pryor Mountain horses along the Montana-Wyoming border. They're hoping that'll stabilize the size of the herd, but he said it's too soon to tell and we got no business removing horses until we know more."

"Hell, I'll admit I don't know crap about what's been going on," Chip added. "But I'll side with Trace. You know him, he's smart and always reading up on things. I've never known him to go in half-cocked on something."

Other customers who'd overheard the conversation weighed in, most of them agreeing it was too early for another roundup. What Nikki found fascinating was how much these men respected Trace's opinion, even the old-timers. They were interested in where Jesse stood as well, but that wasn't a surprise. He was older, more serious and well educated.

Trace was so laid-back, and seemed to cruise by on a shrug and a smile. But most of these people had known him his entire life. They'd watched him grow up, become a man, they knew there was substance behind the smile. When he had an opinion on something important, they took notice.

"What you damn fools are forgettin' is that the land is being overgrazed in the meantime, which means hungry animals." It was Sam's voice.

Nikki turned to see him coming from the back room with his empty mug. She really hadn't meant to ignore him or the others playing pool. The discussion had drawn her in.

His comment was met with general disgust.

"Trace said all that was taken into account when they thinned the herd and started the program." Chip glared straight at Sam. "You think for one minute Trace would let animals starve if he could help it?"

"What I think is that all you dumb bastards just love kissing McAllister ass. You sound like a bunch of little girls out here. Ooh," he mimicked, in a shrill tone, "Trace said this, Trace said that, Trace said I should go drown myself so I believe I will." He set his mug on Nikki's tray, and boy, did she get a whiff of his boozy breath. "It's damn pitiful," he added in his natural drawl, then winked. "I'll take another one, darlin'."

Her guilt over ignoring him vanished. "If you knew how much I want to pull out your lashes, one by one, every time you wink, you would stop." She narrowed her eyes. "Which is highly recommended in case that was too subtle or you're too dense."

She sidestepped him to check on the other pool players, not even smiling when everyone laughed.

"You boys hear that?" Sam said, spreading his hands. "She's crazy about me."

Nikki almost smiled then. She sighed instead. God, the man was like an untrained puppy—cute sometimes, but more often making you mad by peeing on the carpet. Or maybe that was giving him too much credit. She hurried to collect orders, hoping to squeeze in a minute to call Trace and warn him about Aaron, while Sadie poured beers and mixed drinks.

It was crazy how much pride she'd felt listening to these men talk about Trace. She had nothing to do with the respect he'd earned by being thoughtful and levelheaded. At the table behind Chip and Jerry, she overheard an older rancher tell his friend that since his son moved, Trace was the guy he knew he could count on in an emergency.

How horribly she'd misjudged him in February. Or had she really? She wasn't someone who shared easily. She certainly wasn't big on admitting her fears or the incredibly stupid choices of her youth, but she'd let her guard down with Trace, more than once. So something inside her was giving the green light. She just hoped it wasn't her heart getting confused. Falling for him would still be a mistake even if she did trust him.

This thing they had was fun, comfortable and exciting.

She'd like to believe it could last, but she knew better. She really needed to remember that. Easy to risk everything when you had nothing to lose. Loving then losing Trace? That could kill her.

HE WAS SITTING in his truck when she pulled up to the house. She parked her pickup behind him instead of her regular spot. They both climbed out at the same time.

"You boxing me in for a reason?" His teeth flashed in the bright moonlight as he walked toward her.

Had she remembered to leave the porch light on she'd be able to see that slow heart-stopping smile of his. "I don't want you running off before I'm done with you."

"Well now, that sounds promising." No hat tonight, which she was surprised to find she missed. The snug worn jeans made up for it. He stopped not three feet away and looked her up and down. "You went to work like that?"

"Um, yes." She glanced down at her usual jeans and stretchy blue V-neck top. "What's wrong?"

He made a sudden grab for her, scooping her up and making her squeal. "What's wrong?" he said, using a shocked tone and hugging her to his chest. "You can't be looking that gorgeous when I'm not there to protect you."

Nikki laughed, something she did a lot around him. She looped her arms around his neck, her eyes level with his smooth chin. "My feet aren't touching the ground so don't—"

His kiss cut her off. He took his time, angling his head and pressing his lips against hers, softly at first, then more firmly. She flexed her hips against his body and he stilled for a moment, then his tongue swept past her lips and swirled into her mouth. He tasted of wintergreen, and she was so, so glad she'd remembered to pop a mint herself.

"We should go inside," she whispered, dragging her mouth

away from his since he wouldn't stop kissing her. "No use giving the hands a show."

"Those guys are asleep."

"So, you have something against a nice soft queen-size bed and clean sheets?"

"I'm partial to kitchen counters myself." He'd switched to her neck, slowly planting moist kisses headed in the direction of her neckline.

She pushed her fingers through his hair, grabbing two handfuls and forcing his head back to see if he was serious. The teasing glint in his eyes earned him a yank.

"Ouch." He made a face. "I knew I should've gotten a haircut today."

"No, don't." She bit her lip. "Sorry. It's your hair. Do what you want."

"If you like it long, I'll keep it this way."

"Would you put me down? Please."

He swooped in for another quick kiss, then let her slide down his body. "Wait," he said. "Let's do that again."

Grinning, she took his hand and led him to the flagstone walkway. "We're going inside. Hey, I told you the front door was unlocked. Why did you wait out here?"

"I didn't feel right going in without you. Anyway, I wasn't waiting long and I used the time to return Aaron's call."

She'd wondered about whether they'd connected after she gave Trace the heads-up. "Were you able to have a civil conversation?"

"Oh, yeah. Aaron's okay. Just doing his job. I don't agree this time, that's all."

"Some of those guys tonight were getting awfully heated."

"Who? Eli and Lefty?"

She pushed open the door and pulled him inside. "Eli, Chip, Jerry, a few others I don't know by name. Even Sam put in his two cents."

Trace made sure they were locked in. "Two cents is about all that boy has to work with. He make you mad again tonight?"

"Sam is Sam. I'm trying not to react. Hey…" She giggled when he hooked an arm around her waist and hauled her up against him. Her body responded instantly, nipples beading, breaths coming quicker, dampness between her thighs….

"You smell good," he murmured, burying his face in the curve of her neck and shoulder.

"Oh, please, I smell like a bar. I'm taking a shower."

"Hmm, sounds like a good idea. I could use one, too." He plunged his fingers into her hair and gave her a light scalp massage.

She smiled because he smelled fresh and clean and a little like pine soap. "I didn't invite you," she said, letting her head loll back and her eyes close.

"I'm inviting myself."

"Trace, you are just—" She sighed and lifted her lashes. "You're amazing."

He stilled, aiming an expectant frown at her. "I'm waiting for the punch line."

"I hope you have all week." She brushed a kiss across his lips. "Do you have any idea how much admiration and respect the people here have for you?"

Surprise flickered in his face. He blinked, shaking his head and flushing. "Come on…" He lowered his arms and took her hand. "Let's go use up the hot water."

If she touched his cheeks she knew they'd be warm. He was embarrassed and she really should drop it, but she didn't understand why he'd prefer people to think he was a guy who got by on his looks and charm.

A sudden realization stunned her. No, it was her, that's what *she'd* thought. And so did the Sundance guests who chased him and flirted and made fools of themselves because all they saw was the sizzle but not the substance. The people who lived here, the ones who understood him, knew otherwise. To them, Trace was a man to be taken seriously.

"Okay, cowboy." She slipped her hand into his. "Show me what you got."

when you got to the river, they must tired. The
dark or even look that full of ... clock keep time
before ... Bryson. There was a mark, a great ridge
on ... Daisy knew so. She looked like mud quilts. "You got
wet mud quilts."

15

TRACE SOAPED THE back of her shoulders and watched the sudsy water sluice down her spine to the curve of her backside. Her skin looked as silky as it felt under his lips. She'd pulled her hair up into a messy knot, and he was trying his best not to get it wet, but sometimes he'd get distracted by the curve of her hip or the delicate slope of her neck.

"I think you already got that spot," she said, glancing back at him.

"You sure?"

"Yes, all three times."

He smiled and soaped the other side. "When you were going to community college, did anyone ask you to pose nude for art class?"

"What?" She laughed, and spun around to face him. "No."

"Fools." He circled the pad of his thumb over a taut pink nipple. "Though I can't deny I'm glad. I'd hate walking into a gallery and seeing you naked on a wall for everyone else to look at."

Nikki slid her palms up his chest, leaning into him, amusement dancing in her pretty dark eyes. "So, you go to art galleries often?"

"Nope."

"How many have you been to?"

He felt the right side of his mouth lifting. He ought to out-right lie. It would be harmless enough yet wipe that smug expression off her face. Skimming his hand along her hip, he waited until the right moment and said, "None," just as he slid his hand between her thighs.

She gasped and arched against his chest. "Sneaky."

The friction of her stiff nipples rubbing against him tested his willpower. "I forgot to soap down here." He parted her folds with the tips of his fingers, dipping inside only enough to make her tense.

"Pretty sure you didn't miss that spot, either," she whispered, ending with a soft moan that went straight to his cock.

"Better safe than horny."

She laughed and tugged at his chest hair.

"Isn't that the saying?" He braced his other hand against the tile wall for balance so he could better explore her. His fingers delved deeper, while he used his tongue to relearn the contours of her mouth.

She made the best damn sounds. Whimpers, moans, some of them a combination of both, others vibrating softly from her throat like a purr. She'd teased him about being quick on the draw, and he was a bit touchy about that because she wasn't wrong. What she didn't know was that it was all her fault. He hadn't had a problem like that since he was seventeen. She made him want her all the time, even when they were apart. If he so much as thought about the way her eyes flashed when she laughed, he wanted her. If he pictured her full pink lips parting right before they kissed, he wanted her. Hell, he could probably watch her fry an egg and want her right then and there.

Fortunately for him, he wasn't having a problem reloading quickly. What did worry him some was the degree of his infatuation. Something was off. He understood how watch-

ing her strip or kissing those lips could make him ache with
a desperation that was humbling. But when they weren't even
in the same room? Thinking about her still made him feel as
if he was going to explode just as he had as a teenager. The
difference now was that he cared about what was right for
her instead of just his own satisfaction.

Maybe he needed to tell her this physical reaction wasn't
normal for him. She might think he was lying, or maybe she'd
be flattered that she reduced him to a helpless boy. That didn't
sit well. Flattered was okay, but not the rest. Another alternative could be to wait it out…after they made love a few more
times it was likely he'd settle down. Or hell, maybe he'd better start jerking off an hour before he planned on seeing her.
They'd made love before they got into the shower, and while
he was already hard again, he wasn't ready to pull the trigger.

He dragged his mouth from hers to find that sweet spot
behind her ear. Her breathy moan came on cue, and he smiled
against her skin.

"I think we've been in here long enough," she murmured,
tilting her head back and almost getting her hair drenched.

"Okay, we'll get out." He put his arms around her waist
and lifted her.

"What are you doing?" She clutched his shoulders. "I
thought we were getting out."

"We will." He hefted her up a bit more, and she hooked
a leg around his middle. "Put the other one up there, too."

With both of her legs wrapped around him, he kissed her
right breast, then latched on to her taut nipple. He was careful using his teeth, not so much when he rolled and swirled
his tongue over her tender skin. She pushed into his mouth
every time she arched back and if she didn't stop, he was
going to embarrass himself again.

With one hand cradling her firm backside, he kept her anchored to his waist, and used his other hand to tend that slick nub he knew would push her to the edge.

Her body tensed and she hid her face against the side of his neck, her short nails digging into his shoulder muscles.

"Kiss me, Nikki," he said, holding on to her ass when she started to squirm, and rubbing her faster.

She brought her head up, and looked at him, her eyes dazed. "I like that," she whispered sweetly, a little shyly.

"This?" He kept rubbing her, keeping the pressure and pace steady, though tightening his hold.

She nodded, and pressed her mouth to his, letting him coax her lips apart. He waited for her tongue to enter and touch his, then sweep inside. That's as far as she made it before she started whimpering, panting, teasing him with that soft purr. And puffing quick hot breaths into his mouth while she came.

Nikki dried off his back, lingering on his ass, smiling when he flexed the muscles there. Her legs still weren't all that steady. She wouldn't totally relax until they were horizontal.

And had condoms within reach. That's what was scary about getting tuned up in the shower. She'd had to really slam on the brakes. At one point she'd barely been able to think beyond wanting him inside her.

"Okay, I'm dry enough," Trace said, turning to face her, and cupping her breasts. "And I'd prefer to keep a layer of skin, if you don't mind."

"And if I do?"

"I'll have to convince you otherwise." He leaned over, forcing her head back, knowing she wanted to make him break eye contact first. "I like that you're short."

"Why?"

"Want me to show you?"

"No." She pulled away and scrambled to the bedroom, wishing she'd thought to turn back the quilt and sheets.

"What did you think I was gonna do?" he asked with that mischievous smile that usually meant she was in for a treat.

She pointed to the other side of the bed before he touched her and made her forget what she was about to do. "You get over there and help me with the quilt."

"Yes, ma'am." He yanked his side back, ignoring her attempt at neatness. He caught her frown and said, "You know we're just gonna mess it up again."

"True." She laughed, happy, really happy, almost scary happy. Scary because the last time she'd felt this same light-headed giddiness had been with Luis. The high had only lasted a few days and involved too much tequila. It hadn't ended well.

Thinking of Luis reminded her of the last phone call to her mom. Shockingly, he'd shown up at her mother's apartment looking for Nikki. She hadn't seen or talked to him in over a year. Although Nikki harbored no hard feelings toward him, she had nothing to say to him, either. She hated that her mom had to run interference, but it was a relief that he found out Nikki had left Houston. Luis was another shameful part of her past she'd worked on forgetting.

"Nikki?"

She blinked, saw that Trace had already crawled into bed and was staring at her.

"You okay?"

"Where are the condoms?"

"Right here." He held up a handful of packets that he'd left on the nightstand.

"So optimistic." Grinning, she slid in beside him.

"What I lack in stamina, I make up for in frequency," he said, and they both laughed, although he flushed a bit. "Just so you know…that crack you made about me jumping the gun…that little problem I've been having is totally your fault."

"How?" She snuggled up to his chest, his arms around her,

keeping her warm and making her feel safe. Even knowing it wasn't forever, being with Trace still felt perfect.

"Other than being sexy as hell, I'm not sure. All I'm saying is this isn't the norm and I'm hoping it's temporary." He removed the clip holding up her hair and tossed it on the nightstand. "See?" he said, finger-combing the long strands that fell all over the place. "Just touching your hair, I'm getting hard again."

She checked to see if he was teasing because it didn't sound like it, and he really was semi-aroused.

Their gazes met. "And those eyes." His voice lowered and the tender smile he gave her nearly melted her heart. "Those beautiful brown eyes. I have no defense." He brushed the hair away from her face and kissed the side of her mouth. "And these lips…" He pressed a soft kiss at the other corner. "It's a wonder I can keep my mind on anything else."

A wave of shyness swept her. "You're such a player," she said, giving him a light tap on his chest. Regret was instant. She saw the hurt in his eyes.

"I can't blame you for thinking I'm no better than a tomcat. But those women out at the Sundance, they don't mean anything— No. Wait a minute." He frowned. "Have you ever seen me seriously flirt with one of the guests?"

"You've got to be kidding."

"I'm talking about since you've come back. No kidding now, at the Sundance or at the Watering Hole, can you name one time that I flirted?"

Nikki got up on her elbow and leaned back to get a good look at his face. "You flirt all the time, though I'm not saying you shouldn't. It's your business."

"Now you think about this," he said, no teasing in his gaze at all. "I usually respond when they flirt, at least I try to be pleasant. Sometimes they're annoying as hell and it's all I can do to make myself smile."

"Trace, stop. You don't owe me an explanation." Laying her cheek back on his chest, she ran her hand down his belly. "We have more important things to do."

"This is important to me," he said quietly, covering her hand and bringing it to a halt. "It's only you, Nikki. I'm not seeing anyone else." He kissed her hair. "I don't want anyone else."

She didn't even know how to respond to that, or to the flutters he'd set off. Was she supposed to say it back? Thank him? Briefly she considered asking him to be more specific, then discarded the idea. "Okay," she finally mumbled when it appeared he wasn't going to help her out.

He sighed, released her hand and cupped the back of her head. "So where were we?"

Good. This part she knew how to handle. She brushed her lips across his right pec, started to work her way lower, but he slid down, startling her with an openmouthed kiss that left her without air. His tongue demanded entry, then made a thorough sweep she could feel all the way to her core.

It wasn't just his kiss that sent her reeling. Every touch made her hyperaware that it was Trace's hand, Trace's fingers. Each gasp was filled with more than lust. He wanted only her. This good man, the one she'd dismissed so flippantly. No wonder she didn't know how to handle the pure want in his gaze.

She spread her legs, needing him closer. The way his eyebrows rose as his pupils dilated made her flush even more than his intimate caress.

When he was settled, resting on his elbows, his body blanketing her own, he smiled. "I'm not guaranteeing a thing," he said. "You drive me crazy, you know that? Straight out of my mind. And when I'm in you, no matter how I try, I can't seem to control myself."

She brushed her fingers across his cheekbone, then curved

her hand to the back of his neck. "Just the way I like you. Out of control."

His eyes staying on her face, Trace turned to kiss her arm. "I know something else you might like."

"Oh?"

He slid down further, and she could feel the whisper of moist breath on the skin between her ribs, the pressure of his warm lips just below her navel. She sucked in a breath, waiting, trying to watch, but she could only see the top of his head.

The first glide of his tongue sent a jolt through her. She automatically bucked, and he held on to her hips, keeping her still, and using his tongue to drive every last thought from her head until she completely shattered.

NIKKI HEARD THE COLLIES barking and glanced out her bedroom window. She didn't recognize the blue Cadillac bumping along the gravel driveway, but then she hadn't expected to. It was two minutes to four. The attorney was right on time. If only a flat had delayed him long enough for her to leave for work. Though she supposed that wish was a little unkind.

The man was only here to do his job, and she'd promised Matt she'd behave. Sitting quietly and listening wouldn't kill her. It didn't mean she had to agree or accept anything from Wallace. She still hadn't gotten over the shock that he'd named her in his will at all. However, both she and Matt were offended on Lucy's behalf. Loyal to a fault and she hadn't even gotten a mention. They knew because Matt had asked Frank Kessler if Lucy should also be present.

After checking her hair in the mirror so she could leave for the Watering Hole as soon as they were done, she stopped at her bed. She'd made it up, something she did about every other day, but this morning she'd left out Trace's pillow. Picking it up, she lifted it to her nose. She could still smell him. Some of the dread drained from her. If the attorney made her edgy, she'd daydream about Trace, she decided, or replay last night.

Oh, God, that could get her in trouble. Maybe it was better she wasn't all starry-eyed. Or thinking about Trace at the moment. If she was in too good a mood, no telling what she might agree to.

She hurried down the stairs and headed toward the voices coming from the den. Sitting on the red leather couch, papers spread on the coffee table in front of him, Frank Kessler looked out of place. He wore a sharp navy blue suit, yellow tie and shiny black shoes, his gray hair slicked back. She would've guessed he was from New York, not Billings, Montana.

He rose as soon as he saw her and extended his hand. "Nikita Flores," he said, "it's a pleasure to meet you. Frank Kessler."

"Um, I go by Nikki." She didn't care for his weak handshake or the intense curiosity in his small dark eyes.

Matt had already claimed the chair that matched the couch, so she perched on the edge of the floral-patterned chaise close to the stone fireplace.

Mr. Kessler smiled and gestured to the unoccupied side of the couch. "I promise I won't bite."

She returned the smile. "I might." Then darted a grudging glance at Matt. He wasn't amused. "Just kidding," she said to Mr. Kessler, who appeared unfazed. "I'm fine here."

"First off," he said, "please accept my condolences on the loss of your father."

A snide remark nearly tripped off her tongue, but she drew in a breath, reminding herself the goal was to get this reading over with. "Thank you."

"Matt has requested that we keep this short because you have to go to work." He'd slipped on a pair of glasses and was sifting through several legal-size papers while he spoke.

"The Gunderson Trust is quite straightforward. The land and house, including any and all structures, are covered by the trust. Paternity hasn't been challenged, and since Wallace legally acknowledged you as his daughter, Nikki, in the eyes of the law—"

"When?"

Kessler looked at her over the rim of his glasses. "The beginning of March…I believe it was a couple of weeks after you and Matt had visited him. He signed an affidavit verifying your relationship to him, and then he updated his will."

She wasn't sure why she'd bothered to ask. What did it matter? Wallace had always known she existed. Legally recognizing her didn't make a damn bit of difference. "Sorry. I shouldn't have interrupted."

"Ask anything you want, Nikki," Matt said, and she noticed his expression seemed strained. "Now's your chance."

"I'm good for now," she said.

"Feel free to stop me at any time." Kessler seemed patient and professional, but something about him bugged her. "Let's see," he said, his attention going back to the document. "In accordance with the terms of the trust, the land and structures, as I mentioned, now belong equally to the two of you. What gets tricky and isn't clear is ownership of the livestock, which is worth a substantial sum and we'll get to that in a minute.

"Equipment, inventory, vehicles registered to the Lone Wolf, those sorts of things obviously aren't covered by the trust, which was drawn nearly a hundred years ago. Those items are considered personal property and Wallace has left them to Matt. I have an itemized list for each of you. Any questions so far?" He looked up until they both shook their heads.

No point arguing now. Nikki knew division of the land and house was something she and Matt had to sort out in private, which should be a short conversation, given she wanted nothing. But knowing Matt, it wasn't a discussion she was looking forward to. He'd been okay earlier, but now he seemed irritable. She hoped it wasn't over Wallace leaving him all that stuff and not including her. She didn't give a crap about any of it.

"Now, about the livestock." Kessler's gaze moved over the words on the next document. "Fortunately you two are on good terms, that makes things easier," he murmured, half to himself. "That's not always the case…"

Nikki yawned, tuning out Kessler and wishing she'd made coffee. After Trace had left at eight-thirty she'd gone back to sleep. And still she'd only managed to get a total of five hours. Poor Trace had to go move cattle to another pasture, though he'd promised to grab a nap before meeting her at the bar later.

Last night had been sheer heaven. He knew exactly how to touch her, knew where she was the most sensitive and above all, he'd shown her a tenderness she hadn't known existed. Normally she didn't like waking up with a guy. She wanted them gone long before it was time to jump in the shower. But everything was upside down when it came to Trace. Several times today she'd found herself plotting ways to get him to stay over tonight.

"Nikki?"

At the sound of Matt's voice, she straightened. Both he and Kessler were staring at her, and she had a feeling she'd missed quite a bit. "Sorry, what was that?"

"You might want to listen to this," Matt said, his expression more relaxed.

Kessler read directly from the will. "'To my daughter, Nikita Flores, I bequeath the balance of my cash holdings at the time of my death.'" The attorney switched his gaze to a ledger sheet. "As of this morning, including interest, that amount is $172,548."

Nikki blinked. "I don't understand."

Matt smiled, leaning forward, his elbows resting on his thighs. "That money is yours, Nik. Wallace left it to you."

She would've thought she heard wrong if Matt hadn't looked so pleased. This was crazy. She really didn't want anything from the man, but this was huge. That kind of money could change her life. Truly give her a fresh start.

"However, there is a stipulation." Kessler's face went blank and he focused solely on Nikki. "You only get the money if you sign your share of the Lone Wolf over to Matt."

She felt as if someone had punched her in the stomach.

"Bullshit." Matt glared at the older man. "Nobody can mess with the trust. I know that for a fact."

"You're right," Mr. Kessler said calmly. "Nikki couldn't sell her half to anyone, but she can waive her claim and sign it over to you because you're a Gunderson."

"So is Nikki."

"No one's disputing that, Matthew." Kessler removed his glasses and rubbed the bridge of his nose. "Wallace wanted you to have the Lone Wolf. That's all. I will say this, I personally think this is his way of making it up to you for past wrongs."

Matt's anger radiated from across the room. "Screw him. The money is yours, Nikki. You're not signing over any rights."

"I'm afraid that's not up to you." Mr. Kessler sighed. "Look, keep this simple. Legally, you'll need to sign the waiver in order to release the money. After that you're free to do what you want. Do you understand?"

Numb, except for the ache in her chest, Nikki got his meaning. But she didn't care about the Lone Wolf. Right now she didn't even care about the money. Wallace was trying to buy her off, and that hurt more than she thought possible. He'd been a sick old man on his deathbed, and yet somehow he managed to get in that extra slap in the face even after death.

She had to give it to him. It took effort to be that much of a bastard.

Matt was saying something to the attorney, maybe even to her, but she hadn't been listening. "I'll need time to think it over," she said, cutting Matt off and getting to her feet. "Is that all?"

Kessler frowned. "Well, no, there's more."

"Do you need me?"

The older man slowly shook his head. "I guess not."

"Nikki, wait." Matt looked heartsick.

"I'm fine." She forced a smile. This wasn't his fault. She didn't want him to feel bad. Wallace had been a jerk until the end. It shouldn't have been a surprise, and it sure as hell shouldn't make a difference. A sob broke in her throat, and she hurried to the door.

16

NIKKI HEARD A NOISE, turned her head and saw Trace, but not Gypsy. "What are you doing here?" She dabbed at her cheeks to make sure they weren't damp before he got too close. She hadn't cried really, just got a little teary. "Were we supposed to meet today?" she asked, so confused she couldn't think straight.

"No." He jerked a thumb over his shoulder. "I have my truck. Guess you didn't hear me drive up."

"I thought you were moving cattle." She slid off the rock she'd been sitting on for the past hour and dusted off her butt while she waited for him to reach her.

"I was." He left the trail, cut through the tall grass and put his arms around her. "Rough day, huh?"

"Is that a shot in the dark or did you talk to Matt?"

"He called."

Nikki sighed. Pressing her cheek against his chest, taking comfort in the strong steady beat of his heart, she felt some of the tension leave her body. "He shouldn't have done that."

"Of course he should have. If it were Rachel, I'd have done the same for him."

Matt and Rachel were getting married in a few months so

it wasn't at all the same. But Nikki appreciated the sentiment. "He didn't know I was here, though."

"He said you were upset…" Trace brushed a kiss on her forehead. "I figured you might come here." He sighed. "Wallace always was a bastard. That didn't change. I know it's hard, but don't let it get to you."

"Wow, Matt told you everything."

He leaned back and studied her face, touching the outside corner of her eye with his thumb. "You mind?"

She blinked, hoping there were no tears ready to fall. "I would've told you myself…eventually. It's not about the Lone Wolf or the money."

"I know that." He sat on the huge rock she'd used as a bench and pulled her onto his lap.

Nikki started to object…but it felt nice being cocooned by his chest and arms. "I hate that you left work. I'm really okay."

"You think I could do anything but come find you?" He stroked her back, rubbed her arm. "Remember that thing about you not being alone anymore?"

Dammit. So much for no more tears. Sometimes kindness was the worst…

"Hey." He ignored her efforts to hide her face and caught her chin. "Did I just do that?" He looked into her watery eyes, the alarm in his expression restoring some of her calm.

"Yes, you're being too nice. Stop it."

"Sorry. I can't do that." He touched his lips to hers, the gentle kiss meant only to soothe.

"How did Matt sound? Is he okay?"

"He was worried. I called him as soon as I spotted your truck and he seemed relieved. Didn't tell him where you were. No need to give up our favorite make-out spot."

Nikki smiled. "He was so angry, even with the attorney, who was only doing his job." She watched a squirrel scurrying up a tree with something in its mouth. "Now that I've had time to think, for Matt's sake, I'm glad Wallace did what he did."

"You might want to fill me in more," Trace said, frowning as if he couldn't see her point. "Matt gave me the gist but he was pissed and not too clear."

She wasn't thrilled to recap the meeting, but it was a good test to see if she truly was making peace with Wallace. "You know about the Gunderson Trust," she said, and he nodded so she skipped that part, summed up the rest, digging for composure when she got to the one provision in the will. "The money he left, it's a lot, around $172,000." Trace's brows shot up. Apparently Matt hadn't told him how much. "Basically he wants me gone, even though he's dead. I get the cash if I sign over my rights to Matt."

Trace didn't look surprised, only furious. "I know…what I don't get is why you're okay with Wallace being a manipulative jackass or how you can believe that helps Matt."

"At first I was mad and hurt that he thought he had to protect his precious family land from me. After all, I'm not a 'true' Gunderson, only his bastard." She shook her head when Trace started to object, and regretted her bitter tone. Clearly she had more work to do on herself. "But the attorney said something that made me think. I'm not sure that stipulation had much to do with me. Wallace might've been trying to make amends to Matt. He wouldn't care about the money, not with what he's stashed from his winnings. But Matt loves the Lone Wolf."

"Nice thought, except there's no way Matt would be satisfied with you being cut out. He probably hates Wallace even more now."

She sighed, understanding the logic. She herself despised Wallace more for what he'd done to Matt than for abandoning her. "After the hurt and anger dies down, I'll talk to him. Wallace was screwed up. But I want Matt to believe that his father had tried to make things up to him the only way he knew how."

His brows puckered, Trace studied her with no less concern. "You're taking this a whole lot better than I imagined."

"You should've seen me an hour ago. I thought, wow, Wallace was scum and *he* thought I wasn't good enough to be a part of his family."

"Jesus, Nikki." Letting out a harsh breath, he forced her to look at him. "Don't ever go there. You're amazing."

She couldn't help but smile. "And you're…" She touched his stubbled jaw. "I was so wrong about you."

He gave her a crooked grin. "You figured I was just another pretty face, and hollow inside like a chocolate Easter bunny."

"Actually, yes." She laughed. "Not the chocolate bunny, that part didn't occur to me."

Trace hugged her, his quiet growl the sound of pure contentment. "That's a lot of money you're about to get. More than enough to go back to school if you want. They have a few good colleges in Kalispell. Not that I'm being selfish."

Nikki stiffened. "I haven't decided if I'm going to accept the money."

"Why wouldn't you?"

"I never wanted anything from him. You know that."

"Hell, Wallace isn't here. You'd only be hurting yourself by turning it down."

She slipped off his lap. "I'd know the money came from him."

Trace caught her hand. "Don't be hasty. You need time. And don't forget about school," he said while doing light circles on her wrist with his thumb. "Is your hesitation about the Lone Wolf? You know Matt would never let you give up your share."

"I don't want the Lone Wolf, either. I don't even know if I'm cut out for this slow country life." She hadn't meant to raise her voice or be quite so honest, but it shocked her to see the raw disappointment in his eyes.

"Maybe not," he said grimly, tugging her close again. "But if you don't take the money and just disappear, Wallace wins." Trace put his hands on her waist. "You're still emotional, and you and Matt have a lot to discuss. Promise me you'll take your time to decide."

She nodded, not sure if he'd pulled her toward him or if she'd stepped forward. He cradled her between his spread thighs, his arms wrapping around her and hers circling his neck. Their foreheads touching, neither of them moved. He was right. She was still emotional. For the better part of an hour, she'd thought about the past, from the mess with Garrett and the prom to how she'd foolishly tried to find comfort in Luis. Worst of all was how often she'd hurt her mother.

She didn't want to do that to Trace, too. He was so amazing in many, many ways, and much more than someone like her deserved. Wallace had been a bastard, all right. But who was to say he was wrong? Maybe she really wasn't good enough. Maybe she never would be.

TRACE MISSED OBLITERATING his thumb by a hair. He threw the hammer down and cursed his stupidity. "That's it. I'm done for the day. You quit, too, if you want," he said to Josh. "These warped boards will still be here tomorrow."

Tempted as he was to leave the tools scattered, Trace crouched down and started throwing everything into the toolbox. The way they landed all helter-skelter, he'd never be able to close the damn thing.

"I'll do that," Josh said. "Go."

"Nah, that's all right." He'd feel guilty as hell leaving his friend with the mess. Bad enough Trace had been moody since seeing Nikki, no need to let Josh take the brunt of it.

"I'm not trying to be nice." Josh collected the rags. "It's self-defense. Get out of here before I end up on crutches."

A grudging smile tugged at Trace's mouth. "I haven't been that bad."

Josh gave him a long look. "You almost ran over my toes with the four-wheeler. And I'm pretty sure you've used every cussword you know in English and Spanish."

Trace gave up on closing the toolbox. "Not all of them."

Josh took it from him. "You going to the Watering Hole after supper? I'll buy you a beer."

That was part of Trace's problem. He couldn't decide if it was better to go see her or stay away. What he really wanted to do was talk to Matt about her, but he knew that would only lead to trouble—if Nikki went behind his back and discussed him with Rachel, he'd sure be pissed.

"Yeah, I'll go. But I'm buying. I reckon that's the least I can do." He watched Josh patiently rearrange the tools and close the box. "When do you leave to see your girl?"

"Not for three weeks. Fourth of July weekend." Josh's grin was wider than the Grand Canyon. "Can't come fast enough."

"You going all the way to New York?"

"Nope. Haley's meeting me partway."

"Where?"

Josh's grin faded. "Why?"

Trace shrugged. "Just curious." It was more than that. Haley had been a Sundance guest when Josh met her. She lived in Manhattan, and Trace had wondered how that would pan out for them. Josh had never doubted they could make it work, but Trace had. He hoped he wouldn't be put to the same long-distance test with Nikki. "Come on, where are you guys meeting?"

Josh sighed. "Disneyland."

"What?"

"You heard right."

They were heading out of the barn but Trace stopped and laughed. "You haven't seen Haley in how many months, and you're taking her to Disneyland? Son, you need your head screwed on tighter."

"It's not me." He held up his hands. "Haley wants to go there. I didn't argue." Josh narrowed his eyes. "If Nikki wanted to go to Siberia, tell me you wouldn't be packed in two minutes."

"Shut up." Trace started walking again, veering off toward the house.

"You wanna ride with me to town?" Josh called after him.

"No, I'm taking my truck."

"Right." Josh's laugh grated on his nerves. "In case you-know-who wants to go to Siberia."

Trace flipped him off without a look back. A guest could've seen him, but so what. His mood wasn't getting any better, and he figured he ought to skip dinner. Sitting at the table and trying to be nice would be torture. He wasn't even hungry. And he sure as hell didn't want to make small talk.

What a fool he'd been to think Nikki could be happy living here. She'd get bored sooner or later. Bored with Blackfoot Falls, bored with him. It wasn't so much what she'd said about not being cut out for the country, it was how she'd said it. He had a bad feeling she'd already made up her mind.

It still appalled him to think he'd actually been tempted to discourage her from taking the money. If she was broke, she'd have to stay. But with all that cash, she could set herself up someplace real nice. Man, he couldn't stand to think about her leaving. He had no right to ask her to stay, he knew that, but if the time came, he just might beg her.

That would be something. He never imagined he'd have to humble himself for a woman. Not that he thought he was too good for a little humility. Finding a willing woman had always been easy for him. The guys used to tease him about being able to pick and choose. It had been all in good fun, but it also had been the truth. He didn't like this new game plan.

He stopped in the mudroom to scrape his boots. They were in terrible shape but not so bad they'd harm the wood floors. Rachel would yell if she saw him sneaking in with them on, but he didn't care. Besides, he thought he'd heard her on the porch with the guests. It was beer and margarita time for them. And the perfect opportunity for him to creep upstairs unnoticed.

He opened the door to the kitchen and she stood right there in front of him, dropping a can into the recycle bin.

Her gaze went straight to his boots, eyes narrowing to a glare. "What are you doing?"

"I don't want to hear it," he said, putting up a warning finger. Hilda stood at the stove, and she turned in surprise at his rough tone. "Trust me. Bad time to get into it with me," he added to make sure Rachel backed off.

"I know," she said softly. "I really hate Wallace. I do."

"Have you seen Matt?"

She shook her head. "We talked on the phone. I'll see him later. How's Nikki?"

"I know she went to work." He rubbed the tension tightening the back of his neck. "Count me out for dinner."

"Can I at least make you a sandwich?"

"No, thanks. I'm going to town…" He sighed. Hell, everyone knew about him and Nikki at this point. "To the bar. If I get hungry I'll grab something at Marge's."

Rachel nodded. "Go. I'll see you later." She blinked, then her eyes rounded with surprise. "Maybe at the Lone Wolf," she said, laughing and blushing. "Oh, God."

"Ah." He got it. If he spent the night with Nikki it would be kind of weird knowing his kid sister was down the hall with Matt. Trace just laughed. "We bump into each other in the dark and I'll pretend I don't know you."

"Same here." She bit her lip and glanced at Hilda, who kept turning over pieces of sizzling fried chicken, while paying them no attention. Though she must've heard.

Rachel abruptly turned away, trying not to laugh, and he raced out of the kitchen and up the stairs to his room in record time. He lingered in the shower, letting the warm spray hit the back of his neck and stiff shoulders. He had to stop giving his thoughts free rein. Whether Nikki stayed or left, him worrying about it wouldn't change a damn thing.

Ten minutes later, the idea that she could pack up and leave at any time still rattled him no matter what he told himself. With Wallace gone, and Matt busy with setting a new course for the Lone Wolf, there wouldn't be much to keep Nikki around here. Trace wanted to think she'd stay for him, but he hadn't come out and asked her to, or told her how he felt about her. Of course he still hadn't quite narrowed that down yet.

He dried himself off, pulled on clean jeans and took a brown Western-cut shirt out of his closet. The guys would razz him again for wearing his good clothes, and he was in just the right mood to tell them where to shove it.

The ride to town went by quickly. Already there was no street parking in front of the Watering Hole. He saw Nikki's pickup next to the bank and grabbed a spot two trucks away.

Music spilled out onto the sidewalk. The heavy wood door was no match when someone cranked up the jukebox. He would've liked it a whole lot better if the bar wasn't so crowded, but nothing to do about it. He'd barely made it inside when someone whistled, then he heard a catcall and laughter. It was the shirt. Screw them.

Nikki stood at the end of the bar where she turned in her drink orders, looking over her shoulder to see what the noise was about. She saw him and smiled.

He actually felt a strange sensation in his chest. Man, it was going to be hard to walk over and not kiss her. But she looked relaxed as if this was any other night, and for now that was good enough. She moved over to make room for him, and he didn't hesitate.

"This is early for you," she said once he crowded in between her and a young cowboy sitting on a stool.

"I skipped supper." He almost touched her cheek, but diverted his hand to plow through his hair at the last second. "Everyone else seems to have had the same idea."

"It's been crazy busy since Sadie unlocked the door." Her gaze moved over his shirt. "You look nice. Smell nice, too," she whispered, swaying against him, her lids at half-mast.

"Don't go starting anything we can't finish," he muttered, afraid his cock mistook that as an invitation to party.

"Oh, right. Sorry."

"Trace?" Sadie was a bit farther down the bar, mixing a drink. "Beer?"

"Don't worry about me. I can wait."

"Oh, shoot, I was about to help fill mugs." Nikki scribbled something on her pad, then swung to the other side of the bar.

He waited until she had a pitcher and mugs lined up. "Before I forget, we should set a time for a riding lesson tomorrow."

"Oh." She fiddled with the tap. Once the beer began flowing, she nodded. "Good idea. I'd prefer the afternoon if that's okay."

Relief surged through his body. In the few seconds it took for her to agree, he'd realized how much he needed to hear she didn't plan on going anywhere…at least not tomorrow. "Just let me know when and I'll be at our spot."

With a fretful frown, she met his eyes. "About later," she said softly, her voice tinged with disappointment. "It sounds as if you're not coming over tonight."

One more rush of relief and he was going to need to sit down. "I haven't been invited yet."

Nikki's smile lit up every dark cloud hanging over his heart. "Silly boy, I want you every night."

The relief that flowed through him nearly knocked him sideways. He might not be certain about where he and Nikki were headed, but the idea that he wouldn't have the chance to find out had been killing him.

She wasn't leaving tonight. Tomorrow things would seem better. And after that…he had no idea, but at least time no longer felt like a fight he couldn't win.

17

Nikki was starting to get cold feet. Every time the door opened, dread kicked up another notch and she couldn't be sorrier she'd made that deal with Karina. So much had changed between Nikki and Trace since the night she'd thought Karina was trying to pick him up. He wouldn't think the woman's real proposal was funny, and now neither did Nikki. Oh, he might've been a good sport had Karina approached him at the Sundance or in private. But here at the Watering Hole in front of Sam and the others, he wouldn't be amused.

In the three days since the will had been read, Nikki still hadn't completely made up her mind about whether to accept Wallace's money but it no longer ate at her. The more time she spent with Trace, the more she saw the appeal of sticking around, at least until she figured out for sure what she wanted to do with the rest of her life.

Truthfully, the thought of leaving him behind was hard to contemplate. At least for now, when things felt so right. She'd been enjoying her hot nights and jam-packed days with him too much. He'd even coaxed her on top of Gypsy for ten whole minutes yesterday.

While she had time between customers, she washed mugs,

ordering herself not to check the clock. Again. When her mind occasionally drifted to the decision she had to make, she always seemed to hear Trace's voice telling her not to let Wallace win. Matt's solution was for her to sign over her share, accept the money and then he'd reverse the process the very next day.

It took a few seconds to realize her phone had buzzed. It was Trace. She saw that Karina was busy studying the juke-box, and Nikki motioned to let Sadie know she had to step outside for a minute. She answered on her way to the door. It opened and Trace entered, grinning, his cell phone pressed to his ear.

"I miss you," he said, to which she responded with a groan and "You big dope."

His laugh drew Karina's attention. Great. Too late for Nikki to drag him outside. She sighed and nodded at an older cowboy signaling for a pitcher refill.

Trace followed her to the bar and grabbed a stool while she slipped around to the other side. "Come on." Staring at her, his grin faltered. "You can't be mad."

"No, but you might be." While filling the pitcher, she looked past him and watched Karina close in.

"Why?" He started to turn his head, caught a glimpse of Karina and snapped back to face the bar.

"I leave tomorrow, cowboy." Karina slid onto the empty stool beside him. "Last chance for me to buy you a drink."

"No, thanks. Just came by to visit Nikki."

Karina smiled at her. "You know how to make an apple-tini or should I wait for Sadie?"

"I can manage," she said.

Karina waited until Nikki started on her appletini, then turned to Trace. "I have a business proposition for you."

He lifted a brow. "A what?"

"A business proposition. This has been a working vacation for me. A scouting trip." Karina reached into the neck-line of her low-cut blouse and brought out a business card. She passed it to Trace.

He seemed reluctant to accept it. Finally he did, then frowned at the writing. "Okay," he said, drawing out the word.

"My company is staging a campaign to find a cowboy to be the face of our latest line of fragrances."

"Why are you telling me?" Trace narrowed his gaze on Karina, but not before glancing around.

"I think you'd have a great shot at it. We're doing some-thing fun and different to engage consumers in the selection process. We're streamlining the list of candidates by mak-ing a calendar and—"

"Hold on right there." He lowered his voice and slid a quick look to his left, then at the door when it creaked open. "I'm not interested," he said quietly, putting down her card by her drink.

Nikki's breath caught. He looked so embarrassed and she hated, hated that she'd played any part in this. How could she have thought this was funny? A week ago she'd barely known him. Not the real Trace. She'd stubbornly clung to a stereo-type she'd adopted the first night she'd met him in February. It was different now. She knew better, but he was going to be mad and she couldn't blame him.

Karina started in again, trying to convince him with flat-tery and large sums of money. Trace, without being rude, tried his best to get her to tone it down. The few folks sit-ting at nearby tables had turned toward them, their curiosity piqued. Even Sadie had moved closer.

Nikki cleared her throat. "Karina, it's not going to hap-pen. You'll have to find someone else."

The woman swung her a disappointed frown. "You were supposed to help convince him. Thanks for nothing."

Trace stared at Nikki. His expression of disbelief branded her a traitor.

"I need to explain," she said.

"You sure do." He surprised her with a short laugh. "A calendar?"

"Yes." Karina clearly misread his reaction and jumped back in. "You'd be perfect as Mr. March."

Trace shook his head, his lips pressed thin. "She's right. Not gonna happen."

The woman sighed, but seemed otherwise unfazed. She took a final sip of her drink, reached into her cleavage again, then laid a ten on the bar. "Keep my card in case you change your mind. I may come back through Montana next month." She got off the stool, paused to tilt her head and study him a moment. "Maybe Mr. July. Tight button-fly jeans, no shirt, behind you a spray of fireworks against the night sky."

Nikki pressed her own lips together to keep from laughing at the look of astonishment on Trace's face. It really wasn't funny, and she was so lucky he didn't seem furious with her.

"Think about it." Karina shrugged, gave him a saucy wink and walked off.

"Mr. July," Trace muttered. "Shit."

A hand from the Lone Wolf called out, "Oh, Mr. July," in a high-pitched voice and earned a glare from Nikki that shut him right up. The laughter that followed was predictable, but Trace ignored it all.

"So you were in cahoots with her," he said, and there was a hint of hurt in his eyes. "That's surprising."

"Oh. No. It's not like that." Nikki took a deep breath. "When she explained why she was here, I thought it was funny and asked to be there when she told you. I barely knew you then." She leaned on the bar and almost took his hand before she stopped herself. "I forgot all about it until today. I was going to warn you. That's why I left a message."

"I guess I blew that part." He moved his hand closer to hers. They weren't touching, but they might as well have been.

"Thanks for not being mad," she said, still amazed he hadn't even raised his voice. "Even though you had every right."

"I'm a pretty laid-back guy. Usually willing to hear someone out." Smiling, he leaned closer. "Or let her make it up to me."

Nikki let out a loud laugh that drew more than a few looks. She didn't care, and it seemed that neither did Trace. But then she noticed a customer waving his empty mug at her and she straightened with a sigh. "I have to get back to work."

"Well that sucks." Trace let his gaze slide down her body as though he had much better plans for her.

"Stop it right now, McAllister," she warned, and picked up her tray as she came around the bar.

The door creaked open as it had a dozen times in the past hour. Normally she ignored it unless she was expecting Trace. She didn't know what made her look now, but she turned, and felt the blood drain from her face.

Luis.

How? He was supposed to be in Houston. It wasn't possible that he could be here. Her mother promised she hadn't told him where Nikki was living.

His dark hair was shorter and he wore nice jeans, not his usual baggy ones. The blue knit shirt was not his style, and didn't hide the tattoo sleeve that crawled from his wrist up the side of his neck. He couldn't have looked more out of place.

Her feet felt like lead weights. She couldn't seem to move, only watch his gaze pan the room and wait for him to get to her. Her tray was still loaded and she needed to set it down or risk spilling everything.

Luis finally spotted her. She found no relief in the faint curve of his mouth. A smile could go either way with him.

He could be cruel when he was using. Nikki didn't care that he'd sworn to her mom he'd been clean for a year.

It finally registered that the room had grown quiet except for the country music coming from the jukebox. She had to do something. She glanced at the tables closest to her, then set the tray down on the one that had space. Everyone could sort out their own drinks.

She saw him start for the bar and hurried to intercept him, wiping her clammy palms on her jeans. She was able to head him off. But only because he stopped when he saw her coming.

"Hi." She tried to swallow around the lump of panic lodged in her throat. "What are you doing here?"

"Hello, Nikita." Luis moved to kiss her, but she sidestepped him before realizing he'd only been going for her cheek. His touch on her arm was light, then fell away. This wasn't the same man she remembered. "I understand," he said quietly, giving her room.

Obviously unaware of the drama, someone from the back yelled for their beer. Nikki automatically turned and caught Trace's eye. She gave him a small shake of her head and hoped he stayed put. "I'm working," she told Luis while subtly walking him toward the door. "I really can't talk." She saw Sadie retrieve the tray and carry it to the back.

Of course everyone in the bar stared at them.

"No hurry. I don't drink any more but I can have a soda while I wait," Luis said, studying her face. "You look good."

"You shouldn't be here."

"I had to come. I got myself clean. Just like I promised you I would." He sounded more urgent. "I want you back. You said you'd give me another chance if I turned my life around."

"Luis, I was a kid when I said that." She could barely remember the promise she'd made in another life. "I've changed, too."

"I have savings now. Not drug money. I work at my cousin's body shop. Totally legit. A few years and I can buy it from him." He touched her cheek. "Everything I've done is for you, baby."

She pushed his hand away. "I'm not going back to Houston."

"Then we'll go someplace else. Start fresh."

"No, Luis. I wish you hadn't come." She'd always hated the loud country music from the jukebox. Where was it now when she needed it? "Please just leave."

Luis looked past her, his shoulders squaring, and she knew it had to be Trace.

"Nikki, you all right?" he asked from just behind her.

"Fine." She turned and forced a smile for him. "It's okay."

Trace met her eyes. Her weak assurance hadn't been enough.

"You heard her." Luis stayed calm, at least for him, but some of the old belligerence bled into his voice. "Go back and drink your beer, cowboy. And mind your own goddamn business."

"See that's the thing." Trace gave him a thin smile. "Nikki *is* my business, and she doesn't want you here."

"Please stop." She held on to Trace's arm and put her other hand up to Luis. "Please, both of you."

Luis swore. "Tell me how my wife is your business."

Nikki couldn't breathe. Her chest tightened and her throat closed. She reeled at Trace's shocked expression, but it was nothing compared to the pain in his eyes.

TRACE WAITED FOR her denial. This stranger with the tats had to be lying. So why wasn't she saying anything? She just stared, looking guiltier by the second. What the hell? "Nikki?"

She sucked in air, putting a hand to her throat, still staring at him, shame written all over her face. "It's not like that…"

She briefly hung her head, then looked at the other man. "Luis, just go. If you ever cared for me, you'll leave. Now."

Indecision flickered in his eyes. "I only came to get what's mine," he said, and stroked her arm.

Trace watched her delayed reaction in pulling away. "Sorry, dude," he said to the guy, anger and stunned humiliation digging their hooks deeper into him. "My mistake."

"Please, Trace." Her voice was so faint he almost hadn't heard her as he walked around them and out the door.

He got to the sidewalk, thought about stopping and bending over until his head cleared. The truck was still a block away. He pushed on.

Nikki was married? Jesus. That wasn't the kind of thing that could slip someone's mind. He hated to believe the guy, and he wouldn't have if only she'd spoken up. Even if she was legally separated, that would've been okay with him. Things might've gone differently for them until she was divorced, hell, he didn't know.

He jogged the last few yards to his truck, climbed inside with his heart pounding as if it would burst. Did Matt know she was married? Rachel?

It didn't matter because every time Nikki had kissed him, each time they'd made love, she'd lied to him. Not just words gave a lie teeth and she'd taken plenty of bites. What hurt worse was that they'd confided in each other. She'd confessed some pretty heavy stuff, so had he. To think he'd been humbled by her trust... How could he have missed it? He'd thought he knew her. More than any woman he'd ever met. The irony was, he'd finally made up his mind that tonight was the night. He was going to come right out and prove to her that he was in this thing one hundred percent.

He'd believed with everything he had that Nikki was not only brave and strong and independent, but honest down to the bone. It'd never once occurred to him that she could be hiding so much of herself. Not after all they'd been through.

He stuck the key in the ignition and started the truck. His gaze went back to the Watering Hole door. No one had left since him. She was still in there with that guy. Her husband.

As he pulled out of his spot, the fire inside him turned cold. He should have listened to his instincts. Realized he wasn't thinking straight. Twenty-seven was too young to go all in on a relationship. Maybe not for some guys, but for him? His gut had warned him, but that voice had been drowned out by his damn hormones.

He drove slow, careful. Everyone in the bar had just seen him get squashed like a bug. By tomorrow morning, he doubted there was anyone in town, hell, in the county who wouldn't have heard about how she'd made him look like a fool. Just thinking about facing Sam again made Trace's insides crawl.

Why hadn't she told him? Was it because she'd known all along she was going to go back to Luis? Did she love the guy? Is that why she'd made such a point of warning Trace not to get serious?

His cell rang. Nikki's tone. He could have answered the call, but he was too damn angry. So angry, he'd pulled over on the side of the road not too far out of town. Listening to her voice mail telling him she wanted to explain made him ache with disappointment and embarrassment all over again, and he wanted to throw the damn cell out the window. She'd had the chance to explain when he was standing next to her in front of everyone.

Trace sat in the dark, trying to make sense of things. Was that guy still at the bar? She clearly hadn't wanted him there. Dammit. How was Trace supposed to run off in his righteous fury if Nikki needed him?

Maybe he was the biggest fool in Montana but he couldn't

just leave. She hadn't wanted Luis there, and no matter what, Trace wasn't about to drive off without knowing she was okay. For all he knew, Luis had abused her, and that's why she'd left him.

"Well, shit." Trace slammed his hand against the wheel. That was another possible angle. But she still should've told him. Trusted him with the truth.

He turned the ignition again, and made a U-turn to get himself back to the bar. To Nikki. It would be hell walking into the Watering Hole, but there was more at stake than his pride.

He needed to make sure she was safe.

"DON'T YOU GET IT? I'm not like that anymore. I worked all these years—"

"Luis, look, I'm happy for you," she said, as she stared down the street, hoping to spot Trace's truck. She didn't see it, but at least they weren't having this conversation in front of half the town. She turned back to Luis. "And I'm proud. You've done everything you said you would. But it's been a long time."

He snorted and curled his hands into fists. "You think it was easy getting out of that life?"

"I know it wasn't. It hasn't been easy for me, either. And I wasn't—"

"Using. Or in the gang."

She nodded. "Listen, what you did took courage. And you'll do great at the body shop. But not with me."

Luis exhaled sharply. "I suppose it was too much to hope for. But I had to try."

"It wouldn't work anymore. I'm not that girl."

He reached up and touched the side of her face before he turned and walked down the street. She watched him climb into his Chevy, then pulled out her cell phone and hit Trace's speed dial, still not sure what to say. Of course, it went to voice mail just as it had five minutes ago. She wouldn't leave another message. She'd already asked him to come back so she could explain.

Why hadn't she just said right then that Luis was lying? No, she should have told Trace the whole story. She'd been dreaming when she thought she could really have a new life, that all of her sins were in the past. She'd dared to think she didn't have to live and die in the same three square miles of her childhood. But she'd let her guilt, her shame, get the best of her.

She had to find him, to tell him the truth and to admit she'd been a fool for not telling him everything. She wasn't nearly as brave as he thought she was. The truth was, she'd been a coward, running from her past. Maybe she should keep on running. She'd take Wallace's money and start a whole new life, somewhere no one knew her. Now she knew better than to fall for a pair of green eyes and a broad chest. Love was for other people. Not for the likes of her.

Tears welled, and she swiped them away with the back of her hand. *Wallace, you win.*

Nikki's breath caught at the terrible thought. No. He wasn't right about her, dammit. She was better than that. Stronger. She'd made mistakes, and this one might just kill her, but this time she wouldn't be running from her mistake—the real mistake would be to run and leave the most amazing man she'd ever met.

The only thing she could do now was to own up to everything. To be the woman Trace thought she was. She'd stay, finish her night at work, knowing everyone in there would be staring and talking about her. But that didn't matter. She'd come too far to let the old Nikki have her way. The brave Nikki was going to walk back into that bar with her head up.

TRACE STOOD OUTSIDE the door to the Watering Hole, dreading the spectacle. Nothing a bunch of drunk cowboys liked more than a free show, and they'd already gotten the first act. He thought about waiting for the place to close, but screw that. His pride had cost him too much already. Now that he'd seen her truck was still there, he wasn't going to let anything stop him from walking inside and seeing for himself that Nikki wasn't in trouble.

As he pulled the door open, the music hit him like a wave, but just his luck, the goddamn song ended. Every eye was on him.

His gaze went to the bar, and there she was. She hadn't seen him yet, but the sudden silence made her turn. Her look of uncertainty and fear made the rest of the world disappear. He made it across the floor without feeling a step. "Are you okay?" he asked.

She nodded. "I was sixteen. I was hurting after Garret. I was an ass. I'm so sorry."

"So he was telling the truth?"

Her cringe made him ache. "No. Well, not exactly. We went over the border and got married. My mother had it annulled by the end of the week."

"Why didn't you just tell me? I thought you trusted me."

She let out a small whimper. "I do, but I was ashamed. I'd already told you some things about my past, but I was afraid to admit how crazy it had gotten. I'm not the girl next door."

The crack of a pool rack breaking apart split the quiet, and someone coughed, but Trace didn't care. "I know that," he said. "I don't want the girl next door. I want you, just the way you are."

"You don't, though. You don't know—"

"We sat in this very bar back in February, and you told me all I needed to hear about who you were. I was hooked. Still am. You're not the only one who's been holding back.

I should have told you before tonight." He leaned over and caught her hand. It was ice-cold and felt so fragile. "Rachel told me a long time ago that when I finally fell, I'd fall hard. I hate to admit it, but she was spot-on. I love you, Nikki. I kept telling myself I was too young to say those words, but not saying the words doesn't make it less true."

NIKKI OPENED HER MOUTH, but nothing came out. She was still too shocked. "Are you sure?"

"Well, hell, honey, just ask anyone here. You've got a lot of witnesses."

"Oh, God." Her hand covered her mouth as she realized where they were. They might as well have been standing in the middle of the street in broad daylight. No, this was worse. Jerry and Eli had turned their chairs away from their table to get a better view. Sadie at least pretended she wasn't listening. Nikki closed her eyes, wishing everyone but Trace would disappear.

"You gonna leave me hanging out here in the wind?"

Snapping her eyes open, she leaned forward, but she couldn't reach more than his hand over the bar. "What? No. Oh, no. Me, too. I mean, I'm pretty sure. That I love you."

He smiled. "I'll take it. I'm just glad you weren't halfway to Houston. I would have hated making that long drive to go get you. I shouldn't have stormed off."

"Oh, I knew you'd be back."

"How?"

"Something your mom said. Of all three boys, you're the most like your dad. You definitely have the McAllister pride, but you also have the McAllister honor." Nikki walked around the bar until she stood right in front of him. "I didn't know how it would turn out, but I knew you'd let me explain."

"My mom said that?" He looked stunned, a little emotional. "I'm like my dad?"

Nikki nodded. "She did."

"That's a hell of a thing to hear. Thank you. But I didn't come back because of honor, sweetheart." He pulled her close until she was pressed right up against him and he was looking straight into her eyes. "I came back because you're the best thing that's ever happened to me."

She pressed her lips together, trying hard not to cry. The only man who made a difference thought she was just fine the way she was. He loved her. He'd even said it in front of everybody.

When he kissed her, the whole place burst into applause, but she could still hear Sadie's gravelly voice saying, "It's about damn time."

* * * * *

Her Last Best Fling

BY
CANDACE HAVENS

Award-winning author and columnist **Candace "Candy" Havens** lives in Texas with her mostly understanding husband, two children and three dogs, Harley, Elvis and Gizmo. Candy is a nationally syndicated entertainment columnist for FYI Television. She has nterviewed just about everyone in Hollywood, from George Clooney and Orlando Bloom to Nicole Kidman and Kate Beckinsale. You can hear Candy weekly on The Big 96.3 in the Dallas-Fort Worth area. Her popular online writer's workshop has more than two thousand students and provides free classes to professional and aspiring writers. Visit her website at www.candacehavens.com.

For those in the military and police and fire departments, who put their lives on the line for us every day.

_1_

AFTER NINE MONTHS of hell in the Middle East—stuck in a hot, dark cave—Blake Michaels welcomed the deluge pounding his windshield. Heavy rain might keep the curious townsfolk from showing up at the Lion's Club. His mom had moved the party when she discovered a good portion of Tranquil Waters wanted to be there for the hero's return.

He was no hero.

He was a man who served his country, and happened to be in the wrong place at the wrong time.

The gray, wet weather mirrored Blake's mood. He wasn't fond of crowds, at least since he'd returned to the States. The time away had changed him in ways he'd only begun to explore.

He appreciated the thought of a party in his honor, but being around that many people at one time was enough to give a guy the cold sweats. His doctors had promised the anxiety would eventually pass. Almost a year in solitude with only a guard, who never spoke for company, had left him with a few issues.

Once, in the hospital afterward, the nurses had found him huddled in a corner of his room. He never wanted to repeat that night.

He'd had a complete blackout, an "episode" they called it, and it scared the hell out of him. That was when he started to take the therapists more seriously.

As he came around a curve on the highway, a flash of white popped up before him. Brakes squealed as his Ford slid to a stop. His breath ragged from trying to steer away from the woman and the giant animal struggling against her. She held the animal while simultaneously trying to push its hindquarters with the toe of her candy-red high heels into the backseat of her car. This was a problem as her tight pencil skirt only allowed her leg to move to a certain height.

Crazy woman.

The dog outweighed her by at least fifty pounds. She'd have better luck putting a saddle on the black-and-white creature and riding to wherever she wanted it to go.

If they didn't get off the two-lane road fast, someone would plow into them. No way would Blake allow that to happen.

A dog isn't worth her losing her life.

He paused for a second.

Dang if he wouldn't have done the very same thing. He loved animals. Scotty, the therapy dog at the hospital, gave him hours of companionship while he went through the hell the docs called physical and mental therapy.

Straightening his truck on the shoulder, Blake hopped out.

"Here," Blake said as he shoved the beast into the back of the Ford SUV.

As he did, the woman teetered on her high heels and fell back. He caught her with one hand and pulled her out of the way. Slamming the door with his foot so the dog couldn't get out, he steadied her with his hip. Pain shot through his leg, and he sucked in a breath.

"Are you okay?" He kept her upright with his hands around her tiny waist. The sexy librarian look with the falling curls hiding her face, nearly see-through, rain-soaked blouse and tight skirt over sexy curves did dangerous things to his libido.

Down, boy. Down.

"Thanks," she said as she glanced back at the dog. "I'm fine. I better get Harley back to the shelter. This is the second time this week she's broken out. Her owner passed away, and she keeps trying to go home. If you ask me, it's the saddest thing ever to see an animal suffer." She waved her hand. "Well, there are worse things in the world, but it's sad that she doesn't understand that he's gone."

"You could have been killed," he said through gritted teeth, although more from the pain in his leg than being upset with her.

Stiffening, she turned slowly. When their eyes met, a clap of thunder boomed. She jumped and stumbled. He held on to her to keep her from falling down.

Tugging out of his grasp, she raised an eyebrow. "Yes, I'm aware of the danger." Her chin jutted out slightly. "Which is why I stopped to get the dog. She was a danger to anyone else who might cross her path. Thank you for your assistance."

He'd offended her without meaning to. The nurses were right, surly had become his natural state. "I— uh…" He wasn't sure if he should apologize. With his luck, he'd only make it worse.

"Mr. Clooney's rooster Pete says the thunderstorms are going to be pretty bad the next couple of days," she said as she climbed into the vehicle. "And that darn rooster is never wrong. Perhaps you should think about staying inside so you aren't tempted to help poor defenseless animals."

With that, she slammed the door shut.

Did he just get the brush-off?

Mr. Clooney's rooster? Wait, how was that annoying creature still alive?

He remembered when his brother poured half a bottle of cold medicine in the rooster's feed so they could sleep in one morning during the summer. If anything, the somewhat drunk rooster crowed even louder the next morning.

The SUV sped off toward town.

Yep, that was definitely the brush-off.

It'd been a while since he'd spent time with a woman. Well, besides, the doctors and nurses at the hospital. He'd done four tours in a row, only taking a few months off occasionally to see his mom while trying to forget everything he'd gone through the past two years.

This final tour was one he couldn't put on the "man shelf." That's what his therapist, a woman who was exceptionally bright and never let him get away with anything, had called his ability to shove things that upset him to the back of his brain. Every time he tried to redirect the conversation away from his recent past, she called him on it.

Blake shoved a hand over his newly shorn hair. He'd let it get longer in the hospital, but his mom didn't like it that way.

And hell if he wasn't just a big ole mama's boy. Blake and his brother, J.T., would do anything for her. She'd held their family together after their dad died when he and J.T. were teens.

He might not like the idea of the party, but eating home-cooked meals his mom made was high on his list of favorite things. He could suffer through any inconvenience for that.

Thunder hit again, and the black-haired woman's heart-shaped face popped into his mind with those almost-translucent green eyes that had seen too much of the world. He wondered if the thunder might be an ominous sign that he should stay away from her.

He grinned.

Nope, that wasn't going to happen. The last thing he needed was to chase some skirt, but there was something about her. She'd been dressed sexy, but she didn't suffer fools gladly.

That was something he admired.

He liked a challenge. This was a small town, and he was about to be at a party with some of the best gossips in Texas—and that was saying something in this state. A type like the sexy librarian would surely be a topic of conversation. His mom hadn't mentioned anyone moving into town during their chats, so the woman had to be fairly new to Tranquil Waters.

After parking the truck in front of the Lion's Club,

he ripped off the wet shirt. He had an extra hanging in the cab. Once he was dressed in his blues, he steeled himself for the oncoming tide of good wishes.

"For he's a jolly good…" voices rang out as he swung open the door and stepped inside. In other circumstances, he would have run back to the truck. But he smiled and shook hands, all the while thinking about that woman with the raven hair and killer red heels.

Perhaps having half the town at his party wasn't such a bad thing.

Facing the blue-haired gossip brigade, he gave them his most charming smile.

"Ladies, you haven't changed a bit," he said. "If I didn't know better I'd guess you were selling your souls to keep that peaches-and-cream skin of yours."

His mother rolled her eyes, but stood on tiptoes to give him a hug.

"You're up to something," she whispered.

Oh, he was definitely up to *something*.

"BRAN MUFFINS AND fake butter. That was one knight in shining armor," Macy complained to Harley as she wrapped wire around the lock on her cage. She never swore around the animals in the shelter as she believed they'd been through enough trauma, without listening to her temper tantrums. So when she wanted to use angry words, she thought about foods she hated.

"Doesn't it figure that ten minutes after I vow no more men forever, he shows up?"

The dog made a strange noise that sounded like

"yes." Great Danes did have their own language. And she bet Harley understood every syllable she said.

"Oh, no. He has to be so hot that steam came off of him. And me." She fanned her face. The heat from the encounter still on her cheeks.

"Here he comes galloping on his horse to the rescue." Macy's last two relationships were nonevents, except for the part where they'd cheated on her. Three weeks ago she'd discovered the man she thought she might marry was having what he called "a meaningless relationship" with an intern at the paper.

Well, it had meant something to Macy.

Harley made a strange sound.

"Fine, it was a truck he galloped in on, but still."

The dog whined again.

"Lovely girl, I'm sorry. I've been going on and on about me, when you have much more to be sad about." She squatted as much as her skirt would allow and petted Harley through the kennel.

The handsome face of the knight was one she recognized. Though his dark brown hair had been cropped close to his head, it was those dark brown, almost-black eyes she couldn't forget. The marine, who'd been captured in Afghanistan, had returned home. She'd been headed to the welcome-home party to cover it for the newspaper. That wasn't the kind of thing publishers did at larger papers, but this was a small town. Darla, the reporter assigned to the story, had to pick her kid up from school and take him to the dentist. And the other two reporters had the flu.

Thinking that it would be a quick in-and-out, Macy had decided to cover the party.

Well, until she found Harley soaked to the skin.

She loved animals. They weren't as judgmental as humans. Since she was sixteen, she'd been volunteering at various shelters around the world. Every time she took a new job, that was one of the first things she did. Well, except for when she was in the Middle East. She didn't have time to breathe then, let alone help anyone else.

In the newspaper business, one had to move a lot. There was constant downsizing and she had to go where the jobs were. That was how she'd landed in Boston—until the fiasco that was her almost-fiancé throwing their comfortable life into the proverbial toilet.

Harley nudged her.

"I promise as soon as the fence guy gets done, you are moving in with me. If this rain would stop, they could finish." This was the first pet she'd ever adopted. The old girl had one green and one blue eye. The sorrow in them tore at Macy's heart. She was an orphan, too, and she'd bonded with the dog ever since she'd caught her trying to get back home the first time.

Her great-uncle Todd, who had been Macy's only remaining relative, had willed her the town's newspaper. For months she'd been trying to sell it with no luck. When she walked in on her ex and his meaningless plaything, she decided moving to a small locale wasn't such a bad idea. Along with the paper, her uncle had left her a beautiful house overlooking White's Lake. She'd decided to put an eight-foot fence along two of the four-acres of the property so Harley would have a place to roam.

"Great Danes need a lot of space." She smiled and scratched the dog's ears.

"Hey, I thought you went to the party," said Josh from the door as he slipped booties over his shoes for sanitary purposes. He was the local veterinarian who donated his services to the shelter.

"I was on my way, but Miss Harley got out again. I caught up with her on the highway."

Josh tickled the dog under her chin, his fingers poking through the cage. It was a large eight-by-eight-foot space, but it wasn't big enough for the hundred-and-seventy-five-pound dog.

"Nice knot with the wiring there. Do you sail?" He pointed to the impenetrable knot she'd devised to keep Harley in.

She shrugged. "Something I picked up from my dad. In the summer we'd go sailing." Those weeks were some of the happiest of her life. Her parents were journalists, so it was in her blood, but it meant they traveled the far ends of the earth, leaving Macy at home.

"So are you heading over to the hero party?"

Feeling as if she'd stood in a rainstorm for an hour, which she did, she decided she'd be better off going home. "No, I'm heading back to my place to change."

She noticed Josh wasn't meeting her eyes. He did everything he could not to look at her.

She glanced down. Her white blouse was completely sheer and she was cold.

Great. Wonderful. Lovely.

"Well, Cecil is up at the front, so I guess I'll be going," she said as she made a quick exit.

Josh was a nice guy. They'd even tried to date once. But discovered there was absolutely no chemistry, which was probably why he was doing his best not to look at her nipples protruding through the sheer fabric of her shirt and nude-colored bra.

Unless she wanted to be the fodder for more town gossip, there would be no party in her future.

The lovely scent of wet dog pervaded her senses as she made the short drive home.

Five minutes later, she turned on the fireplace in the main family area. The front of the place had a Gothic Revival exterior. The back was full of windows. She loved the water. Living near it made her feel close to her dad.

After constantly chasing the next big story, the pace of Tranquil Waters nearly killed her at first. But she'd grown accustomed to the quiet. Her whole life she'd heard Texans were incredibly kind, and they were— However, the ones here didn't trust outsiders, especially Yankees, of which she was one, having spent most of her formative years in the Northeast.

A hot shower was in order. Then she'd bundle up and see what Mrs. Links, the housekeeper who worried that Macy was wasting away, left in the fridge for dinner. The housekeeper came in three times a week, even though Macy was perfectly capable of cleaning up after herself.

Mrs. Links was another part of her strange inheritance from Uncle Todd. He'd provided for her weekly allowance until the time she no longer needed employment.

Macy didn't have the heart to ask the nearly seventy-five-year-old woman when that might be. For someone who made a living by asking the tough questions, Macy had a soft spot when it came to animals and her elders.

As the warm water sluiced across Macy's body, her mind drifted to the marine. Those biceps under her hands were of a man who wasn't afraid of hard labor. Marines had to stay fit, and she had a feeling he'd have washboard abs, as well.

Men with great abs were her weakness.

You swore off men.

The smell of his fresh, masculine scent. Those hard muscles, the warm smile, even after all he'd been through.

The blood thrummed through her body.

She hadn't been with a man in what felt like forever. That was all. He was hot, and any other woman would feel the same way after looking into those sweet chocolate-brown eyes.

Turning down the water's temperature to cool her body, she wondered how long she'd be able to resist the marine.

2

VIOLENT THOUGHTS CROSSED Blake's mind as Mr. Clooney's rooster crowed, waking half the town—so much for the extra rest. Shoving the pillow over his head, he closed his eyes and willed himself back to the dream about the woman in the red heels. The rooster crowed again.

"I'll kill that bird some day," he growled as he rolled out of bed. Too many years in the military had him up, showered and sipping coffee ten minutes later.

His mother had taped a note to the fridge that said, "Muffins are in the warming drawer. Love, Mom."

At five in the morning, she'd probably already been at the feed store for at least an hour. She liked to get the paperwork done before the place opened. Even though she didn't need to be there anymore, she'd insisted on keeping the books and visiting with customers when they came in. She'd built the business from the ground up while his father traveled the world with the military. She believed in having roots and wasn't much for leaving the town she'd been born in. Their relationship worked, because when they were together, they treated each other as if no one else existed in the world. Well, except for Blake and his brother.

Their parents made certain their boys had an idyllic childhood in the town centered between two lakes. They lived on the edge of town, which had exactly four stoplights, a couple of grocery stores and various shops on the rectangle, as they liked to call it. When the town was first built, there was no real plan. When they finally decided they needed a courthouse it was built in the heart of the rectangle of shops and businesses.

But Tranquil Waters had changed while he was deployed. He remembered laughing about the letters from his mom talking about how the town council had decided that they could have a Dairy Queen and a McDonald's on the same side of the highway.

They also—thanks to the lakes and artists and writers who populated the town—had a good tourist industry year-round. It was almost Halloween and he hadn't seen a house yet that hadn't been decorated. There were several haunted B and B's and even a large corn maze on the Carins' pumpkin farm.

Everything seemed so simple in a small town. It didn't take a CIA spook to find out that the woman he'd run into on the highway was the new publisher of the town newspaper.

"That Yankee girl just doesn't understand our ways," complained Mrs. Lawton. "She reported that old Mr. Gunther was thrown in jail Saturday night.

Well, everyone knows he's spent every weekend in
that jail cell for the last twenty years. Ever since his
sweetheart of a wife, Pearl, passed—God rest her
soul—he's just been longing for her. Poor man. What
he needs is a new woman, a younger one to keep his
mind off his troubles."

While she had glanced around at the other women
in her circle, Blake had a feeling she wanted to be
the new woman to occupy Mr. G's thoughts. Blake
grinned as he sipped his punch. Didn't matter that
she'd just turned eighty-five and Mr. G had to be
nearing a hundred.

"She has that huge house, darn near a mansion,"
Lady Smith chimed in. Her name was Lady, and for
some reason everyone in town called her Lady Smith.
Out of respect, and the fact that she was a friend of
his mother's, Blake had once called her Mrs. Smith
when he was about ten. She'd scolded him and told
him she was a Lady, and he'd do well to remember
that in the future.

The town was full of oddballs, and he'd been one
of them. As a kid, he'd run around dressed like Davy
Crockett for two years and no one had said a word.
Apart from his brother, who was more a Spider-Man
fan.

"She's got more money than she knows what to
do with. Imagine, putting the paper on the inter—
whatever those kids use nowadays," Lady had complained. "People here like to hold a newspaper in
their hands. And she doesn't seem to understand that
there are some stories that just aren't fit to tell. I've
written countless letters to the editor, but she never

prints or listens to them." Lady waved her hand in the air dismissively.

"Darn Yankee."

How dare she tell the truth about Tranquil Waters. The nerve of the woman. Blake found himself chuckling as he rinsed his cup in the sink.

His mother probably didn't need his help at the feed store. But he didn't want to sit around stewing. It almost always sent him in the wrong direction.

He wondered where Macy—he'd finally learned her name—might be. Likely still in bed, if she were smart. Any sane person would be at this hour of the morning. Pulling the truck out of the drive, he saw something run past.

Blake blinked a few times and followed the blur.

"It can't be."

The monster dog he'd recently stuffed into a car sat on the porch of a white-framed house with a for-sale sign in the yard. The spot was about five blocks from his mom's house.

The way Harley stared at the door, as if willing it to open, broke his heart. Blake had seen a lot of awful things through the years, but kids and animals in distress were his weaknesses. He'd do anything to protect them.

Macy was right. Unlike a human, the dog couldn't understand her master was gone.

Exiting the truck slowly, he stepped up the stone path. She glanced back at him, with the saddest puppy eyes. One of the eyes was blue, the other green.

He hadn't seen her eyes when he'd been dealing with the hindquarters.

"Hey, pretty girl, what's up?"

He held out his hand, but she turned away from him. Lifting a large paw, she hit the doorknob.

Damn dog. His heart lurched. Not sure what he should do, he sat down on the top step next to her. He could drag her to the truck, but he didn't have the nerve. If he gained her trust, maybe she'd go willingly. He had a feeling being at the house was about more than just returning to where she felt safe.

"I'll sit here with you until you decide what you want to do next," he said softly. He didn't have anything better to do.

The dog pawed at the door again and growled.

Blake leaned back against the railing. He could have sworn the dog said, "Let me in."

I am losing it. Now dogs are talking to me.

"Did you just say, let me in?"

The dog pawed his shoulder.

Yep, he was crazy.

"Oh, girl, sorry, I don't have a key. I'd let you in if I could, but I don't have one. And I have a code I live by. Breaking and entering isn't an option."

She barked and then leaped off the porch.

As quick as his sore leg allowed him, he got up and followed her around the side of the house.

When they reached the back porch, she pawed at the door handle and attempted to open it with her mouth. She snarled when it didn't budge.

"Well, we tried," he said.

She cocked her head, and he swore she rolled her eyes.

Taking off to a chipped birdbath in the middle of

the lawn, covered with dirt, she pawed the rocks surrounding the base of the concrete fixture and barked. Blake limped out to the fountain, more to appease her than anything.

There on the ground was a key.

"Okay, dog. Now you're freaking me out." If she had had two legs instead of four, she could pass for human. And she had to be one brilliant pup to relate the key to the door.

As he unlocked the door, he noticed someone peeking over the fence.

He pointed an accusatory finger at the dog. "Fine, but if we get arrested you're taking the rap." He patted her on the head. Before he could turn the knob and open the door himself, she nosed it open and stood in the small kitchen, as if waiting for him to come inside. Once he was in, she closed the door with her nose.

Blake had never seen such a thing. The few dogs he'd had when he was a boy could sit and lie down, but that was about it.

Harley woofed and trotted to the living room, where she sat in front of a wingback chair. She nodded at him, as if she wanted him to sit down in it. More out of curiosity than anything, he did. A paw shot out and pushed so hard on the chair he worried he'd go head over heels.

But he didn't fall.

The dog ducked beneath the chair and tossed out several stuffed animals, a ball and chew bones that had seen better days. Once she had her stash from under the chair, she moved the items one at a time to the charcoal-gray sofa. The booty soon became a pillow as she lay atop her toys, sighing as if she'd been on a long journey.

"Poor girl," Blake whispered. The sight of her relaxing choked him up.

"That's the first time I've seen her sleep since he passed," a feminine voice whispered.

Head snapping around, he took in Macy Reynolds's tight jeans, pink hoodie and those furry boots women wore when the thermometer dipped below seventy. The town was having an unusually cool October, and the temperature hung around the fifty-degree mark. A sleepy angel with no makeup, and more beautiful than she'd been the day before.

"I saw her running past my mom's house when I left this morning and I decided to follow." He held up a hand. "I swear she made me unlock the door. She showed me where the key was."

"I believe it. Evidently the drama was about her missing toys. I don't blame her," Macy continued to whisper. "I'm kind of fond of my stuff. I don't have that much, but what I do have is precious to me."

Odd since he'd learned she inherited her uncle's house. He assumed she had tons of stuff.

"What?" She checked her clothing as if she might have missed a button.

"Nothing. I…heard last night that you inherited your uncle's new mansion."

She scrunched her face. "Yes, he— Yes."

"For the record, I haven't been stalking you. Some of the gossips at the party were talking about it."

She smirked and moved to the sofa to sit beside Harley.

"Is there an expiration date or something on being the subject of town gossip? I've never lived in a place where other people were so in your business. Usually, as a reporter, I'm the nosy one. It's disconcerting. And I don't think they like me very much, although I'm doing my best to turn their local into a paper that resembles more than tractor reports."

He laughed, and the dog opened an eye and glared at him.

"Unfortunately, until the next interesting person moves to town, it'll be all about you."

"Yes, but the hero has returned." She nodded in his direction. "Can't you be the subject of conversation for a while?"

"Nah. I'm not nearly as interesting as a Yankee woman who wears pencil skirts and sky-high heels. And according to the gray hairs, you have a scandalous past where you combed the world reporting on everything from celebrities to wars. Some man broke your heart, and you're here hiding away."

Her eyes opened wide. "Wow. They are good. I wish they'd be as generous with their words with me. Honestly, I know heads of state who give more in an interview than people in this town."

She hadn't bothered to deny any of what he'd said, so it must have been true about combing the world and the man who was in her life. He wondered if that relationship was really over. He shrugged. "Give it some time, they'll come around."

"Will you talk to me?"

He frowned. "I thought that was what we were doing."

"No—I mean, yes." She waved her hand. "In an interview. The *Tranquil Waters News* should do a feature on the town hero."

That was the last thing he wanted.

"There isn't a lot these folks don't already know. I've been gone for about seven years. I'm back, a little worse for the wear but alive. There isn't much more to tell. I was doing my job but happened to be in the wrong place at the wrong time."

She sighed, not unlike the suffering sound the dog had made. "I should have known. You're no different than the rest."

The disappointment in her voice forced him to do something he promised he never would.

"All right, if you want to talk, that's cool, but not right now. I need to get to the feed store to help my mom." Small white lie, but he had to stall to gather his thoughts. "I was on my way there when I saw Harley." At least that part was true.

She glanced from the dog to him as if she were trying to discern the truth. "We could do something a little less formal, if that would make you more comfortable. How about tonight? I could make you dinner at my place."

He almost laughed at the look on her face as if she couldn't believe she just asked him to dinner.

"If food is involved, I'm there. If you're sure?"

She nodded. "How about seven-thirty?"

"See ya then." He stood.

"Don't you need the address?"

He chuckled. "The house is where the old Gladstone farm used to be, right?"

"Yes. It overlooks the lake."

"Trust me. I know that area very well." More than once, he and his friends had thrown a party at the old barn, which had been torn down years ago.

"Do you need help with the dog?"

"No, I'm going to go grab my laptop and work here so she can rest. I have a feeling she'll follow those toys wherever I take them."

"Okay, see ya later." He patted the dog and walked out the front door.

He had a date. Well, it was technically an interview, but he was practiced at giving nonanswers. He'd done it his entire military career. All of his assignments were classified, so he couldn't share anything.

Hope she won't be too mad when she finds out I'm as tight-lipped as the rest of Tranquil Waters.

He started the truck engine. The last thing he wanted was the sleepy angel mad at him.

"WHAT WAS I thinking?" Macy blurted into the phone. "You don't invite people you're interviewing to dinner."

"Yes, you do. It's just the dinner's at a restaurant most of the time," her friend Cherie chimed in. "Chill, girl. You're going to have a heart attack. This guy must be superhot to make you so nervous."

Macy slipped on a pair of flats. After his comment about the heels, she realized she'd been trying too hard. Except for those over sixty, this was more of a jeans and T-shirt town. She was perfectly comfortable in that attire.

It wasn't until her breakup with Garrison that Cherie, her nearest and dearest friend, forced her to leave Boston and took her for a makeover in Manhattan. They tossed out everything she'd owned and decided to start fresh with a sexy new wardrobe. Add a brand-new haircut that was perfect for her shoulder-length curls. And a newfound passion for accessories. Cherie had convinced her that shoes and purses were really works of art.

She didn't have to twist Macy's arm very hard.

But if Macy wanted to fit into the landscape of Tranquil Waters, she'd have to scale back on the big-city wardrobe, etc.

"*Superhot* doesn't cover it," she said honestly. "*Scorching* might come close. He puts that gorgeous action-adventure star Tom Diamond to shame."

"Wait. Hotter than Tom Diamond? The man who will be my husband someday, even if I have to shoot him with a tranq gun and stuff him in my trunk? I think it might be time for me to visit Texas."

"You are welcome anytime. I certainly have the room. And yes he's that handsome, and he's sweet to dogs and loves his mother. You know how tough that is for me. He's like a triple threat. But I have to keep this professional. The last thing I need in this gossip-hungry town is to date its hero."

"So you want to date him. Hmm."

"Stop analyzing me and putting words in my mouth," Macy complained. Cherie never stopped being a psychiatrist, but it was her only vice so Macy put up with her.

"You said the words. I'm just placing them in the proper order for you."

"Privacy is impossible at any of the restaurants in town. I'm sure that's why I came up with making the dinner. I wanted him to feel comfortable, to share as much as possible."

"He's a war hero, you know there's not much he can say," her friend warned.

"This isn't my first time." She'd been to almost every war zone in the world the past five years. It had only been the past twelve months that she'd decided to take a permanent position out of the line of fire. Little did she know it was just as dangerous at home.

She'd been shot at, kidnapped twice by insurgents and lost in the middle of the desert. None of that had been as bad as her ex's betrayal.

"Stop thinking about that jerk. He's not worth it."

"How did you know?" Macy laughed at her friend's incredible insight.

"He called here looking for you again. For a hot-shot newspaper publisher, he's not very good at finding people."

Macy snorted. He was one of the best reporters ever, and if he truly wanted to find her, he would. But she'd told him if he did, she'd only turn him away again. It was the truth.

"Of course, I told him to stuff it up his—"

Lights flashed across her bedroom window. "Oh, man, he's here early. Darn those marines and their punctuality."

Macy stared down at the melee of clothing on her bed and picked up the frilly black blouse on top.

"Put down the black, and choose the red. Men love red."

"That was scary. Fine. Red it is. I love you and I wish you'd come see me. It's a nice town but—I still feel very outsiderish."

"Oh, girl, don't you worry. They'll love you as much as I do. Just give them some time and the chance to get to know you. Charm the pants off that marine. That will be a great start."

The doorbell rang and Harley barked twice.

The big dog had settled in just fine. Macy had even bought the dog her own couch for the family room. The fence had been finished that afternoon, and they'd reinforced the gate with two different kinds of locks.

She turned off the phone.

Harley sat patiently at the door waiting for their guest.

Shoving her curls out of her face, Macy took a deep breath and turned the knob.

Oh, shoot, the man is beautiful.

Dressed in dark jeans, cowboy boots and a dark blue button-down under a leather jacket, he was way beyond scorching.

Her normally agile mind couldn't think of the word, but she knew there was one.

This is work. This is work. This is work.

He cocked his head and stared down at Harley.

"Did she run away again?"

"What?" Macy forced her hand to stay still even though she wanted to wave it in front of her own face, which was suddenly too warm even though the temperature outside was in the low fifties.

"Harley? You know the dog?"

He smiled at her as if he were humoring her.

"Uh, sorry. I'd been on the phone and I'm a little—uh—" *Hot for you.* No, that wasn't right. "Out of sorts. Please come in. And Harley lives with me now. She would have been in here days ago, but the rain kept the ground too wet for them to finish putting the fence in."

He handed her a colorful bouquet of chrysanthemums in a vase. "These are a present for your new home." In his other hand he held a large paper bag. "I didn't know what you were cooking so I brought a couple bottles of wine, some dark beer and, er... green tea."

She took the flowers and led him to the kitchen. "Thank you, these are beautiful, but you didn't have to bring anything."

He shrugged and sat the bag down on her quartz countertop. "It's the south, if you don't bring a housewarming gift on the first occasion you visit, or to any party you're invited to, they'll talk about you for years."

"I'll have to remember that," she said. Not that she'd been invited to anything, but maybe some day.

"I probably should have mentioned my kitchen skills are somewhat limited. But I make a mean beef stew. I put it on earlier today, so it should be ready in a few minutes. And I have bread and salad."

"Sounds good to me. In general, I like food, so it doesn't matter too much what it is. After C-Rats, I can, and have, digested everything from guinea pig in Machu Picchu to some weird toad in Africa. I'm not sure that last one didn't lead to a night of hallucinations."

She laughed. "I'm pretty adventurous when it comes to food, but I've never eaten either of those."

"You get to a point where just about everything really does taste like chicken." He smiled and her heart did a double thump.

Oh, heck, I'm in trouble.

She forced a smile.

"Now I feel like maybe I should have tried for something more exotic." She examined the wine bottles he'd brought. He'd surprised her with his choices. She didn't know much about wine, but neither bottle was cheap. "Do you have a preference?"

"Whatever you want is fine with me. I'll be drinking the tea."

At her quizzical look, he explained. "The docs are weaning me off the painkillers for my leg. It's best if I don't drink as it can create an allergic reaction. Although, me and my buddies at the hospital suspected they only told us that so we don't find out how the painkillers are with alcohol. They deal with a lot of addicted vets there."

"We can't have that. Tea it is. The last thing I need is alcohol. It tends to loosen my tongue, and I'm not the one who needs to do the talking tonight."

She caught the tightening of his lips before he turned away. "I don't mind," he said. "If you want a glass of wine. It won't bother me."

"No," she said lightly. "I've grown fond of tea since moving here. Cracks me up that they drink it iced even in the dead of winter."

"Staple of the South," he said, pulling a large plastic pitcher with a lid out of the bag. "Usually it's black tea. I have this friend from China who told me that green tea has healing properties. It also clears away some of the fogginess from the drugs."

"I've heard that, too." She'd forgotten about his injuries. Except for a small limp, he didn't seem to be in much pain. But she'd met plenty of marines and she knew how tough they were. If he had to take drugs, the injuries were severe. The journalist in her wanted to know specifics, but it would wait.

"Before we eat, would you like to see the house? Actually, most of it is my uncle Todd's taste. But I have a few touches here and there."

"I like the stonework on the outside mixed with the pale brick. It blends into the rocky hills behind the house."

"Yes, that was one of his ideas—for it to blend into the landscape. Though, I think it's kind of fun that he added a Gothic touch with some of the windows and the roof alignment.

"Did you know my uncle? I mean, you've been gone awhile, but before?"

"I didn't know him. I probably heard his name around town, but I wasn't much interested in the newspaper when I was a kid. And some might say I was a little self-absorbed back then. I like to say, I was a teenager."

They laughed.

She took him through the family area where Harley plopped down on her sofa. The television was on

Animal Planet, which seemed to be the dog's favorite along with anything on PBS.

He smiled. "She's made herself at home there."

"Oh, that couch is hers. I even had them put extra down in it and then had that wrapped in plastic and an outdoor fabric. Great Danes have joint and bone aches most of their lives. I wanted Harley to have a soft place to rest. Just a minute, I need to change the channel for her."

Picking up the remote, she set it on one of the PBS *Nova* specials. Harley grunted her agreement.

She'd learned about the dog's television preferences earlier in the day when she'd sat with her at her former home. If Macy tried to watch a channel Harley didn't like, the dog would voice her displeasure.

Not that she was spoiled or anything.

The house was a Texas T shape. The various hallways fed into the center area, which was the main entertaining space. "Down that hall are two bedrooms. There's another guest bedroom down that hall—" she pointed "—and the master bedroom and study are down that hall," she said.

It didn't seem appropriate to take him to the bedrooms. "There's a loft upstairs with two more bedrooms. But it isn't really worth the trip up. Let me show you the study. There are a lot of Civil War antiques in there. My uncle was a collector." The rest of the house had been furnished in rich warm tone-on-tone colors. It was a comfortable place to relax at the end of the day. The only room that was slightly feminine was the master bedroom and bathroom, which Macy had decorated.

Macy opened the door to the study and smiled when Blake muttered, "Woooee. This is a museum."

His eyes traveled over the glass cases filled with small items and guns from various Civil War battles.

She'd had the estate appraised and this room alone was worth a couple of million. The study had been outfitted with special equipment that would protect it from fire and anything else Mother Nature might throw at it. The whole house was a bunker of sorts, concrete surrounded by stone. The windows could withstand an F-5 tornado. That was good because in this part of the country hurricanes and tornados happened at least once or twice a year.

"I don't have the heart to auction off these things. Other than the newspaper, this was my uncle Todd's only passion. I can feel his spirit in here, and I just can't let go of his stuff."

Blake blew out a whistle. "I'm no expert, but even I know this is one incredible collection. There are people who'd pay big money for it, but I understand how you feel. My dad collected baseball caps and cards. We still have an entire wall of his hats, some are from teams that no longer exist, and a few are hats his dad had given to him. There's an original Yankees cap in the bunch, but my mom hides that one when her friends come over.

"It was never even a question if we'd keep them. And I feel the same way about them, as you do."

She smiled. "Sounds like you really loved your dad."

Flipping off the light switch, he followed her out the door and to the kitchen.

"Has the interview started?" His voice had changed and he sounded as if he suspected her of trying to get him to talk about his past.

"No. Mere curiosity. I thought I'd feed you before grilling you." She winked at him.

"Then, yes. My dad was a hero to my brother and me. He's the reason I went into the military, albeit he was air force. He was a pilot until he decided to retire and help Mom with the feed store. He was a tough old goat, and my brother and I didn't get away with much when we were kids."

"I met your mom when I first arrived. I had to get a lawn mower and other gardening tools."

He chuckled.

She served up the bowls of stew. "Your mother found me frowning as I checked out the lawn mowers. She dug around in her pockets and handed me a card that had the number of a teenager who does yards. Her exact words were, 'He's a good kid. For four acres it'll be about a hundred dollars a week. If he tries to charge you more, tell him I'll knock him upside the head.'"

Blake laughed. "Yep, that's my mom."

"I loved her. She was one of the few people who was genuinely kind to me. I'd heard Texans are a friendly bunch. And, okay, everyone has been nice to my face. But I get the strangest looks. And as I mentioned earlier, they haven't been exactly welcoming."

He carried both of the bowls to the other end of the counter where there were stools and place settings. "Like I said earlier, soon someone will move to town and then you'll be one of the gang. Just give them more time."

She smiled. "My friend Cherie told me the same thing. I'm not sure why it bothers me so much. I never knew any of my neighbors when I lived in New York, Paris or anywhere in the Middle East. Most of the time I lived out of hotels."

At the mention of hotels, his jaw tightened. She'd read what she could find on him, and knew that he'd been in Africa when he sustained his injuries. He was protecting a visiting American ambassador there. He and most of his men were hit by enemy fire, but they'd saved the ambassador and other dignitaries that day. The soldiers had earned Purple Hearts.

"Don't be too worried about it," he interrupted her thoughts. "Small-town life isn't always what it's cracked up to be. Eventually, you feel like a part of the community when everyone knows your name. It can be a wonderful thing, or a curse." His eyebrow rose.

"A curse?" It hadn't been that bad.

"Oh, yes. And especially if a certain high school girl's dad finds you in the barn with her, um, counting hay straws. He calls your dad, who gives you the I'm-disappointed look in front of the entire town when he finds you later at Lucky Chicken Burger sharing a box with your friends." He looked to the heavens. "People still talk about how he watched as my mom dragged me out by my ear. One of the most embarrassing days of my life."

She nearly sputtered her stew, she laughed so hard. "I can't imagine your mother doing that. She talks so highly of you. She's so proud."

"Now she is. That day, not so much. I was grounded for six weeks after that and wasn't allowed to go on dates alone with a girl until I left for college. If we didn't go in a group, I wasn't given permission to go. I had to write letters of apology to the girl, her parents, my parents and our minister."

He shook his head as she started to laugh again. "Sure, it sounds funny, but back then—my friends and my brother never let me forget it. I ran away to college so fast, it was no joke. Joined the marines to help pay for my bachelors and MBA.

"I was determined I would never come back to this place, but I'm a mama's boy. I probably shouldn't admit that. I missed her and dad so much by the end of that first semester, I hitched a thousand miles to get home by Christmas Eve. Of course, my mom read me the riot act because I could have been killed on the road."

"Still, I bet she was glad to see you."

He nodded. "It wasn't long after that my dad got sick. So I was grateful we had that Christmas together."

A chunk of carrot caught in her throat as she watched the memories pass across his face. There'd been a deep family love there. She envied him that. He grew silent.

She swallowed and had a drink of tea. "My parents traveled a lot for their jobs. We didn't get to have many holidays together. I kind of envy you that."

"What did they do?"

"Journalists. My mom wrote for magazines, my dad was on air for different TV affiliates."

"Are they still at it?"

Macy bit her lip. "No. They were killed in a small-plane crash on their way to report on a new orphanage in India. Happened about eight years ago. Uncle Todd was my last living relative. It's just me now."

Blake frowned. "Sorry. I didn't mean to bring up such painful memories."

She patted his arm. Her fingers tingled from the contact. "You didn't. We were talking about family. I just wish I had what you had and have with your mom. I believe the world would be a better place if more parents were like yours.

"I'm lucky that I have great friends all over the world. They helped me when I lost my parents. I was doing an internship in Bosnia with a newspaper and the military guys I'd been following arranged for me to get a flight home on one of their transports. One of them even flew with me and stayed until Uncle Todd could get to the base. I never forgot that. Kevin Donaldson was his name. He had two kids and a wife who adored him. Anytime I was stateside, they insisted on me coming to visit.

"Wow. Look at me telling you my whole life story. Who is interviewing whom, here? I never talk to anyone like this."

He winked at her. "It's the green tea. Has mystical properties in it."

They both laughed.

"Do you want another bowl?"

"Sure. The stew is good. I miss home cooking."

She handed him another full bowl and shoved the plate of French bread at him so he could reach it. "I—I did some digging. As I mentioned, I've covered the military for years for various assignments. I know you can't tell me exactly what happened, although I do know about the ambassador. That's a matter of public record. And that you guys saved him and the others who were investigating the ammunitions camp someone had discovered in the Congo."

"You have done your research." His voice was guarded again.

"I don't want to ask you anything I know you can't answer. What I would like to know is how it happened. Several of your men were hit, but luckily everyone survived."

He sat his spoon in the bowl and stared down at it.

"Some were luckier than others," he whispered.

Her brow furrowed. "Do you mean the injuries?"

"Yes, and the nightmares. Some of us are having a tough time letting go what happened there."

"What did happen?"

His deep brown gaze cut to her. "You know I can't give you details."

She sighed. "Was it an ambush? From what I've figured out so far, you guys had a peaceful week there until you were getting ready to leave. Then all hell broke loose."

As if Harley had sensed the tension, she nudged between them and put her head on his thigh.

He sucked in a breath.

"Is she hurting you?"

"No. It's just sore, like a bruise. Mind you, her head is like a ton of bricks."

"It is very large. She accidentally bumped my nose earlier with her head when I put food in her bowl, and I thought for sure I'd have black eyes."

He smiled, but it was weak.

Stupid. As professional as she was, it bothered her to realize she'd triggered such old memories—hurtful ones from the look of concern on his face.

That was it. He wasn't just a hero. He was a man. That would be her story. No one needed to read about his nightmares of that terrible day, or the darkness that clearly haunted him. How often had she told that story? Heroes deserved to be recognized, but maybe she could focus on who they were after they came home, rather than who they were then.

So many soldiers were affected by the experiences they'd gone through. Some—not in a good way. But some said that it made them more aware of how small the world could be.

"I have chocolate chip cookies for dessert. Actually, I was going to show you the best way to eat them."

"Well, I thought you ate cookies with your mouth." He gave her an odd look, and she rolled her eyes.

"Ah, where is your sense of food adventure? In fact, I'm going to take that adventuresome nature of yours to a whole new level."

"Bring it on, Macy. I can take whatever you've got."

The seductive, whiskey sound of his voice and his choice of words did all kinds of naughty things to her.

Be careful.

But it was too late. She'd already crossed the line with Lieutenant Blake Michaels, and she wasn't at all upset about it.

3

BLAKE TOSSED AND turned in his bed. Thoughts of Macy in those jeans and that lacy red top made it impossible for him to sleep. He'd wanted to kiss her as soon as he saw her lick the whip cream from her lips. That pink tongue had darted out and all he could think of was capturing it with his mouth. He'd wanted to cover her in the white confection and lick every inch of her.

Damn. He had it bad for her.

He sat up on the side of the bed. He needed a shower, a cold one.

Why did she have to be a reporter? If she had any other occupation he'd be doing his best to get in her bed. He couldn't remember when a woman had affected him the way she did. Her laugh, smile and the way she walked with those lovely curvy hips swaying back and forth held his attention.

He thought back over their conversation. Even though she'd pried, she did it respectfully. True to her word, she hadn't asked him a single thing he couldn't answer. And when she dug a little too deep, she'd backed off and made them chocolate chip cookie pies, her version of the whoopie pie.

She was hot. Smart and funny. The perfect combo.

But he couldn't risk hanging out with a woman who might reveal secrets he prided himself on keeping. He might slip up, get carried away. And the last thing he needed was for his superiors to see something like that in the newspaper.

He'd been thinking about taking the honorable discharge on offer, and maybe settling down like his friends Rafe and Will. They'd all met when Will was their captain on missions in Iraq and Afghanistan.

Will had retired and Rafe had been in charge the day of the ambush. Rafe had all points covered. There was no way they could have anticipated the assault. There would have been a lot more casualties if they hadn't been so prepared.

Before the memories pulled him into the darkness, Macy's smile flashed before him.

Damn. Damn. Damn.

He needed to go for a run, but the docs said it would be another three weeks before his leg could take the pounding.

The town might be small, but they did have a health club that was open twenty-hour hours, specifically for folks who worked shifts.

Grabbing his swim shorts, he pulled on a pair of jeans and a T-shirt. Throwing on his leather jacket, he was at the club in less than five minutes. A swim would be the only thing to burn off the excess energy. It was his substitute form of meditation since he couldn't run. The club was nearly empty at four in the morning, and for that he was grateful. He didn't have to make conversation or smile. The sleepy girl at the desk waved him by when he flashed his membership card.

Diving into the water he struck out hard, his arms and legs going at a blistering pace. After twenty or so laps, he slowed down and cleared his mind. The blank slate, his therapist suggested to calm his nerves, was hard for him to find some days. Tabula rasa, she'd called it. It was a challenge to find it when the sexy woman's face kept popping up over and over again.

Then there was his mother who had waited up to pepper him with questions when he'd returned the night before. Macy had nothing on his mom, who kept giving him strange looks and then smiled when he said he was tired and needed to sleep.

He'd never understood women, and his mom was the most confusing of them all.

"I don't know what that water ever did to you, but I hope you're never that mad at me." Macy's voice penetrated his concentration. He nearly gulped a mouthful of water as he stopped abruptly. He was at the end of a lap, and she stood above the lane in a formfitting navy swimsuit.

Hell. The woman was trying to kill him.

His cock was so hard it hurt. He leaned up against the wall and put his arms on the side of the pool to hide the evidence.

What was he, twelve?

Get yourself under control, Marine.

"I have to give up running for a few more weeks and this is the way I meditate."

She chewed on her lip. "I thought you did yoga, or sat and chanted to mediate."

He smirked. "That's awful closed-minded for someone who has traveled the world. Some people do. But I have trouble shutting off my brain if I'm not moving. When I sit still— Well. I have insomnia and sometimes exercise is the only way I can get myself to calm down."

She sat down and dangled her legs in the water. "I hope it's not because of what we talked about last night," she said worriedly. "It's my nature to push at people until they give me what I want. I tried not to do that with you, but sometimes I just can't help myself."

He couldn't tell her the truth, so he lied. "No, it wasn't that. Well, maybe a little. But not in the way you think." He'd made a fool of himself. "Why are you here?"

She pointed through the window where a man had Harley on a treadmill. "One of the trainers from the rescue shelter is working with Harley. The treadmill is made for people who have bad joints."

"She didn't seem to have any trouble running around the other day."

"No, but she shouldn't have done it. Running like that is bad for her. We're trying to teach her to walk at a fast pace on the treadmill. This was the only time Jack could do it. He's a vet tech at the shelter and his shift starts at seven.

"I thought while they worked out, I'd come do some laps. I didn't realize it was you until you made that last turn. I guess, though I never thought of it that way, swimming is my meditation, too. I do it more to make the puzzle pieces of my life and the stories I tell fit together. When I'm doing something physical, it helps me figure stuff out. And like Harley, I have a bad knee. I like running, but it doesn't like me."

He glanced at her left knee, there was a round puckered scar there, and then a long line that intersected it. His head snapped up, his eyes met hers. "You were hit."

She nodded. "About three years ago. It was a through-and-through, but did some ligament damage on the way out. Nothing like what you've experienced."

The thought of her being harmed brought out his protective instincts. He pulled himself up out of the water and sat beside her. "You don't have a limp."

"Nah. I had some great physical therapists." She traced the scar on his right leg. "Wow, that's nasty. Must really hurt."

Her touch had an instant affect on him. Thankfully her eyes were fixed on his right leg and knee. The scars went from his midthigh through his knee and calf. In all he'd taken three bullets in the one leg. And another one in his back. "It's a lot better than it was six weeks ago. What were you doing when you got hurt?"

"Researching a feature on the Arab spring. A demonstration I was covering got out of hand. Had to run for the border the first chance I got, and we were attacked. We were lucky that the marines were waiting on the other side.

"I got hit. They fired back. Luckily a navy surgeon fixed me up right away and then sent me to a good surgeon and physical therapist in Florida where he had a practice."

"You shouldn't have put yourself in danger like that." The words had more of a bite than he'd meant them to. "You could have been killed."

She pulled her fingers away from his leg as if he'd shocked her. "Uh, it's my job to report the tough stories. And trust me, I've been through worse."

Lifting her curls, she pointed to an ugly scar on the back of her neck.

The air left his lungs.

"That was the one that really scared me." She stared at the water.

He reached out and touched the wound.

She jerked away. "But that's a story for another day. I need to get my workout in. I'm sorry I interrupted yours." She stood and he noticed her toenails were painted a violet color. Something about that made him smile. Then he remembered what he'd done.

"Sorry I touched you. I can't stand violence against women. It—It's one of my triggers."

"Triggers for what?"

"A story for another day," he repeated the phrase back to her. Then he grabbed a towel and wrapped it around his waist. "Have a good swim."

4

WHEN BLAKE TOUCHED Macy it was all she could do not to wrap her arms around him. No one had ever looked at her so tenderly or been so concerned. Her ex had been the one who sent her out on some of her roughest assignments. He'd expected her to be able to handle herself, and she did. But there was a small part of her that wished he'd worried about her once in a while. She should have known something was wrong when she called to tell him that she'd been shot and all he'd worried about was how she was going to get him the story.

She'd made the surgeon wait an hour so she could pound out ten pages and email it to the paper.

Blake would have been frantic worrying about her.

Hey, you are not turning into one of those women.

She refused to be the type of woman who needed the man in her life to save her. Macy prided herself on her independence.

Jumping into lane five, she sluiced through the water. When she thought of the marine, she tried to focus on the story she wanted to tell. But it was complicated. She didn't quite have all the pieces yet. She needed to talk to his mother and others who knew Blake. Well, duh, the whole town knew him.

She wanted a different perspective.

The idea was just out of her grasp. She pushed herself harder and harder until ten laps later she was out of breath and hanging on to the edge of the pool in the same way Blake had earlier.

She glanced through the window to see how Harley was doing. Jack gave her double thumbs-up and she smiled.

Why couldn't she go for a guy like Jack or even his boss, Josh? They weren't the subjects of a story and, as far as she knew, they didn't have any battle scars. Though, she sometimes wondered about Josh. He'd been wounded in some way. It was that haunted look in his eyes.

No one knew better than she did how those scars and secrets could weigh a soul down.

The treadmill slowed, and Jack gave Harley a treat. Climbing the ladder out of the pool, she dressed quickly.

Professional ethics kept her from loading Harley into her car and driving straight to Blake's house. She wanted to comfort him. To hold him in her arms and maybe even slip her legs around him and absorb some of the pain he'd experienced.

When would she realize, she never did simple.

After drying Harley off with a towel, she got her settled in the SUV without any fuss. The dog was too tired to fight her. She lay across the backseat looking exhausted.

As Macy pulled up the long drive to her house, she quickly slammed on the brakes.

Harley growled at her.

The marine plaguing her thoughts sat on the tailgate of his truck more handsome than any man had the right to be.

What was going on?

Her body heated. One glance in the rearview and her cheeks were the color of primroses on a bright sunny day.

Every cell in her body screamed at her. She needed him just as much as he might need her.

Oh.

Cherie would start charging her by the hour.

But before she called her friend, she had to find out why the Blake was here in her driveway. His expression said the weight of the world was resting on his shoulders.

She let Harley out of the backseat.

"Hey," she said as the dog ran up to Blake. He bent over and rubbed the animal's ears.

Macy tried her best not to be jealous, but it wasn't easy.

One small touch from Blake, and she already craved more.

"Hey," he said eyeing her warily. "Sorry I just showed up. We need to talk."

"About?"

"The fact that I touched you without your permission. I was taught better than that. I can write you a letter of apology if you'd like, but I thought it might mean more if I said it in person."

She laughed. "Letters are so old-school. You could have texted me."

He shrugged. "I kind of like the old-school ways, besides, I didn't have your number. And there's something else."

"What's that?"

"I really want to kiss you."

She was in big, big trouble, she could confirm, because she wanted that, too.

"Wow. For a marine, you really aren't afraid to tell it like it is." Macy gave him a smile that didn't quite meet her eyes. He'd made her uncomfortable, but he had to speak his mind. If she told him off, so be it, but he had to let her know how he felt.

If he'd learned anything the past six months, it was that life was short. And from his therapist, that the truth was important.

"It's true. It's who I am. And I understand you and I can't— Well, that is, you have ethics. Some journalists don't anymore, but I can see that you do. We have a connection. I'm fairly certain you've noticed it."

She nodded.

Good, at least the attraction wasn't one-sided.

"But you're writing a story about me and that's a conflict of interest."

"Yes, it is."

"So, I think I have a solution."

She sat next to him on the tailgate and petted Harley.

"Don't write the story."

Immediately her back stiffened. "I can't do that."

"Why not? You're the publisher of the paper, right? Your uncle left you the whole thing, so you make the decisions. Or you could have someone else write the story, though, I'm going to be honest—I wouldn't trust anyone else."

She sighed. "Why do you have to be so—you."

He chuckled. "I'm not sure what that means, but do you agree with me?"

"The story is already compromised because you do strange things to me, Lieutenant Michaels."

He lifted her chin with his fingers and waited. She nodded her approval.

"Strange things?"

"Yes," she said softly. "I always seem to be too warm when you're around."

"Hmm. Maybe you have a fever." He held the back of his hand to her forehead. Then let his fingers trail down her cheek. He leaned in to kiss her.

Harley let loose with a harsh bark.

They broke apart chuckling.

A giant head was eye level with them. Harley's paws were up on the tailgate, and she gave them a look that said break it up.

"I think she's hungry," Macy suggested. "I should feed her."

The dog grumbled.

"Do you mind if I help?"

Macy pursed her lips.

"Hands off, I promise. I won't touch you again until you ask me."

"This isn't a good idea," she said.

"What? Feeding your dog? Surely she would disagree."

Since Macy didn't tell him to leave, he followed her into the house. Keeping his distance so she wouldn't feel pressured.

She needed time to get used to the idea. Hell, they'd only met a couple of days ago and here he was trying to kiss her.

He remembered about the ex. Maybe that wasn't over.

She winced. "I'm trying to fit in and I don't think dating the town hero will help my case."

"See, that's where you have it wrong. I could be just what you need to ingratiate yourself to the town. If I approve of you, well, it doesn't look so good on them if they don't accept you."

She placed the dog's water dish on a raised stand where Harley was mowing through her food. "I'll think about it."

He winked at her. "You do that. I'll pick you up at seven to take you out to eat."

"No," she said. "I mean it. I'll think about it. It hasn't been that long since I got out of a bad relationship. I'm not ready to date yet."

He shrugged. "Who said anything about a relationship? We're sharing a meal. We won't call it a date. We'll call it a mutual companion outing. Besides, you'd be doing me a favor. All the gray hairs keep throwing their daughters at me. You can be my shield."

That made her laugh. "I'm pretty sure you can

defend yourself just fine, Lieutenant Michaels. You don't need me."

He smiled. "But we had dinner last night. Why can't we do it again?"

"Last night it was about work. And frankly, I don't think it's a good idea to leave Harley alone while she's getting used to her new surroundings. I plan on taking her to the office with me so she doesn't feel abandoned."

Rubbing his chin, Blake eyed the dog. "If I can solve the problem with Harley, will you go to dinner with me?"

She bit her lip. He really loved when she did that.

"I'm not sure how many times I can say this isn't a good idea."

"Fine. I agree. It's not a good idea, but I'm having trouble focusing because I keep wondering what it would be like to kiss you. To hold your hand in mine."

"And spending time with me is going to solve that dilemma?"

"Maybe we'll get lucky and you'll bore me to tears. Or I'll be allergic to your perfume. You might like a movie I despise. I'm kind of a movie snob." That last bit was true. In college, he'd refused to date any woman who hadn't seen his two favorite films, *To Kill a Mockingbird* and *North by Northwest,* they were now followed closely by *Zero Dark Thirty*.

Movies were his favorite escape, and he took them seriously.

Shoving her curls behind her ears she stared at him.

"So, I'd really be doing you a favor by sharing

a meal at this mutual companion outing? We'll get bored with each other and then we can move on, right?"

"Exactly," he told her, but he didn't believe it for a minute. She was bright, funny and beautiful. A triple threat as far as he was concerned. Blake didn't want to think about the future. For now he just wanted the clever journalist with the curvy hips any way she'd take him.

5

AMANDA PELEGRINE, the receptionist at *Tranquil Waters News,* put down her nail file and eyed Macy warily. For once, Harley was on her best behavior and strode in as if she owned the place. Macy was certain it had nothing to do with the giant box of dog treats and sack of brand-new toys she had in her hand.

Amanda, who was not Macy's biggest fan, sneered. "I'm allergic to dogs."

Good. Maybe you'll quit.

She'd wanted to fire the useless female since the day she took over the paper. But her uncle's will stated she had to wait three months before making any staffing changes.

He'd left her with an angry receptionist, who looked like something from the circus with her fuzzy raspberry sweater, two-inch-long green nails and fascinator that looked like a dead bird on a perch.

Having lived in big cities, Macy was used to all kinds of fashions, but she'd never seen someone like Amanda.

In addition to the snarky witch, she had one re-porter, Darla, who was amazing, but eight month's pregnant with her second child.

The only columnist was Hugo, who was eighty, possibly ninety. Old enough that he couldn't remem-ber what year he was born. He couldn't hear or see, but the man could write. He used an old manual type-writer, which meant someone else had to scan his sto-ries into a computer.

Twice a week Macy stopped by to pick up his col-umns. She always had to make sure she scheduled an extra hour for each visit because Hugo was just as good at telling a story as he was at writing one.

He'd seen so much, and she enjoyed listening to him talk about the good old days.

"Well, Amanda, she'll be coming here with me every day. I'm happy to give you a severance pack-age, otherwise, I suggest you invest in some antihis-tamines."

"Maybe I'll just talk to my friend the lawyer about working conditions." Her heavily colored eyebrow rose into her bangs. She wore so much makeup it was impossible to tell her age.

If Macy had to wager a guess, it would be some-where around twenty-seven, but that was debatable.

She hadn't meant to sound rude, but she'd grown weary of the woman's constant negativity. "You do that." She only had to wait one more week before giv-ing her the heave-ho.

"No reason to get testy. By the way, you have some messages." She stuck out her hand with a pile of pink notes.

"It's only nine in the morning."

The woman shrugged. "Some might be from the last couple of days. I cleaned off my desk when I was looking for my good nail file and I found them."

Stuffing the messages in her pocket, Macy's mouth formed a thin line. "In my office in fifteen minutes," she said through gritted teeth.

"But I have a—"

"Amanda, my office in fifteen," she said harshly as she entered her office. She slammed the door.

Harley whined.

"Sorry, old girl, but she is too much." Rolling out a furry mat that had gel on the underside, she put it behind her desk. Then she added a stuffed toy along with one of the chewies she'd bought at the discount store just outside of town.

Lucky for her, Great Danes were notoriously lazy. Once the dog was comfortable, she'd probably sleep most of the day.

Macy's phone rang. "Call from Boston," Amanda said snidely. "Same guy."

"Tell him I'm in a meeting."

She hung up before the receptionist could question her decision.

She had no interest in talking to her ex. The man had tried to apologize countless times. But she'd caught him red-handed, meaning in bed with his intern. Not one to give into hysterics, she'd turned on her heel, picked up her laptop and walked out with only the clothes on her back.

The week before she'd found him cheating, she'd received a visit from her uncle's attorney. At first, she thought she would sell her inheritance and use the proceeds for an amazing honeymoon.

But after what had happened, she decided it was a sign to move in a new direction. She'd been a high-profile, far-flung reporter for a long time. She had the awards and reputation to prove it.

So instead of planning a honeymoon, she gave two weeks' notice at the Boston paper and told HR she was taking two of the six weeks of vacation owed to her. She waited until she knew her ex was in a meeting, and went to the condo and packed up everything she owned.

A gypsy, always on the road, she didn't have much other than her clothes, shoes and a few pieces of art she'd picked up during her travels.

She then bought a car and drove to New York to visit Cherie. After a couple of days of being analyzed by her best bud, she knew her choice to move to Texas was a great one.

As soon as she saw her uncle's house, it felt like home, a feeling she hadn't experienced in years. It had surprised her how easy it'd been to walk away from the life she'd thought she wanted and the man she was supposed to marry. That was when she'd known—the obvious reason aside—he wasn't Mr. Right, after all.

Still, she had no desire to speak to him.

A knock on the door interrupted her revisiting the past.

"Come in."

Harley raised her head to see who entered and then lay back down. Amanda stood in the doorway.

"Have a seat." Macy pointed to the chair.

Eyeing her warily, she sat.

"As you know, the three months are almost up. I wanted to give you notice now so that you have time to find another job." Macy picked up a folder. "This is the severance package my uncle had in his files. I will honor it, even though—" She'd been about to say, "you don't deserve it." She shoved the folder across the desk.

"You're firing me?" Amanda's face crumbled. Huge black mascara tears dripped down her cheeks. "I knew it. Why don't you like me?"

Seriously?

"You've been hostile to me ever since I arrived. The missing messages today are just one in a long line of problems with you being inept at your job."

A good manager would have found a way to cushion the blow, but Macy was at the end of her patience with the woman.

"It is nothing personal. It's business. I need to employ people who are efficient and can carry extra duties when necessary. I can barely get you to answer the phone, and that's your only job. I've had to do all the admin, customer service and deal with circulation. That's on top of writing, editing and publishing the paper."

The woman sniffled.

Closing her eyes, Macy gathered her thoughts.

"I—thought you were going to get bored fast and hire someone to take over, so I didn't think it was worth getting to know you or impress you," Amanda said finally. "And you never asked me to do those things. You told me to answer the phone, so I did. I noticed the second week you were here that the accounts receivables were a mess, so I've been doing those. It takes me a little longer than it took Todd, but he'd been doing it for years. And I sort of had to teach myself those first few weeks. You never even said thank-you."

Her eyes popped open. "What?"

"That I was doing so much of the accounting. I'm pretty sure I've done it right, but you might want to have an accountant look over the books. My mom was able to help me with some of it, but once the treatments started, well. You should probably have the figures double-checked."

Macy groaned inwardly. She'd assumed her uncle used a firm to monitor the accounts receivable or payable. There was still so much she had to learn.

The first order of business was to find a good accountant to go over those books.

"We all thought you'd sell the paper, or quit and fold it up. So I didn't see any sense in putting forward any extra effort other than the day-to-day stuff until you figured out what you wanted to do.

"And you were so serious and businessy when you arrived. You didn't treat us any differently than the file cabinets, the gray ones you didn't like. I asked those first few days if I could help you with something, but you looked at me like I was a crazy person.

"I know I don't dress as fancy as you do. But clothes are how I express myself. And I've been studying so hard. I hid the books when you walked by because I was afraid you'd get mad if you saw me. I wanted to talk to you about it. I was hoping, since you were a woman, that maybe you'd give me a chance. But you make me so nervous, I don't know if I'm doing anything right and I sure don't want to ask for a favor."

Staring down at the files on her desk, Macy thought back. She'd been off on her own for so long that she was used to doing everything herself. When she was on assignment, it was expected.

And she'd been sullen and angry when she first got to Tranquil Waters. Had she taken it out on the staff? Did she have the scary face, her game face, on as Cherie called it, when she was walking around town? The same face she had when traveling, so that no one bugged her? No wonder folks thought she was some mean, Yankee shrew.

"That doesn't explain your hostility, Amanda, and what do you mean you've been studying hard? I've seldom seen you without a nail file in your hand."

"You know how you don't know how to act so you act like the other person even though you don't know why someone hates you…. I guess that's what happened. When a person is mean to me, I just do the same back. I'm kind of flaky. I'll give you that.

"You're some important war correspondent, I figured being professional maybe meant being mean. I saw that old movie *The Devil Wears Prada*. That editor was horrible."

Was the woman really taking her cues from a film?

"Yes, but that was fiction. I don't expect you to fall all over yourself, but I do insist on common courtesy." She held up the messages. "And this—this is bad."

The woman scrunched her face. "I considered

throwing them in the trash so you wouldn't find out. It took everything I had to give them to you. When you came in yesterday, you were in such a hurry that I didn't get a chance to pass them on. I stuck them under the phone so I'd remember, but Mrs. Dawes, the cleaner, must have moved them."

Macy gave her an incredulous look.

"I know, I know. But I mean it. I've been studying journalism at an online college. I have to do it like that because my mom is sick and I have to be home to watch my brothers at night when my dad's at work. So in the mornings, I'm tired and can barely keep my eyes open. The nail file thing is a kind of way to trick myself. I hate the sound, but it keeps me awake.

"I promise I'll try to be better. I'll do whatever you ask, just give me two more weeks."

Amanda folded her hands in her lap. The tears continued to roll down her face, and each one churned Macy's stomach a little more.

She felt sick. If the story was true, and her instincts said that it was, Macy had indeed been horrible with a capital *H*.

Journalism 101 was to find out the real story. Everyone had one, and most of the time they were fascinating.

"May I ask what's wrong with your mom? And you should know, as an employee, you do not have to tell me."

"Breast cancer. It's her third time with it. My grandma and aunts all died of it. But she's doing better. This last round of chemo and radiation has taken its toll, but the docs say her counts are good. Dad drives her to Houston once a week for treatment.

"She just doesn't have any energy. I'm the oldest of four, and all under sixteen. So I help out around the house and try to give them money when I can, since Mom can't work right now."

Shame on you, Macy Reynolds. Shame on you.

Dear God, she'd almost fired the poor woman and had the entire family out on the street.

The journalist in her told her to stop right there, that she was being too soft. If Amanda worked at one of the top one hundred papers, she'd be out. Everyone had to do the job of five or six people these days. When Macy started out as a reporter, she'd had to turn in only three columns a week. Her last job in Boston, she'd had to do a minimum of eight, and help with copyediting and online coverage.

But the *Tranquil Waters News* was not a top one hundred paper. She was certain it wasn't even ranked, though for a small paper, they had a good circulation.

"I see. That is unfortunate." Her words sounded cold, even to her. But she'd never been great at the touchy-feely stuff. Except when it came to Harley, that dog turned her into a pile of emotional mush.

"So, you've been studying journalism. What year are you?" She forced a smile.

"I'm a junior. I was all set to go to Texas State, but then Mom got sick again, so I enrolled online."

Rummaging through the old desk, Macy found her personnel file. She was only twenty years old.

Holy hell. That explained so much.

But they had to set some ground rules.

"Are you really allergic to dogs?"

The girl glanced at Harley. "No, but I'm scared to death of them. One tried to bite me once when I was a kid and I've never been able to get close to a dog since. I'm sorry, but that's the truth."

Macy nodded. "This one won't hurt you. She is the friendliest dog. Aren't you, Harley."

The dog lifted her head and cocked it sideways. A low grunt of what sounded like her agreement followed.

Amanda laughed.

"She'll hang out with me most days," Macy explained. "So it might be good if you two tried to be friends. I won't force it, but if you're going to make friends with a dog, this is the one to start with. I promise."

"I'll try."

"Okay. Well, if you're staying, we'll need some changes. Ones that you and I will decide on together."

"I'll do whatever you want, no problem." Amanda held up her hand as if she were swearing an oath in court.

"Good. To begin with, you'd better give me the lowdown on my other employees."

Macy listened carefully to each backstory. Amanda knew it all, which showed she had a propensity for getting the truth out of folks. Not a bad trait for a budding journalist.

"I'll come up with a code of conduct and expectations for you to sign off on. And we'll consider the next two weeks as a probation period," Macy said. "If that goes well, we'll extend it.

"As for your wardrobe, I don't want you to feel like you can't express yourself, but I do want to offer you suggestions on proper attire for the office."

Amanda made a weird face. "I don't have any old lady clothes or sexy librarian stuff like you wear," she said. "But I could maybe tone it down a little."

"How about we compromise with one bright color a day? And maybe jeans that don't show more than they should?"

"Fine by me. Would you like me to get you a coffee?"

Hmm. That sounded good. "Tell you what, you like those lattes from the café. Why don't you get one and I'll take a black coffee. Here's some cash. And then, please find out when everyone can come in for a staff meeting. We need to chat."

"That's going to be a bit tough on Hugo, but I can give him a ride from the nursing home if that's okay with him."

"We'll figure it out. I'd also like to talk to the printer, and before you leave today, I need access to those books. I'll hire an accountant this afternoon."

"Got it, Boss!" She hopped up. "Coffee, and then I'll make the calls. Thank you!"

Macy smiled. "You're welcome."

Amanda turned back when she reached the door. "Uh, there's one other thing."

Macy's eyebrow rose, but she didn't say anything.

"I have to write a feature story for one of my classes. I know it's a lot to ask, but if I can find the subject, can you just edit it for me? You know, like a real editor would?"

Someone long ago had done that for Macy, and life really was about karma. "Sure. Just bring it to me when you're ready."

A bright smile lit Amanda's face. "Wow. You really aren't the complete witch we thought you were."

When she shut the door, Macy snorted.

Well, at least there's that.

6

FOR THE PAST two days, a certain newspaper publisher had avoided Blake. She'd claimed that she was too busy with work. He didn't consider it stalking when he'd driven by the newspaper office on the way to the feed store and noticed her car was there.

No. It wasn't stalking.

For the life of him, he didn't understand why he couldn't get her out of his head.

Well, except for the fact that she was sexy as hell, smart and funny when she wanted to be. The waitress at the Lone Star Café had been gossiping about the new lady with the giant dog when he had his breakfast that morning.

"She's so uppity. Have you seen her walking around? That sneer on her face. I want to tell her that she'll catch more bees with honey, but she tips good so I ain't sayin' a darn thing," the waitress said.

Obviously, not everyone saw Macy the way he did. But then, he had heard her story. Orphaned, world traveler who was in search of a home. He knew that last bit because he felt the same way.

He was lucky that he had his mom, and that would always be home. Nevertheless, he was at a crossroads in his life. Again, he was lucky that he had many opportunities open to him. A marine to his core, the idea of desk duty didn't sit well with him. Pushing papers might be great for some folks; he liked to stay active and to be challenged.

There were a couple of business opportunities. He could take over one of the divisions of the security company he'd invested in with Rafe and Will. And his brother, J.T., had mentioned a number of other businesses that were looking to expand into Tranquil Waters. He liked the idea of being in on the ground floor of something and watching it grow.

His phone rang. He didn't recognize the number, but he picked it up.

"Hello."

"Lieutenant Michaels, this is Amanda from the *Tranquil Waters News* calling for Ms. Reynolds. She's in a meeting right now, but she wondered if you might be available to stop by the office either today or tomorrow afternoon."

Ms. Reynolds, eh. "Today is fine. What time?"

"Four-thirty will work well with her schedule."

"Fine by me."

They hung up.

She didn't call him herself, but she wanted to see him. Was she going to pawn his story off on another reporter?

He'd already told her that he wouldn't trust anyone else.

Glancing at the clock, he realized he had about an hour before the meeting.

She had a penchant for sweets. She said it was one of her few vices when she showed him her version of a whoopie pie.

Blake knew exactly what to do.

STANDING IN FRONT of the bathroom mirror at her office, Macy pushed her curls into some semblance of a style and reapplied her lipstick. She tried to convince herself that it wasn't for Blake's benefit.

Liar.

I need to look my best so I can convince him that my new plan for the story is a great one.

She wasn't sure he'd see it that way. Mentally, she prepared counter arguments for many of the points he might bring up.

Her eyelashes, which were much lighter than her hair color, were barely visible. She pulled out the mascara Cherie had insisted she buy on her shopping spree and applied a coat to one eye.

As she did the other, someone knocked on the door. She jabbed the stick into her eye, leaving a trail of black down her cheek.

"Banana shakes." Her least favorite flavor.

"Sorry, but your four-thirty is here. You told me to let you know as soon as he arrived," Amanda said.

"Thanks. I'll be there in just a minute."

Gathering up some tissues, she dabbed at the eye and did her best to remove the black makeup.

Most of it came off, but…that's when she remembered the sales woman telling her that she'd need an oil-based cleanser to remove it entirely.

Wonderful.

Both eyes were red now and watering. Why was it that if you poked one eye, both of them did that? This was useless. She could call out to Amanda and cancel the meeting, but Blake would know she was here.

She had no other choice.

When her nose started running, she did the only thing she could. Tucking a good chunk of toilet paper up her sleeve, she went to the reception area to meet Blake.

Concern etched his face when he saw her. "Did something happen?" He reached out to touch her, but then pulled back.

She remembered what he said about not wanting to touch her until she asked.

"I was going to lie and say allergies, but I'm not so good at lying. I stuck my mascara wand in my eye and now my face has turned into a faucet."

Blake coughed to cover a chuckle. But she knew what he'd done, and she smiled.

"Yes, I am beauty and grace." She curtsied.

"Do you want to postpone the meeting?" he asked.

"I'm okay, as long as you don't mind my weepy face."

"That face is beautiful no matter what is going on."

"Such a flatterer. I bet you say that to all the women."

"No, only one woman." He said it so low, she wasn't sure she heard him right.

Clearing her throat, she motioned to the chair across from her desk. She'd cleaned out all the file cabinets that had crowded the space and moved the heavy, carved desk so that it faced the door. She'd painted the dull army green a bright cream and brought in some art. She spent most of her days in the space and she liked that it was comfortable.

He set a box from the café on her desk. Then he pushed it toward her. "These are a peace offering for invading your space the other day. I should have called before I came by."

She grinned. "You surprised me, but I didn't take offense. I'm just not in a space where I can—" She lifted the lid on the box. "You got Mrs. Chesaline to make her éclairs? But she only does that on the second Tuesday of the month. I was waiting at the door last week at 5:00 a.m. when I found out what day she made them."

"I heard." He grinned.

She shook her head and frowned. "This town. I swear everything you do is circumspect."

"Yes, but it has its advantages, as well. When you need a helping hand, it's there. You'll see."

She wasn't so sure about that. It was easy for the handsome marine. The town hero home from the battlefield. Not so much for an uptight reporter who was too nosy for her own good.

"I appreciate you taking the time to come over. I've been tied up in interviews all day."

"Who were you interviewing? That is if you can tell me," he said.

"Oh. Uh. Actually, I'm hiring a couple of reporters. Well, I'm hoping I can find reporters who can also edit and lay out pages. I found an ad salesman, next up I need an accountant."

"Is that why you called?" He leaned forward and she caught his pine scent. It wasn't fair that he was beautiful and smelled so good.

"Excuse me?"

"About the accounting position. I don't practice but I do have my license."

She'd forgotten about him having an MBA. The man was so much more than eye candy, which made him so darn appealing. As if he needed any help.

"Well, you know. If you don't mind consulting until I can find someone for us full-time, that would be appreciated."

He nodded. "I can do that. I have something on for tonight, but I'll take a look tomorrow."

Wait, what kind of plans did he have? Was it a date? Why should it matter to her?

Because you know he wants to kiss you.

They had chemistry. But he was so hot he probably had that with every woman he met. He didn't seem like a player, but her track record wasn't the best when it came to men. She no longer trusted her instincts in that regard.

"Tomorrow. Yes. Listen, I appreciate you stepping in temporarily, but that isn't why I asked you to stop by."

He started to say something, but stopped.

Her eyebrow rose. "Please, go ahead."

"I was hoping you asked me for personal reasons."

She smiled. "I'm afraid you're going to be disappointed. It's about the interview. The one for your story."

He leaned back in his seat and eyed her suspiciously. "Are you doing the interview?"

"Hear me out, please."

Frowning, he stood. "Look, I understand this is what you people do, but I told you. I'm not interested in talking to anyone else."

"Why, because you like me?"

"I do, but it's because I trust you. And I've read your work. Whatever you wrote, it would be fair." His voice had grown raw and deep.

She'd touched a nerve.

"You're right. It would be fair if I did the article. And I'm flattered you know that. But what I have in mind goes far beyond just you. The person is someone you'll trust even more than me."

He crossed his arms. "Who?"

"You."

He huffed. "I'm no writer, and it doesn't make sense for me to do a story on myself. You should know I'm not a big fan of games." He was to the door in three strides.

"Hey, I'm sorry. I didn't explain it well. But I'm not exactly sure what it was I said that set you off."

He didn't turn around, but he didn't open the door.

"I thought it would be interesting if you interviewed other veterans, there are so many at the nursing home and the Lion's Club. Not really about war, but about what it's like to come home. How hard it is for families and friends who weren't there to understand what you've gone through." She stood, but didn't move toward him.

Instead, she continued. "The first time I came home from Afghanistan, I couldn't process what had happened. I tried to pretend like it was another life. But after a year of being stressed about everything, even if I'd ever live to write my next story—" She took a deep breath and pushed the painful memories away.

"I was in the newsroom in Boston. One minute I was packing up to go home and the next I was huddled, shivering at my desk unable to speak.

"My uncle Todd came to the rescue again. He'd covered Desert Storm. He got it. And he's the one who called my friend Cherie, who happens to be a psychiatrist. Between the two of them, I was able to talk about it.

"And Cherie taught me coping mechanisms. So thankfully I was able to go back. I had to go back. A lot of important stories needed telling. You get why I had to go back? You've done it time and again yourself, but many people don't. But what we don't always realize is that it not only takes a toll on us—you and I—it takes a toll on our family and our friends."

As he turned to face her, a myriad of emotions passed over his face. His knuckles turned white as he gripped the back of the chair he'd been sitting in. She didn't worry, though, and she certainly didn't fear him. This was his way of channeling anger.

"Being overseas in such conditions—it changes us, Blake. Sometimes for the better, other times not. As much as I'm a loner, I'm a lot more compassionate than I ever was. A journalist must be objective, but even I had to examine my life when I got home again."

She took her seat and gestured for him to take his. "I want to tell you something off the record. Something no one, except Cherie, has heard me say. I'm telling you because I know I can trust you."

"You can trust me," he said gruffly.

Why did she feel the need to confess? She didn't talk to anyone like this.

He sat in his chair. "You don't have to tell me right now," he said. "I believe you. And I'm sorry I—lost my temper. I'm trying very hard to simplify my life. Get up in the morning, do my job, go to sleep at night. I need that kind of routine right now. Things have to be easy."

"I get that. I suppose it's why I'm a workaholic. It happens to be the one constant in my life. We really are a lot more alike than either of us wants to admit."

A long silence followed before he spoke up. "Your idea for the veterans story and their experiences back home is a great one, but I'm not a writer. And you've been there, anyway. Seems to me you'd be perfect for the job."

"Thanks for that. But they'd still be talking to a reporter. I feel like…" She paused. Frustrated she wound a curl around her finger. "This might be really positive for them. I'll help you write the stories, but you need to be the one to do the interviews. How these men and women learned to assimilate back into society could be important for soldiers who are still coming home."

"They have programs," he said, crossing his legs. "Most branches of the military have a system in place where they work with families and do just that. Assimilate."

"Yes, I know, but how you'd write the story would be completely different. Everyone who comes home deals with it in his or her own way. That's why this will work. Readers will be able to say, 'Hey, that's the way I felt.' Or, 'No wonder my dad spent so much time alone in his study.'"

"It all sounds kind of therapist-like to me," he said.

She knew exactly what he meant. "It would be if I had a psychologist writing the stories. I tell you what, how about you do one or two interviews and see how it goes? If it's not your thing—I won't say another word about it."

Harley grumbled beside her and then made her way around to Blake where she placed her head on his lap. Her stomach made an appalling noise.

"Do you need me to walk her?" Blake asked as he stroked the dog's head.

"No, she only went out an hour or so ago. It's time for her dinner, though, and she gets two *c-o-o-k-i-e-s*." Harley's head popped up and she immediately began to drool on his shoe. "You cannot spell!"

Blake laughed. "I'm not so sure about that. I need to get going. I'll think about what you said. Maybe I'll have an answer for you tomorrow when I come check your books."

"You'll still do that?"

"Said I would, and I always keep my word."

"Thank you. I do appreciate it, and I promise I'll

do my best to find someone to help me on a more permanent basis."

"There's something else you should think about," he said.

"What's that?"

"The story you were about to tell me. I saw that look in your eyes. I know it well. If we eventually do this, you should share your own story with readers. It isn't just the military that is overseas and comes back wounded physically and mentally."

"That's true," she admitted. "But I'm not so sure people would be interested in my story, especially in this town. I'd kind of like to keep my head down low. Maybe at some point, fifty or so years down the road, they'll forget I'm the new girl."

"Like you said, the articles could shed some light on why certain people are the way they are. And how they deal with the day-to-day. I have a feeling if the rest of the town knew about what happened to you, it would change things."

Perhaps. But dredging up old memories was the opposite of what she needed. More than anything, she wanted to start fresh. That was what moving to Tranquil Waters had been all about.

7

"HON, I HATE to do this to you, but I need a big favor," his mother said as he walked in the house. The talk with Macy had him riled up and anxious. He wasn't exactly sure why. That look on her face when she thought back to her time overseas, he'd seen it one too many times in the mirror. It bothered him that she'd suffered so much. He wanted to sooth her, to help her forget.

"Blake?" his mother asked.

"Yes, ma'am, whatever you need." He rounded the kitchen and stopped when he saw her worried expression. She had a small suitcase packed.

"Mom? What's wrong?"

She put her hands on her hips. "Momma D isn't doing so well. Your aunt Eloise wants to put her in a rest home, but Momma isn't very keen on the idea. Right now she's in the hospital, and says all she wants to do is be in her own home. She's insisted that she'll heal better with her things around her and being close to her gardens. Even with the full-time nurse, Eloise thinks it's still too much for her at the moment. So I need to go down to San Antonio and look after her for a bit. See what's up."

"Do you need me to drive you? I can be ready in ten minutes."

She put her palm on his cheek. "You are such a good boy. I hate leaving you so soon after you've just got here, but it can't be helped, I'm afraid. I was hoping you could keep an eye on the store. Ray and Tanya pretty much run the place already, I do the books and talk to folks. You wouldn't have to do much. Make the bank deposits. Give Ray a hand with the inventory. You've done it all before when you were a kid. Nothing has changed, except it's all on computers now."

Well, he'd said he needed purpose and routine. Crazy how the universe worked sometimes. "When I saw Momma D on my way up, she seemed fine."

His mother waved dismissively at him. "She's old and a cold can turn into pneumonia in a heartbeat. But don't you worry about her. She's a tough old broad."

He frowned. "Seems like I'd be better off helping you guys down there than I would be here. Like you said, Ray has a handle on things."

"Oh, no, honey. I'll feel better if you're here. I'm going to sit around and gossip with her. And I'll make sure her gardens are ready for the winter. You know how much I love doing that stuff. She has only the one television, so I imagine we'll sit around watching her programs with the sound blaring."

There was that. When he'd stopped by on his way up to Tranquil Waters, he spent the day with this grandmother. She was his mom's stepmother. Her mom had died when she was only three, and Momma D had become the only mother she really knew.

She was nearly deaf, but she didn't miss much. When he visited her, she was in her parlor, which was what she called the living room, watching her afternoon soaps at an earsplitting octave.

But she'd taken one look at him and shaken her head. "Boy, you need a hug." Then she'd held out her arms. Damn if she wasn't right. He'd ended up spending the night there because he loved being in her presence. She was a positive light, and he needed that in his life.

"Your brother will be by in an hour. I asked him to bring you some dinner because I didn't have time to cook."

"Mom, I'm perfectly capable of taking care of myself. I've been doing it a really long time."

"Don't take a tone with me, son. Besides, I want you to grill your brother. Mona who works as a teller at the bank says she could have sworn she saw your brother in the parking lot, in his truck, with a woman in there. She had red hair. I never thought your brother would go for a redhead."

He snorted. In another five minutes, she'd have J.T. married off with five carrot-orange-haired kids.

"I'll take your bag to the car. Is there anything else you need?"

She scrunched up her face, and glanced around the kitchen. "No— Oh, if you don't mind, maybe you could take the sack of seeds on the workbench and put it in the car. And there are two rosebushes by the garage I'm going to take to Momma. They are heirloom, and you know how much she loves them."

It was a bit late in the fall to be planting, but it was San Antonio so the weather stayed pretty warm throughout the year.

Fifteen minutes after she left, his brother rolled up in the driveway in his truck. He didn't bother knocking, just walked through the back door like everyone else in town did. His mom's house was known as a gathering place.

"Stupid jarhead can't even fix a meal on his own." J.T. put a sack from the diner on the kitchen counter. Except for the paint color on the walls, which was a warm yellow, not much had changed in the light-filled kitchen since he was a kid. There were good memories in that kitchen of holiday baking, birthdays and his dad cooking dinner while encouraging Blake and J.T. with their homework. His mom was at the feed store a lot in those early years, so the men in the family had to learn to do for themselves, which wasn't a bad thing.

"Shut it, nerd. Did you bring me a chocolate donut this time?"

The nerd stuck two chocolate donuts on a plate.

"Why didn't you tell Mom you had already planned to come over and watch the game?" The first Mavericks' basketball game of the season started at seven.

"Brownie points, dude. It made me look good to bring dinner to the poor, broken jarhead."

"I'll show you broken if you don't stop calling me jarhead. Come on, nerd, I set up the TV trays in the family room. And thank you again for buying Mom that fifty-six-inch flat screen for Christmas last year. It's the best gift you've ever given her."

They chuckled at that.

"You could have come out to my place," his brother said.

"Not if I want to drink this," he raised one of the two beers he was holding in his hands. Earlier that day he'd visited the local doc for a checkup. He was down to half a pain pill a day. His leg continued to hurt like hell, but it only reminded him that there was still work to do on his body. The doc had given him permission to have one beer, maybe two, a day.

"I have a perfectly fine couch you could sleep on."

He shrugged. Time to have a little fun.

"So Mom says you're getting engaged to some redheaded chick. Who is she?"

J.T.'s beer spewed from his mouth onto his burger. "What the—?"

"Some lady at the bank saw you. Therefore, it must be true." Damn, he'd missed giving J.T. a hard time. The surprise on his brother's face was priceless.

He laughed so hard his gut hurt.

"Sometimes I hate this town," his brother growled. "She's not some chick. Her name is Anne Marie and she's a colleague. We were not on a date. We'd been at a conference in Houston. The rest is none of your business."

Blake held up his hands in surrender. "Hmm. I think he doth protest too much."

"Just watch the game, jarhead."

For the next two hours they did. Screaming at the

refs, who called fouls on everything. It was close but the Mavs won.

They clinked beer bottles.

Blake was relaxed, truly so. He almost felt like a normal human being. He'd been on for so long, he forgot what it was like to let go. Even in the hospital it had been one operation after another and then intense physical therapy.

He took a long breath.

The psychiatrist said he needed time. He understood now. Bit by bit it was coming back to him, how to live a life where he wasn't constantly looking over his shoulder or listening for changes in the wind. He'd never stop being a marine, but he could learn to be calm and enjoy things again. Maybe even sleep more than three hours at a time.

His mind wandered through his conversation with Macy. Could he do what she asked? It might dredge up a lot of issues he didn't want to think about. Then again, sometimes it helped to talk about what happened.

He sipped his second beer.

Then there was his other problem. The one that had kept him awake and unsettled ever since he'd seen her beautiful face in the pouring rain. Never in his life had he felt such a pull toward another person.

It was as if she had an invisible rope tied directly to his heart. He'd met her a couple of days ago, and he—what?

He'd almost lost his temper earlier, and she hadn't backed away one bit. She'd glanced at him, noticed his clenched hands and then looked him straight in the eye.

And she was right. They did have a great deal in common. What would it hurt to date? See her a few times, and get her out of his system. If he wrote the story she asked for, she couldn't use work as an excuse. He wouldn't take any payment for the accounting he'd do, or for writing the article.

So technically she wouldn't be his boss. She'd have to edit the piece, which might give her an out. But he'd find a way around that.

I know what I have to do.

8

THE SUN DIPPED below the lake and the wind gusted. Standing on the back deck of her uncle's place, Macy threw the ball for Harley. The dog loved to run, a little. It wasn't long before Harley kept the ball in her mouth and walked past Macy into the house where she dropped it into her basket of toys.

Chuckling, Macy shut the door and locked it. Using the remote, she turned on the fireplace, and padded to the kitchen to see if her marinara was ready. She'd made the sauce in the slow cooker earlier in the day. Her housekeeper had the next two weeks off while she cared for her ailing grandson, who had chicken pox. From what Macy could discern, the itchy disease had made the rounds of most of the elementary school and a number of day cares. They'd done a small feature about how to care for children and adults with the disease.

Macy didn't mind being on her own. If she had a choice, she'd let the housekeeper go. But she didn't. After setting a pot of water on the stove to boil, she picked up her cell phone to make sure she hadn't missed a call.

His call.

Blake had left a message at the office that he was busy at the feed store. He said he'd let her know when he could come by to do the accounting. It was almost five-thirty and he hadn't contacted her.

He was either really busy, or he might have forgotten.

Why was she disappointed? She'd heard through the Tranquil Waters grapevine that his mother was out of town for some reason.

"Cassidy Lee said she happened to spot Blake out behind the store, loading lumber into a truck." Macy had eavesdropped on the waitress's conversation as she lingered by the register at the café to pay for her lunch. The waitress in question had the rapt attention of a table full of women. "He had his shirt off, and she said it took everything she had not to walk up to him and start licking his abs. It's not a six, it's an eight-pack, ladies. And he has those sexy cut-ins on his hip. I asked her about the scars from his injuries, and she said, 'What scars? I was too distracted by those muscles.'"

The table of women whooped.

"Imagine how hot he must have been to take his shirt off when it's so chilly outside." One of the women fanned her face. "I think I might have to stop by the feed store to pick up some—" she paused for a few seconds "—seeds."

The other women tittered and joked.

Blake was a hot commodity in this town. Most of

the men his age and a little older were for one reason or another not available. She'd learned that bit of news from Amanda, who said she went to Austin if she wanted to dance because then she didn't have to worry about some guy's wife giving her a hard time the next day.

While Macy waited for the water to boil, she cleaned up the mess Harley had made around her food bowl. The dog had no manners when it came to drinking and eating. She was well behaved otherwise, so Macy had no real complaints.

Once the noodles were ready, she put her meal together but skipped the garlic bread since her favorite jeans were a little tight. She should probably up her visits to the pool. She hated dieting and her knee still bothered her, so running was out.

Taking a bite of spaghetti, she closed her eyes and moaned about the delicious flavors. The sauce recipe had come from a chef she'd met when she was in Italy, covering the launch of a new political party.

Her cell vibrated on the counter.

Thinking it was Blake, she answered it.

"It's about time," Garrison, her ex, said. The man's voice was as smooth as silk. But the instant she heard it, she cringed.

"Don't hang up. I can hear you breathing. Look, something's coming down the pike and I wanted to give you a—"

"I'll make it simple for you. No. Whatever it is, whatever you think you need to tell me, my answer is no. Don't ever call me again."

She pushed the off button.

The nerve of the man.

Her phone buzzed again. She thought about ignoring it, but she knew he'd just keep calling.

"If I have to change my number to avoid you phoning me I will. I have no interest in anything you have to say. So take whatever is coming down the pike and toss it somewhere, away from me."

There was a long pause. Finally, she'd gotten through to him.

"Um, your receptionist gave me this number to call," Blake's whiskey-coated voice said.

Ahhh!

"Blake, I'm so, so sorry. I— The call before you— Uh, never mind. Yes, of course I wanted you to call."

"Are you okay?" he asked.

"What do you mean?"

"The call. Is someone harassing you?" His voice was measured, but she heard that protective side of him.

"Yes, but it isn't anything I can't handle. It's my former boyfriend. I really am sorry about that. I should have checked my caller ID."

"Do you still want me to look at your books?"

"Yes, but I'm at home. Do you mind coming here, or I can bring them to your house. I've got the ledgers. Everything else is on my laptop. My uncle kept two sets."

"Let me get something to eat, and I'll be over."

"I made spaghetti," she said quickly. "It's my special sauce. That is if you like spaghetti, if you don't—"

"That sounds great. But I have to warn you, I'm

pretty tired. I may not be able to go over everything tonight."

He'd worked hard all day at the feed store and he was still recovering from his injuries. What was she thinking? "I'm being selfish, Blake. You're so strong that sometimes I forget—"

"I'm fine." The steel in his voice made her smile. Never, ever talk about a marine's stamina. She should have known better.

Before she stuck her foot in any deeper, she opted for telling him, "I'll have your food ready when you get here."

"I'm about five minutes out. See you then."

Five minutes? She glanced at herself in the window. Sloppy sweats, mussed hair, her reading glasses on top of her head.

As she ran for the bedroom she gathered her hair into a messy knot on top of her head.

The washer dinged. All of her jeans were wet. She had a choice, flannel pajama bottoms with Dalmatians on them, or the sweats. She went for the dog pants. Then she tried to find a top that kind of matched. She found a black cotton cami that was a little tight, but it would do.

Harley watched her go back and forth as if she were playing both sides in a tennis match.

"I know. But there's no reason I can't look half-decent. It's not like I threw on a sexy cocktail dress."

She wiped the day's mascara off the under part of her eyes and swiped gloss across her lips.

Harley woofed. The truck could be heard pulling into the long drive.

Spritzing perfume, she dashed through it so he wouldn't know she'd only just put it on.

Running to the kitchen she filled a large bowl with noodles and sauce, and set it next to hers. When he rang the bell, she inhaled a deep breath and released it.

Before she reached the door to let Blake in, Harley was there with the handle in her mouth. The door opened about two inches.

"Macy," Blake called.

She cackled. "Harley opened the door, come on in."

He praised the dog every which way and followed Macy to the kitchen.

"Don't you dare tell her how smart she is," she said, laughing. "You could have been a serial killer. I'm going to get a bolt installed higher up, I guess. Or one of those locks that slide down from the top."

He chuckled. "I'm pretty sure she knows how smart she is."

She and Blake ate and chatted about his mom going to take care of his grandmother, and how the store was busier than ever this time of year because it carried hardware, seeds and gardening equipment, holiday decorating items, as well as the stuff for livestock and pets.

"Mom had this great idea to start a pumpkin patch in one of the outer buildings near the store. Normally the pumpkins would be outside, but with all the rain, she was worried about mold. I'll be happy when Halloween is over this weekend so we can get that building clean. We have to check every pumpkin every day to make sure they're okay."

They cleared the dishes, which she put in the dishwasher while he found containers and put the food in the refrigerator. He was a man used to working in a kitchen, and she liked that about him.

"If you're sure you aren't too tired, I've got the laptop set up in the family room. There's a table in there that I use as a desk so I can monitor you-know-who's television viewing habits."

"Now that I've eaten, I feel more awake," he said. "Let me take a look."

She sat on the couch while he sat at the table and wrote things down as he went through the computer files. Every few minutes she'd steal a glance at his profile. But she had to stop before her body overheated. The man made her feel crazy good.

Would it be such a bad thing to scratch the itch? He hadn't said he'd do the story, nevertheless she'd promised him no one else would get the assignment. That took the ethical problem out of the equation.

She had no desire for anything long-term. So far as they were discreet and no one in town would know. They could use his accounting for the paper as a cover. Friends with benefits. She'd never had one of those before.

"Why are you looking at me like that?"

She blinked and realized he was staring at her.

"Uh. You're very handsome."

That sly grin spread across his face. "Huh. Okay."

He turned back to the computer, but continued to grin.

He knew.

"You do bad, bad things to me, Mr. Marine."

The grin grew bigger.

"I haven't touched you," he said, still facing the screen.

"Oh, but you don't even have to," she whispered. Maybe she had one too many glasses of wine with dinner. The room seemed very warm.

That made him look at her.

"Ms. Reynolds, are you coming on to me?"

"Yes, sir. I believe I am. What are you going to do about it?"

He sat there for a few seconds, his dark brown eyes catching her gaze as if he were searching for answers.

"What about your ethical dilemma?"

"I'm not writing the story, so it's no longer a problem. I wouldn't be dating the subject of one of my stories. You'd just be another guy."

"So if I ask you on a date, you'd say yes?"

She nodded. "With a few conditions."

He leaned an elbow on the table, but didn't take his eyes off her. "I'm not surprised."

"They're nothing wild. First, we keep it simple. You mentioned that you need simple right now and so do I. So we set some ground rules, and everyone is happy."

"And those would be?"

"We are discreet and exclusive."

He frowned. "Why discreet? Are you ashamed to be seen with me?"

"Don't be silly. You're the hottest man I've ever seen. *Ever*. I'd be more than happy to show you off to anyone who would look. But I'm new to the town, and— I don't know. I just think it would be best. That is, since we are keeping it simple."

Now that she'd said it out loud, it seemed over the top.

"Listen, normally, I'd have no problem. But one of the benefits of our mutual companionship, other than the obvious, is that it would detract a lot of the ladies from pushing their single daughters at me. My brother saw a picture of me on a social media site today loading feed bags into a customer's truck. I didn't even know someone was taking pictures. And why would anyone care?"

She smiled. "Remind me to find out what site that is. I want a copy. I heard you had your shirt off."

He huffed. "This is what I'm talking about. How about we hold hands in public or something. Let me take you on a few dates. People date all the time. It doesn't have to mean forever."

"Okay. I see your point. And since I want this to be exclusive, for however long it lasts, it would make sense for others to know. And in this town, it's probably impossible to be discreet."

"Yep. So we're friends who date. Is there anything else?"

"Well, I was kind of hoping that there would be benefits besides dating."

He frowned. "Like what?"

She chewed on her lip. Did he really need her to spell it out for him? "When the time comes, if you're into it, maybe we could—you know."

He grinned and cocked the right side of his mouth. "I'd definitely be into that."

"Me, too." *In fact, we can start right now.*

"So will you go out with me on Halloween? A friend of mine is throwing a party."

She bit her lip. A movie or dinner date was one thing. Meeting his friends was another.

"You're going to say no, aren't you?"

"Uh, well, it depends. It seems a little fast to be meeting the friends. But that isn't the reason I'm hesitant. I promised to help out at the shelter that night. We're dressing up our pets in costumes and handing candy out to kids to raise awareness about the facility."

"Not a problem. I'll help you, and then we'll go to the party afterward."

"Deal. Is it a costume party?"

"Yes, but it doesn't need to be anything fancy."

"Okay. Cherie is sending me a costume to wear for the shelter event. She is really into Halloween and has a ton of stuff in storage. It will probably be a giant pink rabbit or something, so I apologize in advance."

He laughed. "That's some friend."

"You have no idea."

He stood and went over to the couch where he stuck out his hand. When she put hers in his, he pulled her to her feet.

"It's a bit preemptive, but I've wanted to do this since the day I met you."

His mouth was on hers before she blinked. His lips were softer than expected. When his hand cupped her chin, she sighed with pleasure.

"You taste so good," he said against her mouth.

"It's the sauce," she whispered back as he trailed kisses down her neck.

"No, babe, it's you." Then his mouth returned to hers and their kiss intensified, so familiar, so easy, as if they'd done this a million times before.

When he lifted his head, they both gasped for air. "I think I'd better go," he said, leaning his forehead against hers. "I'm not sure I can control myself much longer. I want you so bad it hurts."

She glanced down, reached out and caressed him.

Hissing, he broke away from her. "Macy, please. I—"

"I want you," she said. "Now." She met his gaze and smiled a warm, wide smile.

"But I planned to take you out and woo you," he said. His voice strained.

"Woo me? Do people still say that?" She undid the buckle on his jeans.

"Yes. I say that. Remember, this is Texas. We like to court our women." Even though he didn't have much of an accent he put an extra twang in there.

"I'm a Yankee woman. We don't need wooing. We just need hot, fit marines who make us think of naughty, naughty things to do."

He chuckled. "I'm beginning to like the North better and better every second. Are you sure?"

"Yes," she replied as she tugged his head down to hers.

9

AFTER THEY MADE sure Harley was settled with the largest rawhide bone he'd ever seen, Blake trailed the raven-haired siren to her bedroom. The rest of the house was decorated in rich leather and textured walls. But her room had white walls, white furniture and most of the bedding was the same color. Only the pillows on the bed were pale blue.

He was about to comment on her style, it fit her in a feminine but classic way, when she slipped off her top. A lacy black bra with a tiny red bow in the center cupped her lush breasts.

"You're beautiful."

Her cheeks turned pink. She had no idea how attractive she was.

She pointed to him.

"Your turn."

She was nervous, he could see the slight tension around her eyes and the trembling in her fingers. He was sensitive to her emotions. As if his body and mind had been tuned to her like a radio dial.

He slipped his T-shirt off.

Her mouth formed an O.

"Wow, you're amazing." She didn't hold back.

He liked that about her.

"You're gorgeous, so much so that I can't get you out of my head. You've been keeping me up nights. Once I saw you doing everything you could to heave Harley into the back of your car, I knew I wanted you."

She slipped her baggy pajama bottoms off, and he sucked in a breath. The panties matched the bra. A red ribbon bow on each hip held the tiny triangles of fabric together. Her long legs were those of a runner, strong and firm. Curvy hips, sparkling eyes, and those breasts, she was all woman, and his fantasy come true.

It occurred to him that in seconds she would see the evidence of that, but he didn't want to stop the game.

"Oh" was all she said as he undid his zipper and his hard cock revealed. "It's a— That is, okay, yes. It's really— Yeah. Impressive."

He chuckled.

"Beets!" she said suddenly and put a hand to her temple.

Was she ill?

"Beets?"

"We don't have condoms. At least, I don't." She shook her head. "Tofu turkey!"

"Do you always say food names when you're upset?"

"What? No, it's that I don't like to swear. My

mouth, uh, let's just say hanging out with military types and reporters has left me with a mouth like a—"

"A marine?"

She smiled. "Yelling curse words upset the animals, so I say foods I'm not super fond of to keep from saying the things I shouldn't. Do you have any condoms?"

"Not on me. But I have an idea."

She smirked. "It better not involve driving to a store and buying some. I don't think I can wait that long."

No way he could wait that long, either. Besides, he was worried that she might change her mind. He'd respect her wishes, of course, but he'd also be very disappointed.

"Hold that thought." He rezippered and left the house, heading for the driveway.

Opening the toolbox in the back of his truck he dug around for the first-aid kit. There he found two foil packages. When he'd gone through boot camp it had been drilled into his head that you always packed protection.

He kissed the packets before slamming everything shut and bolting for the door. Praying they hadn't lost the moment, he found Macy curled up in her bed with the covers to her neck.

He tossed the packets to her, and she caught them in the air.

"Quick reflexes," he said as he pulled off his boots and shoved away his jeans. "Is everything okay? You can still say no. You can always say no. I want you to know that."

She rolled her eyes and as a welcoming gesture tossed back his side of the covers. "Blake, I was freezing. That's why I got in here. I want you and I don't want to wait any longer." He slid in. She grinned as she ripped open one of the foil packages and leaned over him.

"Slow down," he said, coughing out a laugh. "You don't have to be in such a hurry."

"But I am." She palmed his erection. And he was about to lose that sense of control he'd warned her about.

"We've got all night." He struggled to get the words out without moaning.

"Yes, but I've been fantasizing about you, about us like this, for days." Before he could stop her, she rolled the condom down over him. When she had finished, he caught her wrist and brought her fingers to his mouth and kissed them.

Damn, that might have been the sexiest thing any woman had ever said to him, which made him all the more determined to make this last. Moving her onto her back, he propped her underneath him.

His right hand slid between them, his fingers seeking her heat.

She smiled and arched her back, clearly wanting and welcoming him.

"I want to do this. For you, Macy," he said, speaking softly into her ear. Her body arched again. "Knowing every inch of you is important to me." He rose up and sat back. It wasn't the most comfortable position for him, but he didn't care about the pain. "Put your legs over my shoulders, baby."

She started to say something, but she stopped. Taking one of the larger pillows, he tucked it under her. He intended to give her every pleasure he possibly could and this would make that easier.

"I—"

"What?" he asked, as he touched her breasts, teasing her.

"I haven't really…" she said, leaving the thought unfinished.

"That sounds like a challenge, Macy."

"No, it's—"

She drew in a sharp breath as his mouth stoked her rising passion. Encouraged by her growing cries and murmurs, he was intent on satisfying every inch of her.

When she called out his name, her body quaked in its release and she reached out for him. He gathered her in his arms and held her tight.

"I need you, Blake." Her body had almost stopped thrumming. "Now."

"Bossy, aren't you?" He dropped a quick kiss on her lips. Tossing the pillow aside, he rolled on to his back. With his leg the way it was, it would be easier if she was on top. His thigh was throbbing, but so were other parts of him.

A limp noodle, he drew her to him. Her soft thick hair had fallen from its messy knot creating a dark veil around her silver-green eyes and high cheekbones. She was so sexy.

His hard cock poked playfully at her belly. She smiled at him. "Finally." Lifting up, she positioned herself on him and sighed as she rocked back and forth.

He matched her pace. It wasn't easy with his beautiful nymph riding him with wild abandon. She increased their tempo and he groaned out his approval.

As her muscles contracted, he held on—barely—and told her to open her eyes.

The moonlight streaming through her window bathed her face in a gorgeous way, and her eyes met his.

"You're incredible," he told her.

She moved faster, pressing into him, never slowing until they'd lost their grip and climaxed together. Losing control had never felt so good.

"That was better than any dream," she whispered tiredly as she fell onto his chest.

He cradled her and murmured sweet words that made her sigh. In minutes, she was fast asleep.

A whine from the doorway had him sliding out from under his beautiful fairy, and pulling the comforter up to keep her warm.

She grumbled but her head stayed on the pillow.

He slipped on his jeans and T-shirt and let Harley out via the back door. He watched her as she ran around the yard a few times. The moon reflected off the lake, and he envied Macy this view.

At the thought of her name, something tugged in his gut, a warning that he might be headed for trouble.

Making love to her was definitely not going to scratch his itch. It only made him want her all the more.

Slow. He reminded himself. She'd just run from a

bad relationship, and he was in no shape to start anything serious. It wouldn't be fair to either of them.

Harley bounded inside and gulped some water. She then grabbed a chew toy and made for her bed. Lying next to the toy, she went to sleep.

What a dog.

He'd never seen anything like her, and he just loved her.

Her owner was equally unusual in a way that called to him.

Shutting off the lights, he considered his next move. He should go home, but it didn't seem right to leave Macy without saying goodbye.

Digging in his pocket, he found one of his pills. After breaking it in half, he drank it down with a glass of water. He slid back into bed with Macy.

"Thanks for letting her out," she said as she snuggled against his chest. He tightened his arms around her, bringing her close.

"No problem. Go to sleep, angel."

"You wore me out," she said quietly. "I don't have a choice."

That made him smile.

"You didn't have to stay, but I'm really glad you did." Her words were soft and heartfelt.

"I may be gone by the time you wake up for work. But trust me, I'd like to stay for the next couple of days. Right here in this bed with you."

"Mmm. I like having friends like you."

Friends? In the plural?

As far as he was concerned, he would be her only

friend like this for a very long time. The thought of another man's hands on her— Hell.

He'd already become one of those possessive blockheads.

She didn't deserve that.

He looked down at her sweet face.

But dammit. She was his.

10

WHEN MACY OPENED her front door to him two days later, Blake's jaw dropped open. He looked at her from head to toe, his eyes resting a bit longer on her midsection and breasts.

She scoffed and turned away. "I'm going to kill Cherie the next time I see her," she grumbled. "I can't wear this. It's—it's…inappropriate."

"Sexy as hell," Blake said at the same time.

"Maybe if it was only you and me, but I'm not wearing this genie costume to pass out candy to little kids."

Closing the door behind him, he followed her into the house. "It's not as revealing as you think," he said. "All of you is covered. It's that some of the material is flesh-colored. And you're not pretending to be from the Arabian Nights or something—that's a kids' story. Besides there are ballerinas, princesses and fairies running around all over the place."

She rolled her eyes. "It's not really a kids' story! A king kills a thousand virgins after he defiles them.

Most of the kids are under seven. And it's too late. I don't have anything else to wear."

"It's cold out, and the temperature might drop down to the thirties. Maybe you could just wear a sweater or something. The skirt isn't that bad with all the scarves." He eyed her appreciatively. "Do those scarves come off one by one?"

The man really did have a one-track mind.

She growled at him.

"That's good," he chuckled. "We can just paint your face to look like a tiger. By the way—hello. I missed you a lot today."

He snagged her and wrapped his arms around her. Instantly, she forgot her troubles as his tongue tangled with hers. Pressing herself into him, his hard cock poked back.

That she could do that to him pleased her. More than she wanted to admit. Every time he looked at her, she felt like the most beautiful woman in the world.

She'd smiled so much today that Amanda asked her if she was okay. When Macy gave her the afternoon off to get her brothers ready to trick-or-treat, the shock and gratitude on the young woman's face had been truly remarkable.

"As much as I want to stay here, I have to get to the animal shelter. I'm the only one who has a key to the locker where all the candy is stored. Mariel, the office manager, didn't trust herself with it. So I had to hide all the candy in my locker."

"We better get going. Where's the beast?"

"Outside. Chasing the geese dumb enough to land within her radius. She's been after them for at least an hour. I'm not worried about her catching one. Every time she gets close to them they honk at her, and she runs away. It's one of her games she's made up. I'll get her."

When she returned, he had Harley's leash and a few toys for the dog to play with while they handed out candy.

Blake had spent the past few nights here, rising early in the morning to be at the feed store. But their lovemaking in the evenings was epic. No man had ever taken her to such heights. She was kind of angry that she'd been missing out on so much.

In his arms, Macy knew it was the safest she'd ever felt. Even though it was only a temporary harbor, she enjoyed it. And he slept when he was with her. Plagued my insomnia and night terrors, he'd had neither since they'd been together.

He'd admitted as much the night before last. She'd laughed it off and said it was because she wore him out. But the look in his eyes, that deep, searching gaze of his, told her it was much more than that. She'd become his port in a storm, as well.

Scary how intimate and intense a relationship could become when both parties were in need of the same thing. They read each other on a more profound level. And he was kind and generous to a fault.

In a mere few days, her cold, jaded heart had realized it had been missing out on what a real relationship could be.

Except, that this was just a fling.

I must keep telling myself that.

Harley, who sat in the back of Blake's truck, on her

special blanket, licked Macy's elbow. It was almost as if she wanted to tell her, *you'll be okay. You have me.*

Reaching behind, she scratched the dog's ear.

And for that I'm grateful.

It didn't take them long to arrive at the animal shelter, but still, bunches of children dressed in an array of costumes had already climbed the hill and gotten there ahead of them.

Blake had assisted with the carving of several pumpkins, which adorned the front porch and the lobby. For safety's sake they had put battery-operated candles inside the jack-o'-lanterns. A good idea, since the first thing Harley did was step in one on the way into the building.

She freaked out until Blake was able to get her paw out of the offending orange ball. Harley growled at it.

"Bad jack-o'-lantern, bad." Blake wagged a finger at the pumpkin, which seemed to please the dog.

Blake put Harley's dragon ears and scales on her. They'd been another gift from Cherie. The scales covered the dog's back and buckled around her belly and neck. The ears were on a headband of sorts.

She pranced around as if she were the queen of everything.

"You are the cutest dragon I've ever seen," Blake muttered as he scratched her behind the ears.

Back outside, Macy kept her coat on. She got a kick out of watching Blake interact with all the kids. He'd worn jeans and a T-shirt that had the *Avengers* logo on it. He'd told her he wasn't much into costumes.

By eight, the crowds had thinned out. That was fine since they were almost out of candy.

"That went by a lot faster than I expected," he said.

"You were great. The kids loved you, and you definitely know your superheroes."

He laughed. "I love to read, and comic books were cheap when I was a kid. I had a habit of losing library books, so my mom only let me take one out a week. Comic books were a cheap alternative."

The man was nothing but contradictions. He was definitely more than a pretty face. He was as tough as they came, but he was also intelligent and thoughtful.

Everything a woman could want, and then some.

And he wanted her.

"What's going on?" he asked as he shifted into Drive and steered the truck away from the shelter.

"Hmm? Oh. Honestly, I'm sort of awed by how amazing you are. What I don't understand is why me? When you could quite obviously have a fling with any woman you wanted."

At the stop sign, he glanced over at her. "That you don't see how beautiful, smart and funny you are is one of the reasons I like you so much. Why would I want anyone else when I have you?"

If Harley's enormous head wasn't on the armrest between them, Macy might have moved into his lap right then and there. "You really do always know what to say."

The street he turned onto was crowded with cars on both sides. She loved this part of Tranquil Waters. Many of the houses had been built in the early 1900s. The neighborhood was decked out in fall colors and

Halloween decorations. People were out in their yards chatting while kids ran around in their costumes.

"It's going to be a hike to find somewhere to park. Do you want me to drop you off in front of my friend's place?"

Definitely not. The last thing she wanted to do was walk into a party where she knew no one—in a skimpy genie costume. "I'm up for a walk. I had my fair share of candy tonight. Are you sure it's okay to bring Harley?"

"Yep. Jaime loves dogs."

She'd never brought a dog the size of a horse to a party.

"No! I can't believe I forgot."

"What?"

"A gift. Your rule about always bringing a gift to a party. I've been rushing around and I didn't remember to get anything."

He grinned. "Don't worry. I've got us covered. I had flowers delivered earlier today from the both of us. One of those fall bouquets. Jaime loves flowers."

Wait. Jaime was a girl? He'd been telling her stories the past couple of days about how he and Jaime were always in trouble together as kids.

Before she could mention it, they were at the door of one of the largest homes on the block. A wraparound porch and two-story columns gave it a plantation house feel.

The open door led into a foyer the shape and size of a rotunda. It was a fit for the Southern mansion. Dark wood floors graced the area, and a huge round table with a bouquet of flowers sat below a crystal chandelier. There were two staircases with banisters draped in magnolia garlands.

"Oh. My. God! It's my favorite marine." A woman in a formfitting Catwoman suit threw her arms around Blake and kissed him hard on the mouth.

And he didn't seem to mind a bit.

"Hey, stinky. What's up?"

"You're late," she said when she stepped back and eyed him up and down. "And you aren't wearing a costume. I told you that you had to wear a costume."

"You know I don't do costumes. I was giving a hand out at the animal shelter, which is why I'm late." That seemed to remind him that she was standing there. "This is my friend Macy," he said as he put an arm around her shoulders.

The happy smile faded from the woman's face as she gave Macy the once-over.

"You that Yankee newspaper editor?"

"Jaime, be nice," Blake warned, but with a playful tone to his voice.

Refusing to back down, Macy jutted out her chin. "Yes."

"This is who you're dating? Do we not have enough women in the South that you have to start in on the Northerners?"

Blake pointed a finger at his friend. "I *really* like her, so play nice. I mean it."

Her hero. Macy smiled up at him.

"What, for goodness' sake, is that?"

Harley cocked her head.

"That's Macy's dog, Harley," he answered.

Jaime glanced back at Macy. "Great Dane?"

"Yes."

The woman smiled at her. Then she put two fingers to her mouth and blew an earsplitting whistle.

A dark gray, almost blue, Great Dane with silvery eyes trotted into the room.

"Harley, this is Bruno."

"If you don't want that costume shredded in the next five minutes, I suggest you take if off of Harley. Bruno gets jealous when other dogs have things he doesn't. Though, I'm definitely going to get him a costume for next year because that dragon outfit is too cute."

Macy wondered if the dog might attack Harley, and she put herself between the two animals.

"Oh, don't worry. He wouldn't hurt a fly. But he would try to get that outfit off of her for himself. He loves everything with ruffles, patterns and either brown or green."

Blake took the costume off of Harley and she shook herself.

"Now, Bruno, play nice. Take her out to the clubhouse."

The dog glanced back at his owner and nodded.

Were all Great Danes so smart?

"Are you sure they'll be okay?" Macy wasn't worried about Bruno being with Harley, she was concerned as to how Harley would interact with him. She got along with the other dogs at the shelter, but she'd always been supervised.

"I'm sure," Jaime said. "Blake, go say hello to everyone. I want to speak to your Yankee lady."

Blake stared at Macy. "I think that might make her uncomfortable. It's probably best if I stick around."

Macy appreciated that he wanted to stay by her, but she wasn't a child.

"Don't worry, I won't bite her," Jaime promised. "Besides, anyone with a dog like that is okay in my book. Great Danes are sensitive and bright, and extremely needy. They take a lot of love, time and patience. That's something your Yankee will need if she's going to train you up, as well."

Blake rolled his eyes.

Macy laughed.

Jaime made a shooing motion with her hands. "Go on. She'll join you in a minute."

"I'm okay," she assured him. "I'll find you when we're done."

Curious about why Jaime wanted her alone, she encouraged him to go.

Jaime reached out to shake her hand. "Sorry about that. I'm a bit protective of him," she said. "He's like a brother to me."

Weird, she'd never seen anyone kiss a brother like that, but Macy kept her mouth shut. She shook the woman's hand.

"You have a great house," Macy said. Her mind was awhirl with questions.

"Belonged to my great-grandma. We've tried to keep the restoration accurate, but it isn't easy."

She motioned for Macy to follow her.

"We'll put your coat in here." Jamie stood in front of a long hall closet and held out her hand for the garment.

"I—that is, my costume's quite revealing."

The woman judged her warily. "It can't be any more revealing than mine, or some of the others in here. Tara has a French maid's outfit on. Every time she bends over to get some food, she flashes her red thong to the entire room. It can't be any worse than that."

Macy slipped off the coat, feeling exposed.

"Well, you are as pretty as he said. It's not fair that you have those legs and that chest."

She wasn't sure how to respond to that…compliment?

"He's head over heels for you."

"What?" The sudden change in topic had Macy's mind spinning.

"Blake. We've never seen him like this over a woman. He called every single person at this party and told them they'd better welcome you or else." She laughed at Macy's grimace. "I know. But he's protective that way. I like the fact that you stood up to me back there. I have a feeling you and I could be friends. But there's just one thing you should know."

"What's that?" Macy walked next to her as they entered the living room full of people.

"If you hurt him, I will do the same to you." The threat was undeniable. "And I always mean exactly what I say."

Macy was about to tell the woman to back off, but she was equally protective of Blake. "If it makes you feel any better, I think he's the most incredible man I've ever met."

Jaime seemed to be in shock. "Oh, you have it just

as bad for him. Interesting. I can't wait to see how this plays out."

She wasn't sure about what to make of that comment, but across the room she spotted someone she knew.

"Excuse me, I see a friend of mine."

Josh, the veterinarian from the shelter, stood by a bay window talking to another guest.

When he saw her, he smiled brightly. "Hey," he said and hugged her, "I didn't know you'd be here." He left an arm around her shoulders, which she didn't mind at the moment. She was grateful to have at least one other person, besides Blake, be nice to her.

She shrugged. "I'm on a date. He was the one who was invited."

Josh's eyes widened in surprise. "Good, good. Seems like you're assimilating into the town really well. Let me introduce you to Brendan Tucker. He and his wife, Jaime, are the hosts of the party."

Macy shook the man's hand.

"I met your wife," she said, searching for something polite to say.

The two men laughed. "She can be a bit much, but she's a sweetheart once you get to know her," Brendan said.

"I'll have to take your word on that. Frankly, I've dealt with insurgents who were less scary."

The men howled.

"So who's your date?" Josh asked.

"I am," a deep voice said from behind them. "And I'd appreciate it if you'd get your hands off my woman."

"Blake," Macy admonished. It made little sense. Why would he act so jealous? It was ridiculous. They barely knew each other and Josh was a genuine good guy.

"Who's going to make me?" Josh said with heat in his voice.

What was happening here?

Macy ducked away from Josh's arm and stood apart from the two men. They were glaring at each another.

"I am, jerk." Blake stepped forward.

"Now, fellas. You know Jaime will have a fit if you break anything. Everyone calm down," Brendan cajoled.

"Why did you have your arm around Macy?" Blake growled at Josh.

"She's my friend. We went out a couple of times when she first came to town. What's the big deal? You aren't still mad at me after all this time? I wasn't the one who made you write those letters."

"Wait a minute," Blake whispered harshly. "You two dated."

His snapped around to look at Macy as if she were some kind of traitor.

She'd had enough.

"I don't know what's wrong with the two of you, but you're embarrassing me."

"Answer the question, Macy. Did you date my former best friend?"

His former best friend?

Oh. Ohhhh. This must be some male feud and

she'd stepped right into the middle of it. "Two times," she replied.

"And that was it," Josh said. "We knew from the get-go that we weren't right for each other. But we are friends. She volunteers at the shelter so we see each other occasionally."

Blake's mouth formed a thin line. He focused in on Macy. "You never mentioned that you went out with anyone in town."

"You never asked. And anyway, nothing happened with your former best friend. You're acting so foolish. Both of you."

With that she stomped out in search of her dog. She would not put up with that kind of arrogant behavior from any man. She and Blake were casual. He had no right to—

She froze in midstep. Hadn't she felt the same about him when his friend Jaime had kissed him?

I was as jealous, just not as vocal about it.

"Hey, genie, why don't you come over here and grant me my three wishes?" a man in a Frankenstein costume called out. A crowd stood around him.

They all laughed.

She turned her back on them.

"Told you the Yankee girl was a witch."

These people were beyond rude.

"You know what, Frankenstein, so much for that Southern hospitality you folks talk about. I'm proud to be from the North. In fact—"

"George, are you giving Macy a hard time? Because if you are, I'm going to have some serious words with you," Jaime said as slipped her arm through Macy's in a clear sign of solidarity. "This is Blake's girl, so that means she's like family. And you know how I feel about my family. You all apologize right now."

Without hesitation, apologies were quickly issued.

"Forgive me, Macy," George said. "I'd blame the whiskey, but sometimes I'm simply an old fool. Just ask my three ex-wives."

The crowd chuckled, the tension evaporated instantly.

Macy looked to Jaime so they wouldn't see her smile. "You didn't have to do that," she told her.

"I meant what I said. I'm sorry about before. This couldn't have been fun for you what with friends fighting, George being his stupid self and me acting like, well, we know what I was acting like."

Macy shrugged. "I've been to worse parties."

Jaime guffawed. "You're all right. I need to check on the caterers in the kitchen. Come with me?"

What she really wanted was to go home, but she followed Jaime.

The kitchen bustled with servers and food preparers sprinting around and shouting.

"Pietro, those mushroom caps are a hit."

One of the guys in a chef's hat blew Jaime a kiss before opening one of the ovens to put in a tray of what looked like hors d'oeuvres.

Walking along the kitchen island, big enough for a dozen bar stools, Jaime inspected the food. Then she grabbed a plate and took food from several of the trays. She handed the plate to Macy. "This one's for you."

She loaded up another plate. "This one's for me. I

never get to eat when I throw parties, but I'm starved.
Come on, let's go check on the dogs."

"Are Blake and Josh all right, do you think?"

Jaime laughed. "My husband is there, and they're
scared to death of him. They won't get too out of
hand."

"Why are they scared of him?"

"Because he's the only man who can tame me, so
he must be one real son of a gun. And he is. I talk
tough, but I'd do anything for that man. The love of
my life, and he knows it."

Next door to the kitchen was the breakfast room,
which looked out over a pool area. Macy could see
Harley chasing Bruno around the cabana. The two
dogs stopped for a second, and then Bruno began
chasing Harley.

"They're pals already, see?" Jaime sat on one of the
loungers and leaned back a heated lamp nearby. She
put the plate of food on her chest and started eating.

Macy sat on a lounger next to her.

"Sorry," Jaime said after swallowing a bite-size
quiche. "I haven't had anything but water and vegetables for a week so I'd fit in this damn costume."

Macy grinned. "Hey, it worked. You look incredible."

"Thanks for that. And I really am sorry about earlier. When we heard Blake was injured this time, well,
we're all kind of protective of him. He's always been
such a stand-up type of guy. And I didn't lie, he is
like my brother. He has dated in the past, obviously,
but—I've never seen him like he is with you. I noticed him when Josh hugged you. He'd been giving

you the loving eyes from across the room, and then it was like a cartoon. I was surprised steam didn't come out of his ears when Josh put his arm around your shoulders.

"And shame on Josh for egging Blake on. That's one of those man things, pushing each other's buttons, I guess."

Macy should have seen this coming. It hadn't been that long since she'd been away from Garrison, although it sure seemed like it.

"I went on a couple of friendly dates with Josh, nothing happened," Macy offered. "But for some reason Blake seems to think I should have been a nun before I met him. Bunch of macho nonsense, if you ask me." Macy bit into something with bacon and cheese in the shape of a ball. It was heaven.

"Yes, it is. Things seem to be moving fast between you two."

Macy winced. "I'm not sure what I'm supposed to say. We both agreed that this would be a casual arrangement."

"Blake's way past casual," Jaime said.

"It's only been a couple of days. I mean, I've known him maybe two weeks. Don't get me wrong— I like him a lot." More than she would admit to one of his best friends. "I'm not sure what to do. Maybe I should slow it down until we both get our bearings."

"Good luck with that." Jaime pointed toward the house.

"There you are," Blake said worriedly.

"See ya, kiddies. I need to get back to my party. Blake, behave yourself. Macy, it was so nice to meet you. I mean that. I'm going to stop by the paper soon and take you to lunch."

"I'd like that," Macy said.

Blake took Jaime's place on the lounger, but he sat sideways facing Macy. They sat in silence for a full thirty seconds.

"I'd like to blame it on the pain pills or too much alcohol, but the truth is I haven't had any because I knew I'd be driving," he said quickly.

Macy stared down at her plate, no longer hungry.

"There's no excuse for that kind of behavior. I just saw his arm around you, and— I promise you it will never happen again."

"You embarrassed me."

"I embarrassed both of us. And I'm truly sorry, Macy."

She still didn't meet his eyes, but she noticed he wrung his hands.

Give the guy a break.

She lifted her head. "I should be flattered about the show you put on in there, but I'm not. I don't like bullies and I'm certainly not someone's possession. I don't belong to you, Blake. I'm an individual. I've been on my own for a long, long time."

He sighed. "You're right. It's a mess. Do you want me to have somebody drive you home? Or I'm happy to do it, if it's okay with you. I just don't want you to be afraid of me."

Macy shook her head. "I'm not afraid of you. I could never be afraid of you. You wouldn't hurt me, no matter what the circumstances. But it does bother me that you think I would be scared of you. You're one of the kindest men I've ever met. And so gentle with Harley…and me. And I don't think any of those guests would appreciate having a hundred-and-seventy-five-pound dog in their backseat, so yes, I'm okay with you taking us home."

"We're okay, then?"

"We are but you have to remember I'm not your favorite toy that you get upset when someone else touches it." She frowned. "That didn't come out right."

"You kind of are," he said under his breath.

"What?"

"Not a toy, but you are my favorite person. Ever."

She couldn't hide her smile. "Stop with the Mr. Charming routine. I'm supposed to be mad at you."

He smiled back.

They said their goodbyes, found Harley and climbed into his truck.

"I was beginning to worry, though. You did seem a bit too perfect," she finally said when they exited off the highway and turned onto her street.

"I'm a lot of things, Macy, but I'm far from perfect."

A few minutes later they were in her driveway.

"Thanks for the ride," she said. As he went to switch off the truck, she stopped him. "I'm really tired. I think Harley and I will say good-night here."

That emotionless mask slipped over his face, he nodded. "I understand."

"No," she said, as she opened the door for Harley, "I don't think you do. It's as much my fault as it is yours that this thing between us has been moving at the speed of light. You were the one who suggested wooing. I haven't forgotten that. A little space would be good so we can both think about what it is we want."

"You," he said. "I just want you."

She stepped up and leaned into the truck to kiss him lightly on the lips. "I want you, too. But with our recent histories, it's not such a bad idea to take a break."

He gave her a brief nod.

Harley ran over to the gate Macy used regularly to get into the house. It was the closest entrance to the driveway. The truck didn't move until she'd gone in and put on the lights.

He slowly backed out of the driveway and she sighed when the headlights hit the road.

Picking up her phone, she dialed Cherie.

"I'm the biggest idiot in the world," she said.

"Tell me something I don't know," her friend replied.

11

"I'M AN IDIOT." Blake stomped upstairs to his bedroom. "Certifiable." Stripping, he turned on the shower as hot as he could stand it. He'd gone and lost the best thing that had ever happened to him.

As much as he wanted to blame Josh, it was his fault for acting like a jealous goof. For the life of him, he didn't understand why he'd lost his cool.

That wasn't true.

He stuck his head under the water.

The woman tied him in knots; she was unlike anyone he'd ever met before. And he didn't know what to do with himself.

Hell, he couldn't even remember what he'd said to Josh. And for a few seconds, when he found out they'd been on a date, he'd been furious. The image of his friend possibly kissing her—or worse—had made him livid.

Because she was his.

He slammed a fist against the tile.

Get a grip, man.

You break something in your mother's house there really will be something to answer for. Leaning both arms forward, he let the hot water run down his back.

She'd just gotten out of a relationship with an idiot, and here he was acting like one. He didn't treat women that way, and if his mother ever found out she'd be so disappointed.

That was the answer. He had to talk to his mom. She'd know how he could persuade his favorite journalist to give him another chance. It meant confessing what he'd done, and she wouldn't be happy. But she'd give him good advice; she was always wise when it came to relationships. Until the day his dad died, his parents had had one of the best marriages he'd ever seen.

He wanted that with Macy. It was too fast, and his head knew it. But his heart told him she was the one.

Now he had to convince her of that.

After finishing the shower and checking close to make sure he hadn't broken one of the tiles, Blake picked up the phone.

"What were you thinking?" his mother bellowed, she didn't even bother to say hello. "I did not raise you to act that way!"

Someone, probably Jaime, must have already called her to say what a moron he'd been at the party.

"Yes, ma'am. I don't have an excuse."

"I agree, young man. If I were there I'd box your ears. That poor girl, in a house full of people she didn't know, and then you went all King Kong on her."

"Shame on you," he heard his grandmother say.

Why did I call? He glanced at the heavens.

"You aren't telling me anything I don't already know. I feel like the world's biggest jerk. And I swear it will never happen again."

"What have I told you about swearing?"

"Yes, ma'am. Please, tell me how to fix this."

"*That's* the most sensible thing you've said all night."

"Halleluiah!" shouted a chorus of women.

"Mom, am I on speaker? And who else is there?"

"Yes, and just a few ladies from Momma's quilting circle."

Blake palmed his face.

"You listen to what we have to say, boy," Momma D shouted. She didn't seem too sick to him. "We'll explain to you how to set things right with that Yankee, and you don't mess it up again. You hear me?"

"Yes, ma'am."

"Now get a pencil, this is going to be a long list," his mother ordered.

And a very long night.

THREE DAYS HAD gone by, and except for two texts, she hadn't heard from Blake or even seen him and it wasn't for a lack of trying. Twice she'd gone to the feed store to pick up food for Harley, and then later some nails that she didn't need, but he wasn't there.

The first text had been an apology. She'd already forgiven him so it wasn't necessary. At the end he had asked about the types of questions he could ask the servicemen and -women for the story. He'd said that he'd meant to tell her the night he worked on her books, that he wanted to do the articles, but he'd been distracted by other things.

By her throwing herself at him, she was certain.

She sent him a text back explaining that he didn't have to apologize, and she was looking forward to seeing him soon. She also emailed him a bunch of questions for the interviews and offered to help him in any way necessary.

He'd replied with, "Thank you."

That was it.

She reread her email again to make sure she hadn't said anything he could misconstrue, but she hadn't.

Stupid marine. She missed him. As much as she didn't want to admit it to herself, she had become quite attached to him.

More than likely she'd wounded his pride. What if he decided she was too much trouble and had moved on? She thought about the women at the café who were so enamored with the half-naked marine. He was bright, gentlemanly and as hot as they came.

And she'd been upset because why? Oh, yeah, because he'd cared for her so much that he went all crazy macho for her.

Cherie was right. She was a class A idiot.

"Some guy beats his chest for you, and you have to be all I'm Miss Independence and don't you dare like me too much," Cherie had chastised.

"But men should not be allowed to—"

"What? Be men. He was staking his territory. It's classic male behavior. Could he have handled it better? Yes. But they don't call them male rivalries for nothing, doll. There's history there. Probably a lot of crap you know nothing about. He apologized profusely and you came back with you needed a break. How else is he supposed to interpret that?"

"But he got so weird when he found out Josh and I dated a couple of times. It was strange."

"Macy," Cherie scolded, "you are not this dense. Oh, wait, you were attached to that boss of yours."

"Geez. All right. I get it. But explain to me how I can feel so much for him so fast. I thought I was in love with Garrison, but it doesn't come close to what I feel for Blake. It scares me. And it's hot and wonderful now, well, it was. But doesn't that kind of thing burn out fast. Isn't it better to slow it down before we both get hurt?"

Cherie barked out a loud laugh. "Honey, when you feel what you do, there's no meaningful reason to slow things down. You said it yourself, you're afraid. And you've been hurt, so your defenses are up. That's actually a good thing. But from everything you've told me, this guy's the real deal. If you get your heart broken, at least it was by a guy who deserved you. Oh, and the sex is great. Do you have any idea how difficult it is to find a guy like your marine?

"I haven't found a single one and I've been looking. Trust me. You need to be a grown-up and reach out to him."

Pursing her lips, she tried to forget the rest of her conversation with Cherie and focus on the story in front of her. It was deadline day and she didn't have any more time to waste. An hour later, she'd edited two pieces and had all but the ad pages ready to go.

The quality of talent in a town as small as Tranquil Waters had genuinely surprised her. It was full of artists and writers. Many of whom liked the idea of more reporting about the community writ large. She'd even found a good photographer to cover local sports.

High school football was a religion to many in this region and state. She'd discovered that if she had sports photos on the front page, then circulation went up. In turn, she'd hired a couple of freelancers to do personal stories on the most popular players and their families and neighbors. Next on her to-do list was to tap into other important local hobbies and interests.

Now when she went into the café, people actually smiled and waved at her. All it took was a little effort.

Everything at work seemed to be falling into place. Meanwhile, her heart was breaking.

This wasn't the first time and it probably wouldn't be the last that the aspects of her life would not be in harmony all at once.

Blake's friend Jaime had even called to find out whether she was okay. That was how Macy found out he was in a foul mood and that no one wanted to be around him. She'd advised Macy to sit tight and wait for him to realize what he'd done wrong, which was the exact opposite of what Cherie had said.

Amanda knocked on the door frame of Macy's office. "I'm running down to the diner to get a cheeseburger and some caffeine. Do you want anything?"

Turned out Amanda was a darn good writer. She made a lot of grammatical errors, but those were easy to correct. Teaching someone to have a voice that comes through in his or her writing was something else.

Amanda had it, and had created a column geared for students. It covered everything from homework tips to saving for proms to how to graduate without a load of debt. She referenced students of all ages and backgrounds, and even added personal tidbits from things that her family did and said.

"Yes, if you don't mind. And I'll treat."

Sweets were necessary if she wanted to survive the afternoon. She might as well wallow and get fat since she had abysmal luck with men. And really, after all the friendly advice she was more confused than ever about what she should do.

"I'll take a cheeseburger, as well. But get me whatever kind of ice cream they have. If they have pints or whatever, that will work. I just need something gooey and full of sugar."

Amanda smiled. "Have you ever had the chocolate fudge ripple from Dory's Dairyland?"

She shook her head.

"I've got you covered. Oh, by the way, your friend—the hot marine—dropped this by." She handed Macy a flash drive.

Macy gulped hard. "Did he say anything?"

Amanda thought for a minute. "Just that this was a sample, and if you didn't like it you can email him with changes." She turned to walk away, and then stuck her head back in the office. "And, Harley. He said to tell her that he missed her. A lot."

With that, Amanda was gone.

"Hmm, at least he misses one of us," she said as she plugged the flash drive into the USB port.

I just wish it were me.

12

STAYING AWAY FROM Macy was slowly killing him. He'd peeked through the window at the paper and watched her as she worked on her computer. He felt silly, but he couldn't help it. Before she turned, though, and saw him, he rushed to the front door to go in and leave the flash drive for her. His mother's advice was to give Macy what she wanted. Time and space.

But he worried each day that the longer they were apart, the easier it would be for her to walk away from what they had.

And they definitely had something. It wasn't just about her being his. He knew that now. His pride had felt threatened that night, but it was more about him finding the thing that made him whole.

He hadn't slept much since they'd parted. She calmed him and being in her presence had become a sanctuary of sorts. He hadn't fully recognized all she'd done for him.

She was the first woman who knew him inside and out, and still accepted him. Wanted him, in fact.

Which was probably why her rejection had felt like a fatal blow.

His mother said it was only a rejection, but it still felt like life ending to him.

After parking his truck behind the feed store, he went straight to the room in back. His mom sat there, reviewing something on the computer.

Taken by complete surprise, he blurted out, "What are you doing here?" Try that again, he told himself. "I mean—"

"Momma D is feeling better, and she insisted I was cramping her style. I came back for a couple of days and then I'll go down on the weekend to check on her again. You look awful, son."

"Thanks, Mom."

His cell rang. He frowned.

"Who is it?"

"Her," he said.

"Quick, answer it before she hangs up."

Blake stared at the phone for another second, and pushed Answer. "Hello."

"Blake." Macy sounded as if she'd been crying. "I need you to come to the office right away."

"What's wrong? Are you hurt? Is it Harley?" He picked up the keys he'd thrown on the desk and turned without so much as a see ya to his mother.

She cleared her throat. "No, I'm sorry. I didn't mean to worry you, but this is time sensitive and I really need to see you now if you can make it."

"I'll be there in five."

He was there in four.

Striding in, he bolted straight past the reception-ist, who didn't seem shocked to see him, and into Macy's office.

She had her head down while petting Harley, who was sprawled out on the floor. When the dog saw him, she jumped up and then ran full force into him knocking him into the chair.

"Harley! Down, girl! Blake, did she hurt you?" Macy went to his side and grabbed the dog by the collar. "Sit, Harley," she commanded.

Harley obeyed immediately but kept her attention on Blake. He could have sworn she smiled at him, her tongue hanging out of the side of her mouth.

"No, she's okay. Hey, girl," he said and affec-tionately scratched behind her ears. She nuzzled his neck and he wrapped his arms around her. He'd truly missed the giant horse of a dog. She proceeded to sit in his lap like a human would and they nearly toppled over backward.

"That's enough!" Macy exclaimed, waving at the dog. "You really missed him, I get it. I missed him, too. Now get off of him and get back to your spot. Now."

Harley looked back at him.

"Better do what she says, girl."

The dog huffed and returned to her gel-pad dog bed.

"Sorry about that. She's excited to see you."

Macy grabbed a tissue and dabbed her nose. He remembered how she'd sounded on the phone. "Macy, tell me what's wrong."

"Nothing's wrong. I mean, yes, there are some things we need to talk about but—these stories you wrote—"

She paused.

Something *was* wrong with them. "I told you I'm not a journalist." He wasn't upset. Maybe a bit disappointed. He'd enjoyed meeting and talking to past military personnel, especially the older vets from long ago.

"Not a journalist?" she scoffed and then smiled. "They're brilliant. Choked me up a little they were so good. There are a few style points I'll need to fix, but other than that, they're okay to print. That's why I called you. I'm going to pull the front page. I'd like to run the first two stories right now. And then, if you're up to it, make it a weekly series."

She liked what he'd done. "Uh, I'm not sure they're front-page worthy," he said, "but thanks."

"I'm the publisher, I decide what is worthy of the front page. And for the record, this has nothing to do with you and, well, what's been going on with us. I want to make that clear."

So it was just business. "Sure," he said. "Feel free to make the changes you think are necessary. I'm glad you liked the stories."

He stood.

"Where are you going?"

He frowned, confused. "Was there more?"

Standing, she walked over and shut the door and the blinds. "Sit down, Blake."

He sat.

She picked up the phone and dialed.

"Davis, I'm sending you new copy for the front page." She paused to listen. "Yes, I know we already did the front page. But I have something better. Make sure you and Sam both look at it, and then send it on to the printer."

She hung up the phone.

Her longs legs moved in front of him, and she sat down on the edge of her desk. She wore dark denims that hugged her hips and were tucked into those stiletto boots he loved. She leaned over and her shirt gapped slightly, giving him a glimpse of purple lace.

"Are you seeing someone else?"

His head popped up. "Why would you say something like that?"

She bit her lip. "You haven't even tried to talk to me since what happened the other night."

He leaned back so he could focus on her face, because her breasts were distracting him.

"That's what you wanted. You said things were going too fast and that I was possessive. Time and space apart, I believe, was mentioned. So I've been doing that."

Crossing her arms, she stared at him. "I meant in regard to that one night. I was embarrassed and hurt. By the next day I was over it. But you didn't answer my question. Are you seeing someone else?"

"Who would I see?" he asked incredulously. "You've ruined me for anyone else."

It was the truth. No way in hell would he ever feel about another woman what he did for Macy.

She gave him a Cheshire cat–like smile. Then she

bent over so her arms were on the arms of his chair, her breasts eye level.

"You're seducing me," he said gruffly.

"Maybe." She slowly leaned in and kissed him.

"What would convince you? This?" She nibbled on his ear.

He coughed and kept his hands at his sides.

She edged her knees on either side of his legs in the large leather chair. Her heat rubbed against his cock. "Or maybe this," she teased and tormented, as her hand went to the fly of his jeans.

Gently, he seized her wrist and stopped her. "Macy, I'm going to lose it right here and now if you don't stop." Then he pulled her to him and ravaged her mouth.

"Not here," he said when he finally let her go.

"Why not?"

"Because when we do this, I'm going to make you moan my name so loud that everyone in town will know what we're doing."

She cocked an eyebrow. "Well, then. I suppose we'd better hurry home. I only have about an hour before the final proofs are ready."

"No. We aren't rushing this again. I'm taking you on a date. We'll have a nice dinner and—" She rubbed her heat over his strained cock.

"Stop distracting me."

She pouted. "What other things are we going to do on the date besides eat? Because I have food at home we can cook. And a soft bed where you can make me moan all night long."

Pulling away from him, she stood. "Unless you're not up for it?"

He chuckled. "When you want something, it's no holds barred, isn't it?"

"It is. So, Marine, I see this going one of two ways. I can make love to you in the restaurant of your choice in front of the customers, or you can come to my place and we can negotiate further."

He swallowed hard. "Will those boots be part of the negotiations?" He had a vision of her with nothing on but those damn boots.

"They could be, but before you leave, there's one more thing."

"Anything you want, babe, it's yours."

"From now on, if we have a disagreement about the terms of our mutual companionship, we discuss it. Calmly. And if I say I need a little time, I'm talking hours—at the most, a night. Understood?" She knelt in front of him and unzipped his jeans.

"Yes," he groaned. "Macy, I'm never going to be able to walk out of here if you keep doing that."

"By my clock we have an hour to fill before I look at those final proofs, so we're going to have some fun."

Her head dipped down and she slid her tongue along his shaft.

"Macy," he said, gritting his teeth, "this feels, you fee…"

Pushing her hair away from her face, she stared up at him. "I know, Blake. I feel it, too."

Before he could say another word, her mouth was on him again.

13

HAVING HER COFFEE in the backyard while tossing a chew toy to Harley, Macy was at peace. Even happy, maybe. When had she ever been able to say that? She had a home that was hers, and a dog that she loved and who loved her. It was like a dream that was never within reach when she'd covered so many stories and crisscrossed the globe.

Most of her adult life had been lived around some conflict. Adrenaline-fueled jaunts pursuing one lead and then the next. She accepted that was how she would spend the rest of her days, knowing that life might be cut short because of the job.

But now—that was no longer true.

Spending time in Tranquil Waters, learning to fit in, the intimacy with Blake—not just the sex—was beyond anything she'd ever experienced. All of these connections made her realize there was so much more to life than adrenaline and airports.

After the sixth throw of the toy, Harley ambled up to her. Macy sat down in a padded deck chair. Even in November, the weather was warm enough that she could be outside in a sweater and still feel comfortable. The same couldn't be said of what it was like in Boston at this time of year.

Her phone buzzed in her pocket, Harley lay at her feet. The dog had short spurts of energy and then she was tired for eight hours.

"You're up early," she said to her friend.

"It's your fault." Cherie yawned.

"Why is that?"

"Your ex won't stop calling me. He has something urgent he needs to talk to you about. He insists you call him now. And I'm supposed to tell you that it isn't personal. It's job related."

Macy frowned. "I don't want to hear anything from him, job related or whatever."

"Seriously, you need to talk to him. *Opportunity of a lifetime* was just one phrase he used. Said he owed you, and this was the big one."

"Last time I saw him, I seem to remember his 'big one' entertaining an intern."

Cherie coughed. "Hold on there. You made a joke."

"I discovered I have a sense of humor, go figure."

"Oh, Macy. Your marine must be something special if he's loosened you up enough to make jokes."

"He is something special," she said wistfully.

"You don't even sound like your old self. I thought you'd signed off on men for good?"

"I did. I have no clue how long this is going to last with the marine, but it's intense. I've— No matter what happens, it will have been worth the broken heart— At least in this case I've learned something about myself and what I want in a relationship."

"You have fallen in the deep end without your water wings again."

Definitely. But she hadn't lied. Nothing about the past few weeks would change if she had a chance to do them over again. Except perhaps, the three days they'd been apart. She was still ticked over the time they wasted.

"I always did like to take risks."

"So when do I get to meet him? You can and you will send me a picture."

"I promise, soon." Part of her didn't want to share Blake, it was new and seemed almost too good to be true. "Listen, I need to get to the office."

"Fine. Don't worry about me. I'm just the one waking up at the crack of dawn to give you news of limitless opportunities."

Macy laughed.

"Please, by all that you hold dear, call your ex. I wouldn't put it past him to hop on a private jet and fly down there to speak to you in person."

Ugh. Something she definitely did not want.

"Fine. And you know, Cherie, you can block his calls."

Cherie grunted. "I did, and then he called my assistant, which is the only reason I'm awake before ten."

AN HOUR LATER she was at the newspaper office. Harley was in her favorite spot sleeping. Deadline day was always a long one for Macy. She had to edit and design the pages and make sure everything was electronically delivered to the printer on time.

In spite of the pressure, the new staff and other changes had made a positive difference and everyone had settled into a comfortable routine.

"Hey, I'm going to do a latte run. Do you want a sandwich or something to go with yours?" Amanda asked. Today she wore a pair of dark jeans, cowboy boots and a T-shirt promoting a punk rock band that had seen better days—the shirt, not the band. At least the outfit was a step in the right direction and Macy wasn't blinded by the color choices.

Glancing at her cell phone she saw that it was almost lunchtime.

"Yes." She pulled cash out of her purse. "And get yourself and Lance something, as well."

"Do you mind answering the phones? Lance is upstairs installing the new computer equipment."

"Not a problem."

Harley barked. The dog grabbed her leash from its hook and sat expectantly in front of Amanda.

Amanda rolled her eyes but smiled. "Yes, you may come, but you have to stay by the bicycle rack and if you try to trip me to get the food this time, there will be no more walks for you."

"You don't have to take her with you. That's a lot to juggle."

"It's okay, I know she just gets excited and can't help herself. Besides, she's a guy magnet. Everyone wants to know what kind of dog she is, because she's so big."

Laughing, Macy followed them to the door.

She slipped her fingers around Harley's collar. The dog looked at her. "You behave, or no cookies for you tonight."

Harley did her signature move and cocked her head to one side.

"I mean it."

Harley grumbled, but licked Macy's hand.

The dog really did understand everything she said. It was spooky sometimes.

After washing her hands, she propped open her office door and the front door of the building so she could hear if someone walked in.

The phone rang as she was passing Amanda's desk.

"Tranquil Waters News."

"I thought you owned the paper, why are you answering the phones?" The smooth voice of her ex was unmistakable.

Figures. As soon as Amanda leaves he would call.

"The receptionist is grabbing lunch. I don't have time to talk. I'm on deadline for our pages."

"Please! Don't hang up." She couldn't remember when he'd last used the word *please*.

"Whatever it is, Garrison, it can wait until tomorrow." She reached down to disconnect the call.

"The Henderson Paper Group wants you to be the executive editor of their online editions," he said quickly. "Aaron Henderson asked for you specifically."

She couldn't believe it. When she'd decided she was tired of traveling, she'd wanted to make a name for herself as an editor. In the six months she was at the Boston paper, which was one of Henderson's largest papers, she'd noticeably improved its bottom line. After streamlining the editorial process, the quality of the information had increased, bringing in more subscribers and consequently more advertisers.

"Are you still there?"

"Yes," she whispered.

"Henderson wants you back and he's bumping you up to executive editor. You're a hot commodity. The different papers in the chain all want you, they're fighting over you. I nearly got demoted when you left, because you had created such a dynamic online version that we were making more money than all the rest of the papers in the group combined."

She hadn't known that, but it pleased her. It meant that people were still interested in hard news, and not just what kind of underwear a celebrity might be wearing.

"You've worked with Aaron, and he's been watching what you've done with the paper there in Texas. From what we can tell, you've increased the ad revenue and circulation. And even though it's a small area without a lot of big news, the quality of reporting is exponentially better that it was six months ago."

"Did you do this?" If this was some bizarre plan to get her back to Boston, she wasn't interested.

This was beyond her dream job. To have creative and editorial input on an entire newspaper chain's online components was incredible. It also pulled at her heartstrings. Journalism, and the way it was reported. Ethics was the one aspect she felt strongest about. Good, objective reporting was needed in the world and this would give her enough influence to make that happen.

"No. In fact, I'd suggested another candidate. But Henderson only wants you. As far as he's concerned, there are no other candidates. He's in New York tomorrow and wants to meet with you personally. By the way, that's where the job would be."

Aaron Henderson had been her first editor, the guy who believed she was tough enough to be a war correspondent when no one else would give her a chance. She owed him. Big.

"That's really short notice."

"I've been trying to get in touch with you for two weeks. Did Cherie tell you I called?"

"Yes, but I've been busy." That was true.

The very least she could do was hear Aaron out. And she had to admit that it was a bit of an ego boost that they'd been watching what she did with the local paper.

"There's a first-class ticket waiting for you, all you have to do is claim it. The flight is at nine tonight. Once you land, a car will pick you up and take you to the hotel. You'll meet with Aaron there at ten the next morning. Are you in?"

Was she? Glancing around her office, taking in all the little changes that now made it hers...she knew it would be difficult to walk away. And what about her relationship with Blake? He had said he didn't plan on living in the small town for the rest of his life, but would he want to live in New York?

Before she spoke to him about it, she wanted to

know the fine print of what she was being offered. Then she'd make a decision.

"Yes. I'm in."

BLAKE HELD THE papers in his hand. An honorable discharge. There was a time he thought he'd go all the way and retire, but he was excited about new possibilities.

One of which was his mutual companionship with Macy. The other was figuring out his place in the world. He'd invested in his friends'—Rafe and Will's—security business. Anytime he wanted to step into a corporate roll it was there for him. He was already the CFO of sorts, overseeing most of the financials.

It meant a fair amount of travel, but that wasn't so awful. If he settled in Tranquil Waters, he'd need to let his soul free now and again. This kind of job might be the perfect answer. They had asked him to take over the rescue-operations department, as well. He'd coordinate search-and-rescue missions, which was something he'd always wanted to do.

His phone played Macy's favorite song. "Hey, beautiful, what's up?"

"How did everything go?" She didn't sound her normal self. There was hesitancy in her voice.

"Great. I've got my papers in hand, and I just landed at the Austin airport. How is everything with you?"

There was a long pause.

"Something has come up and I need to go to New

York for a couple of days. I could put Harley in a kennel, but I'd rather not."

What was in New York? Obviously she'd tell him if she wanted him to know. He guessed whatever it was was personal given the stress in her voice.

"I'll take care of her. What time do you have to leave?"

"My flight is at nine tonight, so I'd like to get out of here by seven at the latest."

"I'll be there by three. Do you want me to keep her at Mom's?"

"Uh, if you don't mind staying here, that would be better for her, I think. But I don't want to put you out."

"You aren't. Is everything okay?"

Another long pause. "Yes. It's— I've got a lot to process in a very short amount of time. Can we talk about it when I get back? I'll know more about the situation, and—we'll figure things then. Okay?"

Figure what things out? She said "we," so she probably wasn't going back to the ex. Besides, he was in Boston. Was it something to do with a job? He knew if he pressed her for details she'd see it as prying, even though her curiosity about everything was boundless. Macy had a double standard when it came to her privacy.

"Whatever you want." He tried to keep the sting of hurt out of his tone. That she wouldn't share what it was she had to figure out bothered him. Hadn't she been the one complaining that he never opened up?

"I have to put the paper to bed, but then I'll be out at the house. Thank you. I'm sorry I won't get to spend time with you. I've missed you."

Well, there was that.

"I missed you, too," he said.

"Bad timing that I have to leave tonight, but it can't be helped. This— It just came up this afternoon." There was a wistfulness to her words that pleased him.

Why wouldn't she just tell him?

"It's okay. You can make it up to me when you return, which is when?"

"I would imagine late tomorrow night or early the next day. Everything is kind of up in the air. And I'm sorry to be so vague. But I'll know more soon.

"Oh, and can you pick up another bag of food for Harley from the feed store? I'd really appreciate it."

"No problem."

By the time he picked up the food and dealt with a few things at the store it was almost four before he pulled up in front of Macy's house.

A large bark came from the other side of the front door, followed by the rattling of the handle.

"Harley, you stop that. No more opening doors, you brat," Macy chastised.

He chuckled. The dog never ceased to amaze him.

"She's keeping you on your toes," he said as Macy opened the door for him.

Harley held out a paw and he shook it. Then she nuzzled his hand.

"I'm glad to see you, too, girl." He rubbed her ears.

"And you." He kissed Macy as they jointly leaned over the dog's head.

He ended the kiss, but she captured his neck in her hand and held him to her where her lips devoured his.

When she finally broke the embrace, she stared deeply into his eyes. A storm brewed there, but he couldn't get a read on her.

"Are you doing okay?" He shifted the dog out of the way so he could put an arm around Macy's shoulders.

"I am. I don't mean to be so secretive, it's just— it's a job thing. A dream job, to be exact. At least that was what the ex told me."

The ex. At the mention of him, Blake's lips tightened into a thin line. "I see."

She didn't seem to notice the tension he felt, which was good. His ego, where she was concerned, had very nearly cost him their relationship. He wouldn't go there again.

"Yes, that's why I have to go. I don't know if he's telling me the truth or not about this job. But it's working with someone I like a great deal, and who gave me my break in the business. I feel like I owe it to him to at least hear him out."

The ex, or someone else? He couldn't come up with a subtle way to ask, without sounding like a jealous boyfriend. They'd said from the beginning that this was a fling, even though it had come to mean a great deal more to him. But he was the last one to stand in the way of someone's dream. Whatever she decided, he cared for her enough that he would support her.

He was just grateful it was about a job, and not another man.

She moved away from him and headed for the bedroom. "I need to grab my carry-on, and then I'll—" She smiled sheepishly. "I was going to say I'd show you where everything is for Harley, but you know all of that as well as I do. The good news is I went on a cooking binge while you were gone. There's a bunch of stuff in the freezer, and I just put the King Ranch casserole in the oven. It needs to cook about twenty more minutes. The buzzer will ring."

"For someone who doesn't really cook, you've been doing a lot of it lately." He smiled.

"It's your fault, making me watch all those cooking shows. I get inspired and then I get in there and go crazy. It's one of the few ways I can settle my mind. I guess, like running, it's my kind of meditation, only a lot more fattening. As soon as my knee is back in shape, I'll have to start running again so that my clothes will fit."

At the mention of food, Harley barked twice. Her signal for feeding time.

He chuckled as he put his duffel bag on one of the bar stools. "I've got her food in the back of the truck, I'll go get it."

"There are a couple of cups left in the old bag, but not near enough for her nightly feast. And watch it if you eat apples, bananas or peanut butter. She'll leave the roasted chicken on the counter but put one of those down and it disappears in the blink of an eye."

"Noted. Do you need a ride to the airport?"

"Oh, thanks, but since it's such a fast turnaround, I'll just take my car."

"If you get your carry-on, I'll put it in the SUV for you."

She went to the bedroom and returned with the suitcase. Dressed in an ivory sweater, dark jeans and heeled boots, she took his breath away. Dammit. Whatever this business was, it was going to mess things up for them. He knew it instinctively.

And that hit him hard, as hard as any man could punch. He didn't want to lose her.

"What's wrong?" She touched his cheek with her fingertips.

"Not a thing. Though I'm worried slightly about you driving the hour into Austin. The traffic was a bear getting here, and you'll be right in the thick of it."

She kissed his cheek where her fingers had been. "You are the sweetest man ever. I'll be fine. Are you sure everything is okay with you? That was a big decision you made about taking the honorable discharge."

"A decision I'd been thinking about for the last six months or so. I'm good. Like you, I'm taking a look at my opportunities and trying to figure out my next move."

"I guess—it's good that we have so many opportunities. There are a lot of people who don't," she said.

"Yes, we're extremely lucky." He kissed her lightly on the lips. "Say your goodbyes to you know who. I'll go put this in the car for you."

Outside, he took a long breath.

Hell.

What if she got in that car and she never came back? It was hard for people to turn down dream jobs. She was talented, it was no wonder someone wanted her.

But no one wanted her more than he did.

Hauling the giant bag of dog food onto his shoulder, he grabbed the groceries he'd bought with the other hand.

When he got to the door, she was holding it open for him and trying to keep Harley inside. "Oh, I should have called and told you about all the food I'd made."

Once in the house, he set the giant bag next to the kitchen door.

"What? Oh?" He glanced down at his hand with the other bag. "These things aren't for me, they're ingredients for a new kind of dog cookie I wanted to try for Harley."

At the word cookie, the dog came sliding down the hall and stopped at his feet.

"She scares me sometimes," he said, nudging the dog out of the way so he could move things into the kitchen.

"You said it," she agreed. "I find myself being careful about what I say just in case I accidentally use one of her cues. But I swear she understands most of the English language." She sighed. "I guess if traffic is bad, I should get going."

He nodded regretfully.

Wrapping his arms around her, he kissed her.

Pressing her body into his, she intensified the exploration of tongues as if she were communicating something else, as well.

Before he could think too much about it, he was lost in her. Her touch did that to him.

They were panting when they finally separated.

"Never in my life has a man affected me the way

you do," she said softly. "And I don't just mean when we make love."

He sucked in a breath. He hadn't realized how much he needed to hear her say that. "The feeling's definitely mutual," he said.

"I don't want to go," she said softly. "I want to stay here with you."

"I want that, too. So hurry up and get back." He kissed her one more time.

Then he scooted her toward the front door and led her out to the car. Opening her door for her, he waited until she was belted.

"I have to kiss you one more time," he said.

"That's a good idea." She tilted up to meet his lips. "Be safe."

She nodded and gave him a sweet smile. "Take care of my girl."

"Done," he replied, and he shut the door and waved.

Everything was about to change. He knew it in his bones. He waved again though her car was already where the driveway met the road.

Damn.

Harley whined beside him.

"I know, girl. I love her, too."

14

As Macy stepped out of the glass-and-marble shower in her hotel room, her phone beeped. Wrapping a towel around herself, she picked up the cell. A picture of Blake and Harley graced her screen. He had his fingers crossed, and the dog had one paw crossed over the other.

The text read, We're crossing fingers and paws that everything goes well for you today. No matter what happens, we are here for you.

The photo and message were the cutest things she'd ever seen and were exactly what she needed to help with jangled nerves.

The Henderson Paper Group had come to her, not the other way around, and besides, she didn't need the job. Still, she had a bad case of the jitters that the warm shower hadn't calmed.

Taking a deep breath, she texted back, You made my day. Thank you! I miss you!

For someone who didn't use exclamation points in her work, she meant every one of them today.

Do you have time for a call? he texted.

Hearing his voice would be the balm that she needed to make it through the next few hours.

Call me in ten minutes, she texted back.

Someone knocked on her door.

"Hold on," she called out as she yanked on the hotel robe and tied the belt around her waist.

Peeping through the peephole, she frowned.

"I know you're in there," Garrison said.

"Why are you here?" she asked through the door.

"Aaron wanted me to bring you to him. Thought you might be more comfortable if you showed up with someone you know."

"I'll be fine. Thanks, anyway. You can go."

"It won't look good. That is, it won't look good if we aren't playing on the same team. Your group will be answering to me. He needs to know we can get along."

Huffing, she opened the door.

The man always looked gorgeous in a suit. Nowhere as good as her marine, but he *was* a looker.

"Sit." She pointed to the sofa under the windows on the far side of the room. "Don't talk to me. Don't do anything. Just sit there until I get dressed." She scooped up her dress, tights and boots and headed for the bathroom.

Her phone rang as she was putting on her dress and she couldn't open the door.

Mortification set in when she realized Garrison had answered the call.

"She's getting dressed, who is this? What kind of

friend?" He sounded jealous when he had absolutely no right to be. That was so not what she needed.

Slamming the door open, she then rushed to grab the phone out of Garrison's hand.

"I told you to sit," she said, annoyed. She pointed to the sofa for emphasis.

He ignored her. "Sorry, I thought it might be the boss telling you the meeting was moved or rescheduled."

What a lie. He was just being nosy. You could take the reporter out of the newsroom and make him a vice president, but you could never take that need for information out of a journalist. That quest for knowledge never died.

"Blake?"

"Hey," he said hesitantly. "Everything okay there?"

"Yes, sorry. I was in the bathroom and someone decided he'd answer my phone, although I didn't ask him to. So, how are you and our girl?"

He chuckled. "I like that. A lot. We're good. She went for a fast walk with me, as fast as I could go with this leg, anyway. She's tuckered out and laying in front of the fireplace. She moved her sofa in front of it last night while I watched the game. I filmed it for you, but it's too big to text."

She laughed. That must have been a sight. "Oh, I really needed that. Thank you. Great Danes get cold. And their bones get achy. I bought some glucosamine tablets for her, but you have to coat the pills in peanut butter to get her to swallow them."

"Got it," he said.

"Uh, can I be the jealous boyfriend for a minute and ask who that guy was."

Get in line. On the one hand she didn't want Blake to get the wrong idea, but on the other hand she wouldn't lie.

"The ex. He's escorting me to the meeting. It's in the publisher's suite, so they wanted me to feel comfortable. Evidently." She moved into the bathroom when she spied Garrison listening to every word with a giant grin on his face.

"And are you more comfortable?"

She huffed and closed the door. "No. I'd rather not have to deal with him while I'm contemplating everything else that's happening. It's weird. I'm not angry anymore—just…irked because I don't like him much as a person."

Her marine let out a deep breath. "I have to admit, I'm glad to hear that. When he answered the phone—"

"I would have thought the same thing," she interjected. "But, trust me, you have nothing to worry about."

"Time to go," Garrison called to her.

"I heard him," Blake said. "Whatever happens today I support you and so does Harley. Right, girl?"

Harley barked in agreement.

That Blake was so supportive brought tears to Macy's eyes. Most of the men in her past were too competitive to be truly supportive, including Garrison. It wasn't until after she'd broken up with him that she'd seen their relationship had become a game of one-upmanship.

"I wish you were here with me," she whispered, not bothering to keep the want from her voice.

"Ditto, babe. Ditto. Call us and let us know how it went."

"Will do."

As she hung up, she heard Harley bark again.

She loved that damn dog.

And she loved the marine.

Settling down in a small town with them didn't seem like such a wild notion to her.

But the opportunity from Aaron tugged at her. A real chance to make her mark in this environment was so enticing. Still, she first had to listen to what he had to say.

She marched forward and opened the bathroom door. "Right. Let's do this."

"Uh. You might want to put shoes on." Garrison raised his eyebrow.

"Well spotted," she said with dripping sarcasm. "He does that sort of thing to me."

"*He* being the boy back home?" Garrison asked.

"He's a man—a decorated marine to be exact—and yes. Not that it's any business of yours."

"Ah. The lady is a little testy. Was he jealous about your ex answering the phone?"

"He has nothing to be jealous about."

Minutes later, they'd left her room and were in the elevator, heading for Aaron. Garrison used a key card in a slot beneath the row of elevator buttons, he pushed the *P* for penthouse.

They want me.

No need to be worried.

On the short flight up, she realized why she was worried. She was about to get the job of a lifetime, one she'd always wanted.

But there might be a big sacrifice in store for her to take the position.

No. I can't think about that right now.

Just listen to what the man has to say.

Then you can make an informed decision.

As the elevator doors opened, she steeled herself. Plastering a smile on her face, she left the elevator and approached the penthouse door.

This was it.

"You look beautiful," Garrison said behind her. "In fact, your small-town life seems to agree with you."

Forcing herself not to roll her eyes, she raised her hand to knock on the door.

"Say anything like that when we're in there, and you'll really regret it." She had no desire to deal with his games and meaningless flirtations.

"You were always a fierce one," he whispered in her ear. "And one of the biggest mistakes of my life was letting you go."

"You didn't let me go. I ran as fast as I could from your toxic, cheating self, which was one of the best things I've ever done. I've met a man's man, one who honors and respects me. A man who deserves me."

"Sounds boring."

She laughed. "Not even a little bit. He's taught me a lot about my body, enough that I know what I've been missing out on all these years."

She glanced back to see his eyes narrow.

Not her finest moment, to throw such a comment

at him, but maybe she'd save the next poor woman he got together with. Everything had always been about his pleasure.

Jerk.

The door opened and Aaron Henderson ushered her in. She'd been expecting one of his aides to answer and she nearly tripped as she passed by him. He steadied her and then guided her to a sofa in the living room.

"I'm so glad you're here," he said. Dressed in gray slacks and a cream shirt, he looked the epitome of classy casual. But she knew how hard he'd worked to own his newspaper group. At forty-five he'd accomplished more than most people did in double the years. "Can I get you some coffee?" He gestured toward a small tray on a table in front of the sofa.

"No, thank you." Her nerves were jittery enough.

"I'll leave you two to your meeting," Garrison said.

"No, please I'd like you to stay." Aaron nodded to a chair.

Aaron sat in the one opposite her.

Her ex hesitated for a moment, but then took one of the leather chairs to the side of the conversation area.

"Before I explain why I called you here, though I'm sure Garrison has mentioned a part of it, I need to know something. It's a touchy subject, but the truth is important to me if we're to move forward with this arrangement. It's personal and not something an employer would ever ask in the normal course of things. But this is a big step, so we need to be clear."

What the heck was he talking about? There was

nothing she couldn't answer. And Garrison didn't need to be here. What arrangement?

"I'll answer whatever it is," she said, defiant.

"Good. So explain to me why you broke your engagement to Garrison and ran off to the country to run your uncle's paper."

Crap.

AFTER MAKING SURE Harley was settled in the office at the feed store with his mother. Blake headed out to the barn where they kept the hay and fertilizers.

"Hey, Blake," Ray said. "What are you doing out here?"

He shrugged. "Need to work off some energy. Thought I'd help you with the bales."

The other man nodded. "Glad to have the help, but is your leg going to be okay?"

Blake patted his right thigh. "It likes a good workout now and then."

Sliding on his leather gloves, he picked up the first bale and walked it into the barn. After creating a stack of about ten, he worked on the next one.

What if she took the job? And really, why wouldn't she? From what her ex had told her, it was all of her dreams tied into one neat package. If she had to move to New York, what would she do with Harley?

What would she do with him?

No way could he lose her.

He could follow Macy, but would she want him to?

When her ex had answered the cell earlier, he was suddenly so angry. It scared him that his temper rose that quickly. That wasn't him.

You're jealous.

Hell. He'd never been jealous before the night of Jaime's party. He'd dated and even had a few girl-friends. But nothing like the connection he had with Macy. In such a short time she'd become everything to him.

He lived his days trying to find ways to please her and make her smile. And darn if that didn't make him feel good, as well. Being around her was the best therapy there was. She made him laugh and look at the world through her curious eyes. Having seen more than his fair share of the dark side of things, he'd become jaded.

The past few weeks, she'd shown him that yes there was darkness, but there was also light. Her articles and features about the local folks had warmed his heart. She understood the true essence of people.

She'd gone a step further and shared some of the stories of people she had met during her travels. Many of them had the same problems as folks here in a small Texas town. Ultimately, they all wanted the world to be safe for their children, put food on the table and have a decent roof over their heads.

No longer did he think of people as us and them. There were evil people in the world, but there were a lot of good people, too. People he would gladly die to protect. When he was in the thick of it, he hadn't been able to see the truth.

Macy wrote that the world was a melting pot and that everyone was more the same than they were different.

That was one of the ideals she could pursue on a

higher level if she took the job. He knew that before she had any of the details. She had a voice that should be heard, and he would not in any way hinder that.

"Not sure what those bales of hay have done to you, but throwing them around is getting messy," Ray's voice cut through his thoughts.

Blake's eyes took in the chaos around him. Two of the bales had busted and there was hay all over the floor.

"Sorry," he said as he reached for the broom. "I'll clean it up."

"Don't worry about it. Let's get the rest of these bales into the loft. It looks like it's about to rain. Mind if I hand them up to you?" Ray asked.

Stepping up on the ladder, Blake climbed into the loft. A half hour passed before the storm hit, and water poured down on the tin roof of the barn. Normally, it was a comforting sound.

But his mood was no better than it had been before he'd started. Though, his muscles certainly ached now. He'd be lucky to get out of bed in the morning.

"Go on," Ray coaxed him. "I'll clean this up. I'm betting that horse of a dog of yours is giving your mom hell about the thunder."

Damn. He'd forgotten about Harley and loud noises.

Running through the rain and into the back of the store, he slid to a stop outside his mother's office door. She sat on the floor reading a book to the dog.

Blake chuckled. She'd done the same for his little brother who'd missed being struck by lightning by mere inches when he was six, and had been afraid of storms most of his childhood.

The crazy thing was the dog hung on her every word.

"Go check on Tanya at the register. There's news the river might flood. Folks will be stocking up. I'll be there once I get her to sleep." She rubbed Harley's head.

He nodded. Still soaked to the skin, he found Tanya had a long line in front of her.

Entering his code, he quickly opened the second register. "Next in line, please."

Grateful for the distraction, Blake's mind never wavered far from what Macy might be doing. Would she go out with the ex to celebrate?

Stop it. He forced himself to smile as he rang up the total for the nails and plastic tarp old Mr. Davis was buying. He did the same for all of the following customers, too. After the initial rush, the crowd thinned out.

He went to the office to check on his mom and the dog.

"You go ahead and take the dog home. She'll be more comfortable in a familiar place," his mom said.

The dog's head was in her lap on top of the small pillow his mother used for her back when she sat in the office chair too long.

"She looks pretty comfortable to me." He smiled.

She smiled back. "Yes, but my legs are numb from her overly large head, and I'm too old to be sitting on the floor."

After scooting the sleeping dog off his mom, he helped her up.

She stretched. "That's a smart dog you have there."

"That she is."

"For a monster, she kind of grows on you."

He laughed. At the sound, Harley glanced up and gave him the evil eye for waking her from her nap.

"Yep. She's too smart for her own good."

"Well, then. You two should get along just fine," his mom said as she patted his shoulder. "Any ideas on what your next move is? Are you sure you don't want to buy the store? You'd mentioned it when you were in the hospital, but we haven't talked about it since you got back."

That was before he met the woman who'd come to mean everything to him. And he'd also been told there was the possibility that he might not be the same again physically.

That wasn't an option for him, and he'd shown everyone, including himself, that he refused to allow his injuries to dictate the rest of his life.

"While you're gone, Mom, I do enjoy hanging out here, but this is your passion. I think mine is elsewhere. The guys have asked me to take a more active part in the security firm. They have some new ideas that might be beneficial to rural areas especially. So I'll probably be helping them grow the business. As soon as I know my next step, you'll be the first one I tell," he promised.

Giving him the mom-knows-all stare, she said, "You haven't heard from her yet, have you?"

"Mom," he warned.

"Son, I'm not saying anything except that her meeting was this morning and it's nearing five."

"I'm aware. Let it go—please."

She shrugged. "Whatever you say. I'll go help Tanya close up. You're soaking wet, get home before you catch your death."

Home. It hit him that it was Macy's house where he now felt at home.

Yes, ma'am. He was in big trouble.

15

As he braked in the driveway and put the truck into Park, Harley woofed. "Let me turn off the engine at least." He patted her back. As soon as he opened his door and got out, she leaped past him and ran for the house.

She must be hungry.

The dog opened the front door before he could get there. That wasn't right. He was certain he'd locked the door when they left earlier in the day.

"Hello, pretty girl. I missed you, too," Macy said as she greeted Harley. "I was a little concerned about you two. I tried to call, but no one answered."

She glanced up at Blake. He could see the concern on her face.

"You called my cell?" He went to take the phone out of his pocket, and discovered it wasn't there. "Well, that explains it," he said. "I must have lost it when I was working with Ray in the barn this afternoon."

Harley soon had her pinned against the fridge demanding to be fed. He grabbed the towel he'd left by the garage door and wiped the rain off of the dog's coat before she ruined the sexy dress Macy wore. She had on high-heel boots, and her hair was done up in that haphazard way that made her look like the sexy librarian.

Though, they'd never had a librarian in Tranquil Waters that ever looked like that.

"I missed you," she said. There was something in her expression that he couldn't quite understand.

"And I missed you. I'm surprised you're here."

"Where else would I be?" She smiled but it didn't quite meet her eyes.

Hell. She was going to take the job.

She held up a hand. "I haven't made a decision yet," she said as if she could read his thoughts. "In fact, I don't want to think about anything right now. The flight into Austin was one of the bumpiest I've ever been on, and I've flown on a lot of planes. Then the traffic this time of day getting out of Austin through the rain was enough to turn me into one of those road-rage maniacs. I could never understand how people got so angry in the car, but I do now.

"All I want is a hot bath and a glass of wine, and I want you to join me."

His body was instantly at attention. Who was he to question if she needed some time?

"Red or white?" he asked. He had a bottle of champagne in the fridge, which he planned to surprise her with if she took the job. But now wasn't the right moment.

"You pick. And do we have any chocolate? I really, really, really need chocolate."

He laughed. "You go start the bath. I'll bring in the treats."

"Deal," she said. "Come on, Harley, have a seat on the couch. *Bad Dog!* is just starting."

"Make sure it's not one of the animal rescue episodes. It upsets her when she sees other animals in pain," he said. He'd made that mistake the night before and ended up sleeping next to her on the floor. It was the only way she'd calm down.

"I should have told you about that. In my rush, I must have forgotten."

As he opened the cabernet sauvignon, he tried not to think about Macy. But he knew the truth.

Finding the box of chocolate truffles he'd bought for her to celebrate, he placed them and the wine on a serving tray he found next to her fridge.

As he passed Harley on her couch she glanced up at him. "Tell you what? You stay there for the next hour or so and behave, and I'll give you two more of these." He put a dog cookie down in front of her. Harley cocked her head and he swore she winked at him. Then she settled back on her sofa to watch her favorite channel.

Balancing the wine, glasses and chocolates again, he found Macy already to her neck in bubbles.

He placed the drinks and plate on the small round table next to the tub and poured the wine.

Handing her the filled glass, he smiled when she moaned with the first sip. His cock twitched, as well. Indeed, one small moan and he was hard.

"Are you sure you want to share the bath, you look pretty comfortable."

She reached out and tugged on his jeans. "Hey, these are already wet."

"I suppose you may not have noticed, but it's raining outside, and wrestling with your dog to get her into the truck was no easy feat. I am grateful that the thunder had stopped by the time we got home. I had to tell her a story on the way as she tried to hide from the noise.

"What kind of story?" She pointed to his shirt as if to say, "Hurry up and strip," so he did.

Her eyes followed him appreciatively as he slid into the tub across from her. Even with his size, he could stretch out his sore legs. His body warned there'd be a steep price to pay for lifting all those bales of hay.

"Mom watched her while I was out in the barn. When I came back, she was reading a romance novel to her. Harley hung on her every word. I swear she understood her."

Macy popped a chocolate in her mouth, and then she shook her head. "I'm not surprised. She's so smart. Sometimes I forget that she's a dog. I talk to her like I would any friend."

"If it makes you feel any better, I do the same thing. But don't tell anyone I said that."

She watched him for a moment from under her lashes. "Tell me about your day," she said before having a large sip of wine.

As he shared the minute details, she shifted around so that she rested against his chest. His legs stretched out along hers, his hard cock pressing into her back. He put his arms around her and drew in her scent.

She was his.

No matter what she told him, he had to find a way to stay in her life. Compromise wasn't one of his strong suits, but he could learn if it meant being closer to her.

"Weren't you afraid of hurting your leg?" she asked.

"Huh." Then he remembered what he'd been telling her about loading hay into the barn. "No. It's good to work out once in a while and push harder than I normally do. Helps build up strength." At least that was what his PT had told him a few months ago.

"So you're feeling okay?" As she asked she turned to face him. She was on her knees, the bubbles creating a pretty swirling design across her breasts.

"Right now, I feel great," he said as he reached out and rubbed his thumb across one of her taut nipples. It hardened even more at his touch.

"I need you," she whispered.

Not nearly as much as he needed her. Leaning down, he teased her sensitive skin with his tongue.

She hissed in a breath.

"I've wanted you since I heard your voice on the phone this morning," he said and raised his head to kiss her. As his tongue played with hers, his fingers found her sex. He stroked her until she arched back and cried out.

"Yes," she moaned. "Yes."

Then she gently moved on top of him.

He shifted forward so she could wrap her legs

around him. She gripped his shoulders as she rode him, his arms strained to keep them as one.

Their bodies rose and fell, and the water sloshed around them. The overwhelming sensations as he filled her had him gritting his teeth for control.

"Please, Blake. Don't hold back. I want to feel all of you."

He smiled and upped their rhythm. He savored every word, every sound that came from Macy's lips.

Throwing her head back, her face radiant, her body began to quiver. Her muscles tightened around him as the orgasm rocked her, and he could hold on no longer.

"Mine," he whispered fiercely as he climaxed.

"Yes," she said. Her lips on his.

When he tilted her forward, so he could see her eyes, a tear streamed down her cheek.

"What is it baby? What's wrong?"

Chewing on her lip, she shook her head.

"You took the job." It was more of a statement than a question.

"Not yet. I— We need to— What we have is so intense. I don't think I can live without it. We said that this was a fling. That we weren't serious."

"We ran past serious the first night we made love," he said as he moved a damp curl from her eyes.

"I thought so, too. That's why I don't want to make this decision, and it really is a life-changing one, without discussing it with you. I have no right…"

He smiled. "I love you, Macy," he told her. "I'm with you no matter what you choose to do."

It took a minute for his words to register. "I love

you, too." She put her arms around his neck and hugged him. "This is strange, right? We've only known each other a few weeks."

He agreed. "But I don't think that's anything we can control."

She shivered.

"Let's move to where it's comfortable," he said. "I think this conversation is going to need more wine, and maybe some of that casserole you made."

She frowned. "Except for the chocolates and wine, I haven't been able to eat all day," she said as he helped her up and into the large walk-in shower. The glass curved so that there was no need for a door.

"Well, no decision should be made on an empty stomach—at least that's what my mom always says." As the warm water sluiced down their bodies, he gathered her close to him. "We will figure this out. I promise."

She smiled and squeezed him tight. "Why does life have to be so hard?"

He kissed the top of her head. "Got to get through the bad to get to the good," he told her. And he meant it.

Could he support her if she went off to New York and left him and Harley behind? It was no place for a dog as big as she was.

It wasn't lost on him that he was prepared to sacrifice a great deal for that damn dog—and even more so for the woman in his arms.

AFTER A GOOD MEAL, which Blake insisted Macy eat, they snuggled on the couch. Automatically, she changed the channel to Nova. The dog watched entirely too much television, but she'd probably done so with her former owner.

There had been times when the television popped on while Macy had been in the bath, or outside in the backyard or garage. And the channel always seemed to land on one of Harley's favorites. When Macy arrived back in the room, the dog would look around as if she had no idea how it had happened.

"This is where I want to be," she said. "Next to you, with the dog watching our favorite shows. Well, her favorite shows." She grinned as she looked up at him.

"I'm kind of fond of our time together, as well," he said. "But being comfortable isn't the same thing as being happy. I care for you too much to let you turn down a lifelong dream."

She gathered her knees up under her and rested her chin on them. Could she handle a new relationship, and a very time-consuming job? What would she do with Harley? The thought of giving her up was just impossible. She loved the dog.

"Tell me what the job entails."

She explained that she would be in charge of all of the online components for the publishing group's papers. They would use a specific strategy to grow their online content, and use a more uniformed format. She'd have almost a hundred people on her staff located across several countries. Henderson wanted to bring her old-school principles to their online content, which was sorely needed.

Stories went up too fast, a lot of facts went unchecked. They'd all agreed, after the very uncomfortable conversation about her ex and why she left, that it was time for them to create a place in Henderson Newspaper Group where people could go to find solid journalistic principles and legitimate stories online, in a timely manner.

Blake whistled and put a hand on her shoulder. "That's impressive. And you have to know it's a huge honor that they think so much of you."

She nodded. Her ego, in between bouts of bone-crushing insecurity, had been buffed more than once during the meeting in New York. She questioned whether she was up for the job, but they believed in her so much that she stopped doubting herself. "Yes. But I'm really torn. I love the life I've created here with you and Harley. The town has even begun to accept me. And I feel like I've made a real difference with the paper."

"True, though now you can take your plans and strategies and ideas out to the wider world," he encouraged. "Talk about making a difference."

She cocked her head to the side and glared at him. "I want you to say, 'you can't leave. You're my woman.' All cavemanlike." She frowned.

"I will, if that's what you actually want. But what kind of man would I be if I kept you from fulfilling your dreams?"

"The kind of man I usually fall for," she snorted. "Many guys wouldn't want their significant other running off to parts unknown to manage a company—at least, part of it, that is."

"Macy, if we've learned anything over the last few weeks, it's that there's nothing *usual* about us."

"You're right." She imitated her receptionist's gesture and bumped fists with him.

He chuckled, but it wasn't a happy sound.

"This relationship is just beginning," he said. "We fell fast for one another. But maybe, like you said, it's good that we slow down to figure out what we want to do next. I'm not sure myself. Moving to New York would be somewhat easy for me, since I own part of a security firm there. But I feel like my next step should be my own."

"So you think it would be good for us to be apart?" She chewed on the inside of her lip.

He frowned at her. "No. I can't stand the idea of being away from you, but I think it's important that you at least try to do this. Dreams change, but this kind of opportunity is something that you've been dedicated to for a long time. There will be serious regrets if you don't get out there and give it a chance."

She sighed. "Why do you have to be so smart *and* handsome?"

He gathered her into his lap. "You're the good-looking one. I'm going to check into chastity belts online. You can find almost anything on the internet these days."

She sputtered and laughed. "Trust issues, dude. Trust issues."

He winked at her.

"There's only one man allowed to touch me," she whispered as she kissed his neck.

"And who's that?"

"A certain marine who has me going every which way so that I'm constantly confused."

He tapped her chin with his fingertip. "Hey, I'm trying to make this easy on you."

She put her palms to his chest. "It would be easier if you'd just tie me to the bedpost and make me a kept woman."

"Hmm." He looked as if he were genuinely contemplating the idea. "I didn't know you were into that, but I'm sure we could work something out."

Suddenly, she hopped from his lap.

A moment of clarity hit her. "I'm scared," she said.

"You wouldn't be human if you weren't," he spoke softly.

"No, not about the job. About losing you." How long would he wait while she was supposedly achieving her dreams?

"Hey, I'll be here. And maybe at some point I'll join you. That is, if we can sort out what to do with you know who."

Macy's heart jumped to her throat. She'd momentarily forgotten about Harley, she'd feel awful leaving the poor dog behind. They really had become family.

"That's going to be hard. I don't think there's a dog park big enough in the city to contain her."

"Well, you won't have to worry about it for a few months. Take the job, and give yourself time to get settled. Once things are in order, then we'll discuss what happens next for us."

"You always say you aren't so great with compromises," she said as she kissed the stubble on his chin. "And yet, you're a lot better at them than I am."

"Only when it comes to you. So, are you going to call Henderson?"

She shrugged. "I will call him, but not tonight. This is our time, yours and mine. His newspaper can wait. In fact, I have until Friday to let Aaron know of my decision and I'm going to take those days. Once I say yes, things will move very fast."

"We have two whole days?" His eyebrows waggled. She didn't have the heart to tell him that a lot of those hours would be spent trying to make sure she had the Tranquil Waters paper seen to. She wouldn't allow it to fail, especially since they'd all worked so hard. Her gut churned. There was so much here that she'd have to leave behind now.

Blake might believe her mind was made up, but she wasn't so sure. There had to be another answer, she was just too tired and wired to think clearly.

"Yes!" she said and kissed him smack on the lips. "So have your wicked, wicked way with me, Marine."

"How about those ropes and bedposts you were talking about," he joked and sent her a naughty grin.

"Oh? What would your mother say?"

"Are you going to tell her?"

She lifted her T-shirt over her head. "Do I look like a girl who would kiss and tell?"

And with that, she was lost in the sweet company of the man she loved.

16

WHEN HE JOINED the marines any hint of a distracting emotion was driven out of him. The words, "Separate yourself from the situation and get the job done," had been seared into his brain.

But that concept wasn't working so well today. While Macy packed, he'd made her eggs, bacon and waffles. He'd taken Harley out for a walk, and added a new playlist to her phone.

He did these things to keep his mind off the fact that in ninety minutes he'd be driving her to the airport, and there was every chance it'd be a month, maybe more, before he could see her again. The gnawing in his gut reminded him of those timely words from the military, even though he was trying to ignore the raw tension.

Whenever his brain began playing the what-if game, he occupied his mind by thinking of other gifts Macy could unwrap when she got to New York. She'd been given a corporate apartment in a fancy building with a doorman, so at least her place would have proper security. And Henderson had insisted she accept the car and driver he provided. He didn't want her wasting valuable time in the subway tunnels with no internet. The car had been specifically outfitted to be a mobile office for her. In the first few weeks she's be traveling to New Jersey, Upstate New York, Virginia and D.C., and after her most recent flight home, she wasn't thrilled about all the travel.

Henderson arranged for the car, and told her when she had to go to the Midwest and Pacific Northwest, she'd have use of the company jet. She had her boss on speakerphone when all of this was discussed, so Blake couldn't help but listen in. He'd never seen someone's eyes almost pop out of their head, but hers were close.

"So, Ms. Corporate Executive how does it feel to be traveling in style?" he asked after she hung up.

"Weird. I'm used to being the one in the middle seat in coach between the lady with the snotty two-year-old and the guy who's decided to be my new best friend on a fourteen-hour flight because the paper didn't have it in the budget and my reservation was made at the last minute. I've been in a jeep with no air-conditioning outside of Iraq when it was nearly a hundred and twenty degrees. There was about two years early in my career, when I didn't come back to the States. I existed with two pairs of khakis, four T-shirts and one pair of boots. I'd start every day not knowing where the story might take me. I usually had to bum rides and barter for taxi rides.

"So yes, it's weird." Then she'd taken his hands in hers. "Everything is changing so fast."

He'd kissed her fingers and smiled, even though it was forced. "Yes, but we have each other. And we're good."

She looked as if she were searching for courage. "I've never really had someone I could depend on before. It's—hard for me to—"

"Trust," he finished her sentence.

She nodded.

"After what you went through before you came here, it's understandable. But you have to realize, I come from a mind-set that we are a team. Harley and I are here for you. We'll video chat and text. And we'll both be so busy we won't even notice how long we've been apart."

"Do you genuinely believe that last bit?"

"No. But we can pretend our hearts aren't breaking while we're apart." He'd taken her in his arms. "There's a lot going on here, as well, but I'll find a way to come see you."

As it had done so many times in his life, opportunity was knocking. When he talked to Rafe and Will a few days ago he'd learned about their new idea that involved protection for wireless service in rural areas.

Their strategy was attractive to him, especially after listening to a frustrated Macy grumble about bad connections and loss of online access.

"Promise to never leave Harley on her own?"

He laughed. "Wherever I go, she does. I don't think I'd have a choice. We've seen what she does when she wants something."

"It's a big responsibility to dump on someone," she said guiltily. "I'm the one who adopted her."

"You did, and she's grateful. And I have lots of dog sitters if I ever need a break, though I doubt that will happen. We've become pretty good friends."

Macy snuggled into his chest. "Hold me really tight," she said.

He did.

She kissed him hard. "You are the most thoughtful man. And I saw the songs you added to my phone. I'm going to cry all the way to New York."

He stroked her back and recognized her sweet scent again. Though he doubted he'd ever forget it.

"I don't think I can do this," she choked out.

A lump of emotion sat in his throat. He swallowed hard, it didn't work. "You can, and you will. When you get scared, call me or focus on the adversity you've known in the past and overcome."

Her exploits seemed legendary to him. He had such respect for her and he knew she felt the same about him.

"Got your bags, ready to go?"

There was a tiny sob against his shirt.

Damn. He was just grateful it wasn't him doing the crying.

"Hey," he murmured, and he affectionately tapped her chin.

"I feel like I'm abandoning both of you," she said, glancing down at the dog. Harley was never more than two feet away from Macy since she'd brought her suitcases out of the closet.

"No. Don't think of it like that. You're going on your best adventure yet. You live for that sort of thing.

You'll call us each night and tell us about everything that happened, and we'll do the same."

Her phone rang. She handed it to him, too choked up to answer.

"Hello?"

"I'm calling for Ms. Reynolds," a man stated.

"Yes, she's indisposed at the moment, can I help you?"

"This is Mr. Henderson's assistant. He has sent the jet to pick her up so that she doesn't need to fly commercial. The plane is at a small private airfield about four miles outside of Tranquil Waters. The thing is, it's there now, waiting for her. So if she wouldn't mind bumping up her schedule to accommodate—"

The assistant left the rest up to him to decipher.

"We'll get her there as soon as possible."

"I'll text the address," the assistant said and hung up.

"Macy, there's good news and bad news," he told her. "The good news is you don't have to worry about any plane with crying babies or folks who want to adopt you. The bad news is that Henderson's jet is waiting for you out at the Jones airstrip. They'd like you to leave right now."

Her eyes flashed big. "But—but I'm not ready. I wanted to stop by the paper and make sure—"

"The gang has it handled and I'll be checking in with them often. Come on. I'll get your cases. We'll bring Harley with us."

A half hour later they drove straight up to the plane in his pickup. The sleek jet was luxurious and impressive.

The pilot met them at the door, and the steward took her luggage to stow in the back. The interior had rich leather seats and the walls had dark wood paneling. It reminded Blake of the exclusive club in London where he and Rafe had had Will's bachelor party. Coincidentally, the club wasn't far from his soon-to-be-wife's modeling show. They'd given him a hard time about modeling the jeans in the finale of her show, but he'd said there was nothing he wouldn't do for his woman.

At the time, Blake hadn't understood Will, but he did now. He would do anything for the woman he'd followed into that jet. Harley barked at the bottom of the steps. She and Macy had already said their good-byes. She was probably worried he was leaving, too.

"Wheels up in ten," the pilot said. "There's a storm brewing over the Atlantic, and we want to get you there before it hits."

That was the last thing poor Macy needed to hear.

"Sit here," he encouraged, and she claimed one of the cushy chairs. Her pink cheeks had gone pale at the mention of the storm. "You're going to be fine. You'll get there before the storm, that's why you have to leave now."

"It's going to be okay," she said as if she were trying to convince herself.

"I love you," he said as he knelt down on his good knee.

"I love you, too." She gathered his hands in hers, and he passed the small gift into her palm.

"What's this?" She opened her hand and revealed a silver chain with four charms on a ring.

"The Great Dane charm is self-explanatory. The saber represents me. The typewriter—I looked for a computer but they didn't have one—represents you. And then the heart is us." He turned the heart over so she could read the inscription. "'You are mine.'" He slipped the necklace over her head.

"This way, we'll always be with you, no matter where you are."

Tears streamed down her cheeks. She threw her arms around him and kissed him.

"This is the nicest, most beautiful gift anyone has ever given me," she croaked.

The tears were almost his undoing.

"I got you something," she said and dug into her tote bag. Holding out a small package, she handed it to him. "You've been so wonderful. It's not much, but— Just open it." She smiled through her tears and put the handkerchief he'd handed her to her nose.

"You didn't have to do this," he said as he ripped off the navy-and-red paper. Inside he found a scuba watch. It was the exact one he wanted. He'd been planning on replacing the one he'd broken when he was injured. He just hadn't gotten around to it.

"Read the inscription on the back." She grinned.

"'You are mine,'" he read out loud and then he chuckled.

"Great minds, right?" She laughed, but it sounded weak to his ears. He smiled, anyway.

"You're amazing. I love you so much," he said.

"Five minutes," the captain called to them.

"I better get going. I don't want Harley to hear the engines."

She frowned. "Yes, she won't like that at all. I don't want you to go."

He cupped her chin in his hand and kissed her lightly. "I don't want to, either, but it's okay. Now that we know we have each other."

He held up the watch. "Call me when you land."

She nodded, the tears falling faster down her cheeks.

The jaded journalist never cried, so he had a good idea how much this parting hurt her.

"I love you," she repeated as he headed to the exit.

"Be safe, you're my heart." Then he turned quickly so she wouldn't see the hurt in his eyes. She seemed to read him so well.

Is this what love did to people? Because it was painful.

Took everything he had to walk away from her when she was like that.

Harley whimpered as he hit the last step.

The plane made a high-pitched whining sound.

"Let's go girl, we have to be a safe distance away."

The dog didn't hesitate. She jumped into the cab of his truck. Then her paw pushed the button to close up the passenger-side window.

Backing the truck up first, he then drove out onto the dirt road that lead to the small airstrip.

The ground vibrated as the jet rumbled to life and soon gathered speed down the runway.

Harley barked as the jet was lost in the cloud cover.

"I feel the same way," he said.

Obviously pouting, the dog rested her jowls on the front dash.

"She'll be back." At least he hoped so.

He hadn't lied; it did feel as if his heart was flying away to New York City. He wasn't sure how he'd live without it.

FRIDAY COULD NOT come soon enough, although Macy had to work through the weekend, she could do most of it in her apartment. She'd forgotten what a rush a busy newsroom could be, but it was also draining.

Her team had accomplished a great deal in a short amount of time. The first two days, she put together a top gang of editors, columnists and reporters. Not one of them had turned down the opportunity when she explained her mission.

Not a single one. Jobs were scarce, but it was clearly more than that.

"This could revitalize the industry," her friend Jill, had said. They'd worked together to cover stories in Pakistan and Afghanistan. "Everyone will want in."

Jill was right. If Macy had any doubts about what they were doing, they were gone. By Thursday, she had a long list of everyone she wanted on her team. Most of them had to give two weeks notice, but luckily enough some of them were between jobs and started the day she hired them.

Henderson and Garrison had helped, going out to some of the bigger-name columnists and bringing them in.

Together with the other editors, she'd set up a stylebook and code of ethics. They hired some of the best fact checkers in the business, and nothing made it on the website until it had gone through three editors and at least one of the fact checkers. Every source was vetted.

Closing her laptop, she stuck it in the messenger bag. The lovely leather case had been waiting for her in her apartment when she'd first arrived. A gift from her marine. She'd received one at the apartment each day when she returned home. They had a routine that after dinner, they'd sit down and watch one of Harley's shows while they video chatted.

That hour each night had been her saving grace. It was almost like meditation, separating her from the stress at work and the time she needed to sleep. Not that she did much of that. After they signed off each night, she'd crash. Then she'd wake up at three in the morning to get to the office for the morning edition. There were a couple of nights when she was still at the office at nine. Still, she'd opened up the chat line and she and Blake had talked for more than an hour.

As she punched the button on the elevator, she realized she'd forgotten the flash drive of the confidential employee reports Henderson had given to her. She grabbed it quickly, she didn't want to keep her driver waiting downstairs as it was beginning to snow. Everyone had warned her that with the Thanksgiving holiday coming up in two weeks, and the weather, the weekend would likely turn a bustling Manhattan into a mess. The group's offices were located at Central Park West. She had a small space, but it had a prime view of the park. She didn't care about the size of her office. She'd expected to be in the middle of the newsroom.

But it was nice to have her privacy. By the time she returned to the elevator, it'd moved on. Being so high up it took a while—especially at the end of the day—to get an elevator.

Pushing the button again, she waited.

This time when the doors opened, Garrison stood there.

"Excellent. The boss wants to see us upstairs." He reached out and tugged her into the elevator. She landed against his chest.

"Hands off," she bit out.

"What? Does my intense charm send your senses reeling?" His mocking tone only annoyed her more.

"Uh, no. It definitely does *not*." She stepped to the other side of the elevator.

"You probably don't want to hear it from me, but you've done an amazing job this week." He sounded almost sincere.

"I appreciate your help with Appleton and Carter," she said, mentioning the two popular columnists he'd brought into the fold.

"Didn't have anything to do with me, it's this *mission*—there's no better word for it—that you're—we're—on."

She shrugged. "We're all fed up with the way things have been going with online journalism the past ten years. I only hope a lot of other online publications follow what we're doing."

The elevator doors slid open at the top floor. She and Garrison made their way to the double-etched glass doors that led to Henderson's sanctuary. That was what he called it. It was part office, part art gallery. The man had a passion for painting and sculpture. He'd insisted the arts get equal coverage as the headline grabbing news, which was fine by her.

"And here she is," Henderson said as they entered his inner office. He was there with some of the board members and a couple of vice presidents. He oversaw an entertainment conglomerate that had everything from television shows and films, to online video streaming sites, radio stations and a lot more.

He'd told her, that by hiring people like her, he was able to juggle so many things. "Hire the best," he said. "A hard worker is worth their weight." He had a soft spot for newspapers, which was why he was so interested in investing in the online industry.

Those assembled clapped as she joined them.

Okay, she should have dressed nicer. She'd run out of skirts and tops, and had worn her dark jeans with a T-shirt and jacket. The people around her were in suits, and the women wore dresses that weren't off the rack.

"You've made a tremendous difference and only a week's gone by," Henderson said as he handed her a glass of champagne. "If you folks will excuse us for a minute, I need to speak with our golden girl—pardon me—golden woman," he corrected when one of the women tsk-tsked.

"Sorry. You're a powerhouse. I didn't mean anything derogatory."

"No problem," she said as he ushered her into a conference room adjoining his office. It was almost as large as the reception area outside. The room had the same view as her office, although this was much more expansive.

"I have an instinct when it comes to people," he said as he motioned for her to have a seat at the table. "I was surprised when you left the Boston paper so fast. You were kind last week when I asked you about why. In the end, I found out the truth from one of the other interns who was working there at the time."

She started to speak, but he held up a hand.

"None of it matters now. But I've been doing a little more digging, and before I bring you into this next project, I have to ask you something personal again."

Great, now what? He was a handsome man, she only prayed he didn't hit on her.

He smiled as if he'd read her mind. "Don't worry. It's not like that. I just need to know if there's anything coming up in the next year that might pull your focus."

She frowned. "I'm not sure I understand."

"The marine? Great guy if the reports are to be believed. He's keeping an eye on the paper, oh, and your dog, while you're here, right?"

Chewing on her lip, she thought for a moment. "This is invasive, Aaron, Mr. Henderson. Would you ask a man the same thing?"

He chuckled. "Actually, I would. I have big plans for you, Macy. Your vision and leadership as well as your management skills are outstanding, and we'd like to take them—you—to the next level."

She blew out a breath.

"Over the next year, the plan is to transition you into a vice president's position overseeing your own division."

Wow.

"I'm not really the executive type." She glanced down at her jeans. "I—"

"*You* are perfect because you care about what's important, and we have a serious lack of people like you in the world. So then, you'll understand why I need to know if you're planning to get married and have children.

"And yes, I'd be asking the same if a man were sitting in your seat. This next year is key if we want to successfully implement a number of changes and do so as fast as possible. A vice presidency will mean a lot of travel for you and long days."

Marriage? Geez. She'd only known Blake for a month, though they both admitted they couldn't ever remember not loving each other.

"Some day, maybe," she said hesitantly. "But not anytime soon."

"Would it make it easier if we moved him here and offered him a position?"

That made her laugh. "Uh, no. That isn't a good idea. He has his hands full with a couple of businesses already, one of which he's responsible for getting off the ground. We're committed to one another, but that's all I can say for now. He's incredibly supportive of my choices. At some point, when I figure out the lay of the land here, I'll think about finding more permanent digs so at least Harley can join me."

"That's the Dane?"

She nodded.

He got out his wallet. "These are mine," he said, pointing at a photo of a pair of Irish wolfhounds.

"Amazing. They're bigger than Harley."

"Not by much, I'm sure. Those two keep me sane, and they go everywhere with me, even overseas."

She paused, about to speak.

"With enough money, you can make anything happen," he said, laughing as he pocketed his wallet.

"What I'm trying to say—although I'm not doing a very good job of it—is that we'll work with you when it comes to the personal business. If you need to fly your marine and Harley in for a visit, or have them travel with you anytime, that won't be a problem."

"But this kind of thing just doesn't happen to me. Ever," she said. What he was proposing seemed so surreal to her. "I'm the one who gets the rotten assignments, pinches her nose and moves on to the next story. I'm not used to being treated—"

"Special." He grinned.

"Yes. And besides, I don't understand it. We've recently hired a slew of talented journalists, why me? I asked you that question when you offered me the job, but I really need to know the answer."

He crossed his arms, and glanced out the window. "Because none of them have your passion for what we're doing. They want to be involved, but it takes someone like you to get others to take action. Not everyone has that. You do, and you have more potential than anyone I've ever hired. I wouldn't be surprised if you were doing my job some day."

That made her laugh. "As if." Then she covered her mouth with her hand. "Sorry."

He smiled warmly. "You have only one flaw. You're too hard on yourself. You've put in the hours, done a good job and now opportunity has come your way. How you handle your new responsibilities is up to you. Just remember, we're all human. And even the best of us make mistakes."

She wasn't sure why the conversation had taken this turn. "Did I do something wrong?"

He chuckled again. "No. But you have some tough decisions to make. I know it's a lot to take in your first week around here, but I wanted to make sure you were aware of what's ahead. That way you can plan your strategy. Will you be one of those people who have to decide how to wear many hats? Or will you be married to the job like me? And for the record, there's no wrong answer. I just want you to go forward fully informed of what's expected."

By the time she finished her glass of champagne and snuck out of the reception he'd thrown for her, it was nearly nine. She returned to her office, dealt with a few emails, collected her things and was completely and supremely grateful for the waiting chauffeur when she spotted him.

In the car, she called Blake, but he didn't answer. He was probably in the shower or out walking Harley. When she walked into her apartment, she smiled. There two dozen red roses with a card.

You made it to Friday. We knew you could do it.
Love B & H

She so appreciated Blake's thoughtfulness. After a quick shower, she checked her phone. He hadn't called or texted her back. After ringing the landline at her house and getting no answer, she pulled back her covers and snuggled into bed.

Too much information today. And more than anything she wanted to speak with Blake about it all, especially Henderson's plans for her. She texted Blake one more time and then put her headphones on. Opening her laptop, she began editing a long column about medical research funding.

By eleven, he still hadn't contacted her. It was only ten in his time zone, but she worried that something might be wrong. He was usually so good at returning her calls and texts.

She was about to call his mom, when her phone rang.

"Hello, gorgeous woman of mine!"

"Hey, Marine. Thank you for the flowers."

She could hear a lot of people in the background. Was he at a party?

"You deserve them. I called earlier but your assistant said they were throwing you a reception. I wanted to let you know that I'm at a birthday party for my brother. And don't worry about Harley. She's here with me. She's the belle of the ball. Everyone keeps telling her how beautiful she is. And of course, she treats them like the adoring fans they are. We got a great picture of her wearing a birthday hat. And Jaime made dog cupcakes for Harley and Bruno.

"Dog cupcakes. Can you believe it? What is the world coming to?"

That made her grin. "Why am I not surprised?"

"Sorry I didn't notice your first couple of texts. It's so loud. I couldn't hear my phone. I came outside with Harley, and noticed them. Is everything okay?"

He was out having a good time, and the last thing she wanted to do was ruin his fun with a heavy talk about their future.

"Yes, I just missed you. I want your arms around me."

"We are like-minded that way," he said.

"Blakeeeee, it's your turn," a woman's voice called out.

Blakeeee? Her stomach dropped.

"Well, I guess I better get going. I don't want to hold up the game. Can I call you in the morning? Or maybe we can V-chat?"

"Absolutely," she replied, forcing herself to sound positive. "Have fun tonight."

"I love you," he said, but he hung up before she could say it back.

It was silly for her to be upset. It was his brother's birthday party.

When had she become a woman who was jealous of someone having a little fun? If she'd really needed him, he would have dropped everything to talk to her. That knowledge should have been enough.

But how long could they do the long-distance relationship? So many times the past week, she'd wished

he were there for her to come home to. Selfish, perhaps, but she'd never really been in love. She thought
she was in love with Garrison, but now she knew it
wasn't anywhere close to the real thing.

*It's been only a week, and already you have
doubts? You're tired. Go to sleep.*

But her dreams were filled with Blake dancing
with a bevy of sexy, sultry women. She woke up
cranky and when Blake called, she didn't answer.
After going for a run and working out at the gym,
she realized how ridiculous she'd acted.

It had only been a week. She needed to get a grip.
Walking away from her marine was not an option,
but she also wouldn't give up the incredible chance
she'd been offered.

Picking up the phone, she called Blake.

"WELL, BABE, IT'S no wonder you feel overwhelmed,"
Blake said as he listened to Macy vent. Between her
job and everything else she had going on, she needed
him.

He'd hop on the first plane, but he had half a dozen
important business meetings set up over the next few
weeks.

"Thank you," she said. "I'm sorry it all kind of
poured out. I'm embarrassed about feeling so inse-
cure last night."

"Don't be. By the way that was Tanya from the
feed store giving me a hard time at the party. She
knew you were on the phone. There's only one woman
for me, and that's you. In fact, every time I walk down

the street, people ask how you're doing. You definitely left an impression."

She laughed. "I needed to hear that. And tell Tanya I'm going to get even with her when I see her."

"Noted," he said and laughed with her. He was glad to lighten up her mood.

"I am not this woman," she proclaimed and then sighed. "You know the one who gets jealous and is whiny. It's so selfish of me to want you here when you have a lot on your plate, and besides, I'm so busy that I fall into bed every night and get up before the sun. I think I might be addicted to you. I need those arms around me when I go to sleep."

"Hey, I feel the same. And if you were here, Harley would be less likely to crawl on your side of the bed in the middle of the night. I woke up this morning and couldn't breathe. Her head was on my stomach. Oh, and this is where I found her yesterday afternoon."

She put him on speaker and opened the text when it arrived. The bed was made, but Harley's head was on her pillow.

"I think she might miss you a little." Blake chuckled. "Every once in a while, I find her in your closet. She's just lying in there on a pile of your clothes. I kept washing stuff, but finally gave up. I found some of your old pj's and sweatshirts and made a small pile in the middle of the closet for her."

"That's sweet. I miss you both so much it makes my heart hurt."

"I'm right there with you. Give yourself some grace. Any job is tough that first month, but it's obvious given what he's offering you after one week, that they really believe in you. I know I do. Is this a crazy route to starting a relationship? Yes. But we aren't like everyone else. And honestly, if I stayed in the marines, we would have had to have been separated even longer."

"True. I feel better just talking to you."

"Next time you feel like you did last night, don't be afraid to tell me that you need me. You're there for me and I'm here for you. Don't forget that. Also, any hope of you getting away for Thanksgiving?"

"I hadn't even thought about the holidays much. They're coming up fast—maybe I'll be home for Christmas. But there's still a lot to do here the next couple of weeks. And I've never been a huge fan of Thanksgiving. My parents didn't really do holidays."

Another hiccup. He'd promised his mother he'd be home for this Thanksgiving. It would be the first one in eight years he'd make. He wouldn't disappoint his mom. But even though she put up a good front, Macy needed him more.

"No problem. Christmas will be great," he said without enthusiasm.

It wasn't his favorite option, but that was the way things were.

"It isn't lost on me how lucky I am to have you in my life," she said softly.

"I know and I feel the same, Macy." But he was worried that the longer they were apart, the more she'd withdraw. She was so used to being on her own that she didn't feel comfortable coming to him when she was stressed or having a bad day. Clearly, she thought she should only show him the good side.

No way would he let her do that. It would mean sacrifice on his part, but Macy was worth it. He thought they could wait it out longer. But she needed him now, if for no other reason than to have someone be there for her at the end of the day. And he was the only someone who would be doing that.

After they hung up, he called his brother.

"We need to talk."

18

"Do YOU NEED me to stay?" Joe Pollack, Macy's assistant, glanced at the heavy snow falling outside her office window. She knew he had plans to catch a train and travel upstate to see his family for the holiday.

"No, you go ahead. I'll do a final check on the new sites to make sure there are no bugs, and then I'll be leaving, too."

"Thanks. You do know that Stu and Margaret have been through those sites multiple times today? They're clean, and they even added several upgraded firewalls to make it tougher for the hackers."

Shuffling papers on her desk, she looked up at him. "You know how I am. Once I feel like everyone really understands how important speed *and* accuracy and all of this is, I promise, I'll cut back on the micromanaging."

Joe didn't seem convinced. "Right. That's never going to happen."

She smiled. She couldn't help it. "I've been a bit on the loony side, have I?"

"I wouldn't say loony, more like determined. Uh, very determined."

"Always a diplomat. That's why you are such a super assistant."

"Yes, that and my ability to know when you are in need of coffee. Oh, and let's not forget my special talent to keep you from chewing out those who displease you," he joked, taking the bite out of his words. She'd had run-ins with a few reporters who hadn't double-checked their facts. The stories had been minutes away from going up on the site, when one of the fact checkers had called her to relay the news that there was something wrong.

Macy understood and appreciated the fact checker speaking up, but she made it clear, anyway, that those kinds of mistakes wouldn't be tolerated. Joe had remained at her side just to make sure she didn't actually throttle the reporters.

Admittedly it had been a good idea. One incorrect story could ruin everything they were all working so hard to achieve.

"Don't stay too late. Are you sure you don't want to come with me? My mom's always insisting there's room for one more at the table. She'd love to meet you."

"That's so nice of you, Joe. And I'd love to meet your mom. Be sure to arrange it if she's ever here visiting you. Thanks, anyway, but I'm looking forward to sleeping for a good twenty-four hours. I can't remember the last time I slept in."

He nodded. "You're always the last to leave and

first to arrive. There's been gossip that you actually live here."

"Sometimes it feels like it."

"Did you know, that if you were so inclined, your office has a perfect view of the Thanksgiving Parade?"

No, she didn't know that. Maybe she would come into the office, after all. Other than sleeping, she really didn't have anything else to do. "Cool. Now go on. The crowds at the station are going to be horrible. I don't want you to miss your train."

After he left, she sat back in her chair and blew out a breath. Everyone had worked so hard earlier in the week so they could be with their families. Even Henderson had taken off for Barbados to get away from the subzero temperature.

Even Cherie had abandoned her. She was on a book tour in Europe. Macy had seen her friend only once since arriving in New York. Cherie's book about relationships had hit the bestseller lists and she was more popular than ever.

Macy's cell rang. She glanced at the picture that came up on the mini screen and smiled.

"Hello, Mr. Marine."

"Hello, yourself. Are you still at work?"

"I am, though I did promise myself I'd leave before it gets too late. The weather is taking a turn for the worse."

He coughed. "I heard. I was worried about you getting home."

"Ah, you're too kind. Tony will be here to pick

me up. You don't need to worry. How is everything going with you? Is your mom fixing a huge feast?"

He snorted. "You said, 'fixing.' Our Texas words have seeped into your vocabulary, as for Mom, enough food for five or six families. We were over there the other day and discovered that Harley has a thing for apple pies."

"Oh, no. She didn't."

"She did. But we caught her before she ate the second one off the counter. She didn't feel so good for a day or two, but the vet says she's fine. I was going to tell you about it, but you had so much going on that I didn't want to possibly add to your concerns."

"You have a ton of patience. I don't know how you put up with her like you do."

"I don't consider her a chore. She's fun to have around."

She could hear Harley barking in the background as if confirming the fact.

Macy froze. She wanted to be there with them. Her mouth watered at the idea of homemade apple pie. It was stupid of her to stay in New York. Most of what she had to do was online. She could have gone home.

But it was too late now.

It was the day before Thanksgiving, no way would she be able to find a flight. And the company jet was in Barbados with Henderson. Even if a flight was available, with the snow the way it was, she had little chance of getting out of the city.

"Hey, did I lose you?"

"No. Sorry. I was just thinking how silly I am for

not coming home to see you at Thanksgiving. Work is busy, but—"

"Don't beat yourself up," he said. "If I hadn't promised my mom that I'd spend the holiday with her, I'd be dragging you out of that office right now."

Harley barked again.

"What's going on?"

"She needs to go out. Can I call you back? Or call me when you're on your way home so I know you're safe." He sounded distracted. Well, he probably was. Harley was likely dragging him to the door.

"No problem. I'll call from the apartment once I get there. Love you."

"Love you, too."

Chewing on her lip, she decided to pack it in. Poor Tony probably had a family he'd like to get home to, as well. She could work from her place. If she wanted to. After texting Tony, to let him know that she was ready to leave, she headed out.

In the lobby, she ran into Garrison, who held two bags of food. "Macy, I was just bringing these things up to you. I found this Thai restaurant still open nearby. Your assistant told me you'd be working tonight."

Her ex had been a little too nice the past few weeks, which made her suspicious. But he'd kept it professional, and Henderson had mentioned that his reports about her had been complimentary.

"Can I ask you something?"

He looked surprised. "Sure."

"What's up? Why are you being so considerate, when you've always been so competitive? I half expected you to tell Aaron that I was doing an awful job."

He shrugged. "I may be a cheating jerk, but even I can't deny you're as talented as they come. Besides, he doesn't need any reports from me. The evidence is out there. It's admirable what you've done. And honestly, I've been nice, because I have this horrible fear that you might be my boss some day. He's that impressed with you."

She laughed. "Oh, geez. You're serious aren't you?"

He nodded.

"Well, you don't need to worry. I forgive your past transgressions. I'm in a really good place. I'm happy in my relationship right now. It isn't easy, us being apart so much, but we're making it work."

He smiled. "I'm truly happy for you. Really. You deserve happiness. He's a fortunate guy."

"Thanks. Sorry about dinner, but I'm on my way home." She stared at the bags. "I have plans."

This was Garrison's life. Take-out Thai food the night before Thanksgiving while he worked. All of a sudden she knew that wasn't the life she wanted for herself. It was so clear to her now.

Henderson had asked if she'd be the kind of person who would learn to wear many hats. She was. Because she didn't want to end up lonely like the man in front of her, or like Henderson, for that matter.

"With who?"

"Huh?"

"Who are your plans with?"

The thought struck her as funny because it was so

glaringly obvious, and she laughed. "Don't look so surprised. My boyfriend."

"I thought he was in Texas." He seemed confused.

"Have a good Thanksgiving, Garrison. See you Monday."

With that she was out the door. Maybe she couldn't be in Texas, but they could share a virtual Thanksgiving. It was better than nothing. She couldn't wait to get back to the apartment and tell Blake her idea.

The snow was pretty, though it fell fast and didn't look to be letting up anytime soon. It took an extra half hour to reach her building.

"Tony, stay in the car. You don't need to open the door. And thank you. Have a wonderful holiday."

He turned to face her. "Won't you be needing me?"

She shook her head. "Not this weekend. You take some well-deserved time off. Enjoy."

He tipped his hat to her, and the doorman opened the car door. "Mind your step, miss. It's very slick on the sidewalk." He carefully led her to the front door. The soles of her boots were smooth, and made the slippery walk treacherous even with his help.

"Thanks," she said as she entered into the lobby. The marble floors proved to be as slick as the sidewalk. Just inside the door she slipped, and would have fallen if strong arms hadn't held her up.

"Whoa," a deep voice said.

It couldn't be.

Her marine smiled down at her. Had she fallen and woken in a dream? This could not be real.

"You— It's not—"

He kissed her then, and she lost herself in his embrace.

Harley barked and barked beside them.

"Ah, sweet girl." Macy bent down to put her arms around the dog's massive neck. "I've missed you."

She stood and stared at Blake, her heart soaring. Blake touched her cheek. "How is it you haven't been sleeping, yet you're still so damn beautiful?"

"Also sweet. But how did you get here? Not that I'm complaining." Macy wished the doorman a happy Thanksgiving and she, Blake and Harley headed for the elevator.

"Well, you couldn't come to Thanksgiving, so I brought Thanksgiving to you." He gave her that sexy smile of his and inside she melted a little. She loved this man.

"I can't believe you're here. I feel like time has stood still or something and suddenly I'm going to find out that none of this is really happening. And I do so want it to be happening."

He chuckled. "Let's get upstairs and I'll show you just how real it is," he whispered.

She sighed happily. "How was she on the plane?" With the loud noises, Macy was surprised the dog still wasn't sleepy.

"We drove," he said. "I didn't have the heart to put her in the cargo hold. And I had some business in North Carolina. We've been on the road the last few days."

"Why didn't you tell me!" she said as she pushed the button for her floor. "I was searching for flights while we were on the phone, but it was ridiculous considering this is the busiest day of the year."

"That and the airports are shut down." He gathered her in his arms. "We wanted to surprise you."

"You did." Her heart felt light. She was excited and at peace all at once. "Surreal. This is what it feels like. There's no better word for it. Wait, Harley's on the elevator, but pets aren't allowed in the building."

"She is. Evidently, she's the exception."

"I bet Henderson had something to do with that. He's a big fan of dogs."

"She did get me into your apartment. I hope that's okay. I had some things to drop off there before I could find a place to park and walk the dog."

"Make yourself at home. Whatever I have is yours."

She opened the door and was assailed by the smell of delicious food.

She turned to glance at him, and he shrugged. In her kitchen, she found his mother and brother, up to their elbows in dressing.

Throwing her arms about their necks, she kissed each of them on the cheek. "I'm so happy you're here. I can't believe you guys did this. Thank you, thank you."

"It's nothing, dear," his mother said, smiling. "Let me get my hands out of this corn bread, and I'll give you a proper hug."

She looked up at Blake who smiled at her.

"You did all of this. How?"

"Harley and I drove, but Mom and J.T. flew in this morning. We knew about the weather. They've been cooking all day. You're a part of the family now, and it wouldn't be right to celebrate without you. Besides, we heard you have an excellent spot to watch the Thanksgiving Parade. Mom's a fan, so she had no problem packing everything in dry ice and shipping it here."

Macy put her hands to her cheeks. "No one's ever done anything like this for me. You guys are incredible."

"It's what families do," J.T. said as he nudged her with his shoulder.

"Why don't you and Blake relax? Dinner should arrive in just a bit," his mother said.

Macy was baffled.

"All of this," J.T. said, waving at the cluttered counter, "is for tomorrow's lunch. We ordered pizza for tonight. It's a family tradition, or at least it was when Blake and I were kids. Mom was always too busy getting ready for the big day to take time to cook dinner the night before, so our dad would order pizza. And there's no better place to carry on that tradition than here."

Thankfully, the kitchen was well stocked with dishes and pots and pans, none of which had been used since she'd moved in. Most of her meals were eaten at work, and then she'd order in most nights.

But sitting around the dining room table with Blake's family, well, it was the best gift anyone could have given her. The brothers gave each other a hard time, their mom butting in to tell them to behave. They were a proper family.

Her parents loved her and cared about her, but they

didn't understand the importance of having this kind of time together.

She wouldn't make that mistake. Macy wanted it all. The family squabbles, the general silliness that came with hanging out with people who knew you better than you knew yourself—and the love.

A few hours later, she and Blake were in bed. Harley had passed out in the living room, and Blake's mom and brother had gone to their hotel.

"I know I keep saying this, but I still can't believe you are here."

He put an arm around her shoulders and leaned over for a kiss. "Believe it," he said and he kissed her again. Desire pooled in her belly. Yes, this was the way one should end the day.

His hand curved around her hip, and he drew her nearer. Wrapping his arms around her, he held her tight.

"This is home," she said against his chest.

He kissed her mouth, her cheek, behind her ear. "Yes, that's the way I feel. It doesn't matter where we live, as long as we're together." He went back to kissing her lips.

"I've got to tell you something, Blake, so just listen, okay? You don't have to say anything."

Blake tensed.

"I mean it. Just listen to what I have to say." She poked his chest as she glanced up at him. "I need to do this before I chicken out."

"Okaaaay," he said slowly.

She met his eyes. "I love you, Blake Michaels. And I want it all."

As her words sunk in, a slow smile split across his face.

"That's a good thing, since I love you and I want it all. In fact, I'm willing to do whatever it takes to make that happen."

"Wait." She lifted her head. "What are *you* saying?"

He gave her a sheepish grin. "I've been making a lot of changes over the last few weeks. I wanted to tell you, but it wasn't until a few days ago that I knew everything was going to fall into place the way I wanted it to. As long as you're all right with what I'm about to ask."

What was he talking about? What kind of changes? "You can ask me anything," she said honestly.

"How would you feel about Harley and I moving here full-time?"

Uh, it would be a dream come true. She slugged his arm. "How do you think I'd feel?"

"Hey, no need for violence." He rolled over and pulled her on top of him.

"I can't believe you were making all these plans and didn't tell me. I've been devising all these scenarios trying to figure out how I can split my time between here and Texas." She sat up straighter, fully aware that he was hard as a rock underneath her.

"So you like the idea."

She laughed. "Of course. It's what I've wanted all along, but I didn't feel right asking you to give up everything you had there to move here with me."

"If you'd asked, I would have done it. But a couple of weeks ago when you were so sad, I realized I didn't care if you wanted me to be here or not, you needed me. I'd do anything for you." He took her wrist and brought her forward and kissed her.

"I want and need you," she whispered, "more than you will ever know."

"Trust me, I do know. I'll have to go back and forth for a while. J.T. will help me out. I'll be based here, though. And it's good timing, too, for the security business my friends and I have. We're thinking of expanding and opening an office here. Besides my financial duties, the guys want me to take charge of implementing the new ideas we've got going and do a forecast for a possible office here. It's a lot, but as soon as I made the decision to be here with you, it all fell into place."

She kissed him, lightly at first, and then she deepened the kiss, putting everything she had into it. "I'm so glad. And what about you know who?" she asked.

He twisted one of her curls around his finger. "You know who will be happy having us and her toys. At some point we should maybe consider trying to find a house outside the city, but there's a great dog park not far from here. She loved it."

"You really have thought of everything."

Something was still making her nervous, and she realized it was because she was so happy.

"You don't think it's too soon for us to cohabitate?" he asked, his expression serious.

She shook her head. "You know it isn't. Like you said, there may be some bumps along the way, but if you're riding over them with me, we can cruise through life together."

"That was a terrible metaphor." He laughed.

"Yes. Yes, it was."

"Have I mentioned how much I love you?"

She glanced at the nonexistent watch on her wrist. "It has been a good ten minutes since the last time. I was beginning to wonder."

Growling, he reversed their positions.

She smiled, and put her hands on either side of his face to hold him close. "Show me, Blake," she said, "show me how much you love me."

Capturing her lips in a long and passionate kiss, he left her breathless. Just from the kiss alone she was ready for him.

"Not so fast, sweetheart," he said as he nuzzled her neck. His mouth paid equal attention to each of her breasts. As he moved down, kissing all the way, she cried out. Having him here with her meant everything to her.

He caressed her, tempted her, touched her exactly as she wanted to be touched. He was amazing, so strong and also so tender.

Her orgasm was searing and swift. She felt it from her head to the tips of her toes. It made her shudder and call out his name.

"Now," she said, shutting her eyes, anticipating him.

"No." He teased her into yet another orgasm. This one robbed her of all control. "Blake, Blake…" she whispered.

He stroked her thighs, moving onto his knees. The intensity of passion in his gaze was enough to make her shudder again.

He entered her slowly, carefully, filling her, completing her.

"Yes," she said, matching the intimate movement of his hips.

As they raced to the edge together and leaped, he kissed her thoroughly. Every bit of love he felt for her was in that kiss, and she returned it.

He was her marine, body and soul.

19

HARLEY BARKED AS Santa passed by the window. Blake's mom clapped, and the woman wrapped in his arms laughed so hard he couldn't help but smile. They were all in Macy's office enjoying the parade.

J.T. shook his head in wonder. "How does she know it's Santa?" he asked.

"Who knows? But she does have a thing for presents and toys," Macy answered.

They laughed.

"Dear girl, that parade was too exquisite for words," Blake's mom said. "So much better in person and beyond anything I could imagine. I am surprised that even with all the snow on the sidewalks, so many people showed up."

"Yes. It was fun and nice to be able to watch it here in my office where it's warm and comfortable. More snow is expected later this afternoon. I'm just glad the skies cleared a bit so they could have the parade. It would have been awful if you came all this way to see it, and then it didn't happen."

His mother pulled her out of Blake's arms and

hugged her. "Macy, sweetie, we didn't come for the parade. We came to see you. No one should be alone on Thanksgiving. I've had a few too many of those myself, and I didn't want that for you." She kissed Macy's cheek. "Let's roll, J.T., we'll take Harley for a walk. You two be back at Macy's place by one so we can eat."

She paused in front of Blake and touched his hand. "It's wonderful to see you so happy, son. It's about time."

He held his mom's hand and squeezed. "Mom, you are the absolute best. I love you."

"Love you, too, son. Don't be late for dinner." She followed J.T. and Harley out the door.

Blake sat on the edge of Macy's desk. She pushed his legs apart and slipped in between them. He leaned toward her and she put her arms around his neck and kissed him.

"This has been on of the best days of my life and it's still early."

He held her close. "I agree. Are you sure you're okay with my family invading your space unannounced?" He'd kept an eye on her throughout the morning. It was almost as if she were afraid of offending someone or saying the wrong thing. He didn't want her to feel that way.

"Blake, I so appreciate what your mom and brother have done for me this Thanksgiving. It's been great. I've never felt like—I was a part of a family. Years on my own, well, you know how it's been. Now that I see what I've been missing out on, I want to make up for lost time. So there's no invasion. I'm ecstatic that you and your family are here."

He kissed her nose. "Good. Because my mom is

very excited about shopping tomorrow. I was hoping I could count on you to handle that one."

Macy laughed. "Always with the ulterior motives. I should have known. But if I'm going out in the wilds of Manhattan and facing all those shoppers, then seriously, you're coming with us." She tugged on his arm and they left her office.

"I had a feeling you'd say that." At the elevator, he helped her on with her coat. He thought about that and all the other things in future that he would want to help her with. Big and small. He planned to spend the rest of his life loving this woman.

She was his everything.

One day he'd ask her to marry him, but not until he knew she was ready. The year ahead represented a lot of change for her. He'd be there for her. He wanted her to achieve her dreams. In fact, he couldn't think of anywhere he'd rather be.

"Hey, Mr. Deep Thoughts. What's going on in that brain of yours?" She was standing in the elevator, waiting for him.

No more living day to day, wondering if it might be his last. From now on he and Macy lived in a world of possibility.

"I'm thinking about the interesting things I can do with you after everyone leaves tonight."

Her cheeks turned a bright shade of pink as she yanked him into the elevator. "Now that's all I'm going to think about during dinner."

He waggled his eyebrows. And then he kissed her.

This was only the start of a long and happy life together.

* * * * *

Give a 12 month subscription to a friend today!

Call Customer Services
0844 844 1358*

or visit
hillsandboon.co.uk/subscriptions

MILLS & BOON®

Why shop at millsandboon.co.uk?

Each year, thousands of romance readers find their perfect read at millsandboon.co.uk. That's because we're passionate about bringing you the very best romantic fiction. Here are some of the advantages of shopping at www.millsandboon.co.uk:

* **Get new books first**—you'll be able to buy your favourite books one month before they hit the shops

* **Get exclusive discounts**—you'll also be able to buy our specially created monthly collections, with up to 50% off the RRP

* **Find your favourite authors**—latest news, interviews and new releases for all your favourite authors and series on our website, plus ideas for what to try next

* **Join in**—once you've bought your favourite books, don't forget to register with us to rate, review and join in the discussions

Visit **www.millsandboon.co.uk**
for all this and more today!

MILLS_WEB